ROYAL BLOOD & SOUTHERN CHARM

THE CHRISTMAS MIRACLE

BY

R.W. DOVE

Dedication

To my loving and supportive wife, Lady Julie Dove, whose unwavering belief in me and boundless encouragement inspire every word I write. This book is a testament to your love and the countless ways you enrich my life. Thank you for being my greatest supporter and partner in all things.

Lord R.W. Dove

Preface

In a world where duty often eclipses desire, the heart's true calling can lead individuals down unexpected paths. In "Royal Blood & Southern Charm: The Christmas Miracle," R.W. Dove invites readers into a captivating romantic tale that weaves together love, sacrifice, and the magic of the holiday season.

The story follows Prince Alexander, a young man torn between his royal obligations and the enchanting love he discovers in the American Midwest. While pursuing his college education, Alexander crosses paths with Rachel, a spirited Southern lady whose charm and warmth illuminate his world. Their friendship blossoms into a deep and abiding love, but it does not come without its challenges.

As Alexander grapples with the weight of his royal heritage, the specter of duty looms large, especially when his mother, Queen Isabella, becomes increasingly wary of his affections for an American. This conflict of heart and heritage highlights the essence of the narrative: the struggle between societal expectations and the transformative power of love.

With the holiday season as a backdrop, the stakes rise when Rachel is called back to Tennessee due to her uncle's medical emergency. This pivotal moment challenges both characters to confront their true feelings and the difficult choices that lie ahead.

"Royal Blood & Southern Charm" is not merely a love

story; it is a celebration of the miracles that occur when individuals dare to follow their hearts. As readers turn the pages, they are invited to find inspiration in Alexander and Rachel's journey and perhaps even discover a reflection of their own stories within theirs.

R.W. Dove extends heartfelt gratitude to readers for joining this enchanting adventure and hopes they enjoy every moment of this captivating tale of love.

TABLE OF CONTENTS

Chapter 1

Beneath The Appalachian Sky

Rachel Rodgers stood by her open bedroom window of her family's small farm in the Appalachian mountains of Tennessee, the cool mountain breeze ruffling her long brown hair. The sun is just breaking the horizon, casting a golden glow over the rolling hills of the farm. It was a moment of peace and contentment, a scene of rustic beauty that had always been her home.

It was her last year at college before graduation, and she was nervous and excited. Breakfast is ready, Rachel, a voice rang out over the crisp morning air.

Rachel's heart raced as she quickly brushed her hair and slipped on her favorite sweater. The smell of pancakes and freshly brewed coffee wafted through the air, making her stomach rumble in anticipation. She hurried down the stairs.

As she entered the kitchen, her mom smiled warmly at her. "I made your favorite! You need a good breakfast to fuel that brain of yours," she said, placing a stack of fluffy pancakes on the table. "Thanks, Mom!" Rachel replied, her nerves slightly easing at the sight of her mother's comforting presence.

"Oh, where is your father this morning?" her mother, Kathy, sighed. Her mother looked out the door across the farm.

Rachel followed her mother's gaze, the vast expanse of land stretching out before them, dotted with the silhouettes of the barn and the grazing cows. The lingering scent of breakfast mixed with the fresh mountain air was comforting, but the absence of her father weighed on her mind.

"He should be back soon, right?" Rachel replied, trying to sound optimistic. "I mean, he always comes back for breakfast."

Kathy turned back to the stove, flipping over a pancake with a practiced hand. "I just wish he wouldn't spend so much time out there alone. It's been a bit unpredictable with the weather lately," she said, her tone tinged with concern.

Rachel sat down at the table, the warm wood beneath her fingers grounding her. "I'll go check on him after breakfast. I can take the truck and drive up to the fields." She felt a surge of determination, wanting to reassure her mother.

Kathy smiled softly, appreciating her daughter's spirit. "You're growing up so fast, Rachel. Just be careful out there, okay?"

With a nod, Rachel poured syrup over her pancakes, the sweet aroma mingling with the warmth of the kitchen. The moment felt right—just her, her mother, and the promise of a new day. But the thought of venturing out into the expanse of the farm still made her heart race.

Rachel's heart lifted at the sight of her father. Max, with his weathered hands and sun-kissed skin, carried an air of calm that instantly eased her worries. "Sorry I'm late!" he chuckled, brushing the dirt from his boots as he stepped inside. "I got caught up checking on the new fence we put up."

Kathy turned to him, relief washing over her face. "We were just starting to wonder where you were! Rachel was about to go out looking for you," she said, a hint of playful reproach in her voice.

Max ruffled Rachel's hair as he walked by, his grin wide. "You know me, always losing track of time when I'm out in the fields. But I wouldn't miss breakfast with my girls for anything." He took a seat at the table, and Rachel couldn't help but smile back at him.

"Pancakes, Dad! Mom made your favorite too," she said, pointing to the towering stack in the center of the table.

"Now that's what I like to hear!" Max exclaimed, reaching for a plate. As he served himself, he glanced out the window, the golden light of the sun illuminating the farm in a way that made everything look magical. "It's a beautiful morning out there. We have so much to be thankful for."

Rachel nodded, feeling a sense of warmth spread through her. The worries of the morning faded away as laughter and chatter filled the kitchen, the three of them sharing stories and enjoying the simple pleasure of being together. For Rachel, this was home—full of love, warmth, and the comforting smell of pancakes.

As they settled into their breakfast, the conversation

flowed easily. Max recounted a humorous story about a stubborn cow that had gotten out of the pasture, leading him on a wild chase through the fields. Rachel couldn't help but laugh, picturing her father sprinting after the animal, his usual calm demeanor replaced by a burst of energy.

Kathy chimed in with her own stories from the kitchen, sharing anecdotes about the day's chores and the antics of the farm's animals. Rachel listened intently, feeling a sense of belonging that only moments like these could bring. The warmth of their familial bond enveloped her, making her forget the world outside for a little while.

After they cleared the table, Max suggested they all take a walk around the farm. "The morning air is perfect for a little stroll, and I want to show you the progress we've made on that new garden plot," he said, his eyes sparkling with enthusiasm.

"Sounds great!" Rachel replied, eager to step outside and experience the beauty of their land. She slipped on her boots, and they headed out together, the sun shining brightly overhead.

As they walked, they admired the vibrant wildflowers that dotted the landscape and the way the sunlight danced on the leaves of the trees. Max pointed out the various plants they had cultivated over the years, sharing his hopes for the upcoming harvest. Rachel listened, soaking in every word, inspired by her father's passion and dedication to their home.

Kathy walked beside them, occasionally stopping to pick a wildflower or to snap a picture with her phone. "This place is truly magical," she said, looking around at the rolling hills and the distant blue mountains.

Rachel felt a swell of pride as she looked at her parents. This farm was not just land; it was their legacy, filled with memories and dreams. She realized that these moments spent together were the threads that wove their family story—a story she was excited to be a part of.

As they reached the edge of the garden plot, Rachel felt a familiar sense of adventure stirring within her. She couldn't wait to see what the future held for them, together on this beautiful piece of land they called home.

Max looked lovingly into Rachel's eyes, I can't believe it is already time for you to go back to college so soon.

Rachel felt a pang in her heart at her father's words. The thought of leaving the farm, even for a little while, always filled her with a mix of excitement and sadness. "I know, Dad. It feels like just yesterday I was packing up for my first semester," she replied, trying to maintain a brave face.

Max reached out and gently squeezed her shoulder. "You've grown so much, Rachel. We're so proud of you and everything you've accomplished. College has changed you for the better, but it's hard to let you go," he said, his voice thick with emotion.

Kathy, who had been quietly listening, chimed in, "You know, we'll always be here for you, no matter how far away you are. This farm will always be your home." She looked around, her eyes glistening with a mixture of pride and nostalgia.

Rachel nodded, feeling tears prick at the corners of her eyes. "I'll miss you both so much," she admitted, her voice barely above a whisper. "But I promise to come back as often as I can. I want to help out here whenever I'm home."

Max smiled softly, his eyes reflecting the love and support he had always given her. "And we'll be waiting with open arms, ready to share a stack of pancakes and stories from the farm," he said, trying to lighten the mood.

"Exactly!" Kathy added, her voice brightening. "And don't forget, we'll send you pictures of all the new plants in the garden and the animals. You'll feel like you're right here with us!"

Rachel laughed, grateful for their unwavering support. "You both make it so hard to leave!" she said playfully, wrapping her arms around them in a tight hug.

As they stood there, the sun rising behind the mountains, Rachel felt a deep sense of gratitude. No matter where her journey took her, she would always carry this love and connection with her. The farm, her family, and their shared moments would forever be a part of her heart.

Chapter 2

Sunset Reflections

As Rachel moved through the familiar rhythms of farm life, she found comfort in the tasks at hand. The crisp morning air filled her lungs as she walked toward the barn, where the horses awaited their morning feed. She smiled at the sight of Bella, the gentle mare, nudging her shoulder for attention.

"Hey there, girl," Rachel said, stroking Bella's mane. The warmth of their bond reminded her of the countless mornings spent here, a routine she would deeply miss.

After feeding the horses, Rachel joined her dad in the garden. Rows of vibrant vegetables and leafy greens sprawled before them. They worked side by side, sharing stories and laughter.

"Remember that time we had a tomato fight?" Rachel asked, laughing as she recalled the messy afternoon. Her dad chuckled, shaking his head. "I still have stains on my overalls from that day!"

As they finished in the garden, Rachel helped her dad prepare the afternoon snack. They made sandwiches and iced tea as she relished the simple joy of being together.

Later, as they washed up, Kathy joined them, bringing a basket of freshly baked cookies. The sweet aroma filled the kitchen, and Rachel felt a sense of warmth enveloping her. They settled around the kitchen table, savoring cookies and reminiscing about their favorite memories on the farm.

With each passing moment, Rachel's heart swelled with love and nostalgia. She knew that while she was embarking on a new adventure, these moments would forever be etched in her heart. As the sun began to set, casting a golden hue over the land, she took a deep breath, cherishing the beauty of her last day on the farm.

As dusk began to fall, the air was filled with the sweet scent of blooming flowers and freshly cut grass, creating a serene backdrop for Rachel's contemplative moment. She watched as the sky transformed into a canvas of warm oranges and soft purples, each hue reflecting the memories she cherished. The gentle creaking of the porch swing matched the rhythm of her thoughts, reminding her of the countless sunsets she had shared with her loved ones.

In that tranquil moment, Rachel thought about her dreams and the adventures that awaited her. Yet, the warmth of home tugged at her heart, a reminder that no matter how far she traveled, the bonds forged on this farm would always be her anchor. She closed her eyes, allowing the sounds of nature and the fading light to envelop her, feeling a perfect blend of excitement and nostalgia.

The memories flooded Rachel's mind like a gentle stream, each one a cherished moment that shaped her into the person she had become. Kathy and Max had taken her in with open arms, their love wrapping around her like a warm blanket on a cold night. She could picture Kathy's comforting smile and the way she had a knack for turning even the simplest meals into feasts filled with laughter and love. Max, with his steady presence, had taught her the value of hard work and resilience, always encouraging her to dream big while remaining grounded in the beauty of their rural life.

Rachel remembered the countless evenings spent in the glow of the kitchen, where stories were shared and lessons were learned. Kathy's soothing voice had always been there to guide her through the tough moments, while Max had inspired her to face challenges head-on, instilling in her a sense of courage and determination.

The accident that had taken her parents away felt like a distant storm cloud now, overshadowed by the vibrant life and love that Kathy and Max had provided. They had turned her grief into strength, teaching her that family isn't just defined by blood, but by the bonds of love and support that one nurtures.

As the sun dipped lower, casting long shadows across the porch, Rachel felt a swell of gratitude for the life they had built together. She realized that no matter where her journey led her, the lessons, love, and memories shared with Kathy and Max would always be her guiding light.

The creaking of the screen door caught Rachel's attention as Max stepped out onto the porch. He carried a warm mug of chamomile tea, a familiar ritual that signaled the end of the day. Max settled into the swing beside her, the gentle motion creating a soothing rhythm that matched the quietude of the evening.

"Thought you might like some company," he said with a soft smile, handing her the steaming mug. The aroma wrapped around Rachel, bringing with it a sense of comfort and safety.

"Thanks, Dad," she replied, taking a sip and savoring the warmth that spread through her. She studied his weathered face, noting the lines etched by time, laughter, and a few worries. "It's beautiful out here," she added, gesturing toward the horizon where the last rays of sunlight danced against the mountain peaks.

Max nodded, his gaze fixed on the view, a peaceful expression settling over him. "It always is, especially when you take the time to appreciate it," he said thoughtfully. "You know, Rachel, I've been thinking about how far you've come. Your parents would be so proud of you."

Rachel felt a lump form in her throat at the mention of her parents. "I wish I could have shared all of this with them," she admitted, her voice barely above a whisper.

Max reached over, placing a reassuring hand on her shoulder. "They're with you in spirit, always. And you've made them proud by living your life fully, just as they would have wanted."

His words resonated deeply within her, and Rachel felt a sense of peace wash over her. As they sat together, sipping tea and watching the stars begin to twinkle in the evening sky, she realized that this moment, surrounded by love and support, was a testament to the family they had created together.

As the stars began to dot the night sky, Rachel and Max fell into a comfortable silence, each lost in their thoughts. The gentle breeze rustled the leaves of nearby trees, creating a soothing melody that harmonized with the distant sounds of crickets chirping. Rachel felt a sense of tranquility envelop her, a moment suspended in time where the worries of the future faded into the background.

Max turned to her, breaking the silence. "You know, I often think about how this farm has shaped us. It's more than just land; it's our legacy, our stories," he said, his voice filled with nostalgia. "Every corner of this place holds a memory."

Rachel smiled, recalling countless moments spent exploring the fields, learning to plant seeds, and watching them grow. "I remember the first time you took me to the old oak tree by the creek," she said, her eyes lighting up. "You told me it was a place where dreams could take root."

"Exactly. And look at you now," Max replied, pride shining in his eyes. "You've planted so many dreams, and I have no doubt you'll continue to grow. Just remember, it's okay to reach for the stars while keeping your roots grounded here."

Rachel took a deep breath, absorbing his words. She felt a mix of excitement and apprehension about the future, knowing that soon she would set out on her own path. But in that moment, she realized how vital it was to honor her past and the love that had nurtured her.

"Do you think I'll ever find my way back here?" she asked, her voice tinged with uncertainty.

Max looked thoughtfully at the horizon, then back at her. "Home is always here, Rachel. It's not just a place; it's a feeling. No matter where life takes you, this love, this connection, will always pull you back. You'll carry it with you."

As they sat together under the vast expanse of the night sky, Rachel felt a renewed sense of purpose. She knew that while her journey was just beginning, the foundation of love and support from Kathy and Max would be her guiding star. She was ready to embrace the unknown, knowing that the heart of her home would always be with her, lighting her way forward.

Chapter 3

The Dance of Destiny

Meanwhile, in the small eastern European country of Slovitia. Prince Alexander was busy getting ready to go to America to finish getting his degree.

Prince Alexander stood in front of a large wooden mirror in his opulent chamber, adjusting his tie with a focused expression. The walls were adorned with rich tapestries that told the stories of his ancestors, and the sunlight streamed through the tall windows, illuminating the room in a warm glow. He was not just any student; he was the heir to the throne of Slovitia, and his decision to study abroad was met with skepticism from his mother as well as the royal court.

As he packed his belongings, he made sure to include a few personal items—a family crest, a journal for his thoughts, and a small globe that had been a gift from his grandfather. Each item reminded him of his roots.

As Alexander continued to pack, his mind wandered to memories of Rachel. He recalled their last conversation before the winter break, filled with laughter and shared dreams about their futures. Would she remember those moments as vividly as he did? He hoped that their friendship had not only survived the distance but had grown stronger in its absence.

With the final touches to his suitcase complete, Alexander took a moment to sit on the edge of his bed, staring out the window at the sprawling gardens below. The vibrant colors of blooming flowers and the gentle rustle of leaves in the breeze reminded him of the beauty he was leaving behind. Yet, he felt a surge of excitement at the thought of new experiences and adventures awaiting him in America.

Just then, his mother, the queen, knocked on his door."Alex, may I come in?" Queen Isabella's voice was soft but firm, a gentle reminder of the bond they shared.

"Of course, Mother," Alexander replied, turning from the window to face her. He noticed the way her expression shifted from concern to warmth as she entered the room, the door closing softly behind her.

"I wanted to check on you before you leave for your adventure in America," she said, taking a seat on the edge of his bed. "How are you feeling?"

Alexander took a deep breath, gathering his thoughts. "I'm a mix of excited and nervous. It's a big step, and I want to make sure I'm ready for everything that comes with it."

Queen Isabella smiled knowingly. "It is a big step, but you have always risen to challenges. Remember, you are not just leaving for yourself; you carry the legacy of our family and the hopes of our people.

Her words echoed in his mind, providing a sense of comfort. "I know, and I want to make you proud.

"These are your last messages from the council," she said, her voice a mix of concern and pride. She knew that Alexander's journey to America was not just about academics; it was a chance for him to experience the world beyond the palace walls.

"Are you sure you won't reconsider and finish your studies at home?" the Queen inquired. Queen Isabella's apprehension regarding Alexander's journey to America stemmed from her desire to maintain the royal lineage and social status. The fear that he might become enamored with someone of lower social standing reflected the historical tensions between love, duty, and the preservation of royal bloodlines. Such concerns were not uncommon among royalty, as alliances and marriages were often arranged for political gain rather than personal affection.

Isabella likely envisioned a future where Alexander would marry a woman of noble birth, thereby strengthening political ties and ensuring that the royal legacy continued unblemished. The allure of adventure and the promise of new horizons in America might pose a threat to those plans, as he could be swayed by romantic feelings for a commoner, leading to potential scandal and upheaval in the royal court.

Mother, I promise to return with knowledge that can help our people," Alexander replied, a hint of determination in his voice. He had always felt a responsibility to his country, and he believed that studying in America would give him the tools he needed to lead effectively, but he longed once more to see his friend Rachel. He was hopeful that their relationship had survived the winter break.

Prince Alexander was hesitant to tell his mother about Rachel, knowing that his mother was already busy finding suitable royal matches. Alexander knew that he had to keep this secret from his mother.

As the weight of his mother's expectations settled in, Alexander felt a pang of guilt twist in his stomach. He understood the importance of his position, and the pressure to uphold the family legacy weighed heavily on him. But the thought of sharing his feelings for Rachel felt like stepping into a minefield, with potential consequences that could ripple through his life and his family's standing.

"Mother, I appreciate your support," he said, trying to keep his voice steady. "I will do my best to represent our family honorably while I'm abroad."

Queen Isabella smiled, her eyes filled with pride. "I have no doubt you will. Just remember to stay focused on your studies and the responsibilities that come with your title. The royal court will be watching."

As she turned to leave, Alexander felt a surge of determination. He couldn't allow the pressure of royal duty to extinguish the flame of his friendship with Rachel. He wanted to explore that connection without the burden of expectations clouding his heart.

Once he was alone, Alexander sat back down at his

desk, his mind racing. He would protect his feelings for Rachel, allowing them to flourish in the background while he focused on his studies and responsibilities in America. He understood that he had to tread carefully, ensuring that his mother and the court would remain unaware of the depth of his friendship.

Later that evening, a farewell gathering was held in the grand hall of the palace. Friends and family gathered to bid him goodbye, their faces a mix of pride and sorrow. Alexander made his way through the crowd, exchanging hugs and heartfelt words of encouragement.

As the night wore on, he found himself standing near a window, gazing out into the night. The stars twinkled overhead, and he couldn't help but wonder about Rachel, about her life on the farm, and the dreams they had shared. Would she be looking at the same stars, thinking of him?

Just then, Queen Isabella approached him, her expression gentle. "Are you ready for this journey, my son?" she asked, resting a hand on his shoulder.

"I am, Mother. I just hope to make you proud," he replied, his voice steady.

"You already do, Alexander. Always remember that you carry the heart of Slovitia with you. No matter where you go, it will guide you," she said, her eyes glistening with emotion.

With a final embrace, Alexander felt a wave of determination wash over him. Tomorrow, he would take the first step into a new world, where he hoped to reconnect with

Rachel and embrace the adventures that lay ahead. As the gathering continued around him, he felt ready to embark on this journey—one that would intertwine their lives once more, no matter the consequences.

Chapter 4

Paths of the Heart

The next morning, the sunlight pierced Rachel's window. The golden rays danced across her room, casting playful shadows that seemed to awaken the remnants of her dreams. Rachel stirred in her bed, blinking against the brightness, feeling the warmth of the sun on her face. It was a new day, brimming with possibilities, and she could already feel the anticipation building within her.

She sat up, stretching her arms overhead and taking a moment to gather her thoughts. Memories of last night's conversation with Max flooded back, filling her with a sense of purpose. Today, she had plans—plans that would take her beyond the familiar comforts of home and into the wider world.

As she sat up, her mind flooded with memories of Jacob and the memories they had made together at school. She remembered seeing his face for the first time at the library. The moment felt vivid, almost as if it had happened just yesterday. Rachel could still picture Jacob, hunched over a stack of books, his brow furrowed in deep concentration. The library had always been her favorite place to escape into worlds of adventure and tranquility, but that day, it became something more.

She had been searching for a book for her English class

when she noticed him, lost in his reading. There was something magnetic about his focus, the way he seemed to be in a world of his own. Curiosity tugged at her, and she found herself lingering just a little longer, stealing glances at him from behind the shelves with her best friend Polly. His dark, well-groomed hair fell in soft waves over his forehead, and when he finally looked up, their eyes met for the briefest moment.

A spark of connection ignited in that instant, and Rachel felt a flutter in her heart. She remembered how she had fumbled her words when she eventually approached him, asking about the book he was reading. They had struck up a conversation that day, their shared love for reading forming an instant bond. From that moment on, the library became their meeting place, a sanctuary where they could exchange thoughts on stories and dreams.

As Rachel reminisced, she thought about the laughter they had shared during long study sessions, the way they would challenge each other to think deeper, and the comfort of knowing they had each other's backs. Jacob had a way of making even the most mundane tasks fun, turning homework into a game and sparking her creativity in ways she never expected.

But with those sweet memories also came the pang of nostalgia. They had drifted apart as life took them in different directions. Rachel felt a bittersweet ache at the thought of missing him, wondering what he was up to now. Did he know how much their friendship had shaped her?

As she sat on her bed, the sunlight pouring in and illuminating the pages of her notebook, Rachel made a decision. She would reach out to Jacob. The memories they had created together were too precious to leave in the past.

With a renewed sense of purpose, she picked up her phone and started drafting a message, her heart racing with excitement and a hint of nervousness. The dawn of a new day also brought the possibility of rekindling a friendship that had once meant so much to her. As she pressed send, Rachel felt a sense of hope wash over her, eager to see where this journey would lead.

As Rachel sent the message, she felt a mix of excitement and trepidation. Would Jacob respond? Would he remember her the way she remembered him? The uncertainty lingered in the air as she set her phone down, trying to focus on the tasks of the day ahead.

After a quick breakfast of toast and fresh fruit, Rachel grabbed her notebook, a cherished companion filled with sketches, ideas, and dreams. She settled at the kitchen table, the sounds of the farm coming to life around her—the distant clucking of chickens, the soft rustle of leaves outside, and the faint hum of a tractor starting up. All of it felt grounding, a reminder of where she came from.

She decided to head out for a walk around the farm, hoping the fresh air would clear her mind. The landscape was alive with color; wildflowers dotted the fields, and the sky was a brilliant blue. As she walked, Rachel thought about the memories she had shared with Jacob, each one a thread woven into the fabric of her existence.

Their late-night study sessions had often turned into deep conversations about their dreams and aspirations. She remembered Jacob's passion for art—how he would sketch in the margins of his notes, bringing characters and scenes to life. He had a gift for seeing the world from a different perspective, which inspired Rachel to push her own creative boundaries.

As she approached the old oak tree, Rachel paused to take in the surroundings. This spot held many memories of laughter and shared dreams. She could almost hear Jacob's voice echoing in the breeze as he animatedly described his latest endeavors. The thought brought a smile to her face.

Suddenly, her phone buzzed, jolting her from her thoughts. Heart racing, she glanced down to see a notification. It was a response from Jacob. Taking a deep breath, she opened the message, her heart pounding in her chest.

"Hey, Rachel! Wow, it's been a while! I remember those library days fondly. How have you been?"

A wave of warmth washed over her as she read his words. She quickly typed back, sharing snippets of her life since their last days at school and how she was preparing to return.

As Rachel hit send, she felt a sense of relief. Reconnecting felt like a bridge back to a part of herself that she cherished. She continued her walk, her mind wandering to the possibilities that lay ahead. Would they meet up? Could they revive their friendship, or perhaps even become something more?

Chapter 5

A Prince Among Commoners

Alexander was preparing to leave the castle when Queen Isabella called out, Jacob Alexander Frederick Kingston the third, were you going to leave without saying goodbye?

Alexander turned around, a sheepish smile creeping onto his face. "I didn't mean to be rude, Your Majesty," he replied, stepping back into the grand hall of the castle. The walls were adorned with rich tapestries, and the golden light from the chandeliers cast a warm glow.

Queen Isabella, with her regal presence, approached him gracefully. "You know how much I value our farewells, especially before you embark on your adventures. It would be unthinkable to let you leave without a proper send-off."

Alexander chuckled softly, "You always know how to make an exit feel significant." As they exchanged pleasantries, the weight of his upcoming journey began to settle in, but the warmth of her words made it feel a little lighter.

I've asked Ivan here to accompany you to America. Ivan had been Alexander's manservant for several years as they had grown up together.

Ivan stepped forward, a look of determination on his

face. "I wouldn't let you travel without me, Alexander. Besides, who else will ensure that you don't get into trouble?" His playful tone was accompanied by a twinkle in his eye, reminiscent of their shared childhood.

Queen Isabella nodded approvingly. "It's wise to have a friend by your side. The journey may offer unexpected challenges, but with Ivan, you'll have someone who knows you well and will be on your side."

Alexander chuckled, appreciating Ivan's unwavering loyalty. "I suppose I could use someone to keep me in check. America is quite different from our home, and I'll need all the help I can get."

Queen Isabella nodded approvingly. "It's wise to have a friend by your side. The journey may offer unexpected challenges, but with Ivan, you'll have someone who knows you well."

It has all been arranged, Ivan will be going to school with you to serve as your guardian while you are in America.

The news took Alexander by surprise, and he turned to Ivan, who was grinning broadly. "A guardian? I didn't realize I'd have a personal bodyguard on this adventure," he teased, raising an eyebrow.

Queen Isabella smiled, sensing Alexander's apprehension. "It's not just about protection; it's about ensuring you have someone you can trust by your side.

Queen Isabella feared that Alexander might be lured off course by a common American and was determined to prevent it.

Ivan chuckled at Alexander's playful tone. "Trust me, you'll want me around. Adventures have a way of leading you into unexpected situations," he replied, his grin widening.

Queen Isabella nodded, her expression turning serious. "Your journey is fraught with risks, Alexander. It is essential to have someone who can navigate both the treacherous waters of living in America and the treachery of women. I need you to stay focused on your mission. Get a fine education and return home to rule over this land."

Alexander's brow furrowed slightly. "You think I could be distracted? By someone… common?"

Isabella's gaze softened. "It's not about your strength, but the allure of new experiences. America is filled with wonders and temptations. I cannot risk you losing sight of your purpose."

"Understood," Alexander replied, a mix of determination and curiosity in his voice. "But if Ivan is my guardian, I'll make sure he keeps his eyes on the prize as well."

Ivan pretended to look offended. "Hey now, I'm not just a bodyguard; I'm here for the adventure too! But I promise to keep you on course, even if it means dragging you back from a dance with a 'common American.'"

Their light-hearted banter eased the tension, but the weight of Isabella's concerns lingered in the air.

Queen Isabella feared that Alexander had already become enamored with an American.

Alexander softly kissed his mother's cheek. Then he and Ivan got into the car to go to the airport.

As Alexander settled into the back seat of the car, he exchanged a knowing glance with Ivan. The atmosphere was charged with unspoken thoughts, both aware of the weight of the Queen's concerns.

"Are you ready for this?" Ivan asked his tone a mix of encouragement and caution.

Alexander nodded, though a flicker of uncertainty crossed his face. "I suppose so. But I can't shake off the feeling that my mother is overreacting. It's just a friendship… for now."

Ivan raised an eyebrow. "Just a friendship? You know how these things can escalate, especially with someone from outside your world. You'll have to tread carefully."

"Trust me, I have no intention of letting it go too far," Alexander replied, though a hint of defiance lingered in his voice. "But there's something about her that pulls me in. It's refreshing."

"Refreshing can be dangerous," Ivan warned, his protective instincts kicking in. "Just remember your duties and the expectations that come with being a prince. Your heart may lead you down a path that could complicate things."

As they approached the airport, the towering structure loomed ahead, a gateway to new adventures but also a reminder of the responsibilities that awaited him. Alexander took a deep breath, steeling himself for whatever lay ahead, knowing that the journey might not only take him physically to another destination but also challenge the very foundations of his heart and duty.

As they settled into their seats on the Royal airplane. Ivan began to inquire more about Rachel.

"Is she really worth the risk?" Ivan asked, examining Alexander's expression closely. "I mean, what do you actually know about her?"

Alexander shrugged, his thoughts drifting back to Rachel's laughter and the way her eyes sparkled with passion. "She's different from anyone I've met. She's driven, intelligent, and genuinely cares about the world around her. It's refreshing to be around someone who isn't just focused on royal duties or social expectations."

Ivan leaned back, crossing his arms. "That's all well and good, but remember that we live in a world where appearances matter. One wrong move and it could create a scandal that would follow you for years."

"I understand that," Alexander replied, a hint of frustration creeping into his voice. "But I can't help how I feel. It's not like I'm planning to run away with her. I just want to get to know her better. Maybe I can learn something from her perspective."

"Just be cautious," Ivan urged, his tone softening slightly. "You're not just a man; you're a prince. Every action has consequences, especially when it involves someone outside your circle."

As the airplane's engines hummed steadily, Alexander stared out the window, pondering Ivan's words. The towering airport structures came into view, each symbolizing the weight of his responsibilities. Yet, amidst the looming expectations, a flicker of excitement stirred within him—an adventurous spirit ignited by the possibility of something real with Rachel. "I'll be careful," Alexander finally replied, determination in his voice. "But I won't deny how she makes me feel. I owe it to myself to explore this, even if it's just a friendship for now."

Ivan nodded, sensing the resolve in his friend. "Just remember, the heart can be a tricky guide. Keep your eyes open."

As the plane began its descent, Alexander's heart raced, not just from the thrill of landing but from the anticipation of what lay ahead with Rachel.

As the aircraft began its descent, Alexander felt the familiar rush of nerves. He knew that stepping off the plane as a prince would draw instant attention, and with his growing interest in Rachel, he wanted to avoid the spotlight for just a while longer.

"Let's switch," he whispered to Ivan, his voice barely audible over the soft roar of the engines. "I need a bit of anonymity right now."

Ivan raised an eyebrow, surprised but understanding. "You think they won't recognize you? You're still the prince, no matter what you wear."

"I know," Alexander replied, glancing at the window where the airport was coming into view. "But I want to connect with Rachel without the royal facade. Just for a short while longer. I just need a little more time."

With a reluctant nod, Ivan agreed. They quickly swapped outfits, Ivan donning a more regal outfit while Alexander slipped into a simple yet stylish ensemble that would blend in with the crowd.

As the plane doors opened, Alexander took a deep breath, stepping out into the bustling environment of the airport. The air was filled with the sounds of chatter, the hustle of staff, and the flash of cameras capturing the royal entrance. While Ivan stepped forward to greet the officials, Alex lingered a step behind, trying to remain inconspicuous.

He kept his head down, slipping past the throng of people. The excitement of being in a new space mingled with the thrill of possibility. He wanted to find her before the formality of the royal duties swallowed him whole.

Alex gathered his bags and was able to leave without being seen by the reporters and their cameras.

With his heart pounding, Alexander maneuvered through the bustling airport, clutching his bags tightly. He could feel the weight of his royal identity pressing down on him, but the thrill of anonymity fueled his determination.

Thanks to Ivan's help and their quick wardrobe switch, he was just another face in the crowd.

As he moved swiftly past the throng of reporters and officials, he kept his head down, careful to avoid drawing attention. The ocean of voices and the click of camera shutters faded into the background, allowing him to focus solely on his goal: to get to the university without being discovered.

He spotted an exit that led to a less crowded area outside the terminal. With a surge of adrenaline, he headed toward it, his pulse racing with the excitement of what lay ahead. The fresh air greeted him as he stepped outside, and he took a moment to breathe deeply, soaking in the freedom of being just Jacob.

He quickly flagged a cab, waving his hand to catch the driver's attention. The yellow car pulled over, and he hopped in, feeling a rush of exhilaration as he settled into the back seat.

"Where to?" the driver asked, glancing back at him."Take me to the nearest park, please," Jacob replied, hoping to find a quiet space where he could think and maybe even reflect on the whirlwind of events ahead.

As the cab weaved through the bustling city streets, Jacob couldn't help but feel a mix of anticipation and nervousness. He was grateful for the chance to escape the royal expectations, if only for a little while. The city outside the window buzzed with life, people rushing about, completely unaware of the prince who was temporarily shedding his title.

The driver navigated through the traffic, and soon they arrived at a small park dotted with trees and benches. Jacob thanked the driver and stepped out, inhaling the fresh air and feeling a wave of relief wash over him. This was exactly what he needed—a brief retreat from the chaos.

He wandered into the park, taking in the sights and sounds. Children laughed and played, couples strolled hand in hand, and the rustle of leaves created a soothing backdrop. Jacob found a bench beneath a large oak tree and sat down, allowing himself a moment to breathe and gather his thoughts.

As he sat there, he couldn't shake the feeling of excitement he had felt earlier with Rachel. The memory of their conversation lingered in his mind, and he realized how much he wanted to explore that connection further. But the weight of his responsibilities as a prince loomed over him, reminding him of the complexities that came with his title.

Jacob pulled out his phone, feeling a mix of anticipation and practicality as he typed a quick message to Ivan. He knew that even a brief escape from the royal duties wouldn't last forever, and having Ivan on standby would ensure a smooth transition back to reality.

"Hey Ivan, I'm at the park near the capital. Can you bring the car around? I'll be waiting near the pavement, I'll be easy to find." Moments later, he felt his phone buzz in his pocket. He pulled it out to see a message from Ivan, "On my way. Should be there in about 10 minutes."

Jacob paced near the entrance of the park, his mind racing with thoughts and emotions. The vibrant sounds of the park—the laughter of children, the rustle of leaves, and the distant chatter of families—created a comforting backdrop, but his heart was restless.

He couldn't shake the feeling of anticipation that had built up during his time with Rachel. Their conversation had stirred something within him, a longing for connection and purpose that transcended the confines of his royal duties. As he walked back and forth, he replayed their dialogue in his head, cherishing each moment of laughter and understanding they had shared.

With each passing minute, the reality of his obligations loomed larger. He was aware that he had to return to the royal duties that awaited him—meetings, press engagements, and the unrelenting expectations of being a prince. Yet, the thought of returning to that life felt increasingly suffocating after experiencing the freedom of being just Jacob.

He glanced at his phone again, checking for any messages from Ivan. Nothing. Just as he was about to send another text, he spotted the familiar black sedan pulling up. A wave of relief washed over him, and he quickened his pace toward the car.

As the vehicle came to a stop, Ivan stepped out, looking around as if scanning for any signs of trouble. "Everything alright?" he asked, his brow slightly furrowed with concern.

"Yeah, just enjoying a moment away from the chaos,"

Jacob replied, trying to keep his tone light. "I think it's time to get you settled into your accommodations," Ivan said as they drove through the city, the skyline dotted with historic architecture and modern buildings. "The Palace has arranged a nice townhome just a short distance from the university for us to stay at."

Jacob felt a wave of relief wash over him. "That sounds perfect. I want to be close to campus, especially with everything I need to manage while I'm here."

Ivan nodded, glancing at him as they navigated the streets. "It'll give you the freedom to focus on your studies and any initiatives you want to pursue without being too far removed from campus life."

As they approached the townhome, Jacob couldn't help but admire the charming exterior. The building had a classic design with a welcoming facade, complete with flower boxes and a small porch. It felt like a home rather than just a temporary residence. "This is it," Ivan announced, pulling to a stop. "Shall we take a look inside?"

Jacob stepped out of the car and took a moment to absorb his new surroundings. He felt a mix of excitement and apprehension about what lay ahead. As they walked up to the front door, Ivan retrieved the keys from his pocket and unlocked it, pushing the door open to reveal the interior.

The townhome was beautifully furnished, with a cozy living area, a well-equipped kitchen, and a modest dining space. Natural light poured in through the large windows, giving the place a warm and inviting ambiance.

"It's fine," Jacob said, stepping inside and taking in the details. "I can definitely see myself living here."

"I thought you'd like it," Ivan replied, following him inside. "You have everything you need to make this your own space while you're here. Plus, it's private, which is essential for someone in your position."

Jacob nodded, appreciating Ivan's encouragement. "I want to make the most of my time here, both academically and personally. This is a chance for me to explore my interests and figure out who I am outside of the royal duties."

As he moved from room to room, Jacob felt a sense of liberation. This townhome represented a new chapter, one where he could carve out his own identity while still honoring his responsibilities. He envisioned inviting Rachel over, discussing their shared passions, and brainstorming ideas for their studies.

"Once you're settled, we can discuss your schedule and any upcoming events at the university," Ivan said, pulling Jacob back to the present. "You'll want to stay connected with your peers and the faculty."

"Right," Jacob replied, feeling a mix of excitement and nervousness. "I want to make an impact, but I also need to find a balance."

"Just remember, you're not alone in this," Ivan reassured him. "I'll be here to support you every step of the way."

Jacob felt a surge of gratitude for his friend's

unwavering support. "Thanks, Ivan. I really appreciate everything you're doing for me."

"From this point on, do not refer to me as Alexander, or Prince, or any royal declaration. From this point out, I'm just Jacob," he said, looking at Ivan with a newfound determination.

Ivan nodded, understanding the weight behind Jacob's words. "I get it, Jacob. This is your time to define who you are outside of the Palace. I'm here to support you in anything you need."

Jacob felt a sense of relief wash over him. Embracing this identity was liberating, and he was ready to dive into life as a regular person, without the constraints of royal expectations. "Thanks, Ivan. I really appreciate your support."

As they continued their conversation, Jacob felt the anticipation building for the upcoming day with Rachel. He thought about the possibilities that lay ahead—friendship, and perhaps something more.

Chapter 6

Heartfelt Goodbyes

The morning light shone through Rachel's window once more as she lay awake, feeling a mix of excitement and anxiety for the day ahead. Today marked a significant transition; she would be moving back to Utah to continue her studies at the university. It was an exciting time for Rachel, but also a reminder of the challenges and responsibilities that awaited her.

Rachel sat up in bed, taking a deep breath as she glanced around her room, which was filled with the familiar comforts of home. She could see her packed bags in the corner and a few mementos from her time at the university scattered around—photos with friends, and notes from classmates.

As she got up and began to prepare for the day, thoughts of Jacob flooded her mind. Their conversation sparked something exciting within her, and she couldn't help but wonder how their connection would evolve now that she was back in town. She remembered the way he had listened to her ideas and how easy it had been to talk with him.

After a quick breakfast, Rachel double-checked her packing list, ensuring she hadn't forgotten anything important. She was ready to make the most of her time at the university and dive deeper into her studies, focusing on getting her business degree with the dream of one day running a business of her own, perhaps something that combined her passion for business and art.

With her bags in tow, she headed downstairs to meet her family, who were waiting to help her move. The chatter and laughter filled the air as they waited for Rachel's sister Sally to arrive.

"Are you excited?" her mother asked. "Definitely! I can't wait to get back into the swing of things," Rachel replied, enthusiasm bubbling in her voice. "I have so many ideas for my classes and projects this year."

Her father chimed in, "You've got this, Rachel. Just remember to balance your studies with some downtime. It's important to enjoy the experience, too." "I will, Dad," she promised, smiling at his advice.

Just then, the sound of someone driving up the old gravel road toward the farm caught Rachel's attention. She looked out the window and smiled as she recognized the familiar old blue pickup truck. It was Sally, her sister, pulling up with a wave and a grin that instantly brightened Rachel's day.

"Hey, Rachel!" Sally called out as she hopped out of the truck, her curly hair bouncing with her energetic movements. "I couldn't miss your big moving day!"

Rachel rushed outside to greet her sister, feeling a surge of happiness at having Sally by her side during this transition. "I'm so glad you came! I was just getting worried you might have forgotten."

Sally gave her a quick hug, then stepped back to take in the sight of Rachel's glowing expression. "I could never forget my favorite sister! Besides, I wouldn't miss this for the world."

Just then, Max and Kathy joined them outside. "Thanks for taking your sister to the airport," Max said, his warm smile lighting up his face. "I wish I could, but the fields need to have their spring plowing done. You know how it is."

Kathy nodded in agreement. "We all have our responsibilities, but I'm glad Sally can be with you today. It's important to have family support during times like these."

Rachel felt a swell of gratitude for her family and their understanding. "I appreciate it, Dad. I'll be okay, and I promise to keep you updated on everything."

Max ruffled Rachel's hair affectionately. "Just make sure to call us and let us know how you're doing. We want to hear about all your adventures!"

"Definitely!" Rachel replied, laughing as she fixed her hair. "And I'll send some pictures of my new place."

With a few more affectionate exchanges and promises to stay in touch, Rachel felt ready to embrace her new chapter. She looked at Sally, who was already glancing at her watch. "What time do we need to head out?" Sally asked.

"We should leave soon", Rachel replied. "Let's get a move on, then! If we are lucky, we can beat the traffic and get you to the airport on time," Sally replied.

As they climbed in and began driving, Rachel felt a mix of emotions swirling inside her, excitement, anticipation, and a hint of nostalgia. She knew that this move was just the beginning of a new adventure, and having Sally by her side made it feel all the more special.

As they drove down the dusty road, the familiar landscape whizzing by, Sally and Rachel reminisced about their days growing up together. The warm sun filtered through the trees lining the road, and the air was filled with the scent of fresh earth and blooming wildflowers.

"Do you remember that time we tried to build a treehouse in the old oak tree?" Sally laughed, her eyes sparkling with nostalgia. "We thought we were so clever until it came crashing down!"

Rachel chuckled, shaking her head at the memory. "How could I forget? We spent hours gathering those old boards and nails, and then it fell apart just as we were about to climb in!"

"Honestly, I think we ended up with more bruises than we did any actual treehouse," Sally said, grinning. "But it was so much fun just being outside and imagining what it would be like to have our own secret hideout."

"Yeah, those were the days," Rachel agreed, her heart warming at the thought. "We were so carefree back then. It feels like a lifetime ago."

As they drove, Sally leaned in, her interest piqued. "Have you heard from Jacob?" "Yes," Rachel smiled, feeling a rush of excitement. "I texted him yesterday."

"What did he say?" Sally asked, her eyes sparkling with curiosity.

"He has been busy learning his family's business, but he still remembered me and the fun times we had," Rachel said with a giggle, her excitement growing with every word. "It's nice to know that even with everything going on, he still thinks about our time together."

Sally smiled, her eyes twinkling with mischief. "That's a great sign! It shows he values those memories and wants to keep the relationship alive. What fun times are you thinking about?"

"Oh, all those late-night study sessions where we ended up just laughing and goofing off instead of actually studying!" Rachel recalled her laughter mingling with Sally's. "And that time we got lost on our hiking trip, but ended up discovering that amazing place called Mirror Lake? I still can't believe we managed to turn that into such a fun adventure."

"Those were classic moments!" Sally said, nodding in agreement. "It sounds like you two have built a solid foundation of shared fun experiences. It'll be great to see how that translates into your time together now."

"I really hope so," Rachel replied, her heartbeat

quickening at the thought. "I just want to enjoy our time and see where things go. I can't help but feel excited!"

"Just be yourself, and let the relationship develop naturally. You've got this, Rachel!" Sally reassured her, giving her a supportive nudge.

As the drive continued, Rachel felt a comforting warmth wash over her, not just from the sun streaming through the windows but from the bond she shared with her sister. The journey down memory lane reminded her of the importance of family and the roots that anchored her, even as she prepared to branch out into new experiences.

Sally's encouragement resonated deeply with Rachel, and she found herself reflecting on her aspirations and the friendships she hoped to nurture. The thought of rekindling her connection with Jacob added an extra ray of sunshine into her life.

Rachel's heart raced with a mix of excitement and nervousness. She hadn't seen Jacob in months, and the memories of their laughter and shared adventures flooded her mind. The car's tires hummed against the asphalt, a steady rhythm that matched her heartbeat.

Sally glanced over, sensing Rachel's shift in mood. "Are you ready for this?" she asked, her voice laced with warmth and support.

Rachel smiled, her anxiety easing slightly. "I think so. It's just… it feels like it has been an eternity." She bit her lip, contemplating the words she wanted to say to Jacob.

Would he still feel the same spark? Would their connection be as strong as it once was?

The airport loomed closer, its towering structure and busy atmosphere promising a world of possibilities. They drove around for what seemed like forever looking for a place to park. As they parked and began to walk towards the terminal, Rachel took a deep breath, allowing the energy of the place to invigorate her spirit.

"Just be yourself," Sally encouraged, linking her arm with Rachel's. "You've got this."

With every step, Rachel reminded herself of her goals, the friendships she cherished, and the opportunity to rekindle something beautiful. This year was about embracing new beginnings, and she was ready to greet Jacob with open arms.

As they entered the bustling airport, Rachel was enveloped by the sounds of rolling luggage, the chatter of travelers, and the distant announcements echoing through the terminal. Each sound felt like a reminder of the world waiting outside, full of adventures and reconnections.

Sally pointed toward the large departure board. "Which flight are you on?" she asked, scanning the list of departures.

Rachel fished her phone from her pocket and quickly checked. "Flight 239 to Salt Lake City," she replied, her voice barely above a whisper. The anticipation was exhausting, and she could feel butterflies dancing in her stomach.

Sally nodded, her eyes gleaming with excitement. "That's not too far! Just a short flight. Are you sure you're ready for this?"

Rachel took a deep breath, feeling the weight of the moment. "I think so. It's just… I haven't seen him in a while. What if things have changed?" Her mind raced with possibilities—what if Jacob had moved on? What if the connection they once shared had faded into mere memories?

Sally placed a comforting hand on Rachel's shoulder. "Change is part of life. But it doesn't mean what you had is gone. You might be surprised at how much you still connect."

Rachel appreciated Sally's optimism, but the uncertainty lingered like a shadow. They settled into seats near the gate, the chatter of other passengers a soothing backdrop to her swirling thoughts.

As they waited, Rachel glanced at her phone, scrolling through old messages and pictures from happier times with Jacob. Each snapshot was a reminder of the laughter and dreams they once shared, a stark contrast to the silence that had grown between them.

"What if I don't know what to say?" Rachel fretted, biting her lip.

"You'll figure it out. Just speak from your heart," Sally replied, her tone reassuring. "Remember, you're not just reconnecting with Jacob; you're reconnecting with a part of yourself, too."

Rachel nodded, knowing that Sally was right. This trip was about more than just meeting Jacob; it was about rediscovering her own aspirations and the friendships that mattered most.

The announcement for Flight 239 broke through her thoughts, and Rachel's heart raced again. She stood up, her palms slightly sweaty. "This is it," she whispered, excitement and nerves bubbling within her.

Sally stood beside her, offering a supportive smile. "Go get 'em, Sis. No matter what happens, you've already taken the first step."

With that, Rachel and Sally stepped toward the boarding gate, ready to embrace whatever came next.

As Rachel approached the boarding gate, she could feel the anticipation building like a wave inside her. The atmosphere was electric, filled with travelers bustling about, some saying their goodbyes, others eagerly awaiting their adventures. Each step felt heavier, yet exhilarating, as she clutched her boarding pass tightly.

Sally walked alongside her, a steady presence amidst the chaos. "Just remember, it's okay to be nervous. It's a big moment," she reminded Rachel, giving her a gentle nudge. Rachel appreciated the support, knowing that her friend was right there to catch her if she stumbled.

As the boarding announcement echoed through the terminal, Rachel paused for a moment, taking in the scene around her. She spotted families reuniting, friends hugging tightly, and the joyful faces of children traveling for the first time. It made her realize that reunions, no matter how small, were often filled with emotion and significance.

As Rachel and Sally approached the security checkpoint, Sally stopped, well, Sis, this is as far as I can go. Rachel and Sally warmly embraced as they said goodbye.

Rachel felt a bittersweet pang in her heart as she hugged Sally tightly. "Thank you for everything, really. I couldn't have done this without you."

Sally pulled back, her eyes sparkling with encouragement. "You're going to be great, Rachel. Just remember to breathe and be yourself. I'm just a call away if you need anything."

Rachel nodded, feeling a mix of gratitude and apprehension. She watched as Sally turned to leave, her figure disappearing into the crowd. With every step away, Rachel felt the weight of the moment settle in. This was it— she was embarking on a journey back into her past, but also into an uncertain future.

Taking a deep breath, Rachel stepped forward to the security checkpoint, the buzz of the airport around her fading into the background. She placed her backpack on the conveyor belt, her mind racing with thoughts of Jacob and their upcoming reunion. Would they fall back into their old rhythm? Would it feel as comfortable as it once had, or would the months apart create a barrier they couldn't cross?

After passing through security, Rachel gathered her

things and made her way to the gate. She glanced at the departure board, confirming that her flight was on time. The excitement bubbled up again as she thought about what lay ahead.

When it was finally time to board, Rachel moved forward with a mix of determination and anxiety. She found her seat by the window, glancing out at the runway as the plane prepared for takeoff. The view was stunning, with planes taxiing and the distant skyline shimmering under the afternoon sun.

Once settled in her seat, Rachel's mind wandered again to Jacob. She imagined how he would look, how he would greet her, and what they would talk about after all this time. Would they slip back into their old rhythm, or would it feel awkward and unfamiliar? The uncertainty was both thrilling and daunting.

The flight attendants began their safety demonstration, but Rachel barely registered the instructions, her thoughts racing. She pulled out her phone again, scrolling through old photos of them, camping trips, late-night talks, and spontaneous adventures. Each image tugged at her heart, reminding her of the connection they once had.

Before she knew it, the plane was in the air, climbing higher and higher. Rachel felt a sense of freedom wash over her as if she was leaving behind the doubts and fears that had been holding her back. She closed her eyes for a moment, envisioning the conversation she wanted to have with Jacob about their dreams, their lives, and the paths they had taken since they last met.

After a brief flight, the plane began its descent into Salt Lake City. Rachel's heart pounded in her chest as they touched down, the reality of the moment settling in. She gathered her belongings, the excitement coursing through her veins. As she stepped off the plane and into the terminal, the familiar hustle and bustle enveloped her once more.

Chapter 7

Friendship and Fearlessness

Following the signs to baggage claim, Rachel's thoughts were a whirlwind of what-ifs. Would Polly be waiting for her? Just as she reached the baggage carousel, she spotted a familiar face in the crowd, Polly leaning against a pillar, scanning the area with an eager expression.

"Rachel!" Polly exclaimed, rushing forward with open arms. The two friends embraced tightly, their laughter echoing in the busy terminal.

"I can't believe you're finally here!" Polly said, stepping back to take a good look at Rachel. "You look amazing! How was the flight?"

"It was great," Rachel replied, a smile spreading across her face. "I felt so free up there, like I was leaving everything behind. But now I'm just excited to see you and catch up."

Polly's eyes sparkled with enthusiasm. "I've got so much to tell you! And I can't wait to hear about your time back home on the farm. I just love your stories about home. But first, let's grab your bags and get out of here."

As they made their way to the baggage carousel, Rachel felt a mix of nostalgia and excitement. The last time she had seen Polly had been months ago, and now with graduation this year, they were both at a crossroads in their lives. She couldn't shake the feeling that this year was going to change everything.

Once Rachel's suitcase appeared, they headed outside, where the crisp Salt Lake City air hit them. Polly pulled out her phone. "I ordered us some food from that cute café nearby. We can catch up over brunch."

"That sounds perfect," Rachel said, her heart racing at the thought of reconnecting with her friend and sharing everything that had happened.

As they walked towards Polly's car, Rachel's mind drifted back to Jacob. She knew she would have to face the conversation with him soon, but for now, she was grateful to be with Polly, ready to dive into their shared memories and dreams for the future.

Once they arrived at Polly's car, Rachel couldn't help but admire the vibrant sunlight reflecting off the windshield. "It sure is a beautiful Spring day," Rachel said cheerfully. Polly tossed her suitcase into the trunk and hopped into the driver's seat, her energy infectious. As they pulled away from the airport, the city skyline came into view, and Rachel felt a wave of excitement wash over her.

The café was just a short drive away, nestled in a charming neighborhood filled with local shops and art galleries. Polly parked, and they made their way inside, the bell above the door jingling cheerfully as they entered. The café had a warm, inviting atmosphere, with eclectic decor and the hum of conversations filling the air.

They settled at a small table near the window, and as they waited for their food, the conversation flowed effortlessly. Rachel shared stories about her life on the farm, waking up at dawn, the smell of fresh hay, and the satisfaction of eating fresh fruits and vegetables. Polly listened intently, her eyes wide with curiosity.

"I always thought it was so romantic," Polly said, taking a sip of her coffee. "Living on a farm seems like such a simple, beautiful life. But I know it must be a lot of hard work."

"It is," Rachel admitted, a smile creeping onto her face. "But there's something so rewarding about it. I love the connection to the land and the rhythm of the seasons. It's grounding."

Just then, their food arrived, and the delicious spread filled the table. As they dug into their meals, Rachel felt a wave of gratitude for this moment. It was easy to forget the stress of the future when she was with Polly, reminiscing about their shared experiences.

After brunch, they decided to take a stroll around the neighborhood. The streets were lined with blooming flowers, and the air was filled with the scent of fresh pastries from nearby bakeries. They wandered into a few shops, laughing and trying on quirky hats and accessories, momentarily forgetting the weight of their upcoming decisions.

Polly paused outside a small bookstore, her eyes lighting up. "Oh, we have to go in here! I need to find something new to read." Rachel followed her inside, the cozy atmosphere wrapping around them like a warm blanket.

As they browsed the shelves, Rachel spotted a book that reminded her of Jacob. It was a collection of poetry about love and longing, and she couldn't help but pick it up. The weight of it in her hands felt significant, like a reminder of the conversation she needed to have. Polly noticed and raised an eyebrow. "What's that you've got there?"

Rachel hesitated but decided to share. "It's a poetry book. I used to love reading poetry with Jacob. It feels… meaningful, I guess."

Polly studied her for a moment, then nodded thoughtfully. "You should definitely talk to him about how you feel. It sounds like you have a lot to say."

Rachel sighed, a mixture of apprehension and determination swirling within her. "I know. I just hope it goes well."

As they left the bookstore, Rachel felt a sense of clarity. She might not have all the answers yet, but she was ready to face whatever lay ahead. With Polly by her side, she felt empowered to embrace the changes and challenges that awaited her.

As they continued their stroll, the sun warmed their faces, and the vibrant energy of the city infused their conversation. Polly, ever the optimist, kept the mood light, sharing stories about her own adventures and plans for the future.

"You know, I've been thinking about applying for an internship in New York City after graduation," Polly said, her eyes sparkling with excitement. "It's a big leap, but I feel like it could be a great opportunity for me."

Rachel smiled, feeling a swell of pride for her friend. "That sounds incredible! You've always dreamed of living in a big city, and I can totally see you thriving there."

Polly grinned. "Thanks! It feels a bit scary, but I think a little fear is a good thing, right? It means we're stepping out of our comfort zones."

Rachel nodded, the truth of Polly's words resonating with her. She realized that facing her own fears—like the conversation with Jacob—was part of this growth. They stopped at a small park, taking a moment to sit on a bench surrounded by blooming flowers and the sounds of children playing nearby.

"Speaking of comfort zones," Polly said, her tone shifting slightly, "what's your plan with Jacob? Are you going to tell him how you feel?"

Rachel took a deep breath, contemplating the question. "I want to. I've been carrying this weight for too long. I need to know if there's still something between us, or if we've both moved on. It's just… what if it doesn't go the way I hope?"

Polly leaned closer, her expression serious but encouraging. "What if it does? You'll never know unless you try. You owe it to yourself to find out."

Rachel appreciated Polly's unwavering support. "You're right. I've been holding back because I'm scared of what might happen. But I can't let fear dictate my choices anymore."

Feeling empowered, Rachel looked out at the park, where life was buzzing all around her. Children laughed as they played, couples strolled hand in hand, and friends gathered on picnic blankets. It reminded her of the beauty of connection and the importance of taking risks.

After a while, they decided to head back to Polly's car, their hearts full of laughter and conversation. As they drove through the city, Rachel couldn't help but feel a renewed sense of purpose. She wanted to embrace the unknown, to be brave enough to face her feelings head-on.

Back at Polly's apartment, they settled onto the couch with cups of herbal tea. The sun began to set, casting a warm glow over the room. Polly flipped through a magazine, but Rachel's mind was elsewhere, focused on the upcoming conversation with Jacob.

"Do you think I should message him before I go to bed?" Rachel asked, feeling a mix of excitement and nervousness.

Polly paused, considering. "I think that could be a good idea. It might set the stage for an honest conversation when you see him."

Rachel nodded, feeling a surge of determination. "Okay, I'll do it. I'll let him know I'm in town and would love to catch up."

With her heart racing, Rachel pulled out her phone and began typing a message. She poured her feelings into the words, expressing her excitement about being back in town and her desire to reconnect. Before she could second-guess herself, she hit send.

As they settled back into conversation, Rachel felt a mix of relief and anticipation. She had taken the first step, and now it was just a matter of time before she faced Jacob. With Polly by her side, she felt ready to embrace whatever came next.

As the evening unfolded, Rachel and Polly reminisced about their childhoods, sharing stories that made them laugh and reflect on how far they had come. The comforting atmosphere of Polly's apartment, with its warm lighting and cozy décor, felt like a safe haven where they could express their hopes and fears without judgment.

"Remember that time we tried to bake cookies and ended up with a giant, gooey mess?" Polly laughed, her eyes sparkling with the memory. "I think we ended up just eating the dough straight from the bowl!"

Rachel chuckled, the memory flooding her with warmth. "Yes! And we thought we were such great bakers. I can't believe we didn't burn the place down!"

Polly grinned, leaning back against the couch. "It's those little moments that I cherish. No matter where life takes us, I hope we always find time for fun like that."

Rachel felt a pang of nostalgia but also a sense of determination. "I want that too. I want to make sure we don't lose touch, no matter how busy life gets."

Just then, Rachel's phone buzzed, breaking the comfortable silence. Her heart leaped as she saw it was a message from Jacob. Taking a deep breath, she opened it, trying to steady her racing thoughts.

"Hey, Rachel! So good to hear from you. I'd love to catch up! When are you free?"

Rachel felt a rush of warmth, a mix of excitement and nervousness. She quickly typed back, suggesting they meet at a favorite coffee shop the next day. After hitting send, she looked at Polly, her eyes wide. "He wants to meet up! I can't believe it."

Polly clapped her hands in excitement. "That's amazing! This is your chance to talk things out. Just be honest with him about how you feel."

Rachel nodded, a wave of determination washing over her. "I will. I just need to remember that I'm not the same person I was before. I've grown, and so has he. I need to approach this with an open heart."

As the evening continued, they delved into deeper topics—dreams, aspirations, and the uncertainties of adulthood. Polly shared her hopes for her internship in New York, while Rachel talked about her desire to explore new opportunities, possibly outside of the farm life she had always known.

"You deserve to chase your dreams too," Polly said, her voice filled with sincerity. "Whatever you choose, just make sure it's something that makes you happy."

Rachel felt a surge of gratitude for her friend. "Thank you for always believing in me. It means so much to have your support."

Later that night, as they prepared for bed, Rachel felt a sense of peace settles in. She knew that the next day would bring challenges, but she also felt a sense of excitement at the prospect of reconnecting with Jacob. With Polly's encouragement echoing in her mind, she drifted off to sleep, her dreams filled with possibilities.

Chapter 8

Whispers of the Heart

The next morning, the sun peeked through the shades as Jacob stretched, the sun shining across his face. Jacob's eyes fluttered open, greeted by the warm, golden rays of the morning sun filtering through the partially drawn shades. He felt the gentle warmth on his skin, a comforting reminder of the new day ahead. Stretching his arms above his head, he let out a yawn.

As Jacob lay in bed, the sunlight wove itself through the shades, casting playful patterns over his muscular physique. The warm glow highlighted the defined lines of his arms and chest, accentuating the strength that lay beneath his relaxed posture. Each beam seemed to bring his form to life as if nature itself was celebrating his presence. The soft sheets cradled him comfortably, and for a moment, he felt invincible.

Thoughts of Rachel flooded Jacob's mind, stirring a whirlwind of excitement and anticipation. He could vividly recall her laughter, the way her eyes sparkled when she smiled, and the effortless connection they shared. Every moment they had spent together replayed in his memory, igniting a sense of eagerness that made his heart race. He envisioned their upcoming meeting, the warmth of her embrace, the spark of conversation, and the little moments that felt so significant. As he lay there, time seemed to stand still, and the prospect of seeing her again filled him with an exhilarating energy, pushing away any lingering remnants of sleep.

As Jacob continued to revel in his thoughts of Rachel, he imagined the way her hair fell softly around her shoulders, catching the light just like the sunbeams that danced across his bed. He could almost hear her voice, a melodic sound that seemed to wrap around him like a warm blanket. The memories of their shared laughter and deep conversations swirled in his mind, creating a tapestry of moments that he cherished.

He thought about the little things that made their connection special—the way they would finish each other's sentences or the inside jokes that made them burst into laughter at the most unexpected times. There was a certain ease between them, a comfort that made him feel at home, even in the chaos of the outside world.

Jacob couldn't help but smile at the thought of what lay ahead, the excitement bubbling within him. He knew that seeing Rachel again would be more than just a reunion; it would be another chapter in the story they were writing together, one filled with promise, laughter, and the kind of connection that could only deepen with time. With that thought, he finally pushed the covers aside, ready to embrace the day and all of the possibilities it held.

As Jacob stepped out of his room, the rich aroma of sizzling eggs and crispy bacon wafted through the air, drawing him toward the kitchen like a magnet. The familiar sounds of clattering pots and pans filled the space, accompanied by Ivan's cheerful humming. It was a comforting scene, one that spoke of home and the kind of morning that promised a hearty breakfast.

Entering the kitchen, Jacob found Ivan standing at the stove, a spatula in hand, flipping the golden-brown strips of bacon with expert precision. The morning light streamed in through the window, casting a warm glow on Ivan's focused face. He glanced over his shoulder and broke into a wide grin upon seeing Jacob.

"Good morning, Good morning your Majesty! Thought you might appreciate a little breakfast to kickstart your day," Ivan said, his voice full of enthusiasm.

Jacob chuckled, feeling grateful for his friend's thoughtfulness. "You always know how to make a morning better. It smells amazing!"

As Jacob settled into a chair at the kitchen table, he watched Ivan work, admiring his culinary skills. The sound of the bacon crackling and the eggs cooking created a symphony of morning delights. Ivan moved with ease, adding spices and herbs, transforming simple ingredients into something special.

"Don't forget, you do not need to address me by a royal title while we are here in America. I want Rachel to like me for who I am, not a title. " Jacob said with a smile.

Ivan chuckled, his eyes sparkling with mischief.

"Alright, alright. No royal titles here in America. Just plain old Ivan and Jacob." He set a generous portion of eggs and bacon in front of Jacob, his grin growing wider. "But you have to admit, 'Your Majesty' has a nice ring to it."

Jacob rolled his eyes playfully. "As long as you don't expect me to start giving out orders, we're good." He picked up his fork, diving into the breakfast with enthusiasm. The flavors burst in his mouth, and he couldn't help but let out a satisfied sigh. "This is fantastic, I was wrong, I may need a guardian."

"Glad you like it! A good breakfast is an important part of the day, especially when you're about to meet a certain someone special," Ivan replied, leaning against the counter, arms crossed.

Jacob nodded, savoring each bite while contemplating the day ahead. "You know, it's funny how things change. Just a few months ago, I couldn't have imagined feeling this way about someone."

Ivan raised an eyebrow, intrigued. "Oh? Do tell!"

With a smile, Jacob began to share the story of how he met Rachel, the initial sparks of attraction, and the blossoming connection that had grown between them. As he spoke, the kitchen filled with laughter and camaraderie, setting a perfect tone for the day ahead. The bond between the two friends deepened over breakfast, each bite fueling Jacob's excitement for what was to come.

"I have taken the liberty of getting us both registered for

our college classes this morning. I have already spoken with the Dean about keeping your identity secret again this year," Ivan said as he ate his breakfast.

Jacob smiled warmly, feeling a wave of gratitude wash over him. "Seriously, Ivan, thank you for always looking out for me. You're a great friend," he said, sincerity evident in his voice.

Ivan shrugged nonchalantly, a playful grin spreading across his face. "What are friends for? Besides, it's fun being your sidekick. Keeps things interesting!"

Jacob chuckled, shaking his head. "You make it sound like I'm some kind of superhero or something."

"Hey, you kind of are!" Ivan replied, leaning forward with enthusiasm. "You've got the brains, the charm, and now a mysterious aura. It's like you're living in a fairy tale."

Jacob couldn't help but laugh at the comparison. "Alright, I'll take that. But seriously, I really appreciate the effort you put into this. It means a lot to me."

Ivan waved off the compliment, his expression softening. "I just want you to have a smooth year. You've got a lot on your shoulders, and I know how much you want to focus on your studies and your time with Rachel. The last thing you need is unnecessary drama."

"True," Jacob agreed, feeling a sense of relief. "With all the pressures of the kingdom, I just want to enjoy college without the added pressure. You've got my back, and I couldn't ask for more."

They shared a knowing look, the bond of friendship evident between them. As they finished breakfast, Jacob felt reassured that with Ivan's support, he could tackle whatever challenges lay ahead.

After finishing his breakfast, Jacob stood up and stretched, feeling a mix of excitement and nervousness. "Hey, just wanted to let you know I have plans to meet up with Rachel at noon at Emma's café," he said, glancing at Ivan with anticipation.

"Oh, Emma's café! That place is said to have the best coffee and pastries," Ivan replied, his eyes lighting up. "You've got to try the almond croissants. They're to die for!"

"How do you know all this?" Jacob replied. Ivan grinned, "I Googled all the cafes in the area."

Jacob chuckled, shaking his head in amusement. "Of course you did! Leave it to you to research everything thoroughly."

Ivan grinned, unabashed. "Hey, I'm just trying to make sure you have the best experience possible! I mean, what kind of royal guardian would I be if I didn't do my homework?"

"True, true," Jacob replied, still laughing. "What else did you find out? Any hidden gems I should know about?"

"Absolutely! Besides the almond croissants, they have this killer vanilla latte that I think you'd love. And the vibe is perfect—cozy, with comfy seating and a totally romantic ambiance," Ivan said, his enthusiasm contagious.

After finishing his meal, Jacob stood up and stretched, feeling the pleasant fullness from breakfast. "Alright, I think I need to go shower before my date," he announced, a hint of excitement in his voice.

"Good call! A shower always helps me feel fresh and confident. " Ivan replied, giving Jacob an approving nod. "You want to make a great impression, especially since it's with Rachel."

"Exactly! I want to look and feel my best," Jacob said, a smile spreading across his face at the thought of seeing her. "I'll just be a few minutes. I don't want to keep her waiting."

"Take your time," Ivan assured him, leaning back in his chair. "No need to rush. You've got this!"

As Jacob headed to the bathroom, his thoughts turned to Rachel. He wanted everything to go smoothly, from the conversation to the atmosphere at the café. A quick shower would help him clear his mind and focus on the moment.

Once in the bathroom, he turned on the water and let it warm up, taking a moment to gather his thoughts. He imagined how Rachel would smile when she saw him, the way her laughter filled the air. He was determined to make this date memorable.

Jacob stepped into the warm shower and stood still for a moment, letting the water run down his muscular physique. The heat enveloped him, melting away the stress of the moment. He closed his eyes and took a deep breath, allowing the soothing sensation to wash over him.

As the water cascaded down his back and shoulders, he felt relaxed. The rhythmic sound of the water hitting the tiles created a calming backdrop, allowing his thoughts to drift. Jacob reflected on his upcoming date with Rachel, feeling a mix of excitement and nerves. He couldn't help but think about how much he enjoyed her company and how effortlessly they connected.

The warmth of the water felt invigorating, and he let his mind wander to the moments they had shared in the past— the laughter, the conversations that seemed to flow endlessly, and the little glances that hinted at something deeper. Jacob smiled to himself, feeling optimistic about the possibilities that lay ahead.

After taking a moment to gather his thoughts, he grabbed his shampoo and began to wash his hair, feeling the tension in his body slowly dissipate. With each wash, he reminded himself to stay present, to enjoy the moment, and to be himself. "You've got this he said, as he stood under the cascading water.

Once he finished rinsing off, Jacob turned off the water, feeling refreshed and renewed. He stepped out and wrapped his towel around his waist. "You can do this", he said as he stared at his reflection in the mirror.

As Jacob entered his bedroom, he was greeted by the sight of Ivan, who had just finished laying out his outfit for the day. "There you are! I took the liberty of picking something that'll make you look sharp," Ivan said with a grin, gesturing to the neatly arranged clothes on the bed.

Jacob chuckled, appreciating his friend's enthusiasm. "Wow, you really went all out, huh?" he replied, eyeing the outfit. It consisted of a fitted navy shirt that complemented his physique, paired with well-fitted trousers and stylish sneakers. A casual yet polished look that would be perfect for his date with Rachel.

"I know how important this is for you, so I wanted to make sure you're looking your best," Ivan said, clearly proud of his choices. "Trust me, this outfit will definitely turn some heads."

"Thanks, Ivan! This looks great," Jacob said, feeling a surge of confidence at the sight of the ensemble. He quickly changed into the outfit, appreciating how it felt against his skin. As he looked in the mirror, he couldn't help but smile at the reflection staring back at him.

"See? You look awesome!" Ivan said, giving him a thumbs-up. "Now, just remember to relax and have fun. No pressure!"

"Yeah, I'll do my best," Jacob replied, feeling the excitement building inside him. He was grateful for Ivan's support and the effort he put into helping him get ready. "I really appreciate you being here for me, man."

"Always! Now, let me grab my keys, and we will get going. You don't want to keep Rachel waiting," Ivan said, clapping Jacob on the shoulder as they headed out of the room together.

With a final glance in the mirror, Jacob took a deep breath, ready to step into the day and make the most of his time with Rachel.

As they walked to the car, Ivan turned to Jacob and said, "Alright, here's the plan. I'll drop you off at the café, and then I'll park a short distance away. That way, you'll have some privacy, but I'll still be close by if you need anything."

Jacob nodded, appreciating Ivan's thoughtfulness. "That sounds perfect. I really don't want to feel like I'm on display or anything. Just some time to relax and enjoy the moment."

"Exactly! You can focus on having a great time with Rachel without any royal distractions," Ivan replied, sliding into the driver's seat. "And if you need a backup—like if you accidentally spill your drink or something—I'll be just a call away."

"Thanks, man! It's good to know you've got my back," Jacob said, feeling reassured by Ivan's presence.

Chapter 9

Double Date Surprise

Meanwhile, at Polly's apartment, Rachel was getting ready with Polly's help. The two friends were in the midst of a fun and frantic preparation session, with Polly fussing over Rachel to ensure everything was perfect for her date with Jacob.

"Okay, let's see that dress again!" Polly exclaimed, clapping her hands in excitement as Rachel twirled in front of the mirror. The brightly colored floral dress hugged her figure beautifully, with a soft, flattering neckline that highlighted her delicate features.

"It feels a bit too much, don't you think?" Rachel asked, biting her lip as she examined herself.

"Not at all! You look amazing. Jacob is going to be blown away," Polly assured her, adjusting the straps and smoothing out any wrinkles. "This is your time to shine!"

Rachel smiled, feeling a mix of nerves and excitement. "I just want everything to go well. What if I trip or say something awkward?"

"Hey, everyone has those moments," Polly replied, rolling her eyes playfully. "What matters is that you're genuine. Just focus on having a good time with Jacob, and everything else will fall into place."

As Rachel applied her makeup, Polly handed her a few accessories to choose from—a delicate necklace and a pair of earrings that sparkled under the light. "These will add the perfect touch," Polly said, helping Rachel put them on.

"Thanks for being my personal stylist today!" Rachel laughed, feeling grateful for her friend's support. Polly had a knack for knowing just what to say to ease her nerves.

Once Rachel was satisfied with her look, she took a step back to admire her reflection. "I think I'm ready!" she said, a sense of confidence washing over her.

"Let's take a quick selfie to capture this moment!" Polly suggested, pulling out her phone. They posed together, both smiling brightly, and Polly clicked the picture.

As they walked to the door, Rachel paused and turned to Polly, her expression reflecting a mix of determination and anxiety. "I can't do this alone. You have to come with me, Polly," she said, biting her lip nervously.

Polly raised an eyebrow, surprised but amused. "Are you serious? You want me to tag along on your date?"

"Yes! Just until I see Jacob, then you can disappear," Rachel insisted, her voice a blend of urgency and hope. "I just need that extra boost of confidence. What if I freak out when I see him?"

Polly chuckled, her heart warming at her friend's vulnerability. "Alright, alright! I'll be your wingwoman for a bit. But you owe me a cupcake from the café afterward!"

Rachel laughed, relief washing over her. "Deal! Thank you so much, Polly. I feel so much better knowing you'll be there for a little moral support."

"Let's go then! I'll give you the pep talk you need on the way," Polly said, grabbing her bag and heading toward the door.

Rachel pulled out her phone and quickly opened her messaging app, her fingers hovering over the screen as she composed a text to Jacob. She wanted to be upfront and ensure he didn't feel caught off guard when she arrived with Polly.

"Hey, Jacob! Just wanted to give you a heads-up that I'm bringing a friend with me. I hope that's okay! I just thought it would help me relax a bit. Can't wait to see you!" she typed, her heart racing a little as she hit send.

Polly leaned over, peeking at the message. "Good call! It's always better to keep things transparent. He'll appreciate it."

Rachel nodded, feeling a mix of anticipation and nervousness. "I just hope he doesn't mind too much. I want him to feel comfortable."

A moment later, her phone buzzed with a reply. Jacob's message popped up: "No problem at all! I'm looking forward to it. See you soon!"

Jacob rested his cell phone on his knee, a sheepish grin spreading across his face. "Change of plans, Ivan. You'll be joining Rachel, her friend Polly, and me."

Ivan raised an eyebrow, curiosity piqued by the unexpected twist. "Oh, so it's turned into a double date? This just got interesting! Who's Rachel bringing along?"

Jacob shrugged, a hint of apprehension in his demeanor. "I'm not sure who her friend is, but I thought having you there would help keep the vibe balanced."

"Smart move! I can definitely help break the ice if things get a bit awkward," Ivan said, a smile beginning to form. "So, do you have a game plan for this?"

"Not really," Jacob admitted with a grin. "I guess we'll just have to wing it!"

Chapter 10

A Dance of Diplomacy

Meanwhile, back in Slovitia, Queen Isabella eagerly prepared for the arrival of Princess Penelope from the neighboring kingdom of Maltiva. The air was filled with excitement and anticipation as the royal court buzzed with activity, ensuring that everything would be perfect for her esteemed guest.

The grand hall was adorned with elegant tapestries and fresh flowers, creating a warm and inviting atmosphere. Queen Isabella, known for her grace and royal hospitality, wanted to make Princess Penelope feel truly welcome.

For many years, Queen Isabella had been preparing her son, Alexander, for a future that would intertwine their lives with that of Princess Penelope. She understood the importance of forging strong alliances to fortify their small nation, and a union between Alexander and Penelope would be a significant step toward achieving that goal.

Isabella had instilled in Alexander the values of diplomacy, kindness, and leadership, knowing that these qualities would serve him well as he navigated the complexities of courtship and the throne. She often spoke of the virtues of Princess Penelope, emphasizing her grace, intelligence, and the potential for a prosperous partnership that could benefit both their kingdoms.

Queen Isabella's worries began to deepen as Alexander's upcoming journey to America surfaced. The thought of her son meeting a commoner during his studies in America filled her with unease. She had always envisioned a future where he would marry Princess Penelope, solidifying their alliance and ensuring the stability of their small kingdom.

Isabella knew that America was a land of opportunity and vibrant cultures, where commoners often held unique charms and perspectives. The Queen feared that Alexander might be captivated by someone outside of the royal circle, potentially jeopardizing her carefully laid plans for the future of their nation.

As the sun began to set, casting a golden hue across the land, the royal household awaited the arrival of the princess. Queen Isabella stood at the window, gazing out at the horizon, her heart filled with hope for the blossoming friendship between their kingdoms. She knew that this visit could strengthen ties and foster unity in a time when both kingdoms needed it most.

When the royal convoy finally approached, the Queen's heart raced with anticipation. She smiled, ready to greet her guest with open arms and a heart full of warmth.

As the royal convoy came to a stop, Queen Isabella stepped outside, her regal presence commanding immediate attention. The air was filled with the sweet fragrance of blooming flowers, and the soft sounds of music played by the court musicians created an inviting atmosphere. The

Queen's heart swelled with pride and hope as she awaited the arrival of Princess Penelope.

The limousine's door opened, and out stepped Princess Penelope, radiant in her elegant gown adorned with delicate embroidery. Her golden hair cascaded down her shoulders, and her bright smile illuminated the evening. Isabella felt a wave of relief wash over her; Penelope exuded grace and poise, exactly the qualities she had hoped for in a future daughter-in-law.

"Welcome to Slovitia, dear Princess Penelope!" Isabella greeted warmly, extending her arms for an embrace. The two women shared a heartfelt hug, instantly establishing a bond of camaraderie.

"Thank you, Your Majesty. It is a true honor to be here," Penelope replied, her voice melodious and sincere. "I have heard so much about your beautiful kingdom."

As the introductions continued, King Frederick, a tall and dignified figure, stepped forward to greet Princess Penelope. His presence commanded respect, and the assembly quieted as he approached. With a warm smile, he extended his hand to the princess.

"Welcome, Princess Penelope," he said, his voice deep and reassuring. "It is a pleasure to finally meet you. I have heard wonderful things about you from my wife."

Penelope curtsied gracefully, her cheeks flushed with a mix of excitement and nervousness. "Thank you, Your Majesty. The honor is all mine. Your kingdom is truly magnificent."

King Frederick, ever the gracious host, motioned to the royal staff. "Please ensure that Princess Penelope and her entourage are well taken care of. Make certain they have everything they need during their stay." The royal staff quickly unloaded the luggage from the convoy of vehicles. King Frederick graciously led his guests into the castle.

As the evening progressed, Penelope felt increasingly at home in the grand palace. The opulent surroundings, decorated with rich tapestries and gleaming chandeliers, were impressive, but it was the kindness of her hosts that truly made her feel welcome. She found herself engaging in light-hearted conversations with Queen Isabella, who was eager to share tales of Slovitia's history and culture.

King Frederick smiled warmly at Princess Penelope, his curiosity evident. "So, what brings you to visit our kingdom?" he asked, genuinely interested in her motivations for the trip.

Penelope took a moment to gather her thoughts, her eyes sparkling with enthusiasm. "Your Majesty, I have long admired the beauty of Slovitia and its rich history. I believe that strengthening the ties between our kingdoms is vital, especially in these changing times. My visit is not only a personal journey but also an opportunity to explore potential collaborations in trade, culture, and education between our realms."

The King nodded appreciatively, impressed by her insight and diplomatic approach. "Indeed, our kingdoms have much to gain from one another. It is wise to foster connections that can benefit both our peoples."

After the royal dinner held in Princess Penelope's honor, the evening air was filled with the sweet scent of blooming jasmine as she and Queen Isabella strolled through the beautifully manicured royal courtyard. The soft glow of lanterns illuminated their path, casting a warm light on the intricate stonework and lush greenery surrounding them.

"Your Majesty," Penelope began, glancing at Isabella with admiration, "this palace is truly breathtaking. I can see why your kingdom is so revered."

Isabella smiled, her heart swelling with pride. "Thank you, dear Penelope. It has been a labor of love for generations. But the true beauty lies in the people and the bonds we build. I hope this visit will be the beginning of a strong friendship between our families."

As they walked further into the courtyard, the sounds of the evening—crickets chirping and leaves rustling in the gentle breeze—provided a serene backdrop. Penelope felt a sense of comfort in Isabella's presence and decided to open up.

"I must admit, I was a bit nervous about this visit. I wanted to make a good impression, especially with your son," she confessed, her cheeks flushing slightly.

"Have you seen Alexander? Is he preoccupied today?" Princess Penelope inquired.

"No, he is currently in America completing his

education. That is precisely why I summoned you," the Queen responded.

I was hoping maybe you could stay here in Slovitia for a short visit so we could get to know each other better. Queen Isabella smiled.

Penelope's heart fluttered at the idea of spending more time with Queen Isabella. "I would love that," she replied, her voice filled with enthusiasm. "It would be a wonderful opportunity to get to know you and your husband, King Frederick, and particularly Alexander, while I'm here."

Queen Isabella's eyes sparkled with warmth. "Excellent! I believe you will find Slovitia quite fascinating. And perhaps, in Alexander's absence, we can share stories about him. He speaks very fondly of you, you know."

Penelope's cheeks flushed deeper at the mention of Alexander. "Really? I didn't realize he thought so highly of me. I have always thought very highly of Alexander, even when we were children playing together," she said, trying to suppress a smile.

"Yes, he has always been drawn to beautiful, intelligent women. I believe you two would have a wonderful connection if given the chance," the Queen remarked, her tone playful yet sincere.

As they strolled through the courtyard, the evening light cast a golden hue over the blooming flowers, creating an enchanting atmosphere.

As Princess Penelope departed the courtyard, King

Frederick emerged from behind a tree. "What are you up to, my dear?" he asked, his expression a blend of curiosity and concern as he turned his attention to Queen Isabella.

Isabella met his gaze with a warm smile, unfazed by his sudden appearance. "I was just enjoying a delightful conversation with Princess Penelope. She's quite charming and has shown a sincere interest in Alexander."

Frederick raised an intrigued eyebrow. "Is that so? I trust you haven't overwhelmed her with fanciful tales of our royal lives."

"Oh no," Isabella grinned. "We mostly talked about Alexander."

King Frederick's brow arched playfully as a smirk danced on his lips. "Really? It seems you couldn't resist the allure of sharing stories about him."

Isabella chuckled, her eyes glinting with mischief. "I may have mentioned a few things, but can you blame me? Princess Penelope appears genuinely interested in Alexander, and I thought it only fitting to share some of his more endearing qualities."

"Endearing, indeed," Frederick teased, his voice light. "I can only imagine the stories you chose to share. Just remember, he's growing into a man now, and he might find your enthusiasm a bit overwhelming and even intrusive."

Chapter 11

A Symphony of Hearts

Jacob and Ivan were the first to arrive at the café. After Ivan parked the car, they stepped inside, greeted by the enticing scent of freshly brewed coffee and delicious baked goods. The fragrant aroma of freshly baked croissants and muffins wafted from the display, filling the air with a delightful warmth.

Jacob looked around the room, his heart racing a little as he eagerly awaited Rachel's arrival.

"Let's grab a table in the corner," Jacob suggested, pointing to a cozy spot with a view of the entrance. He wanted a little privacy but still enough visibility to see when Rachel and Polly walked in.

As they settled in, Ivan leaned back in his chair, looking amused. "So, what's your strategy? Are you going in for casual conversation, or are you planning to impress her right away?"

Jacob shrugged, attempting to play it cool. "Honestly, I just want to be myself. I think if I act too eager, it might come off as desperate and scare her off. Plus, I want her to like me for who I am and not for my title or wealth like so many others do back home."

Ivan chuckled. "Good point. Just keep it light and fun.

If you start feeling the pressure, remember that I'm here to help lighten the mood!"

"Thanks, man. I appreciate it," Jacob replied, his thoughts drifting back to Rachel. He couldn't help but wonder how she was feeling about the date.

Meanwhile, Rachel and Polly were on their way, Polly giving Rachel a pep talk. "Just remember to breathe. You've got this! Jacob seems like a nice guy, and if he's interested, you just need to be yourself."

Rachel nodded, her nerves tingling with excitement and anxiety. "I know, I know. But what if he doesn't like me as much as I like him?"

Polly rolled her eyes playfully. "You won't know unless you go for it! He agreed to meet you, right? That's a good sign."

As they approached the café, Rachel took a deep breath and adjusted her hair. "Okay, here goes nothing!"

They entered, and the warm ambiance immediately enveloped them. Rachel spotted Jacob and Ivan in the corner, and her heart skipped a beat. "There they are!" she whispered to Polly, who gave her a reassuring nod.

With a mixture of excitement and trepidation, Rachel walked toward the table, her heart racing. Jacob looked up just as they approached, his smile widening as he stood to greet them. "Hey, you made it!"

"Hi, Jacob! This is my best friend Polly," Rachel

introduced, feeling a rush of warmth as she took in Jacob's friendly demeanor.

"Nice to meet you, Polly!" Jacob said, extending his hand.

"Likewise!" Polly replied, shaking his hand with a confident smile.

Ivan rose to his feet, smiling warmly. "Hey there! I'm Ivan." Polly gazed into his brown eyes, feeling a flutter in her chest as her heart melted.

As they settled into their seats, the conversation began to flow effortlessly. Jacob and Ivan exchanged tales of their adventures back home, recounting exhilarating hiking and skiing trips in the majestic mountains of Europe. Their playful banter had Rachel and Polly laughing, captivated by the infectious enthusiasm in their voices.

Rachel felt a magnetic pull toward Jacob's genuine smile and the way his eyes lit up as he spoke about his passions. Each story painted vivid images of stunning landscapes and thrilling experiences, and she could almost feel the chill of the mountain air and the rush of adrenaline from their escapades.

Polly, too, was engrossed, enjoying the camaraderie between the two guys and the way they effortlessly connected. She could see how much Rachel admired Jacob, and it only fueled her own excitement about the new friendships blossoming around them.

Polly, meanwhile, found herself enjoying a growing

connection with Ivan. As they chatted, they uncovered a shared passion for hiking and outdoor adventures, which ignited a lively discussion about their favorite trails and unforgettable experiences in nature.

Polly, excited to share her knowledge, mentioned, "You know, Utah is famous for its incredible parks and hiking trails. The scenery is absolutely breathtaking!"

Ivan's eyes lit up at her words. "Really? I've always wanted to explore that area! What are some of the must see spots?"

With enthusiasm, Polly began listing her favorites: "You have to check out Zion National Park; the rock formations are stunning. And then there's Arches—those natural stone arches are just amazing to see in person. Don't forget about Bryce Canyon, either; it's unlike anything you've ever seen."

Ivan nodded, captivated by her descriptions. "That sounds incredible! I love the idea of getting lost in nature like that. I've heard the sunsets in Utah's parks are just magical."

Polly agreed, her excitement palpable. "They really are! There's something special about watching the colors change as the sun sets behind the mountains. It makes every hike worth it."

Their conversation flowed seamlessly, filled with dreams of future adventures and the thrill of discovering new trails together. It was clear that their connection was deepening, spurred on by their shared love for the great outdoors.

The aroma of coffee and pastries lingered in the air as the four of them exchanged stories and laughter, creating a cozy atmosphere filled with budding friendships. Rachel felt a sense of comfort and excitement, realizing that this was the kind of connection she had been hoping for.

As the conversation deepened, they shifted from lighthearted topics to more personal ones, sharing dreams and aspirations. Jacob spoke about his ambitions and the importance of staying true to oneself, resonating with Rachel's own desire for authenticity in relationships.

With each passing moment, the initial nervousness began to fade, replaced by a growing sense of camaraderie and warmth among the four friends. The café buzzed around them, but in that little corner, it felt as though they had created their own world, one filled with laughter, connection, and the promise of new beginnings.

Jacob turned to Rachel, a curious look on his face. "So, have you finished registering for all your classes yet?"

Rachel paused for a moment, a playful smile forming on her lips. "I'm almost done! Just a couple of electives left to choose from. I'm trying to decide between a photography class and one on creative writing. What about you?"

Jacob leaned back, crossing his arms with a thoughtful expression. "I'm pretty much set. I went with a mix of business and some art courses. I think it's important to balance the practical with the creative, don't you?"

"Absolutely," Rachel replied, feeling a spark of inspiration. "I believe that creativity can enhance any field. It's great to see you're taking that approach!"

Rachel sat quietly, her gaze fixed on Jacob as he savored his latte, the steam curling up gently from the cup. A longing stirred in her heart, a desire to connect with him on a deeper level. Each laugh he shared and every glimmer of enthusiasm in his voice made her yearn to uncover more about the person behind that charming smile.

As he animatedly shared another story from his adventures, Rachel found herself hanging on to his every word, captivated by the warmth and sincerity that radiated from him. She felt an irresistible pull, eager to engage in conversations about dreams, fears, and everything in between.

Casting a glance around the table, Rachel noticed Polly and Ivan deeply immersed in their own lively exchange, presenting her with the perfect opportunity to focus solely on Jacob. Gathering her courage, she resolved to take the leap.

"Jacob," she said, her tone steady yet inviting, "what's your favorite memory from our time together so far?"

Jacob appeared taken aback for a moment, then a thoughtful smile spread across his face as he seemed to sift through a mental scrapbook of moments. "That's a fantastic question!" he replied. "I think my favorite memory has to be when you and I attended that outdoor concert last spring. The atmosphere was electric, and we were dancing and singing along to the music. I remember glancing around and seeing you having such a great time."

A warm glow filled Rachel at the recollection. "Absolutely! That night was so much fun. I loved how we completely lost ourselves in the music. It felt as if we were in our own little universe."

"Exactly!" Jacob responded, his enthusiasm contagious. Rachel couldn't help but chuckle, her cheeks flushing at the memory. "We were so carefree! It felt wonderful to let loose and just enjoy ourselves. I'm really glad you were there with me."

Their eyes locked, and in that moment, Rachel sensed a deeper connection blossoming between them. Jacob continued, "It's moments like those that remind me of the value of our friendship and the joy we can share together. I'm truly grateful we met."

Rachel nodded, a soothing sense of belonging washing over her. "Me too. I never anticipated finding someone as special as you."

From there, their conversation flowed effortlessly, each sharing cherished memories and eagerly anticipating future adventures. Rachel felt a blend of excitement and comfort, recognizing that this newfound bond was just beginning to unfold.

Then Jacob and Rachel shifted the conversation back to

their class schedules, eager to find common ground. "So, which classes are you taking this semester?" Jacob asked, leaning in with genuine interest.

Rachel smiled as she pulled out her planner. "I've got a mix of subjects—some core classes and a few electives. I'm really excited about my corporate management course. What about you?"

Jacob nodded, his face lighting up. "I'm taking a couple of business classes, but I also signed up for a photography elective. I've always had a passion for capturing moments, and I figured it would be a fun way to express my creativity."

"That sounds amazing!" Rachel exclaimed. "I'd love to see your work. Maybe we could even collaborate on a project sometime?"

Jacob grinned at the idea. "Definitely! And we should definitely get together to study, too. I could use a study buddy for my business courses. They can get pretty heavy."

Rachel's heart raced at the thought of spending more time with him. "I'd love that! We can help each other out. Maybe we could meet at the library like we did last year."

"Sounds perfect!" Jacob replied enthusiastically. "How about we set a regular study date? It'll keep us both on track."

"Great idea! Let's figure out a schedule that works for both of us," Rachel said, feeling a surge of excitement.

As they continued to discuss their classes and plans to

study together, the connection between them deepened. Each shared laugh and thoughtful conversation made Rachel more eager to explore the possibilities of their friendship, and perhaps something more.

After several hours filled with laughter, engaging conversations, and warm cups of coffee, the four friends decided it was time to stretch their legs and explore the vibrant atmosphere outside. The sun was just beginning to dip in the sky, casting a golden glow over the street as they stepped out of the café.

"Let's take a walk and check out the local shops along the street!" Polly suggested, her eyes sparkling with excitement.

"Great idea!" Ivan agreed, already heading toward the door. Jacob and Rachel exchanged glances, both feeling a thrill at the prospect of continuing their time together in the fresh air.

As they strolled down the street, the cheerful sounds of laughter and music filled the air, mingling with the enticing aromas wafting from nearby food vendors. Colorful decorations adorned the storefronts, creating a lively and inviting atmosphere.

Rachel felt a sense of joy as they wandered from shop to shop, admiring handmade crafts, unique clothing, and delightful trinkets. Each store they entered was filled with its own charm, and the group reveled in the discoveries they made along the way.

"Look at this!" Jacob exclaimed, holding up a quirky piece of art. "This would make a perfect addition to my room!"

Rachel giggled, enjoying the playful banter among them. "You definitely have an eye for unique finds!"

As they continued their journey, Polly spotted a small boutique filled with colorful scarves and accessories. "Let's check this place out!" she said, pulling Ivan inside. Rachel and Jacob followed, their laughter echoing as they browsed through the vibrant selection.

Rachel found herself drawn to a beautiful scarf that reminded her of the colors of the sunset. "What do you think?" she asked Jacob, holding it up for him to see.

"It's stunning! It really brings out your eyes," he replied, his gaze sincere. Rachel felt a warmth spread through her at his compliment.

After spending some time in the boutique, they stepped back out into the street, the laughter and chatter continuing as they explored more shops and shared their thoughts on the various items they discovered.

The evening air was crisp, and the festive atmosphere surrounded them like a warm embrace, solidifying the bond they were forming.

Jacob held Rachel's hand tightly as they strolled down the street, their fingers intertwined. The warmth of his grip sent a flutter through her chest, and she couldn't help but smile up at him. The festive lights twinkled above them, adding to the enchanting atmosphere of the evening.

Behind them, Ivan and Polly walked closely together, exchanging glances and subtle gestures. They couldn't help but notice the chemistry blossoming between Rachel and Jacob. Polly raised an eyebrow and nudged Ivan playfully, a grin spreading across her face.

"Looks like someone's having a great time," she whispered, nodding toward the couple ahead. Ivan chuckled, leaning in closer to catch the affectionate glances that passed between Rachel and Jacob.

"Yeah, they definitely have a spark," he replied, his voice low but filled with amusement. "I think they're really hitting it off."

Polly nodded enthusiastically. "It's about time! They've been dancing around each other for forever. I'm glad to see them finally connecting."

Meanwhile, Rachel and Jacob continued their stroll, unaware of the playful scrutiny from their friends. Jacob turned to Rachel, a soft smile on his face. "I'm really enjoying today. It's nice to just be out here with you."

Rachel's heart raced at his words. "Me too! I love the energy of the street, and having you here makes it even better."

As they walked, they shared stories and laughter, their connection deepening with every passing moment. The world around them faded away, leaving just the two of them wrapped in their own little bubble.

In the background, Polly and Ivan shared knowing glances, happy to see their friends finding joy in each other's company. "I think we should have more outings like this," Ivan suggested, his eyes twinkling. "It's good for them."

Polly agreed, her gaze drifting back to Rachel and Jacob. "Absolutely! It looks like they're on the verge of something special. We should keep the momentum going."

As they continued down the street, the bond between Jacob and Rachel grew stronger, while Ivan and Polly plotted ways to encourage their friends' blossoming relationship.

As they walked along the bustling street, the atmosphere was alive with the sounds of laughter, music, and the enticing aromas from nearby food stalls. Jacob and Rachel found themselves gravitating toward a food vendor selling freshly made pretzels, their mouths watering at the sight of the golden-brown treats.

"Should we get some?" Jacob asked, his eyes sparkling with excitement.

"Absolutely! I've always loved pretzels," Rachel replied, her enthusiasm matching his. They stepped up to the food truck, and Jacob ordered two warm pretzels, adding a side of mustard for dipping.

While they waited, Jacob turned to Rachel, a playful grin on his face. "What's your favorite way to eat a pretzel? Sweet or savory?"

Rachel laughed, considering the question. "I think I'm

team savory all the way! There's something about the saltiness that just hits the spot."

"Good choice! I'm with you on that," Jacob agreed, taking their pretzels as they were handed over. "Let's find a nice spot to enjoy these."

They wandered a little further until they found a cozy bench under a string of twinkling lights. Sitting down, they took a moment to savor the warm, delicious pretzels. Jacob took a big bite, and Rachel watched, laughing as a tiny piece of pretzel flew from his mouth.

"Nice catch!" she teased, wiping a bit of mustard off her chin. "You're quite the pretzel connoisseur."

Jacob chuckled, his cheeks flushing slightly. "What can I say? I'm just trying to impress you!"

Their playful banter continued as they shared stories of their favorite foods and culinary disasters. Rachel found herself feeling more at ease with each passing moment, her laughter mixing with the sounds of the lively street around them.

Meanwhile, Ivan and Polly were a few paces behind, observing the blossoming chemistry between their friends. "They look so happy together," Ivan remarked, a hint of pride in his voice. "It's nice to see Rachel opening up like this."

Polly nodded, her heart swelling. "I knew they had something special. It just took a little push!"

As they finished their pretzels, Rachel turned to Jacob, her eyes sparkling with curiosity. "So, what's next on your list of adventures? Do you have any favorite places you'd like to show me?"

Jacob thought for a moment, his expression thoughtful. "There's this beautiful park a little further down the road. It has these beautiful old trees and walking trails. It's a perfect spot to relax and take in the scenery. Would you want to check it out?"

"Absolutely! That sounds lovely," Rachel replied, feeling a surge of excitement at the idea of exploring more with him.

As they rose from the bench, Polly and Ivan caught up with them, eager to join in on the next adventure. "What's the plan?" Polly asked, her eyes twinkling with enthusiasm.

"We're heading to the park!" Jacob replied, beaming. "Care to join us?"

"Definitely!" Ivan said, and the four of them set off together, the air filled with laughter and the promise of new memories waiting to be made.

As they walked toward the park, Rachel felt a sense of belonging swell within her. The evening was enchanting, and she couldn't shake the feeling that this was just the beginning of something beautiful. The shared moments, the laughter, and the connection with Jacob all felt like pieces of a puzzle falling perfectly into place.

As they entered the park, the ambiance shifted to a

serene oasis filled with the sounds of wind blowing through the tree leaves and distant laughter. They walked hand in hand under the expansive branches of a large, ancient tree, its leaves whispering secrets in the gentle breeze.

Jacob paused, his grip on Rachel's hand tightening slightly as he turned to face her. The world around them seemed to fade away, leaving just the two of them bathed in the soft glow of the setting sun. Rachel looked up at him, her heart racing in anticipation.

In that moment, Jacob leaned closer, his eyes searching hers, filled with a mix of warmth and intent. Without a word, he closed the distance and kissed Rachel with a passionate kiss that took her breath away. It was tender yet electric, a perfect blend of emotion that made her heart soar.

Rachel melted into the kiss, feeling the world around them dissolve into nothingness. Time seemed to stand still as they shared that moment, the warmth of his lips igniting a spark she had been yearning for. She felt a rush of happiness and excitement, realizing just how deep her feelings for Jacob had grown.

As they finally pulled away, both of them breathless, Jacob smiled down at Rachel, his eyes shining with affection. "Wow," he said softly, his voice barely above a whisper. "I've wanted to do that for a while."

Rachel's cheeks flushed, a shy smile spreading across her face. "Me too. I didn't know how to say it, but I'm really glad you did."

Their friends, Polly and Ivan, who had been walking a few steps behind, exchanged knowing glances and wide smiles, excited to see their friends taking this step. Polly couldn't help but whisper to Ivan, "I knew it! They were meant to be."

"Looks like we'll have to keep planning more outings," Ivan replied with a grin, feeling the joy radiating from the couple ahead.

As the weeks unfolded, Rachel and Jacob found themselves drawn to each other in ways they had hoped for but never expected. The countless hours spent in the library became a sanctuary where their hearts intertwined, allowing them to uncover the layers of each other's souls. Rachel would share longing glances, and their whispered laughter transformed their study sessions into something truly special.

As Polly and Ivan observed their friends, they couldn't help but notice the chemistry blossoming between them. Laughter and shared moments painted a beautiful picture of companionship. However, Ivan's mind was clouded with concern, particularly regarding Jacob. He knew that Queen Isabella, with her strict views on relationships and marriage, would disapprove of any union that strayed from her expectations.

Chapter 12

Hearts in Harmony

As summer unfolded, the group of friends eagerly embraced the warm days and the breathtaking beauty of the mountains surrounding them. The trails, winding through tall trees and dotted with vibrant wildflowers, beckoned them to explore. Each hike became a new adventure, filled with laughter, stories, and the thrill of nature's grandeur.

One morning, they set out early to catch the sunrise from a particularly stunning viewpoint overlooking one of the valleys. The air was crisp, and the anticipation hung thick as they trekked up the incline, their spirits high. Polly led the way, her enthusiasm infectious, while Ivan brought up the rear, ensuring everyone stayed together.

Reaching the summit, they were greeted by a spectacular panorama: the sun peeking over the horizon, casting golden rays across the rugged peaks and valleys below. The sight took their breath away, and they stood in awe, feeling a profound connection not just to nature but to each other.

As they settled onto a rocky outcrop, sipping water and sharing snacks, the conversation flowed easily.

As Jacob and Rachel sat close together, the warmth of

the morning sun began to wash over them, casting a golden glow on everything in sight. Their fingers intertwined, a silent promise of connection and support, while Jacob's arms enveloped Rachel, offering her a sense of safety and comfort.

The world around them faded as they lost themselves in the moment. The vibrant colors of the sunrise mirrored the feelings blossoming between them—fiery and passionate, yet tender and serene. Jacob glanced down at Rachel, her face illuminated by the soft light, and he couldn't help but smile at how perfect this moment felt.

"Isn't it beautiful?" Jacob whispered, his voice barely above a breath, as he gestured toward the breathtaking view.

Rachel nodded, her eyes sparkling with joy. "It really is. I could stay here forever," she replied, leaning her head against his shoulder.

In that serene moment, the concerns of the outside world, especially those related to Queen Isabella, felt far away. For Jacob, nothing else mattered but the bond they were forming amid the stunning backdrop of nature. It was a moment of pure happiness, a fleeting escape that they both wished could last indefinitely.

As the sun continued to rise, painting the sky with hues of pink and orange, Jacob and Rachel felt an undeniable connection deepening between them. The tranquility of the mountains provided the perfect setting for their budding relationship, allowing them to share their thoughts and dreams without the distractions of daily life.

Jacob turned to Rachel, his expression serious yet gentle. "You know, I've never felt this way about anyone before," he admitted, his gaze searching hers for understanding. "It's like I can truly be myself around you."

Rachel smiled, her heart fluttering at his words. "I feel the same way, Jacob. It's like you see me for who I really am, and it's so refreshing."

They spent the next few moments sharing stories about their childhoods, their aspirations, and their fears. Rachel spoke of her life on the farm and how life was growing up without her parents, while Jacob shared his passion for photography, revealing how he loved capturing the beauty of nature. Each revelation brought them closer, and laughter punctuated their conversation, echoing through the mountains.

"It must have been difficult to grow up without knowing your parents," Jacob said.

Rachel's expression softened at Jacob's words, and she took a moment to gather her thoughts. "It was… difficult, to say the least," she replied, her voice reflective. "I always wondered about them, why they weren't there. I felt a sense of loss that I couldn't quite explain."

Jacob listened intently, his heart aching for her. "Did you ever get to find out anything about them?" he asked gently, wanting to understand the depth of her experiences.

Rachel shook her head slowly. "Not really. I grew up with my aunt and uncle, who loved me dearly, but they were always tight-lipped about my parents. I think they wanted to protect me from the pain of knowing the whole truth," she explained, her eyes gazing off into the distance as if searching for answers in the mountains.

"But I learned to cope," she continued, a hint of resilience in her tone. "I poured myself into my studies and found solace in nature on the farm. It became my escape, my way of finding peace."

Jacob nodded, feeling a surge of admiration for her strength. "You're incredibly brave, Rachel. It takes a lot to face those kinds of challenges and still come out with such a positive outlook."

Rachel smiled, appreciating his kind words. "Thank you, Jacob. It hasn't been easy, but I've learned that family isn't just about blood. It's about the connections you make and the love you share. I've found that in my friends, and now… with you."

Her words hung in the air, filled with promise and warmth. Jacob felt a rush of emotion, realizing just how special their bond had become in such a short time. He leaned in closer, wrapping his arm around her shoulders, pulling her into a comforting embrace.

In that moment, surrounded by the beauty of the mountains and the rising sun, both Jacob and Rachel felt a sense of hope. They knew that whatever challenges lay ahead, they would face them together, drawing strength from the love they were beginning to nurture.

But as they shared this intimate moment, a shadow of reality loomed on the horizon. Jacob's thoughts drifted to his mother, Queen Isabella, and her rigid expectations. Would their relationship survive the scrutiny of the queen? Sensing his momentary distraction, Rachel gently squeezed his hand, bringing Jacob back to the present.

"Hey, whatever happens, I want you to know that I'm here for you," he said, his voice steady and reassuring.

Rachel looked into his eyes, feeling a surge of hope. "Thank you, Jacob. That means everything to me."

Chapter 13
A Royal Dilemma

Meanwhile, back in Slovitia, Queen Isabella received troubling news from her royal assistant, Patricia Jackson. Patricia, with a serious expression, reported, "Your Majesty, I must inform you that Alexander has made several credit card purchases for flowers at a local florist."

The queen's brow furrowed, her mind racing with implications. "Flowers? For whom?" she inquired, her tone sharp with curiosity and concern.

Patricia hesitated for a moment, sensing the queen's rising agitation. "It appears that the purchases were made on multiple occasions, and the amounts suggest they are intended for someone special, my queen."

Isabella's thoughts turned to her son, Alexander. She knew he had been spending a lot of time with friends lately, and the idea of him becoming romantically involved was both intriguing and worrisome. "Find out who he's been seeing," she commanded, her voice steady but laced with authority. "I need to know if his affections are directed towards anyone who could jeopardize our family's reputation."

Patricia nodded, ready to carry out the queen's orders.

As she left the room, Isabella's mind was already racing with possibilities. She understood that matters of the heart could be complicated, especially when it concerned the royal family. Determined to protect her son and uphold the family's honor, she steeled herself for the task ahead.

Queen Isabella turned to her husband, King Frederick, her face reflecting both concern and resolve. "Frederick, we have a problem," she started, her tone unwavering. "Patricia just informed me that Alexander has been making a series of flower purchases. It seems he might be involved with an American."

King Frederick raised an eyebrow, intrigued but cautious. "Flowers? That doesn't sound particularly alarming, Isabella. Young love can often be innocent."

Isabella shook her head, her anxiety clear. "You don't grasp the gravity of this. It's not merely about flowers; it's about who he might be seeing. If his affections are directed toward someone inappropriate, it could threaten everything we've built for our family. He deserves a suitable wife, not a commoner."

Frederick stepped closer, feeling the weight of her worries. "What do you mean by 'inappropriate'? We can't dictate his heart, Isabella. He's old enough to make his own decisions."

"But not decisions that could tarnish our reputation!" Isabella countered, her voice rising slightly. "His future is tied to the royal legacy. If he becomes involved with the wrong person, it could have dire consequences for both him and the Kingdom."

King Frederick placed a calming hand on her shoulder. "Perhaps we should let him explore this relationship first. We can guide him, but we must also place our trust in him. Let's gather more information before jumping to conclusions."

Isabella sighed, her determination wavering a bit. "You're right, of course. But I can't shake this feeling. I'll have Patricia find out more, and then we can decide how to approach Alexander."

"Remember, my love, Alexander is becoming his own man. We should avoid making hasty decisions that might alienate him. After all, he is the heir to the throne. It's crucial for him to discover who he truly is. I know you only want what's best for him, but we must tread carefully."

Isabella took her husband's words to heart, yet deep down, she felt compelled to prevent Alexander from following his heart. There was a greater good for the kingdom to consider. "Of course, my love," she replied, gently stroking his cheek.

As the conversation lingered in the air, Queen Isabella felt a whirlwind of emotions. She understood King Frederick's perspective, but her maternal instincts were strong. The thought of Alexander potentially being involved with someone deemed unsuitable gnawed at her. The weight of the royal legacy pressed heavily on her shoulders, and she feared the repercussions of a misstep.

Meanwhile, King Frederick remained resolute, believing in the importance of allowing their son to navigate his own path. He admired Alexander's growth and wanted to encourage his independence. Frederick recalled his own youthful indiscretions and how they shaped him into the man he had become. He hoped to instill the same sense of self-discovery in Alexander, even if it meant facing the unknown.

As Isabella contemplated the situation, she considered Patricia's reliability. Patricia had always been a trusted confidante, and Isabella felt confident that she could uncover the truth about Alexander's romantic interests. Yet, the idea of prying into her son's life felt like an invasion of his privacy, she stilled her concerns, knowing it was best for him and the Kingdom.

"Frederick," Isabella finally said, breaking the silence, "what if this relationship distracts him from his responsibilities? He must be prepared to take on the throne one day. This is not just about his happiness; it's about the future of our kingdom."

King Frederick nodded, acknowledging her concerns. "I understand, but we must also remember that happiness can fuel a strong leader. If Alexander finds love, it could strengthen his resolve to fulfill his duties. We must strike a balance between guiding him and allowing him to follow his heart."

Isabella considered his words, her heart heavy with the burden of leadership. "Perhaps you're right. But I still worry about the potential consequences. I'll speak with Patricia and gather information, and then we can make an informed decision on how to approach Alexander."

"Good," Frederick replied, his gaze softening. King Frederick took Isabella by the hand and pulled her close. "We'll work together on this. Let's ensure that whatever happens, Alexander knows he has our unwavering support and love, regardless of the choices he makes."

Isabella smiled faintly, her worries still present but tempered by her husband's reassurance.

As the first rays of sunlight streamed through the ornate windows of the royal chamber, the atmosphere was charged with a sense of urgency. The queen, regal and composed, summoned Patricia with a wave of her hand, her expression one of steely determination. "Patricia, I need you to immerse yourself in the shadows of Alexander's activities in America," she instructed, her voice firm yet laced with an undercurrent of intrigue.

Patricia, a loyal confidante with a keen intuition and unbridled ambitions, felt a thrill of excitement surge through her. She understood the gravity of the queen's request; Ivan's reports had been vague, filled with half-truths and omissions that left much to the imagination. "I will do everything in my power to uncover the truth," she assured the queen, her resolve unshakable.

The queen leaned closer, her voice dropping to a conspiratorial whisper. "I will also summon Princess Penelope for a private discussion. We must strategize and ensure all angles are covered." Her mind was a flurry of thoughts, each one more elaborate than the last, as she envisioned the intricate web of alliances and secrets that connected them all.

"Your mission is urgent," the queen continued, her eyes glinting with determination. "Travel to America and infiltrate the circles surrounding Alexander without being noticed. I want to know every detail, from his dealings to his companions. We cannot afford to be caught off guard. I want to know if an American has ensnared his affections. "

Patricia nodded, absorbing the weight of the task ahead. The queen's ambitious plans were intoxicating, yet she felt a twinge of concern. "And what of the King, my Queen? Will he approve of this maneuver?" she asked, her brow furrowing slightly.

A playful smile danced across the queen's lips, her eyes sparkling with mischief. "Ah, let me handle the King. He may be a formidable presence, but I know how to navigate his concerns. Your focus must remain on Alexander. Knowledge is the most potent weapon we have, and I intend to wield it like a sword. I will not allow my son and future heir to the throne to make a foolish decision, he will regret it. "

The very air in the chamber seemed to thrum with anticipation as the queen's plans began to become clear as glass. Patricia felt a surge of adrenaline coursing through her veins; the chase for the truth was on, and she was ready to step into the fray, knowing that the fate of their Kingdom may very well hinge on what she discovered.

Chapter 14

Tides of Affection

As the seasons subtly shifted, painting the landscape in hues of green and grey, Jacob and Rachel found themselves gravitating toward one another in ways that felt both exhilarating and new. Their study sessions, once relegated to the hushed, studious atmosphere of the library, transformed into intimate gatherings in the warmth of each other's homes. The air was often filled with the rich aroma of freshly brewed coffee or the sweet scent of baked goods, as they took turns hosting each other. Each meeting was marked by an infectious energy, where laughter and shared stories intertwined with their academic discussions, making the pursuit of knowledge feel more like a joyful adventure than a chore.

Polly and Ivan observed this blossoming connection with a mix of amusement and fondness. They often exchanged knowing glances during these study sessions, their hearts warming at the sight of Jacob and Rachel stealing glances and sharing shy smiles. However, beneath Ivan's cheerful exterior lay a simmering worry that he couldn't shake. He frequently found himself lost in thought, contemplating the potential fallout if Queen Isabella were to discover Alexander's secretive relationship with Rachel. The very notion sent a chill down his spine, as he imagined the chaos and disapproval that would surely ensue. It was a concern that gnawed at him, causing him to occasionally drift into silence, his mind racing with scenarios he wished he could dismiss.

Polly, attuned to the subtle shifts in Ivan's mood, sensed that something was amiss. Her instinct was to delve deeper, to uncover the source of his unease, but she hesitated. Instead, she chose to focus on the moments at hand, relishing the lighthearted banter that filled the room and the way Jacob's laughter seemed to brighten Rachel's face. They played games and shared stories, creating a bubble of happiness that momentarily shielded them from the outside world.

One afternoon, as they gathered around a cluttered table strewn with textbooks, notes, and half-empty mugs, Jacob leaned back in his chair, a spark of excitement in his eyes. He casually mentioned Liam, a mutual friend and fellow student known for his adventurous spirit. Jacob's voice brightened as he recounted Liam's invitation for the group to join him at the lake, a popular destination where many of the students would often go to relax from their studies. The lake was famous for its breathtaking sunsets and the perfect picnic spots along its banks, where laughter echoed, and memories were forged.

"Liam wants us to bring some snacks and make a day of it!" Jacob exclaimed, his enthusiasm infectious. The prospect of a day spent outdoors, free from the weight of schoolwork and responsibilities, ignited a spark of excitement in the group. Polly imagined the sun glistening on the water, the gentle breeze ruffling their hair, and the sound of splashes as they playfully waded into the lake.

Ivan's worries momentarily faded as he saw the joy on Jacob and Rachel's faces. Perhaps a day at the lake was just what they needed to escape the pressures of their lives, to breathe, and to enjoy the simplicity of friendship. The idea of their little getaway seemed to weave a thread of hope through Ivan's anxious mind, reminding him that, despite the uncertainties that loomed over them, moments of joy and connection were still very much within reach.

As the anticipation for the outing grew, the group began to plan the details with increasing excitement. Jacob took the lead, suggesting a variety of snacks to pack, from savory sandwiches to sweet treats like Ivan's homemade cookies and fruit. Rachel chimed in with ideas for refreshing drinks, her eyes sparkling as she spoke about homemade lemonade and iced tea, perfect for a sunny day by the water. Polly and Ivan eagerly contributed their own suggestions, transforming the planning session into a lively brainstorming session filled with laughter and playful banter.

The day before their trip, the atmosphere was electric. Jacob and Rachel spent the afternoon preparing, their camaraderie evident as they worked side by side in the kitchen. Flour dusted their noses as they baked cookies with Ivan and Polly, and the sweet scent wafted through the air, mingling with their laughter. Rachel's playful teasing and Jacob's lighthearted responses made the mundane task of cooking feel like an adventure in itself. In those moments, they shared stories of their childhood, revealing little quirks and secrets that deepened their connection.

Later, Polly and Ivan found themselves in a cozy, quieter corner of the apartment, a familiar space where they often gathered to share their thoughts and feelings. Polly observed that Ivan appeared a bit more at ease, a subtle shift that filled her with hope. She leaned in closer, gently nudging him to open up about what was troubling him. "You know, talking about it might really help," she said softly, her gaze steady and filled with concern.

Ivan let out a deep sigh, running his fingers through his hair in frustration. "I just can't shake the feeling that things might not unfold as Jacob hopes," he admitted, his voice tinged with worry. "I wish I could explain more, but for now, I need you to trust me."

Polly nodded, her heart aching for Ivan's concern. "I get that, but maybe we should focus on the good in this moment," she suggested. "Tomorrow is supposed to be a beautiful day, and we're all together. Let's enjoy it and be there for them, no matter what happens."

The morning of the lake trip arrived, bright and sunny, as if nature itself was celebrating their plans. The group gathered early, their energy palpable as they loaded up the car with blankets, coolers filled with snacks, and beach gear. Laughter echoed through the car as they drove, with Jacob taking the wheel and Rachel navigating, her excitement spilling over as they neared their destination.

As they arrived at the lake, the sight before them was breathtaking. The water glistened under the sun, reflecting shades of blue and green, while the surrounding trees swayed gently in the breeze. The sound of laughter and splashes from other groups filled the air, creating a joyful symphony.

As they strolled along the wooden pier, the sun hung high in the sky, casting a warm golden hue over everything. The vibrant sounds of laughter echoed around them, mingling with the soft, rhythmic lapping of water against the weathered posts of the dock, creating a lively and inviting atmosphere. The air was filled with the tantalizing scent of salt and the promise of adventure, making their hearts race with anticipation.

Suddenly, a booming voice cut through the cheerful noise, calling out, "Jacob! Over here!" The group turned to see Liam, an energetic figure perched confidently at the back of a sleek, gleaming motorboat. His dark hair whipped in the wind as he waved his arms enthusiastically, a wide grin plastered across his face. The sight of him, so full of life and excitement, ignited a spark of joy within the group, prompting them to quicken their pace toward the dock.

As they approached, Jacob and Liam met with a hearty handshake, their expressions bright with genuine happiness. "I'm so glad you guys could make it!" Liam exclaimed, his voice rising with enthusiasm as he gestured for everyone to climb aboard. The boat bobbed gently in the water, its polished surface reflecting the sunlight like a mirror.

"Thanks for inviting us!" Rachel chimed in, her voice bubbling with excitement. Jacob and Ivan stepped forward, taking on the role of gallant hosts as they carefully assisted Polly and Rachel onto the boat. They maneuvered the picnic supplies— a sturdy cooler filled to the brim with refreshing drinks and a picnic basket bursting with colorful sandwiches, fresh fruits, and homemade snacks, ensuring everything was stowed securely without causing any spills.

Once everyone was settled, Liam turned the key in the ignition, and the engine roared to life with a powerful growl. The sound reverberated through the air, filling them with a sense of exhilaration. As the boat surged forward, the thrill of speed rushed through them, and they felt a rush of adrenaline as they glided across the sparkling water. The sun glinted off the surface, creating a dazzling display of light that danced around them.

Jacob and Ivan, eager to embrace the warmth of the sun, wasted no time. They quickly stripped off their shirts and shorts, revealing their swim trunks, their skin glistening under the bright rays. Jacob's lean, muscular physique caught Rachel's eye, and her cheeks flushed a deep shade of pink as she took in the sight. Every contour of his body was accentuated by the sunlight, highlighting the definition in his arms and the strength in his broad shoulders. He carried himself with effortless confidence, moving to the front of the boat to assist Liam with steering.

Meanwhile, Ivan settled beside Polly, who was trying to maintain her composure. She found herself casting sidelong glances at him, her heart racing as she took in his sun-kissed physique. The way the sun's rays danced across his skin made him look almost ethereal. She couldn't help but admire the way his broad shoulders and toned arms defined his silhouette. Polly felt a rush of warmth flood her cheeks, momentarily lost for words as she attempted to gather her thoughts.

"So, um… I…" she stammered, her voice barely above a whisper, unable to articulate the admiration she felt. Her heart raced, and she fumbled with her words, feeling a mixture of shyness and excitement.

Ivan caught her eye, a playful smile tugging at the corners of his mouth as he noticed her flustered demeanor. "You okay?" he asked, his tone light and teasing. The warmth in his voice sent her heart fluttering, and the teasing glimmer in his eyes only made her blush deepen.

The atmosphere around them was electric, filled with the sounds of laughter, the roar of the engine, and the splashes of water as they sped across the lake. The sun warmed their skin, the breeze tousled their hair, and the excitement of the day ahead was palpable, creating the perfect backdrop for an unforgettable adventure. With the laughter of friends and the promise of freedom in the air, they felt ready to embrace whatever the day had in store.

As the boat glided smoothly across the shimmering surface of the lake, a palpable sense of exhilaration filled the air. The sun hung brightly in the cobalt sky, its radiant beams dancing upon the water, transforming it into a sparkling expanse that resembled a sea of diamonds. Each ripple reflected the sunlight in a dazzling display, captivating the group as they sped along. Laughter erupted among them, harmonizing beautifully with the powerful roar of the engine and the gentle, rhythmic lapping of waves against the boat's hull.

Jacob stood at the front, embodying the spirit of adventure. His strong frame was silhouetted against the bright blue sky, and the wind tousled his hair, giving him an almost carefree and wild appearance. He inhaled deeply, savoring the fresh scent of the lake mingled with the scent of food in the air, and felt completely alive in that moment.

"Hey, Liam! Can we hit the big waves?" Jacob shouted, his voice filled with excitement, a playful challenge dancing in his tone as he turned to his friend at the helm. Liam, always up for a little adventure, flashed a wide grin, his eyes sparkling with mischief. He tightened his grip on the steering wheel, his knuckles white with enthusiasm.

"Hold on to your shorts!" Liam called back, his voice booming over the wind. With a quick twist of the throttle, the boat surged forward, accelerating as the engine roared to life. The hull sliced through the water with a powerful thrust, creating a substantial wake that sent splashes flying in all directions. Jacob leaned into the wind, laughter spilling from his lips as the boat bounced lightly over the waves, the spray of water glistening like tiny jewels in the sunlight.

Rachel stood just behind Jacob, her heart racing not just from the speed but from the sight of his vibrant energy and carefree spirit. The sun highlighted the contours of his body, casting shadows that accentuated his athletic build. She couldn't help but admire how effortlessly he seemed to embrace the thrill of the moment, how his laughter seemed to brighten the entire scene.

"Wooo!" Rachel yelled, her voice rising above the wind as she felt the exhilarating rush of air against her face. The joy was infectious, and she felt her own excitement bubbling up, matching the energy around her.

As the boat carved its way through the lake, Ivan and Polly shared a moment on the side, their eyes sparkling with amusement as they watched Jacob and Liam's playful antics. The water sprayed around them, creating a refreshing mist that felt invigorating. Ivan turned to Polly, a playful gleam lighting up his eyes. "You know, you can't just sit there looking cute all day; we need to make some waves too!" he said, nudging her gently with his elbow, his tone teasing yet inviting.

Polly raised an eyebrow, a smile creeping onto her face as she felt a flutter of excitement in her stomach. "Oh really? And how do you propose we do that?" she challenged, crossing her arms playfully and leaning in closer to him, her heart quickening at their playful banter.

"Let's jump in and swim! I dare you," he replied, flashing a charming grin that made her heart skip a beat. His confidence was infectious, and Polly felt a surge of adrenaline at the idea of diving into the cool lake, the prospect of adventure igniting her competitive spirit.

"Alright, Mr. Daredevil! You're on!" she declared, her voice filled with determination as she felt her excitement bubbling over.

With everyone in agreement, they prepared for the plunge. Jacob and Liam expertly maneuvered the boat to a quieter cove, the water calm and inviting, the sun reflecting off the surface like liquid gold. As they anchored the boat, Rachel and Polly erupted with energy, shedding their remaining layers and revealing their swim attire, anticipation buzzing in the air.

Without hesitation, Jacob and Liam were the first to leap off the side of the boat, their bodies slicing through the water with powerful strokes. The splash they created was magnificent, sending droplets flying in all directions that sparkled in the sunlight. They surfaced with triumphant laughter, water cascading off them as they called out to the rest.

"Come on in! It's perfect!" Jacob shouted, his voice brimming with enthusiasm as he wiped the water from his eyes, a wide grin stretching across his face.

Rachel stood at the edge of the boat, her heart pounding with a mix of excitement and trepidation. The cool water sparkled invitingly below her, but she hesitated for a moment, feeling a rush of adrenaline coursing through her veins. Jacob's encouraging smile and playful splashes drew her in, making her heart race even faster.

Taking a deep breath, she summoned her courage and took a running start, her feet pounding against the deck of the boat before she leaped into the air. Time seemed to freeze as she soared through the sky, the thrill of the jump exhilarating. When she hit the water, it enveloped her in a refreshing embrace, sending a shock through her body that was both startling and invigorating.

As she resurfaced, laughter bubbled from her lips, and she shook her hair out of her face, her cheeks flushed with joy. Jacob was right there, his eyes sparkling with delight as he splashed water in her direction, droplets catching the sunlight like tiny diamonds. "See? Isn't it amazing?" he called out, clearly reveling in the moment.

Polly stood at the edge, her heart racing as she watched the carefree joy unfold around her. With a determined grin, she turned to Ivan, her competitive spirit ignited. "Alright, let's show them how it's done!" she declared, her voice filled with excitement and challenge. Ivan nodded, a matching grin spreading across his face, and together they took the plunge, leaping off the boat in synchronized jumps that sent up an impressive splash.

As they broke the surface, the group erupted into laughter, the lake around them alive with energy and joy. The sun warmed their skin, the water refreshingly cool against their sun-kissed bodies, and for that moment, everything felt perfect. They swam and played, splashing and racing each other, the worries of the world far away as they embraced the freedom of the day.

As the day wore on, the sun hung high in the sky, bathing the lake in a warm golden light that shimmered across the water's surface like liquid gold. The air was alive with the sounds of laughter as the group splashed and played, their joyous shouts mingling with the gentle waves crashing against them. Jacob was in his element, embodying the carefree spirit of summer. He dove into the water with a graceful plunge, disappearing beneath the surface, only to resurface moments later, just inches away from Rachel. Each time he emerged, he did so with a cheeky grin, water droplets glistening on his skin, and a playful jab that sent Rachel into fits of laughter. His silly faces and antics were infectious, filling the air with a lightheartedness that seemed to erase any worries they might have had.

The sun began its slow descent, painting the sky with hues of orange and pink, signaling the approach of evening. After what felt like an endless span of gleeful splashing and playful competition, Jacob and Ivan took charge, calling the group back onboard the boat. The collective growl of their stomachs echoed in the air, a reminder that it was time to refuel. With eager hands, they quickly unpacked the cooler, revealing a delightful spread of delicious treats: flavorful sandwiches, luscious slices of ripe watermelon, homemade cookies, and an assortment of chilled drinks that sparkled in the sunlight like gems.

Rachel's gaze followed Jacob as he moved about the boat, her heart fluttering with each fluid motion. She found herself completely captivated by him, her cheeks flushing a deep shade of pink every time he bent over to grab something from the cooler. The sight of his sun-kissed thighs, accentuated by snug swim trunks, sent a wave of warmth through her, making her pulse quicken. The way the sunlight danced across his skin, highlighting the contours of his muscles, gave him an almost ethereal quality, and she couldn't help but admire the effortless confidence he exuded.

Polly, seated nearby, couldn't help but notice Rachel's

fascination. "You are not being very subtle, you know," she teased with a playful glint in her eye as she nudged Rachel with her elbow. "He's definitely got your attention!" Her words made Rachel's cheeks heat up even more, but she couldn't fight the smile that crept across her face.

Once everyone was back on the boat, they settled into a cozy spot. Jacob found a comfortable place to sit, and Rachel nestled between his legs, feeling the warmth radiating from him. She laid her head against his chest, relishing the steady rhythm of his heartbeat beneath her ear, a soothing melody that made her feel safe and content. In this intimate position, she could feel the rise and fall of his chest with each breath, grounding her in the moment and making her heart swell with a mix of exhilaration and comfort.

As they settled in, Rachel felt an irresistible urge to place her hand gently on Jacob's thigh, her fingers resting lightly against the warm skin. The touch was innocent yet charged with unspoken affection, and she felt a thrilling connection course through her at that moment. Jacob, fully aware of the effect he had on her, smiled down at her, his eyes sparkling with warmth and a hint of mischief.

"Here, let me feed you," he said playfully, scooping up a piece of ripe fruit from his plate. He held it up to her mouth, his expression teasing as he encouraged her to take a bite. She opened her mouth, and as she bit into the juicy slice, the sweetness exploded in her mouth, but it was Jacob's laughter that truly made her heart race.

"See? Isn't this better than diving?" he teased, offering

her another bite, and she couldn't help but giggle in response. Each morsel he offered was accompanied by light-hearted banter and playful antics. He made exaggerated expressions as he recounted silly stories from their day, his laughter mingling with hers in a beautiful harmony. The air around them felt charged with excitement and warmth, creating a perfect backdrop for the deepening connection they were forging.

As they enjoyed their meal together, the sun dipped lower in the sky, casting a warm, golden hue across the water. The soft glow wrapped around them like a cozy blanket, enhancing the intimate atmosphere on the boat. Rachel stole glances at Jacob, his relaxed demeanor making him even more appealing. The way he effortlessly moved, his laughter ringing out like music, made her heart flutter with every shared glance.

In this cocoon of warmth and laughter, they shared stories, dreams, and playful teasing, each moment pulling them closer together. The world beyond the lake faded away, leaving only their friendship and the promise of more adventures yet to come. Rachel found herself savoring every second, fully aware that these memories would linger long after the sun had set and the day had drawn to a close.

As twilight began to settle, painting the sky in deep indigos and soft purples, the group leaned back, taking in the beauty of the moment. The stars began to twinkle overhead, one by one, creating a breathtaking tapestry against the night sky. Rachel felt a sense of peace wash over her, knowing that this day, filled with laughter and connection, would forever hold a special place in her heart. Each shared smile and playful touch between her and Jacob felt like a promise—a promise of friendship, adventure, and perhaps something deeper that was just beginning to unfold.

As twilight deepened, the atmosphere on the boat transformed into something magical. The soft murmur of the water against the hull became a soothing lullaby, while the stars began to twinkle overhead, casting their gentle glow upon the lake. The sky morphed from vibrant hues of orange and pink into rich indigos and soft purples, creating a breathtaking backdrop that felt almost surreal. Rachel nestled deeper against Jacob, feeling a sense of warmth and safety in his presence, as if the world outside had faded away, leaving only the two of them in their own little universe.

With the sun now beginning to set, the warmth of the day lingered in the air, but a cool breeze began to sweep across the lake, causing Rachel to shiver slightly. Jacob immediately noticed and wrapped his arms around her, pulling her closer into his embrace. "You okay?" he asked softly, his voice low and warm. The concern in his tone made her heart flutter.

"I'm fine, just a bit chilly," she replied, tilting her head back to meet his gaze. The evening light painted his features in soft shadows, accentuating the warmth in his eyes. "But this is perfect."

Jacob smiled, a genuine smile that reached his eyes. "Good, because I'm not letting you go now," he teased playfully, tightening his hold around her. Rachel couldn't help but laugh, the sound bubbling up from her chest. There was something intoxicating about being this close to him, the way he made her feel both at ease and exhilarated at the same time.

"It's been really great hanging out with all of you," Liam said, a warm smile spreading across his face as he looked around at his friends, each one glowing with the joy of the day. The sun hung low in the sky, casting a golden hue across the lake, and the laughter they shared seemed to echo in harmony with the gentle lapping of the water against the boat.

Chapter 15

Twilight Whispers

"I guess we'd better head to shore," Jacob replied, glancing upwards at the horizon where the sun was dipping lower, a fiery orb slowly disappearing behind the mountains. The sky was painted with shades of orange and pink, promising a beautiful twilight. He could feel the cool breeze gently brushing against his skin, a subtle reminder that evening was approaching, and it was time to wrap up their fun-filled day.

"It's starting to get a little chilly," Polly chimed in, her voice slightly shivering as she hugged herself tightly. The warmth of the sun was fading, and the cool air was creeping in, prompting her to seek comfort in her clothing. She glanced around, noticing the way the evening light danced on the water, creating a shimmering effect that was almost mesmerizing.

With a shared understanding, Polly and Rachel began to rummage through their bags for their clothes. Rachel laughed as she struggled to get her shirt over her head, her hair flopping around like a wild mess. "I swear, I'm like a toddler trying to get dressed!" she joked, her laughter brightening the atmosphere even more.

Jacob and Ivan exchanged amused glances, their expressions lighting up with playful mischief as they watched the girls. "Need a hand, Rachel?" Jacob teased, leaning back against the side of the boat, arms crossed, clearly enjoying the spectacle. His eyes sparkled with humor, and he grinned widely, ready to join in the fun.

Once the girls managed to wrangle themselves into their clothes, Jacob and Ivan began to put on their clothes as well.

As Rachel continued to watch her friends, her gaze often drifted back to Jacob. The way the evening light played across his sun-kissed body was mesmerizing. His skin glowed with a warm bronze hue, a testament to the hours spent under the sun during their day of adventure. The light caught the contours of his muscles, highlighting the defined lines of his arms and shoulders as he pulled on his shirt.

In that moment, Rachel felt a flutter in her chest. She couldn't help but admire the way his body moved with an effortless grace, each motion fluid and confident. As he reached for his shorts, the sunlight danced across his skin, illuminating the droplets of water that still clung to him from their playful splashes in the lake. She noticed the way his sun-kissed thighs flexed as he bent down, and her cheeks flushed with color at the thought.

There was something undeniably captivating about Jacob, especially as he dressed in front of her. The snug fit of his swim trunks accentuated his athletic build, drawing her eyes to the way his physique was shaped by the summer sun and the countless hours spent outdoors. She found herself momentarily lost in thought, appreciating the warmth radiating from him, both from the sun and his vibrant personality.

As he turned toward her, catching her gaze, a playful grin spread across his face. "What? You've never seen a guy get dressed before?" he teased, his eyes sparkling with mischief. Rachel quickly averted her gaze, her heart racing, but she couldn't suppress the smile that tugged at her lips.

"Just admiring the view," she shot back playfully, trying to keep her tone light even though her cheeks were still warm. The banter between them was effortless, but in that moment, she felt a deeper connection stirring beneath the surface. Jacob's laughter rang out, filling the air with a sense of camaraderie and warmth that made her heart flutter even more.

As the girls continued to tease the boys, Rachel found herself reveling in the moment, feeling grateful for the opportunity to enjoy not just the beauty of the setting sun but also the beauty of the friendships around her—and especially the one she shared with Jacob. The way he carried himself, confident and carefree, was intoxicating, and as she watched him, she couldn't help but wonder what other adventures awaited them in the days to come.

Their movements were exaggerated, each boy playing to the audience of their friends. Jacob pulled on his T-shirt with a flourish, striking a ridiculous pose as he flexed his arms. "Thank you, thank you! I do what I can for fashion!" he announced dramatically, pretending to bask in the adoration of an imaginary crowd.

Ivan, not to be outdone, joined in on the theatrics. As he pulled on his shorts, he made a show of strutting around the boat, puffing out his chest. "Watch out, world! Here comes the fashion icon of the lake!" he declared, twirling around with an exaggerated flair that sent everyone into fits of giggles.

The girls couldn't contain their laughter as they threw playful compliments at the boys. "Looking sharp, boys!" Polly called out, her eyes sparkling with amusement. "I think you both should model for a magazine!"

Jacob and Ivan, fully embracing their roles as the clowns of the group, responded with even more over-the-top antics. Jacob pretended to pose like a runway model, turning this way and that, while Ivan mimicked a news anchor, reporting on the latest trends in lake fashion. "In breaking news, swim trunks are officially in this season!" he exclaimed, gesturing wildly.

The laughter bubbled up between them, an infectious energy that filled the air. The warmth of their friendship enveloped them, creating a joyful atmosphere as they continued to tease and banter. The boys made silly faces and exaggerated movements, their antics drawing the girls in further. Rachel leaned against Jacob, giggling at his ridiculous expressions, while Polly clutched her stomach, laughing until tears formed in her eyes.

As the sun dipped lower, casting long shadows across the boat, the group savored these final moments of the day together. The warm glow of friendship wrapped around them, the laughter and teasing echoing against the serene backdrop of the lake. The world around them faded, leaving only the warmth of their bond and the promise of more adventures to come. In that moment, it felt as if nothing else mattered, just the joy of being together, creating memories that would last long after the sun had set and the stars began to twinkle in the night sky.

As Jacob navigated the winding road home, the laughter from their day at the lake echoed in the air, a melody of joy that wrapped around them like a warm embrace. In the backseat, Ivan and Polly exchanged knowing glances, observing the undeniable chemistry sparking between their best friends, a connection that was both thrilling and tender.

When they arrived at Polly and Rachel's apartment, Jacob and Ivan assumed the roles of gallant knights, playfully guiding the two ladies toward the entrance of their building. The evening was bathed in a soft glow of street lights, and the air was filled with the sweet scent of petunias blooming nearby, enhancing the romantic atmosphere. Rachel and Jacob's fingers intertwined, their hands fitting together as if they were always meant to be. They exchanged glances that spoke volumes, their eyes shimmering with unspoken feelings, each moment charged with anticipation.

As they drew closer, the world around them faded away, leaving only the two of them in that perfect moment. Their lips met softly at first, a gentle brush that ignited a passionate fire within Rachel, her heart racing like a wild drumbeat. This kiss was everything she had ever imagined and more—

a whirlwind of emotions that swept her off her feet, making her feel as if they were the only two souls in existence.

After the kiss lingered in the air like a sweet promise, Rachel and Polly slipped inside the apartment, but Rachel couldn't tear herself away just yet. She stood by the door, her heart still fluttering with the warmth of their connection, watching as Jacob walked back to his car. When he paused and turned to look back at her, his smile was like a beacon, illuminating the dim evening. In that moment, Rachel felt her heart melt completely, warmth flooding through her as their eyes locked, a silent understanding passing between them—a promise of more beautiful moments to come.

Chapter 16

Whispers of Determination

The following afternoon, Patricia Jackson stepped into the bustling airport, her demeanor a mix of determination and thinly-veiled frustration. The lively atmosphere of travelers rushing about and the constant announcements over the PA system felt overwhelming. Patricia, an ambitious woman with a reputation for being stern and focused, was on a mission to serve the royal family, and she intended to do it flawlessly. The queen had entrusted her with a significant task: uncovering the truth about Alexander's activities, and she was determined to prove herself.

This, however, was her first trip to America, and Patricia found herself grappling with the unfamiliarity of it all. Striding purposefully to the car rental counter, she glanced at her watch, as if time itself were conspiring against her. Once she secured the keys to a sleek black sedan, she marched toward the vehicle, confidence radiating from her. Yet, as she approached the car, she opened the door on the wrong side, her brow furrowing in irritation.

"Of course, I'd pick the side that makes absolutely no sense," she muttered under her breath, feeling a wave of embarrassment wash over her. Climbing into the driver's seat, she took a moment to collect herself, adjusting the mirrors with a stern focus. Driving on the opposite side of the road was a concept she had read about but never experienced, and as she fumbled with the controls, she felt her confidence start to wane.

"Who in their right mind would put the steering wheel on the left side of the car and then expect you to drive on the right side of the road?" she grumbled, shaking her head in disbelief. It was a ridiculous setup that seemed designed to trip up even the most competent of drivers.

With a huff, Patricia steered the car out of the parking lot, her grip on the wheel tightening as she faced the bustling streets. The vibrant city unfolded before her, filled with honking cars and pedestrians darting in every direction. She tried to maintain her composure, but as she mentally calculated her next move, she found herself hesitating at a stoplight, completely lost in thought.

"Just keep it together, Patricia. You can do this," she admonished herself, though her confidence was faltering. As she merged into traffic, she inadvertently turned on the windshield wipers instead of the turn signal, causing her face to flush with frustration.

"This is just a minor setback," she reassured herself, though her stern exterior was beginning to crack.

As Patricia navigated the chaotic streets, her frustration simmered just beneath the surface. With every honking horn and bewildered glance from other drivers, her resolve to maintain her stern demeanor was tested. She glanced at the GPS, its cheerful voice offering directions that felt like they were mocking her. "In 300 feet, turn left," it chirped, but as she approached the intersection, the reality of her situation began to set in.

"Left… or right? Why can't this just be simpler?" she grumbled, her fingers tapping nervously on the steering wheel. She knew she needed to make a decision quickly, but the unfamiliar street signs seemed to taunt her. With a deep breath, she chose to turn left, only to realize moments later that she'd just entered a one-way street going the wrong direction. Panic surged through her as cars rushed toward her, and she instinctively slammed on the brakes, her heart racing.

"Okay, stay calm, Patricia. You can fix this," she told herself, her voice stern as she gripped the wheel. But the truth was, she felt anything but calm. With a deep sigh, she carefully maneuvered into a parking lot to regroup, all the while muttering about the absurdity of American driving laws. "Who thought this was a good idea?" she complained, shaking her head as she pulled into a space.

Sitting there for a moment, she took a deep breath, trying to gather her thoughts. She was a woman of action, known for her decisiveness in the royal court, and yet here she was, lost and fumbling. She glanced at her reflection in the rear-view mirror, adjusting her glasses and reminding herself of her purpose. "You need to find your hotel and then Alexander," she stated firmly, her tone more resolute. "This is just a minor hiccup."

As she prepared to set off again, she realized she had left the GPS on and it was now loudly announcing,

"Recalculating!" The irony wasn't lost on her, and she couldn't help but let out a small, exasperated laugh. "Great, even my navigation system thinks I'm incompetent," she muttered.

After a brief moment of self-reflection, Patricia decided to embrace the chaos. "If I can survive this, I can survive anything," she said, her voice filled with dry humor.

With newfound determination, she pulled back onto the road, her grip on the wheel steadying as she focused on the journey ahead. Each turn felt less daunting now, and even though she still struggled with the occasional mishap, like mistakenly hitting the horn instead of the turn signal, she found herself chuckling at the absurdity of it all.

After a day filled with unexpected twists and turns, Patricia Jackson finally approached the Grand Hotel, its grand facade towering above her with an air of elegance and sophistication. The building was an architectural marvel, adorned with intricate details and surrounded by lush gardens that hinted at opulence. She felt a rush of anticipation mixed with a tinge of anxiety as she stepped through its regal doors, the sound of her heels clicking against the marble floor echoing in the spacious lobby.

Inside, the atmosphere buzzed with activity. Guests checked in, bellhops hurried by with luggage, and the soft strains of a piano filled the air, creating an inviting ambiance. Patricia straightened her posture, shaking off the chaotic experiences of the day as she focused on her mission. She was here to gather information about Alexander, and she needed to project an air of authority.

As she walked to the reception desk, she couldn't help but notice the ornate chandeliers hanging from the ceiling, casting a warm glow over the polished furnishings. "This place is something else," she thought, momentarily distracted by the luxurious surroundings. But she shook her head, pushing aside the allure of the hotel's charm. She had a job to do.

"Good evening, ma'am. How may I assist you?" the receptionist greeted her with a smile, a polished professionalism that matched the hotel's ambiance.

As Patricia stood before the reception desk of the Grand Hotel, she straightened her blazer and spoke with authority. "I am Patricia Jackson, royal representative of Queen Isabella. I have a reservation." Her voice was steady, carrying the weight of her position, yet there was a hint of nervousness that she quickly masked with a confident smile.

The receptionist looked up from her computer, her expression shifting to one of recognition and respect. "Of course, Ms. Jackson. We've been expecting you. Let me pull up your reservation." She typed swiftly, scanning the screen before looking back at Patricia. "You're booked into the Royal Suite. It's an honor to have you here."

Patricia felt a swell of pride at the mention of her title and the acknowledgment of her role. "Thank you," she replied, her tone firm yet cordial. "Please, if you could expedite the check-in process, I have an important business to attend to."

"Absolutely!" the receptionist responded, her fingers flying over the keyboard. Within moments, she handed Patricia a key card. "Here you go, Ms. Jackson. The Royal Suite is on the top floor. You'll find it to be quite comfortable and well-appointed. Is there anything else I can assist you with?"

Patricia accepted the key card, her mind already racing with the tasks ahead. With a nod of appreciation, Patricia turned and headed toward the elevator with the bellhop right behind, her heels clicking purposefully against the marble floor. As she ascended to the top floor, she glanced at her reflection in the polished metal doors. She adjusted her hair and straightened her posture, reminding herself of her mission. The royal family was counting on her, and she would not let them down.

When the elevator doors opened, Patricia stepped into the hallway, the plush carpet muffling her footsteps. The Royal Suite was at the end of the corridor, and she approached the door with a sense of anticipation.

As she entered the suite, she was immediately struck by its grandeur. The spacious living area boasted elegant furniture, a stunning view of the city skyline, and tasteful decorations that exuded luxury. Patricia took a moment to appreciate the surroundings before focusing on the task at hand.

"Alright, Patricia, time to get to work," she said to herself, her tone resolute. She had the bellhop place her bags down as she made her way to the sitting area, pulling out a notepad to jot down her thoughts. The luxurious ambiance of the suite felt like a fitting backdrop for the important discussions that lay ahead.

Patricia was ready to begin her mission to find Alexander, to uncover the truth, and to represent her royal duties with the utmost professionalism. The Grand Hotel, with all its grandeur, was simply a stepping stone on her journey, and she was determined to make the most of it.

As Patricia stood in the grand living area of the Royal Suite, savoring the luxurious surroundings, a polite yet slightly awkward cough broke her concentration. She turned to see the bellhop standing nearby, his expression a mix of patience and expectation.

The bellhop stood there for several moments, his hand still extended, clearly caught off guard by Patricia's response. She furrowed her brow, realizing the awkwardness of the situation. "Oh, alright," she said with a resigned sigh, pulling out a single dollar bill and handing it to him.

As the bill exchanged hands, the bellhop's eyes widened in disbelief. He blinked a few times, processing the situation, and for a brief moment, the professional facade slipped, revealing his stunned expression. It was as if he had expected a bit more for the service he had provided, especially in such a luxurious setting.

"Thank you, Miss Jackson," he finally managed to say, his voice slightly strained as he turned to leave, the dollar bill crumpled in his hand.

Chapter 17

A Mission of Importance

Half a world away in the enchanting kingdom of Slovitia, nestled between lush green hills and sparkling rivers, Queen Isabella busily prepared for the eagerly anticipated visit of Princess Penelope. The air was filled with a sense of excitement, as the queen had grown increasingly fond of the young princess, who represented everything Isabella envisioned for her son, Alexander.

Princess Penelope was not only strikingly beautiful, with cascading golden hair and sparkling blue eyes, but she also possessed a rare grace and charm that captivated everyone around her. Her laughter danced like music through the halls, and her keen intellect made her a delightful conversationalist. Isabella admired how Penelope carried herself with poise, her every movement exuding confidence and warmth. It was clear to Isabella that the princess was not just a pretty face; she had a vibrant personality that could light up any room.

As Isabella arranged the grand hall for the occasion, she meticulously selected the finest silk drapes in royal blue, complementing the elegant gold accents that adorned the room. Exquisite tapestries depicting the kingdom's rich history hung on the walls, while fragrant blooms from the royal garden filled the air with a sweet scent, creating an inviting atmosphere. Every detail mattered to Isabella, as she wanted the visit to be nothing short of magical.

Yet, amid the preparations, Isabella couldn't help but reflect on her son Alexander's headstrong nature. Known for his unyielding spirit, he often clashed with those around him, especially when his mind was set. His stubbornness had caused concern for the queen, who feared it might hinder his ability to recognize the value of true partnership in love. However, Isabella remained hopeful; she believed that with Princess Penelope's warmth, understanding, and innate ability to connect with others, she could gently coax Alexander from his resolute ways.

As the day approached, Isabella's heart swelled with anticipation. She envisioned the moment when Penelope would arrive, her radiant smile lighting up the hall, and she could almost hear the sound of laughter and engaging conversation filling the air. In her mind, she dreamed of a blossoming connection between the two, one that could unite their families and pave the way for a bright future.

"Princess Penelope, please do come in," Queen Isabella beckoned as the young princess gracefully entered the grand Main Hall. The room, adorned with shimmering chandeliers and elegant furnishings, seemed to come alive at her presence. The queen, resplendent in her regal attire—an exquisite gown of deep emerald silk that flowed elegantly with her every movement—extended her hand in a warm welcome.

"I'm so delighted to be here again with you, Queen

Isabella," Penelope replied, her voice filled with genuine warmth. "You look absolutely ravishing!"

"Thank you, dear Penelope," the queen replied, her eyes shimmering with excitement. "It's always a delight to come and visit with you. Tell me, has Alexander returned from America yet?" Princess Penelope inquired, her voice filled with anticipation.

The princess's expression shifted slightly, curiosity mingled with concern. "No, no, not yet," Isabella said, her voice tinged with urgency. "But that is precisely why I have invited you here again. I fear that Alexander's affections may have been hijacked by a lowly commoner in America, and I need your help."

Penelope's eyes widened in surprise, her brows furrowing slightly. "A commoner? But surely he wouldn't be swayed so easily?"

Isabella sighed, her regal composure momentarily faltering. "You see, Alexander is a spirited young man, and while I raised him with the values of our noble lineage, he has always been drawn to adventure and the allure of new experiences. I worry that he may have become enchanted by someone who does not understand the responsibilities of our world."

Taking a step closer, Penelope lowered her voice, her concern evident. "What do you wish me to do, Your Majesty?"

Isabella's gaze softened, reflecting both determination

and hope. "I believe that your presence, your charm, and your understanding of the court could remind him of the life and love he has here in Slovitia. I need you to rekindle the bond between you two, to show him that the heart can find its true home among those who share the same values and heritage."

Penelope nodded thoughtfully, her resolve strengthening. "I will do my utmost to help, Your Majesty. If there's a chance to win back Alexander's heart, I won't let it slip away."

Queen Isabella's smile broadened, a wave of relief washing over her. "That is precisely what I was hoping to hear," she replied, her voice infused with warmth.

With a slight blush, Penelope continued, "Your Majesty, I have always thought highly of Prince Alexander, even when we were just young children frolicking around the castle. I can still vividly remember those carefree days, when our laughter filled the halls and the sun cast playful shadows on the stone walls as we played.

"What exactly did you have in mind?" Princess Penelope asked, her curiosity now piqued.

Queen Isabella leaned in slightly, her voice filled with purpose. "I want you to travel to America and remind Alexander of what it truly means to be in the presence of a beautiful and refined lady. He has been swept away by the excitement of the unfamiliar, and I believe that your elegance, grace, and deep understanding of our heritage can serve as a guiding light for him.

In a land so far from home, where things may seem more adventurous and less grounded, your presence can remind him of the values and traditions he was raised with. Remind him of the beauty of our world, the depth of loyalty and love that he may be overlooking. It is essential that he sees the contrast between fleeting enchantments and the enduring connections that await him back in Slovitia and the royal court."

The princess was taken aback by such a bold request. "Travel to America?" she echoed, her voice a mix of disbelief and intrigue. The very idea felt foreign and daunting, a world away from the familiar comforts of her homeland.

"Yes," the queen affirmed, her tone resolute, a hint of urgency lacing her words. She could see the hesitation flickering in Penelope's expressive eyes, a whirlwind of emotions swirling within her—surprise, uncertainty, and perhaps a touch of fear.

"I understand your reservations," Queen Isabella continued, her gaze softening with understanding. "But I have already arranged for my most trusted assistant to be there, someone who knows the landscape well and can guide you through this unfamiliar territory. You won't face this challenge alone; she will be your ally."

She stepped closer, placing a reassuring hand on Penelope's shoulder, her grip gentle yet firm. "I will ensure you have everything you need for your journey, financial support, travel arrangements, and any resources to help you navigate the urban jungles in America. This is not just a trip; it's a mission, my sweet child. It's an opportunity to reignite the bond between you and Prince Alexander."

Queen Isabella's eyes sparkled with hope. "You have the charm and grace that can remind him of what he is missing. Show him the beauty of our heritage, the depth of loyalty, and the warmth of love that he may be overlooking in his pursuit of adventure. I believe that with your heart and determination, you can make him see that duty is where love and honor reside."

The princess nodded in agreement, her determination growing. "You will see, Penelope, that this is the best path for both you and Alexander. With your grace and elegance, he will come to understand that you bring far more to the table than any ordinary American ever could," the Queen said, gently clasping Penelope's hand.

Princess Penelope bowed gracefully, her heart swelled with purpose. "I would consider it an honor to undertake this task."

Queen Isabella smiled, satisfaction radiating from her. She motioned for a servant to guide the princess to one of the regal bedrooms, a space adorned with rich tapestries and exquisite furnishings, fit for a royal guest.

As the princess was exiting the room, she encountered King Frederick in the doorway. "Ah, Princess Penelope! It is a delight to have you here again," he greeted warmly, though a flicker of curiosity danced in his eyes. "I hope my wife is not being a burden to you," he added, a knowing smile creeping onto his face.

The king had a keen sense that Queen Isabella was up to something, and he couldn't help but wonder what plans were unfolding behind the scenes. His instincts told him that this was more than just a friendly visit; there was a deeper purpose at play.

Penelope offered a polite smile, her thoughts momentarily drifting back to the queen's request. "Not at all, Your Majesty. It is always a pleasure to be in the company of such esteemed royalty," she replied, her demeanor composed, masking the whirlwind of emotions beneath the surface.

King Frederick studied her for a moment, sensing the underlying tension. "I trust you will enjoy your stay, Princess. If there is anything you need, feel free to ask," he said, his tone inviting yet cautious, aware that the tides of royal affairs often shifted unexpectedly. As Penelope continued on her way, he couldn't shake the feeling that Queen Isabella was about to meddle in Alexander's affairs.

King Frederick stepped into the room, his expression serious as he approached his wife. "My love, are you meddling in Alexander's affairs?" he asked, a hint of concern lacing his voice, his brow furrowed with worry.

Queen Isabella turned to him, feigning innocence, her eyes wide with surprise. "Why would you say such a thing?" she replied, her tone light, but her heart raced with the underlying tension of their conversation.

The king crossed his arms, a knowing smile tugging at his lips. "I know you all too well, my love. You've always had a tendency to orchestrate events to suit your desires. I will warn you again to be careful in interfering in Alexander's love life. He is old enough to make his own choices, and those choices must be his alone."

Queen Isabella maintained her composed demeanor, though a flicker of defiance sparked in her gaze. "I would never dream of interfering in Alexander's life. I simply want to ensure he is making good decisions for his future. You know how easily he can be swayed by the allure of the unfamiliar."

King Frederick rubbed his chin thoughtfully, his expression becoming more serious. "Isabella, I can't help but feel that Princess Penelope's visit is more than just a coincidence. Are you really suggesting that you believe this will end well? You know how unpredictable matters of the heart can be."

"Frederick," she replied, stepping closer, her voice softening, "Penelope represents everything that is noble and refined. She embodies the values and traditions we hold dear, and perhaps her presence can remind Alexander of what he truly deserves. He has been so caught up in the excitement of America that he may have forgotten the beauty of his heritage. "

The king sighed, torn between his trust in his wife's instincts and his desire to protect their son. "I understand your intentions, but love is a delicate dance, and the consequences of meddling can reverberate far beyond our intentions. What if this backfires? What if Alexander pushes her away, believing we are trying to control his heart?"

Queen Isabella's eyes narrowed slightly, her resolve strengthening. "I believe in Penelope. She is strong, intelligent, and capable of winning Alexander's heart in a way that no fleeting romance can. Besides, this is not about control; it's about guiding him back to what truly matters."

King Frederick studied her, sensing the passion behind her words. "And what if he finds happiness elsewhere? Shouldn't we allow him to explore those possibilities? What if he falls in love with an American? Can we truly dictate who he should love?"

Queen Isabella placed a hand on his arm, her expression earnest. "I want him to be happy, but I also want him to be grounded. Love should not be a fleeting whim; it should be rooted in tradition and duty. Penelope can offer that stability, and I believe she can help him see the beauty in our traditions."

Frederick looked into her eyes, hoping she would heed his warning while also understanding the depth of his concern for both Alexander and her. "Then let us tread carefully, my dear. I trust you, but remember that the heart is unpredictable. We must be prepared for whatever path Alexander chooses, even if it leads him away from our plans."

"You know the law states that Prince Alexander must marry into a royal line," Queen Isabella said softly, her voice filled with a mix of determination and concern. She placed her hand gently on the king's face, her touch tender yet firm. "I just want the best for him, like our parents wanted for us."

King Frederick sighed, feeling the weight of her words. "I understand that, my love. I truly do. But I also believe that love cannot be dictated by laws or traditions alone. It must be genuine and free. I know you want the best for Alexander, but we must be careful. Matters of the heart can be explosive and unpredictable."

Queen Isabella's expression turned serious as she withdrew her hand, her brow furrowing. "Frederick, I recognize the complexities of love, but we have a responsibility to guide him. The throne requires stability, and marrying into a royal line ensures that he can forge alliances that strengthen our kingdom. We cannot overlook that."

The king nodded, his gaze unwavering. "You're right, but remember that forcing him into a union he does not desire could drive him away from us. We don't want to lose him to resentment. He needs to feel that he has a say in his own destiny."

Isabella's voice softened, a hint of desperation creeping in. "I fear he may not realize what he stands to lose if he continues down this path with fleeting romances. I believe Penelope can provide him with the love and loyalty he deserves—a partner who understands the weight of duty and honor."

Frederick sighed again, rubbing the back of his neck, the tension evident in his posture. "And what if he falls for someone else? Someone outside of our expectations? We must allow him the freedom to choose, even if that choice leads him away from our plans. We cannot control his heart, Isabella."

"I know," she replied, her eyes searching his for understanding. "But I believe that if we give him the opportunity to see Penelope again, to remember what they once shared, he may come to realize that true love doesn't have to be a gamble. It can be a choice, a commitment rooted in shared values and duty."

King Frederick studied her, the fire in her eyes igniting his own resolve. "Then let us proceed with caution. I trust your judgment, but we must remain vigilant. If this backfires, we may need to help him pick up the pieces."

Queen Isabella nodded, a sense of relief washing over her. "Thank you, my love. Together, we can guide him without suffocating his spirit. We can show him that marrying for love and marrying for duty can coexist."

The king smiled gently, pulling her into an embrace. "We are partners in this, just as we have always been. Let's hope that our efforts lead him to the happiness we both envision." The weight of their conversation lingered, but there was a shared understanding that together, they could navigate the complexities of love, duty, and the future of their family.

Chapter 18

Shadows of Surveillance

As the seasons shifted, the world outside transformed into a stunning canvas of vibrant oranges, deep reds, and golden yellows, heralding the arrival of autumn. The trees stood tall, their leaves fluttering gently to the ground, creating a crunchy carpet that crackled underfoot. A cool breeze carried the earthy scent of fallen leaves and distant bonfires, while the weight of impending exams loomed large over the students, filling the air with a mix of excitement and anxiety.

Amidst this whirlwind of deadlines and study materials, Rachel and Jacob discovered their bond growing stronger. Initially, they had been mere classmates, but their shared experiences during late-night study sessions forged a deeper connection. Their relationship flourished, marked by shared laughter, supportive words, and the thrill of overcoming challenges together. Their late-night study marathons became a cherished ritual, where they would sometimes lose track of time, their conversations drifting from textbooks to personal dreams.

Their evenings were illuminated by the soft glow of desk lamps, casting gentle shadows across the room cluttered with notes and coffee cups. The rustling sound of papers filled the air, punctuated by bursts of laughter as they navigated through complex concepts. They often took breaks to sip steaming mugs of cocoa, the warmth spreading through them as they exchanged stories and hopes for the future. The connection they cultivated extended far beyond academics, blossoming into a profound friendship that made the stress of exams feel a little less daunting.

When the day of reckoning arrived, Rachel and Polly could hardly hide their excitement upon learning they had passed their final exams with flying colors. Their joy was infectious, and they embraced tightly, tears of relief mingling with laughter. The thrill of success was palpable, spreading warmth among their friends. Jacob and Ivan, equally elated, joined the celebration, their faces lighting up with smiles that spoke volumes of their shared triumph. They engaged in playful banter, recounting their study mishaps and the moments that had tested their resolve.

In the midst of the festivities, it was announced that Jacob had graduated at the top of his class in business—a remarkable achievement that filled everyone with admiration. He stood tall as he accepted the news, a mix of pride and disbelief washing over him. Selected to deliver the commencement address, he felt a wave of excitement intertwined with nervousness. The group rallied around him, offering words of encouragement and support, sharing their own experiences of public speaking as they helped him prepare to inspire his classmates.

To commemorate their success, the group decided to enjoy a night out at a charming local café known for its warm atmosphere and delectable treats. The café, adorned with twinkling fairy lights, created a magical ambiance that felt like stepping into a fairy tale. The walls were lined with bookshelves filled with novels, and the aroma of freshly brewed coffee mingled with the scent of pastries, creating a cozy haven away from the pressures of school. As they settled around a rustic wooden table, laughter and chatter filled the air, weaving a tapestry of memories that would last a lifetime.

As they indulged in rich chocolate cake, laughter echoed as they reflected on their late-night study sessions, reminiscing about the confusion that had transformed into understanding and the joy of helping one another grasp difficult concepts. Each bite of cake was a celebration in itself, a sweet reward for their hard work. They shared their dreams for the future—Rachel, with her eyes sparkling, envisioned herself moving to the city, where she would pursue a career at a large corporation, thriving in the fast-paced environment. Polly, inspired by her recent achievement, imagined a vibrant career in New York, where her creativity could flourish.

Although Jacob felt a surge of pride in his academic accomplishments, he wrestled with the anxiety of revealing to Rachel that he was the heir to the throne of Slovitia and would soon take on the responsibilities of leadership. The weight of this secret felt heavy in his heart as he contemplated the changes it would bring to his life and the lives of those around him. Meanwhile, Ivan lightened the mood with humorous anecdotes about his own uncertain future, spinning tales of absurd career paths that elicited hearty laughter from the group. He was careful to keep Jacob's secret safe, wanting to protect his friend from the burden of disclosure.

As the evening unfolded, a spirit of camaraderie and optimism enveloped them, each conversation drawing their lives closer together. They shared hopes and fears, dreams and aspirations, creating a bond that felt unbreakable. Beneath the fairy lights, with chocolate cake and laughter surrounding them, they felt ready to face whatever challenges lay ahead, united in their friendship and the adventures that awaited them.

As they sat in the cozy café, the warm ambiance wrapping around them like a comforting blanket, Ivan's attention was suddenly drawn to an unusual sight outside the window. A sleek black sedan was parked across the street, its tinted windows reflecting the soft glow of the café's fairy lights. But it was the figure inside that piqued his curiosity, a strange looking lady with an oversized, extravagant hat and large dark sunglasses that obscured her features.

Ivan's instincts kicked in, and a sense of unease washed over him. The way she sat there, leaning slightly forward, her gaze fixed intently on their group, sent a chill down his spine. It was as if she were studying them, her presence casting a shadow over their celebration. The combination of her eccentric attire and the air of secrecy that surrounded her sparked a troubling thought in Ivan's mind: could it be that the Crown had sent a spy to watch Jacob?

He glanced at Jacob, who was laughing heartily,

oblivious to the tension brewing just outside. Ivan's heart raced as he considered the implications. If this woman was indeed a spy, what could she want? Was she there to gather information about Jacob's activities? The thought was unsettling, and he felt a surge of protectiveness over his friend.

Trying to shake off the feeling of paranoia, Ivan turned back to the group, determined to keep the atmosphere light. He joined in on the laughter, but his mind kept drifting back to the lady in the sedan. He subtly shifted in his seat, positioning himself so he could keep an eye on her without drawing attention from the others.

As the conversation flowed around him, he couldn't help but steal glances toward the sedan. The woman remained still, her expression hidden behind her dark sunglasses, but he could feel her gaze piercing through the glass, lingering on Jacob more than the rest of them. Ivan's heart raced as he considered his next move. Should he say something to Jacob? Alert Rachel and Polly? Or was he overreacting, letting his imagination run wild?

The weight of the secret they were all carrying pressed heavily on him, and he knew they had to be cautious. Whatever was happening, he was determined to protect Jacob and keep their joyous evening from being overshadowed by the ominous presence lurking just outside. With a deep breath, Ivan resolved to stay vigilant, ready to act if the situation escalated.

After some time had passed in the cozy café, Ivan

sensed that it was time to make their exit and see if the ominous black sedan would follow them. The warm chatter and laughter of his friends felt distant as he focused on the figure inside the car. His heart raced at the thought of being watched, and he knew he had to act quickly. To create a plausible excuse for their departure, he decided to feign feeling unwell, rubbing his temples and letting a few coughs escape, hoping to convince the group that he needed fresh air.

"Hey, guys, I'm not feeling too great," Ivan said, his voice slightly strained and laced with concern. "Maybe we should head back to Polly's apartment? A change of scenery might help."

Rachel looked at him with genuine concern, her brow furrowing. "Oh no, Ivan! Are you okay? We can definitely go back to Polly's if that would help you feel better." Her caring nature was evident, and she leaned in slightly, her hand resting on his arm in a comforting gesture.

Polly nodded, her eyes filled with empathy. "Yes, let's get you some water and maybe a snack. That always helps me when I'm feeling off." She glanced around, her mind already racing with ideas for what they could have at her apartment.

Jacob was initially taken aback by Ivan's sudden change in demeanor. The lighthearted atmosphere of their celebration began to shift, and he could sense something was amiss. As he observed Ivan's furtive glances toward the window, he began to piece it together. Realizing that something or someone had caught Ivan's attention, he quickly adapted to the plan, his instincts kicking in.

"Sure, let's head back," Jacob said, trying to sound casual though he felt a growing sense of urgency. "I'll drive."

As they gathered their belongings and made their way out of the café, Ivan seized the opportunity to position himself strategically. "Could I sit up front with you, Jacob? The air blowing on me might help me feel a bit better," he suggested, his tone casual but his eyes sharp with intent, scanning the street for any sign of the sedan.

Rachel smiled, relieved that Ivan had found a way to make himself comfortable. "Of course! I can sit in the back with Polly," she said, her voice brightening as she attempted to ease Ivan's discomfort.

Jacob nodded, though his mind was racing with thoughts of the mysterious lady in the sedan. He hoped that by playing along with Ivan's plan, they could figure out what was going on without raising any alarms. As they all climbed into the car, Ivan settled into the front passenger seat, his body tense with anticipation, keeping a careful watch through the windshield.

Once they were on the road, Jacob began to drive at a steady pace, trying to maintain an air of normalcy. He glanced in the rear view mirror, catching sight of Rachel and Polly chatting, their laughter a stark contrast to the tension that gripped Ivan. Polly's animated gestures and Rachel's bright smile seemed oblivious to the underlying current of anxiety.

With each passing moment, Ivan remained vigilant, scanning the streets for any sign of the black sedan. He fought to maintain a calm exterior, but inside, his heart raced with determination. "Just act natural," he muttered under his breath, a mantra to steady his nerves.

As they made their way through familiar streets, Jacob took a few turns, trying to shake off any potential followers. The streetlights flickered above them, casting fleeting shadows across the car's interior. He felt the weight of his friends' trust resting on his shoulders, and he was determined to keep them safe.

"Did you guys see that new movie trailer that just came out?" Jacob asked, attempting to divert the conversation and lighten the mood. He could sense the tension in the air and wanted to distract his friends from Ivan's discomfort.

"Oh, the one with the superhero?" Polly replied, her eyes lighting up. "I can't believe they're finally making a sequel! I loved the first one!"

As they chatted about movies and the latest trends, Ivan's mind drifted back to the sedan. He remained focused on the rearview mirror, scanning for any signs of the vehicle. The tension in his shoulders eased slightly as he noticed that they hadn't been followed yet, but the nagging feeling that they were being watched still lingered.

Jacob navigated through the streets, taking a few winding turns to throw off any potential followers. The air in the car felt charged with anticipation, and he couldn't shake the feeling that they were being watched. He focused on the road ahead, determined to keep his friends safe while unraveling the mystery that had suddenly thrust itself into their evening.

With the comforting hum of the car and the lively chatter of his friends, Ivan felt a mixture of relief and anxiety. He knew they needed to remain vigilant, and he couldn't shake the feeling that the shadow of the mysterious lady and her black sedan was still looming over them.

As they pulled into the apartment complex, Ivan felt a knot tighten in his stomach when he noticed the black sedan had indeed followed them. It came to a halt on the street, its headlights flickering off and plunging the vehicle into an ominous darkness. The sleek silhouette of the car loomed menacingly against the backdrop of the dimly lit street, and Ivan's pulse quickened as he turned to Jacob, his expression grave.

"I hate to be a damper on everyone's spirits, but I think I should just go home and get some rest," Ivan said, trying to keep his voice steady despite the urgency of the situation. He could feel the tension ripple through the air, heavy with unspoken worries.

Jacob's sharp gaze darted to the rearview mirror, where the dark sedan lingered just out of the direct light. It was clear now that Ivan was aware they were being followed. "I think you're right, Ivan. Maybe we should get you home," he replied, his tone firm yet understanding, a protective instinct kicking in.

Rachel, sensing the shift in mood, leaned closer to Ivan, her brows knitting together in concern. "I hope you start to feel better soon," she said softly, reaching up to hug him tightly. The warmth of her embrace provided a fleeting comfort amidst the growing tension. "Maybe tomorrow we can all go to the mall? I need to pick up a few things," she added whimsically, trying to infuse a dash of normalcy back into their evening.

Ivan managed a faint smile, grateful for her warmth. "That sounds great, Rachel. I'll definitely be up for it," he said, though his mind was still racing with thoughts of the sedan and its mysterious occupant.

Jacob nodded, feeling a wave of relief wash over him as they all agreed to the plan. "I'll walk the ladies to their door," he said, determined to maintain a sense of normalcy despite the underlying tension. He wanted to ensure that Rachel and Polly reached the safety of their apartment without any incidents, even as the shadow of the sedan loomed over them.

As they stepped out of the car, Ivan kept his eyes glued to the black sedan, its darkened windows reflecting the soft glow of the streetlights. He felt a protective instinct surge within him, knowing that he couldn't let anything happen to his friends. Jacob, meanwhile, moved with purpose, guiding Rachel and Polly toward the entrance of their building, his posture exuding confidence even as unease simmered beneath the surface.

The cool night air was filled with the sounds of distant traffic and the rustling of leaves, but to Ivan, it felt eerily quiet. The laughter and chatter from Rachel and Polly seemed to echo in contrast to the ominous presence of the sedan. He lingered by the car, taking a moment to gather his thoughts while remaining vigilant for any movement from the vehicle. Each second felt stretched, and he hoped that whatever was going on would resolve itself by morning.

The following morning, Ivan awoke with the first light of dawn filtering through the curtains, casting soft shadows on the walls of his bedroom. The air was crisp, carrying the scent of fresh coffee brewing in the kitchen. He rubbed the sleep from his eyes and took a deep breath, steeling himself for the challenges ahead.

As he softly approached the window, he pulled aside the blinds, unveiling the street illuminated by the warm, golden light of the rising sun. A wave of dread washed over him as he spotted the familiar sedan parked further up the street, its polished, dark frame nearly merging with the shadows. This vehicle had become an ever present reminder of the lurking anxiety that gnawed at his thoughts.

With a furrowed brow, Ivan turned away from the window, his mind racing. He could feel the weight of the world pressing down on him, and he knew he had to share his thoughts with Jacob. In the living room, amidst the clutter of their shared space—maps, books, and half-finished projects—he found Jacob lacing up his boots, a look of determination on his face.

"I think we need to talk," Ivan said, his voice barely above a whisper. Jacob paused, sensing the gravity in Ivan's tone. "I suspect that Queen Isabella has sent someone to spy on us," Ivan continued, his expression serious. "That sedan isn't just a coincidence. We have to be careful about what we say and do from now on."

Jacob's brow furrowed in concern, and he nodded slowly, understanding the implications of Ivan's words. They both knew the stakes were high; the queen had her eyes on them, and any misstep could lead to dire consequences. As they prepared for the day, a sense of urgency filled the air, the quiet morning now heavy with the weight of their unspoken fears.

Ivan and Jacob set out on their mission to pick up Rachel and Polly, their excitement palpable as they anticipated a day of fun at the downtown mall. The morning sun bathed the streets in a warm glow, but for Ivan, the light couldn't dispel the dark cloud of anxiety that loomed over him. He felt a palpable tension in the air, a sense of foreboding that clung to him like a second skin.

As they drove through the familiar streets, Ivan kept a close eye on the rear view mirror, where the ominous sedan trailed behind them like a silent sentinel. Its presence was unsettling, as if it were a dark omen lurking in the periphery of their cheerful outing. He could see the vehicle's sleek, black exterior, which seemed to absorb the light around it, making it appear even more sinister.

Chapter 19

A Game of Shadows

In the sedan, Patricia was doing her best to remain inconspicuous. Ivan could catch glimpses of her through the mirror, her large hat flopping slightly with the motion of the car, casting shadows over her features. Her oversized dark glasses made her look almost cartoonish, yet there was an unsettling air about her—an aura that screamed of someone trying too hard to blend into the background. Ivan's instincts kicked in, warning him that she was more than just an innocent bystander.

When they finally pulled up to Polly's apartment building, Jacob wasted no time. He jumped out of the car, his energy infectious as he bounded toward the entrance, ready to fetch the girls. Ivan, however, remained behind, tension coiling in his chest as he continued to monitor the sedan. He felt like a sentry standing guard, his eyes darting between the car and the entrance of the building, waiting for any sign of trouble.

Minutes felt like hours as Ivan gripped the steering wheel tightly, his knuckles turning white. The laughter and chatter from the nearby pedestrians seemed distant, muffled by the weight of his thoughts. He couldn't shake the feeling that something was off, that the day wouldn't unfold as they had hoped.

Finally, the door swung open, and out came Rachel and Polly, their faces radiant with excitement. Their laughter filled the air, light and carefree, as they chattered animatedly about their plans for the day. Jacob walked closely behind them, his protective instincts kicking in as he kept a watchful eye on the surroundings.

As the girls approached the car, their joy was contagious, and Ivan felt a rush of relief wash over him. He smiled back, trying to mask his unease. Yet, as he glanced back at the sedan, parked just a few cars away, the knot in his stomach tightened again. It was still there, a dark specter looming over their outing. He knew they had to stay vigilant; today was more than just a trip to the mall, it was a dance with danger, and he wasn't sure how it would unfold.

As they drove toward the mall, the atmosphere inside the car was electric with excitement. Polly and Rachel chatted animatedly, their voices bubbling over with joy and anticipation. The realization that they had all successfully passed their exams and were now set to graduate filled them with a sense of accomplishment and new possibilities.

Polly's eyes sparkled as she shared her dreams of landing an internship in New York. "Can you imagine it?" she exclaimed, her enthusiasm infectious. "If everything goes well, I could be right in the heart of the city, working alongside some of the best in the industry! It's going to be such an adventure!" Her excitement was palpable, and Ivan couldn't help but smile at her optimism.

Rachel, sitting next to her, chimed in with her own aspirations. "I've always thought about moving to a big city," she said, her voice slightly wistful. "The idea of working for a large corporation, making my mark in a corporate environment, it's so appealing!" But beneath her excitement lay a hint of melancholy. She glanced at Jacob, her expression shifting as she recalled his recent revelation. The thought that Jacob would have to return to Europe to take over the family business weighed heavily on her heart.

Jacob, driving with focused determination, sensed Rachel's change in mood but didn't know how to address it. He wanted to comfort her, to explain the duty that awaited him back home, but there was something deeper he was grappling with. He knew he needed to tell Rachel the truth—that he was the heir to the throne of his family's kingdom—but finding the right words or the perfect moment felt daunting.

As the car navigated through the busy streets, he stole glances at Rachel, her brow slightly furrowed as she stared out the window, lost in thought. He wanted to reach out to her, to share his own dreams and fears, but the weight of his secret seemed to hold him back. The thought of leaving her behind, of stepping into a role that felt both noble and burdensome, filled him with conflicting emotions. He had always envisioned a future where they could explore the world together, yet duty called him to a different path.

The conversation in the car flowed around him, filled with laughter and dreams, but Jacob remained quietly contemplative, wrestling with his thoughts. He hoped that someday soon, he would find the courage to share his truth with Rachel, to let her know that his heart was still very much with her, even as his destiny pulled him in another direction.

As they pulled into the mall's parking lot, Jacob maneuvered the car smoothly into a spot, the excitement palpable among his friends. The moment they stepped outside, they were greeted by a vibrant scene. The mall was a stunning architectural marvel, with its high glass roof allowing sunlight to pour in like golden rays, casting a warm glow over the bustling scene below. The air was filled with a mix of enticing aromas, candles, gourmet coffee, and the faint scent of new clothes, all blending together to create an inviting atmosphere.

The mall was alive with activity, shoppers meandering through the maze of stores, their laughter and chatter creating a symphony of sound. Polly and Rachel's eyes sparkled with excitement as they made their way from one shop to another, admiring everything from trendy clothing to quirky accessories. Their giggles echoed as they tried on hats and posed in front of mirrors, reveling in the carefree joy of youth and friendship.

Chapter 20

Secrets and Soap

However, unbeknownst to them, Patricia was shadowing their every move, her efforts to remain inconspicuous proving to be a challenge. She shuffled along, her large hat bobbing slightly with each step, and her oversized sunglasses glaringly out of place. Despite her best attempts to blend in with the crowd, the combination of her unusual accessories and the air of tension surrounding her caught the attention of a few curious onlookers.

As the group continued their exploration, Ivan's focus shifted. He felt a growing sense of unease, particularly as he caught sight of Patricia lingering just a few storefronts behind them. Though the girls were lost in their excitement, Ivan couldn't shake the feeling that she was up to something. His instincts kicked in, urging him to take action.

As they rounded a corner and approached a particularly vibrant shop filled with colorful displays, Ivan seized the opportunity to pull Polly aside. "Can I have that bottle of soap I picked up that's in your bag?" he asked, trying to keep his voice steady even though a knot of urgency tightened in his stomach.

Polly blinked in surprise, momentarily thrown by the unexpected request. "The soap? You mean the musk one?" she asked, her brow furrowing with curiosity about why Ivan needed it. She quickly rummaged through her bag, the sound of zippers and fabric rustling filling the air. Within moments, she retrieved the small bottle, its label adorned with a fancy label, and handed it to him discreetly.

"Here you go," she said, her voice low but laced with confusion. Before she could inquire further about his intentions, Ivan leaned in closer, the urgency of the situation pressing upon him. "Tell Jacob to take you and Rachel to the car, and I'll catch up to you in a minute. I have to do something," he whispered, his eyes darting toward the entrance, where he could still see Patricia's figure lingering in the distance.

Polly's eyes widened, uncertainty flickering across her face. "What are you saying, Ivan? What do you need to do?" she pressed, her voice barely audible, filled with concern.

"Please, just trust me," he urged, his expression earnest and resolute. He could feel the weight of the moment pressing down on him; he needed to act quickly.

Polly hesitated, glancing toward Rachel and Jacob, who were engrossed in their own conversation about a new store they wanted to visit. After a moment of internal struggle, she nodded, sensing the urgency in Ivan's demeanor. "Okay, I'll tell him," she murmured, albeit reluctantly.

With a deep breath, Polly turned and approached Jacob, who was admiring a window display filled with colorful Fall dresses. Leaning in close, she whispered Ivan's message, her voice low and tinged with concern. Jacob's brow furrowed as he processed what she was saying, a protective instinct rising within him. "Alright, let's head to the car," he replied, glancing back toward Ivan, who had taken a few steps away from the group, his gaze locked on the entrance of the mall.

As Polly and Rachel began to walk toward the stairs leading to the exit, Jacob fell into step beside them, casting wary glances back at Ivan. The air felt heavy with unspoken tension, and Jacob couldn't shake the feeling that something was off. The carefree day they had planned was slipping away, replaced by a sense of impending uncertainty.

With each step they took, Ivan remained rooted in place for a moment longer, watching as his friends moved away. He felt a mixture of dread and determination wash over him.

As they continued their way through the bustling mall, Ivan felt the tension building within him as he observed Patricia still lingering nearby. She had stopped in front of a shop window, pretending to admire the display, but Ivan could see right through her act. He needed to create a distraction, a way to ensure that his friends would be safe from whatever intentions Patricia had.

Reaching the top of the stairs leading down to the main level, Ivan feigned interest in tying his shoelaces, bending down with an air of casualness. As he knelt, he discreetly uncapped the bottle of men's soap that Polly had given him. With careful precision, he poured a thin line of the soap along the edge of the steps, ensuring that it would remain unnoticed by Patricia. The scent of musk wafted through the air, a stark contrast to the tension he felt.

Once he finished pouring the soap, he tied his laces with

an exaggerated slowness, all the while keeping a watchful eye on Patricia. Satisfied that he had set his little trap, he straightened up, took a deep breath, and quickly made his way down the steps to catch up with Jacob, Rachel, and Polly.

As he descended, he glanced back to see Patricia still focused on the window display, completely unaware of the danger that awaited her. With each step he took, he felt a mix of anticipation and relief, hoping that his plan would work as intended.

But as he reached the bottom of the stairs, he heard the unmistakable sound of hurried footsteps behind him. Patricia had finally decided to follow. Ivan's heart raced as he quickened his pace, blending in with the crowd of shoppers who were oblivious to the drama unfolding just behind them.

Then, all at once, the chaos erupted. Patricia stepped onto the soapy stairs, her foot slipping dramatically on the slick surface. Time seemed to slow as Ivan turned to catch a glimpse of her reaction. Her feet flew up into the air, and with a loud scream, she lost her balance and tumbled down the steps, bouncing down several stairs in a flurry of arms and legs.

A chorus of surprised gasps erupted from the nearby shoppers as they turned to witness the commotion. Ivan couldn't help but chuckle softly to himself, a mix of relief and amusement washing over him. The sight of Patricia landing in an undignified heap at the bottom of the stairs drew attention from onlookers, who quickly rushed over to help.

"Are you okay?" someone shouted, while others murmured in shock, their eyes wide with disbelief at the scene. Ivan seized the moment, slipping seamlessly back into the group as Jacob, Rachel, and Polly turned to see what had happened.

"What was that?" Rachel asked, her eyes darting toward the source of the commotion.

Jacob frowned, concern etched on his face as he moved instinctively away from the crowd gathering at the bottom of the stairs. "I'm sure it's nothing," he said, leading the way, with Polly and Rachel following closely behind.

Ivan hung back slightly, watching the chaos unfold. He felt a sense of satisfaction knowing that he had created a diversion, at least for the moment. The urgency of the situation was still present, but for now, they were safe, and Patricia had been taken out of the equation, if only temporarily.

After confirming that Patricia was no longer a threat, Ivan felt a wave of relief wash over him. He quickly turned and sprinted to catch up with Jacob, Rachel, and Polly, who were now gathered at the car. A smile spread across his face, bright and jolly, as he approached them, eager to shift the mood back to a lighthearted one.

"How about we go find someplace nice to eat?" he suggested cheerfully, his tone infused with enthusiasm as if nothing out of the ordinary had just occurred. His demeanor was contagious, and he hoped to redirect their attention to the fun and excitement of the day ahead.

Jacob's smile widened in response, his earlier concern fading as he recognized the familiar spark in Ivan's eyes. It was clear to him that Ivan had successfully handled the situation with Patricia, and he felt grateful that their stalker was no longer an issue. "That sounds great! I'm starving," Jacob replied, his voice lightening. He glanced around, taking in the myriad of dining options that the mall had to offer, from cozy cafés to bustling food courts.

Rachel and Polly, catching Ivan's infectious energy, nodded enthusiastically. "Yeah, let's find somewhere less crowded!" Rachel exclaimed, her earlier worries slipping away as the group turned their focus to choosing a place to eat. Polly chimed in, "I've heard there's a fantastic Italian restaurant just a short drive from here. Maybe we could try that!"

The chaos of the past few minutes was fading into the background as laughter and friendly chatter filled the air around them. The group navigated through the parking lot, their energy renewed with the promise of good food and shared moments.

Ivan couldn't help but glance back over his shoulder once more, ensuring that Patricia was still nowhere in sight. Satisfied, he turned his attention back to his friends, grateful for their joyful spirits and the bond they shared. For now, it seemed like they could enjoy their day without any lingering shadows, and he intended to make the most of it.

Chapter 21
Between Pain and Purpose

Patricia's eyes fluttered open as the warm morning sun crept through the gaps in the hotel room's curtains. She let out a soft groan, her body still aching from the accident the previous day. As she shifted in the bed, the movement sent a twinge of pain through her injured arm, now securely wrapped in a sling.

Suddenly, the shrill sound of her phone's ringtone pierced the tranquil silence, startling her. Instinctively, she reached for the device, her fingers fumbling clumsily as she tried to answer the incoming video call. "He… Hello," she stammered, her heart racing, trying to quickly smooth down her disheveled hair and straighten her appearance.

The regal features of Queen Isabella filled the screen, her brow furrowing with concern as she took in Patricia's injured state. "What on earth happened to you over there?" the queen exclaimed, her voice laced with a mix of worry and frustration.

Patricia let out a heavy sigh, wincing slightly as the movement jostled her arm. "I may have had a slight setback in my efforts to uncover what Alexander has been up to," she explained, a hint of resignation in her tone. "I suspect Ivan was behind the accident that caused this."

"Enough of that, Patricia," the queen snapped, her features hardening. Seeing you in this condition, you're in no shape to be driving. I'll have a car sent to the hotel to pick you up." She paused, her expression softening ever so slightly. "Princess Penelope will be arriving in America at noon today, and I need you to bring her back to the hotel."

Patricia straightened her posture, determination flashing in her eyes despite her obvious discomfort. "Oh yes, your Majesty," she replied, her voice unwavering. "I'm still capable of carrying out my mission. This is only a minor incident."

The queen shook her head, a faint frown creasing her brow as she looked at her loyal agent, the weight of Patricia's failure and the toll it had taken on her clearly visible in the queen's expression.

Patricia hurriedly cleaned herself up, her heart racing with a mix of anticipation and anxiety as she maneuvered around her hotel room. Each movement was a careful dance, trying to avoid aggravating the ache in her injured arm. She slipped into a tailored blazer and fitted pants, a combination that exuded both professionalism and a hint of authority. The fabric felt smooth against her skin, grounding her in the moment as she caught a glimpse of herself in the mirror. A deep breath steadied her nerves.

Just as she adjusted her collar, the hotel phone rang, breaking the momentary calm. It was the front desk, their voice crisp and clear as they informed her that a limousine was waiting for her outside the lobby. "I'll be right down," she replied, her voice steadier than she felt, a flutter of excitement and trepidation stirring in her stomach. The responsibility the Queen had entrusted to her weighed heavily, but it also ignited a fire within her.

With renewed determination, Patricia hobbled out of her room, the slight pain in her arm a constant reminder of her recent setback. She navigated the hallway with purpose, the plush carpet muffling her footsteps as she approached the elevator. Each ding of the elevator felt like a countdown to her mission, heightening her anticipation.

Upon reaching the lobby, she spotted the driver standing tall by the front desk, a professional air surrounding him. His calm demeanor offered a sense of reassurance as he greeted her with a warm smile. "Patricia Jackson," he said, his voice steady and inviting.

"Yes, I'm Patricia Jackson," she confirmed, a sense of urgency creeping into her tone. "I need you to get me to the airport right away." The words tumbled out, underscoring the importance of her task ahead.

The driver nodded with understanding, his expression respectful as he walked her outside. The sleek limousine gleamed under the morning sun, its polished exterior reflecting her determination. He opened the door with a graceful motion, and as Patricia stepped inside, a wave of exhilaration washed over her. The interior was a plush sanctuary, soft leather seats inviting her to sink in.

As she settled into the seat, she felt a rush of excitement. This was more than just a ride; it was a means to fulfill her purpose. The gentle hum of the engine combined with the luxurious surroundings wrapped around her like a comforting embrace, momentarily easing her worries.

In that moment, Patricia realized how much she craved this sense of authority and purpose. As Patricia settled into the luxurious interior of the limousine, a wave of thoughts washed over her. This was but a taste of what it must be like to be a royal, she mused, her mind racing with the implications of her current situation. The plush leather enveloped her like a second skin, and the gentle hum of the engine felt like a heartbeat echoing her own excitement.

She gazed out the tinted windows, watching the world outside transform into a blur of colors and shapes. The bustling city seemed to pulse with life, a stark contrast to the quiet weight of her responsibilities. In this moment, she could almost imagine the life of elegance and privilege that came with being part of the royal family—the grand balls, the diplomatic dinners, the adoring public. A smile tugged at her lips as she envisioned the regal attire, the sparkling tiaras, and the dignified poise.

Yet, Patricia knew that beneath the glamorous surface lay immense pressure and expectation. She felt a kinship with the royals, understanding that their lives were intricately woven with duty and sacrifice. This glimpse into their world, even if fleeting, filled her with a sense of purpose. If only for a moment, she could embrace the authority and respect that came with being in service to the crown.

As the limousine glided smoothly through the streets, she reflected on the trust that Queen Isabella had placed in her. The weight of that trust was both daunting and exhilarating. Patricia felt a surge of determination; she was ready to rise to the occasion, to prove that she was capable of handling the challenges ahead.

With each passing moment, she reminded herself that this was just the beginning. The thrill of the unknown beckoned her forward, and she vowed not to let the Queen or herself down. This mission was more than just a task; it was a chance to step into a role that felt bigger than herself, to embrace the essence of duty that resonated with her own aspirations.

Chapter 22

Sweaters and Secrets

Meanwhile, Rachel and Polly were enveloped in a lively discussion, their voices animated as they made plans to meet up with Jacob and Ivan. The warm days of summer were fading into memory, and the sharp, crisp air of autumn was settling in, wrapping around them like a cozy blanket. Each rustle of leaves outside the window echoed the fleeting nature of the season, stirring a mix of nostalgia and excitement in their hearts.

"So, have you and Jacob figured out how to keep your relationship going?" Polly asked, her eyes sparkling with curiosity as she leaned closer, eager to pry into Rachel's thoughts. She could sense the flutter of emotions swirling within her friend.

Rachel's cheeks flushed slightly as she met Polly's gaze. "I really want us to continue seeing each other," she said, her voice soft yet resolute. A hopeful smile blossomed on her face, illuminating her features. "But honestly, I'm a bit lost on the logistics—I don't even know where in Europe he's from!" The uncertainty gnawed at her, but the thrill of possibility was intoxicating.

Polly's face lit up, her eyes widening in delight. "Just imagine! You two could end up sharing an apartment in New York! Picture it—Sunday mornings with coffee, lazy afternoons in Central Park, and endless adventures in the city!" Her voice brimmed with enthusiasm, painting vivid images that danced in Rachel's mind.

Rachel leaned back in her chair, cradling her warm cup of hot chocolate between her hands, taking a moment to savor the rich, velvety taste. A dreamy smile spread across her lips as she envisioned a future with Jacob—one filled with laughter, late-night talks, and shared dreams. "It's a beautiful thought," she said softly, her heart fluttering at the mere idea. "But I do worry that his family obligations to take over the family business might come between us. I want to support him, but what if it pulls him away?" Her voice was tinged with both longing and a hint of fear.

"What exactly does his family do?" Polly asked, her interest intensifying, eager to understand the dynamics at play.

Rachel furrowed her brow, recalling snippets of their conversations. "I think they're in real estate," she replied, a thoughtful look crossing her face. "He mentioned something about them managing properties and looking for new investments. It sounds like a big responsibility."

Polly chuckled, shaking her head in disbelief. "Well, good heavens! With everything going online these days, they could manage properties from anywhere! It sounds like there's a world of possibilities, Rachel! Maybe he can find a way to balance both worlds!" Her laughter rang out, filling the cozy café with warmth.

With their conversation winding down, both friends felt

a surge of excitement as they prepared to meet up with Jacob and Ivan. The prospect of seeing them sent butterflies fluttering in Rachel's stomach, igniting her imagination with visions of what could be, a future filled with love, challenge, and the thrill of the unknown. As they gathered their things, the air buzzed with anticipation, each moment brimming with endless potential.

Rachel and Polly began rummaging through their closets, the soft rustle of fabric mingling with their laughter as they searched for the perfect outfits to embrace the beauty of an autumn day. The golden leaves outside the window danced in the gentle breeze, casting a warm glow that mirrored the excitement in the air.

"Let's find something that screams fall!" Polly suggested, her eyes sparkling with enthusiasm. She pulled out a cozy, oversized sweater in a rich burgundy shade that seemed to capture the essence of the season. "What do you think of this? It's perfect for wrapping up in!"

Rachel nodded appreciatively, holding the sweater against her. "That's adorable! It would look great with your favorite scarf." She turned to her own side of the closet, searching through a delightful mix of textures and colors. She stumbled upon a mustard-yellow cardigan that seemed to radiate warmth. "Oh, I love this one! It feels like a hug," she exclaimed, draping it over her shoulders.

As they continued to sift through their clothes, they shared stories and memories associated with each piece. "Remember this dress?" Polly laughed, holding up a floral midi dress that had once been a staple during their summer outings. "I wore this the day we got caught in that unexpected rainstorm!"

Rachel chuckled, the memory flooding back. "And we ended up ducking into that little café, completely soaked, but we made the best of it!"

They dove deeper into their wardrobes, unearthing scarves, hats, and boots that would perfectly complement their fall outfits. Rachel found a pair of knee-high black boots that she had almost forgotten about. "These! They're perfect for crunching leaves!" she proclaimed, holding them up triumphantly.

Polly grinned, pulling out a plaid scarf. "And this will definitely keep me warm! I can already picture us walking through the park, sipping hot cider."

With each piece they discovered, their excitement grew, fueled by the promise of a day filled with laughter and adventure. The warm hues of autumn began to reflect in their choices, as they layered on cozy fabrics that complemented the season. As they finally settled on their outfits, Rachel and Polly felt a rush of anticipation, ready to step out into the crisp air and embrace the beauty of the day ahead.

Chapter 23

A Heart in Conflict

Meanwhile, Jacob and Ivan were in the midst of getting ready to meet with Rachel and Polly. The air was thick with anticipation, each moment charged with an undercurrent of emotion. Jacob stood in front of his wardrobe, his fingers trailing over various shirts and jackets, but he found it hard to focus on the clothes. His mind was elsewhere, spinning with thoughts of Rachel, her laughter, and the way her eyes sparkled when she spoke.

As he rifled through his clothes, Ivan leaned against the doorframe, arms crossed, observing his friend with a knowing look. "Where do you see your relationship with Rachel going?" he asked, his tone casual, but there was a deeper curiosity in his voice. He wanted to understand just how serious Jacob was about this woman who had clearly captured his heart.

Jacob paused, a smile breaking across his face as he imagined Rachel. "She is the most amazing woman I've ever met," he said, his voice softening with affection. "She's nothing like the aristocrats my mother is always trying to set me up with. Rachel is unique; she's vibrant and genuine. Every moment with her feels real, like I can be myself without the weight of my title hanging over us."

As Jacob spoke, he could feel warmth spreading through

him, a sense of hope and excitement that made his heart race. Ivan watched his friend's face light up, a mixture of pride and happiness reflected in his own expression. It was evident that Rachel had ignited something profound within Jacob, a fire of passion that he had never felt before.

But then, Ivan's expression shifted, becoming more serious as he ventured into delicate territory. "I do have a question, though," he said, his voice lowering slightly. "Have you told her who you truly are? Does she know that you're the crown prince and heir to the throne?"

Jacob's smile faltered, his brow furrowing in frustration and anxiety. "No, I haven't," he admitted, his voice tinged with worry. "I keep trying to find the right moment to tell her." He leaned against the dresser, running a hand through his hair in a gesture of distress. "I want her to see me for who I really am, not just my title. But I also worry about how she'll react. What if she feels overwhelmed? What if she thinks I'm just another prince looking for a trophy?" The weight of his secret hung heavily on his shoulders, and he could feel the tension building within him.

Ivan studied Jacob closely, recognizing the internal conflict that was playing out behind his friend's eyes. "You care about her deeply, don't you? You want her to see you as more than just a royal title," he said, his tone encouraging yet serious.

"Exactly," Jacob replied, his voice earnest, filled with a mixture of hope and trepidation. "I want her to understand my world, but I don't want to scare her away. She deserves the truth, but I need to find the right way to share it with her." The vulnerability in his voice revealed just how much he valued Rachel and the connection they had forged.

Ivan nodded in understanding, sensing the turmoil Jacob was grappling with. "Just remember, if she's as genuine as you say, she'll appreciate your honesty. It might be daunting, but keeping it from her could create distance between you two," he advised gently, weighing the importance of transparency in relationships.

Jacob sighed deeply, leaning against the dresser as he contemplated Ivan's words. The thought of revealing his true identity sent a shiver down his spine, mixing excitement with dread. "I just hope that when I do tell her, it doesn't change everything," he murmured, his voice barely above a whisper, revealing the depth of his concern.

Ivan stepped forward, placing a reassuring hand on Jacob's shoulder. "If she truly cares for you, she'll want to be part of your world, no matter how complicated it may seem. Trust that connection you two have." His words resonated with Jacob, who felt a flicker of hope igniting within him.

As they prepared to leave, Jacob's heart raced. He could already envision Rachel's smile, the way her laughter filled the air with light. But the fear of what revealing his true self might mean for their budding relationship loomed in his mind like a shadow. Would she still look at him the same way? Would the weight of his title change the way she felt about him?

With his thoughts swirling, Jacob took a deep breath, steadying himself for the day ahead. He knew he had to find the courage to share his truth with Rachel, to let her in on the parts of his life he had kept hidden. With one last glance in the mirror, he straightened his shoulders, ready to face whatever lay ahead, determined to embrace the adventure that awaited them both.

Jacob and Ivan climbed into the sleek black car, the familiar scent of leather filling the air as Jacob settled into the driver's seat. He took a moment to adjust the rearview mirror, but his mind was still swirling with thoughts of Rachel. Before starting the engine, he glanced over at Ivan, who was fastening his seatbelt with a serious expression.

"Just remember this, my friend," Ivan said, his voice steady, "it's better that she hears it from you. You don't want someone from the royal family dropping the news on her and purposefully scaring her away." There was a weight to his words, a reminder of the potential fallout if Jacob didn't take the initiative.

Jacob nodded, the gravity of Ivan's advice settling in. "I will tell her," he replied, a determined smile creeping onto his face. The resolve in his voice was stronger now, bolstered by the support of his friend. He knew he had to be brave, to face the truth and embrace the vulnerability that came with it.

With a deep breath, he turned the key, and the engine roared to life, a comforting sound that signaled the start of their journey. As they pulled out onto the bustling street,

Jacob felt a mixture of excitement and anxiety bubbling within him. He could picture Rachel's warm smile and the way her eyes lit up when she talked about her passions. He wanted to share everything with her, the good and the complicated.

Chapter 24

A Heartfelt Vow

As they drove through the city, the autumn leaves fluttered around them, a kaleidoscope of oranges and golds reflecting the warmth of the season. Ivan glanced out the window, then turned back to Jacob. "You know, you're really lucky to have found someone like Rachel. Not everyone gets to experience that kind of connection," he said, his tone shifting to one of encouragement.

Jacob's heart swelled at Ivan's words. "I know," he said, his voice filled with sincerity. "She makes me feel alive, like I can be myself without any pretense. I just hope she can accept all the parts of me, including the crown."

"Trust in what you have," Ivan replied, a reassuring smile on his face. "If she's as genuine as you've described, she'll appreciate the honesty. Just be open with her."

With the city bustling around them, Jacob felt a surge of determination. He navigated the streets with purpose, his focus now not just on the drive but on the moment that lay ahead. The anticipation of seeing Rachel and telling her the truth filled him with a mix of nerves and excitement.

As Jacob drove the car along the curvy canyon road, his heart raced with anticipation and anxiety. The stunning landscape around him faded into a blur as his mind swirled with thoughts of how he would reveal his true identity to Rachel. Each twist and turn of the road felt like a metaphor for the emotional journey he was about to embark upon. Would she understand? Would she still want him after knowing who he really was?

As he approached the top of the canyon road, he saw Polly's car parked, and the sight of Rachel and Polly leaning against it brought a rush of warmth to his chest. They were laughing, their voices light and carefree, a melody that tugged at his heartstrings. Rachel's laughter was like music, a sound that made the world feel right, and for a moment, the weight of his secret felt bearable.

"Look at them," Ivan remarked, breaking Jacob's reverie. He leaned back in his seat, a smile creeping onto his face. "They seem to be having the time of their lives."

Jacob nodded, unable to tear his eyes away from Rachel. Her hair danced in the breeze, the golden sunlight illuminating her features, making her look radiant. Just seeing her smile filled him with joy and a flicker of hope. He thought about the moments they had shared—the warmth of her touch, the way her eyes lit up when she talked about her passions. Those memories were precious, and he wanted to create more of them, but he feared that his truth might shatter everything they had built.

As they got closer, Rachel turned, her eyes catching the sunlight as they sparkled with excitement. The moment their gazes met, his heart skipped a beat. "Jacob! Ivan!" she called out, her voice a melody that wrapped around him like a warm embrace.

Polly nudged Rachel, whispering something that made her giggle, and Jacob couldn't help but smile at the sight. It was a beautiful moment, filled with joy and friendship, and he felt an overwhelming urge to protect that happiness. But beneath the surface, the weight of his secret loomed larger, reminding him that he could no longer hide.

"Hey, you two!" Jacob called out, attempting to keep his tone casual, even though the weight of the moment hung in the air. He leaned out of the window as he pulled into the parking spot, a playful smile on his face. "Enjoying the view?"

"It's absolutely stunning!" Rachel replied, her enthusiasm infectious. "We were just talking about how perfect this spot is for a little adventure. I can't believe how beautiful it is out here." Her passion was palpable, and Jacob felt his heart swell with admiration.

Ivan chimed in, "And you both look like you're having a blast!" His voice was warm, filled with genuine happiness for their friendship.

Rachel laughed, her joy lighting up the air around them, and for a moment, Jacob lost himself in her presence. He wanted to linger in this moment, to bask in the warmth of their connection, but he knew that waiting would only make the reveal harder. The thought of sharing his truth weighed heavily on him, but he also felt a flicker of hope that Rachel would accept him for who he truly was.

Suddenly, Polly pulled out her phone, her excitement bubbling over. "Let's capture this moment!" she exclaimed, urging everyone to gather together for a photo. Jacob felt the warmth of Rachel's shoulder brushing against his as they huddled close, and he couldn't help but smile at her contagious laughter.

As they posed for the picture, Jacob glanced at Rachel, her eyes shining with happiness, and he felt a rush of determination surge through him. This was his moment, the opportunity to be honest and vulnerable. The connection they shared was real, and he wanted to build on that foundation, even if it meant risking everything.

Taking a deep breath, he steeled himself, ready to reveal the truth that had been weighing on him for so long. He wanted Rachel to know him completely, to see the man behind the title, and to understand that his feelings for her were genuine and unwavering.

With the sun hanging high in the sky behind them, bathing the scene in a warm glow, Jacob felt a pressing need to speak. "Rachel," he began, his voice firm yet brimming with emotion, "there's something important I need to share with you." As he gathered his thoughts, the world around them faded into a gentle blur, and he braced himself to take the leap, hoping that whatever unfolded next would justify the vulnerability of opening his heart.

Just then, Polly approached Jacob and Rachel, her laughter ringing out like a bell in the crisp autumn air. "Hey, you two! We need to start walking if we're going to finish this hike before the light fades. You know how short fall days are!" she teased, playfully grabbing Rachel's arm with an infectious energy.

Jacob chuckled, the sound mingling with the warmth in his chest. "Okay, let's go!" he agreed, though part of him wished to linger in this moment.

Rachel turned to Jacob, her eyes glistening with a mixture of mischief and affection. "We'll finish this conversation later," she promised, a soft smile playing on her lips. She leaned in, pressing a gentle kiss to his lips that sent a rush of warmth through him, igniting a spark of hope and longing.

As they pulled away, Jacob felt a moment of suspended time, the world around them fading. The sweetness of that kiss lingered, filling him with both excitement and a deeper yearning to share his truth with her. With a shared glance, they set off on their adventure, but the unspoken words hung in the air, promising that their conversation was far from over.

As they hiked along the winding trail, the crisp air filled with the scent of pine and fallen leaves, Jacob felt a mix of anticipation and trepidation. He turned to Rachel, who was taking in the beauty around them, her hair catching the sunlight. "What was it like being raised by your aunt and uncle after losing your parents?" he asked softly, his voice barely above a whisper, as if he were afraid to disturb the moment.

Rachel paused, her gaze drifting to the vibrant leaves

fluttering in the breeze, each one a reminder of the change and fragility of life. "I really never knew my parents," she began, her voice steady yet heavy with emotion. "My aunt and uncle have been in my life since I was an infant." She looked up at Jacob, her eyes reflecting a mixture of gratitude and sorrow. "My mother was my aunt's sister. When I lost my parents, they took me in as if I were their own. They've sacrificed so much to help me get to college, even though I'm not really their child."

Jacob's heart ached for her, the weight of her words settling heavily on his chest. He imagined her as a child, surrounded by love yet marked by loss. "They told me my parents were in New York when they were in a terrible accident," she continued, her voice trembling slightly as a shadow passed over her features. "I was in the backseat, strapped in, when the car was hit head-on. My aunt says my parents were killed instantly. They always said it was a miracle that I even survived."

The depth of her pain struck Jacob like a physical blow, and he felt a surge of protectiveness toward her. "I can't imagine how difficult that must have been for you," he murmured, his heart aching to comfort her, to ease the burden she carried.

Rachel nodded, her expression turning pensive as she brushed a stray leaf from her cheek. "I've often thought about going to a place in downtown Salt Lake where they can help with genealogy work," she revealed, a flicker of hope breaking through the sadness that lingered in her voice. "I want to know more about where I come from, about my parents."

Jacob's face lit up at the idea, a spark of excitement igniting within him. "We should do that one day!" he exclaimed, his enthusiasm bubbling over like the mountain streams nearby.

A radiant smile spread across Rachel's face, illuminating the cool autumn air around them. "We can do each other's!" she suggested, her eyes sparkling with joy and possibility.

"I would love that," Jacob replied, his heart soaring at the thought of sharing such a meaningful experience. He imagined the two of them sitting together, poring over old records, discovering pieces of their pasts that would weave their lives even closer together.

Suddenly, Jacob halted in his tracks, the weight of unsaid words pressing heavily on his chest. He turned to Rachel, his heart racing as he took in the way the sunlight danced in her hair and the softness of her expression. "I love you, Rachel," he said, his voice breaking with raw emotion, each word trembling with sincerity.

Rachel's eyes widened, surprise and warmth flooding her features as she absorbed his declaration. Jacob felt a rush of vulnerability, the enormity of his feelings spilling out into the open air between them. "Whatever happens to us in this life," he continued, stepping closer, "know that you will always have my heart."

The sincerity in his gaze pierced through the moment,

creating a fragile silence that felt charged with possibility. Rachel's breath caught in her throat, and for a heartbeat, the world around them faded away—just the two of them standing amidst the vibrant colors of autumn, suspended in a moment that felt both monumental and tender.

Tears glistened in Rachel's eyes as she processed his words. "Jacob…" she began, her voice barely above a whisper, filled with awe and disbelief, "I…"

Before she could finish, Jacob reached out, gently taking her hands in his. The warmth of her skin against his sent a shockwave of emotion through him, grounding him in this moment of truth. "I've felt it for so long," he admitted, his voice steadying, "and I just couldn't hold it back anymore."

Rachel's smile blossomed, radiant and full of hope, as she squeezed his hands tightly, her heart swelling in response. "I love you too, Jacob," she finally confessed, her voice filled with a mix of joy and relief. "You've brought so much light into my life."

In that moment, surrounded by the beauty of nature and the promise of their connection, time seemed to stand still. They stood there, hearts intertwined, knowing that whatever challenges lay ahead, they would face them together, united by the love that had blossomed so unexpectedly yet felt so right.

Polly, walking a few paces in front of them, overheard Jacob's heartfelt confession and came to an abrupt halt. Her eyes widened in delight, and a bright grin spread across her face. "He told her he loved her!" she exclaimed, her voice bubbling with excitement.

She turned to Ivan, who was lost in thought, and started tugging on his arm, her enthusiasm infectious. "Did you hear that? Jacob just told Rachel he loves her!"

Ivan looked up, a smile breaking across his face as he processed the news. "Really?" he asked, genuinely surprised but pleased for his friends.

"Yes! Can you believe it?" Polly continued, her eyes sparkling with joy. "It's so sweet! They're perfect for each other!"

Ivan chuckled, the warmth of the moment washing over him. "It sounds like they're on a beautiful path," he replied, glancing back at the pair, who were still caught up in their intimate moment.

Polly couldn't help but bounce on her heels, her excitement palpable. "We have to celebrate this! They've both been through so much, and now they've found each other. It's like a fairy tale!"

Chapter 25

The Ties That Bind

As Patricia glided through the bustling airport, her heart raced with anticipation at the thought of finally meeting Princess Penelope. The vibrant energy of travelers rushing by only fueled her excitement. She imagined the queen's proud gaze upon her, envisioning how her unwavering loyalty and the challenges she had overcome would be rewarded.

Dressed in a tailored business suit that exuded professionalism and sophistication, Patricia carried herself with an elegance that mirrored her determination. The crisp lines of her outfit emphasized her confident posture, while her heels clicked purposefully against the polished floor, each step echoing her resolve. She felt as though the entire airport was a grand stage, crafted just for her. The bright lights overhead reflected in her eyes, illuminating her dreams of recognition and triumph. In that moment, she was not just a traveler; she was a heroine on the cusp of a remarkable encounter.

Patricia hurried through the bustling airport, her pulse quickening as she darted her eyes toward the large screens displaying the arrivals. Each announcement felt like a drumbeat in her chest, amplifying her anticipation. "Gate 12, that's the one," she whispered to herself, a spark of determination igniting within her.

As she spotted the destination flashing brightly on the board, a wave of exhilaration washed over her. The orchestra of voices around her swelled into a harmonious blend of laughter, conversations, and the distant call of boarding announcements, creating a symphony of human connection. It felt almost surreal, as if the very air vibrated with the energy of countless stories converging in this moment.

With every step, her heart raced faster, echoing the urgency of her mission. She could already envision the moment she would finally stand before Princess Penelope, the culmination of her loyalty and dedication. Navigating through the throngs of travelers felt like weaving through a sea of dreams, each person a mere shadow compared to the vibrant hope shimmering in her chest.

Gate 12 loomed ahead like a portal to a new chapter, and she could hardly contain the emotions swirling within her— a mixture of excitement, pride, and the exhilarating possibility of what lay ahead. It was as if the very essence of the airport was cheering her on, urging her to embrace her destiny.

As Patricia scanned the crowd of passengers emerging from the gate, her excitement grew with each familiar face that passed by. Her heart raced, and a sense of urgency filled the air around her. Then, in a moment that felt almost magical, she spotted her—Princess Penelope.

There was no mistaking it; she radiated the essence of royalty. Draped in sophisticated attire that seemed to shimmer with every movement, the princess exuded grace and poise. Her hair cascaded in soft waves, framing a face that was both striking and kind. It was everything Patricia had imagined a princess should be elegant, confident, and unapproachable.

Patricia's breath hitched as she observed the princess engaging with those around her, her presence both captivating and carefully guarded. In that fleeting moment, all the anticipation and effort Patricia had poured into this journey crystallized into a profound sense of wonder. She was filled with an unshakeable determination; this was the moment she had longed for, and she was prepared to embrace it with every fiber of her being.

Patricia's heart raced as she quickly made her way to Princess Penelope, her palms slightly sweaty with nervous anticipation. "Princess Penelope, I hope you had a comfortable flight," she said, trying to infuse her voice with warmth and sincerity, hoping to impress her royal guest.

"First class is not what it used to be," Princess Penelope snapped back, her tone sharp and laced with irritation. The princess's perfectly manicured brows furrowed as she surveyed the bustling airport, her demeanor revealing the weight of her royal expectations. "I know; they'll let just about anyone into first class these days," she replied, her eyes glinting with a mix of frustration and disdain.

"Who are you?" Penelope inquired, her curiosity cutting through the tension.

"Allow me to introduce myself. I am Patricia Jackson,

the personal assistant to Queen Isabella," she stated. "What happened to you?" the princess inquired, noticing Patricia's arm was in a sling.

"Oh, it was just a little mishap while I was keeping a close watch on Prince Alexander," Patricia replied with a hint of weariness in her voice. "Very well, then," the princess said, her tone firm and commanding, "you need to fetch my luggage."

"Absolutely!" Patricia replied, her voice bubbling with eagerness, despite the slight strain in her expression from the weight of her arm in a sling. They hurried through the bustling baggage claim, the air alive with the chatter of travelers and the distant clanking of luggage carts. Each step felt charged with excitement as they approached the carousel, where a sea of bags awaited.

When they finally spotted Princess Penelope's elegant luggage—each piece a striking blend of royal insignias and designer brands—Patricia felt a surge of pride. However, as she reached for the first suitcase, she was met with its unexpected heft.

Princess Penelope strode ahead with an air of regal confidence, her head held high and a slight smile gracing her lips. Meanwhile, Patricia's laughter mingled with the chaos around her as she wrestled with the bags. Each tug felt like a battle, her feet stumbling over the stubborn wheels that seemed determined to trip her up.

The scene unfolded like a comedic play, Patricia's exaggerated efforts drawing curious glances from amused onlookers. With every pull and misstep, she felt a mix of determination and embarrassment, her cheeks flushing with a mix of frustration and laughter.

Finally, they stepped outside into the crisp air, where the sun shone brightly against the polished surface of the waiting limousine. The chauffeur stood at the ready, his demeanor professional as he opened the door for Princess Penelope.

"Here, deal with these," Patricia instructed with a wave of her hand, her voice brisk and authoritative. Without waiting for a response, she handed off the heavy luggage to him, a satisfied smile on her face as if she were shedding the burdens of travel.

In one smooth motion, she gracefully slid into the plush interior of the limousine, the soft leather seats enveloping her like a warm embrace. As Princess Penelope settled into the luxurious confines of the limousine, Patricia couldn't help but notice the subtle shift in her demeanor. Despite the elegant surroundings, a cloud of discontent hung over the princess, her expression clouded and distant.

Princess Penelope's brow was slightly furrowed, and her lips, usually curved in that charming smile, were pressed into a thin line. There was a tension in her posture, as if she were carrying an invisible weight on her shoulders. It was clear to Patricia that something was troubling her.

"Is everything alright, Your Highness?" Patricia ventured, her voice soft and filled with genuine concern, hoping to bridge the gap between the princess's unease and her own desire to help.

"I'm tired, and I need to rest," Princess Penelope replied curtly, her voice tinged with fatigue.

"Very well, Your Majesty," Patricia responded, quickly shifting her tone to one of reassurance. "The queen has secured the best accommodations in the city for us. I'm sure you will be quite comfortable."

But before she could elaborate further, the princess's mood darkened, and she snapped, "Where is Alexander?" The sharpness in her voice caught Patricia off guard, revealing the tension that lay beneath her royal facade.

"I came to America to rekindle Prince Alexander's love for me, not to talk to an assistant," Princess Penelope said, her voice sharp and tinged with a mix of frustration and vulnerability. The admission hung in the air, revealing a deeper layer of her emotions that Patricia hadn't expected.

Patricia's heart sank at the weight of the princess's words, understanding that beneath the royal exterior lay a young woman grappling with her feelings. "I understand, Your Highness," she replied gently, trying to maintain a supportive tone. "But I'm here to help you in any way I can, whether it's arranging meetings or giving you the space you need."

The princess sighed, her shoulders slumping slightly as the tension began to ease. "I just want him to remember how we used to be," she murmured, a hint of longing in her voice. "It feels like everything has changed."

Patricia nodded, recognizing the depth of the princess's

feelings. "Love can be complicated, especially with the pressures of duty and expectation. But you have the chance to show him how you truly feel."

"Once we get you rested from your journey, we can go out later," Patricia said, her tone brightening with determination. "I know where he and his American friends like to hang out. There, you can show Prince Alexander what a real lady is like—not this American adventure he seems caught up in."

The princess's eyes flickered with a mixture of hope and skepticism. "Do you really think that will make a difference?" she asked, her voice softening slightly as she considered Patricia's words.

"Absolutely," Patricia replied confidently. "You have a grace and poise that can remind him of all the things that made him fall in love with you in the first place. Just being yourself will speak volumes. He needs to see the real you again, free from the noise of this new world he's in."

Princess Penelope allowed herself a small smile, the thought of rekindling their connection sparking a glimmer of excitement. "Alright, then. Let's make sure I'm ready," she said, her determination rekindled. "I want him to remember what we had."

"I'm sure when he gets to see and compare you against this American who has ensnared his affections, you will easily win him back," Patricia said, her voice laced with encouragement. She watched as the princess's posture straightened, a spark of confidence igniting within her.

Princess Penelope's eyes narrowed slightly, a mix of determination and competitive spirit creeping into her expression. "You really think so?" she asked, her tone shifting from doubt to intrigue.

"Without a doubt," Patricia affirmed. "You have a charm and sophistication that no one else can match. Plus, you're not just any lady; you're a princess. That carries a weight and allure that will remind him of everything he's missing."

The princess smiled, a hint of mischief playing at the corners of her lips. "Then I suppose I should make the most of this opportunity," she said, a newfound resolve shimmering in her voice. "I won't let him forget what we shared."

Patricia felt a wave of relief wash over her, knowing that the princess was beginning to embrace the challenge ahead. "Exactly! Just be yourself, and let him see the real you, the one he fell in love with."

Chapter 26

Dancing Around the Truth

After an invigorating day spent hiking through lush trails and breathtaking landscapes, the group finally returned to the parking area, their bodies pleasantly fatigued, yet their spirits soaring from the shared adventure. The sun began to dip low in the sky, casting a golden hue over the scene as they approached their cars, laughter and animated chatter filling the air.

Rachel took a moment to breathe in the crisp, pine-scented air, her heart still racing from the exhilaration of the day. She turned to her friends, a sense of fulfillment warming her from within. "What an incredible day! I can't believe how beautiful it was out there," she exclaimed, her eyes sparkling with enthusiasm.

Polly, still buzzing with energy, nodded enthusiastically. "It really was! I think we should make this a regular thing," she chimed, her joy evident as she rummaged through her bag for her keys.

Ivan, leaning against his car, chuckled at Polly's excitement. "As long as you promise to keep the hiking snacks coming, I'm in!" he joked, flashing a playful grin. The group erupted into laughter, the camaraderie palpable.

Jacob, standing beside Rachel, felt a surge of happiness

at being surrounded by friends. Yet, as he glanced at Rachel—whose face radiated joy—his heart grew heavy. He had not yet found the courage to reveal his secret to her, a truth that weighed on him like a stone in his chest. He longed to share his feelings, to open up about his true identity and his royal duties that awaited him back in Slovitia, and what she truly meant to him, but fear held him back. What if it changed everything?

"How about we head home to freshen up and then meet back at the café for dinner and maybe a movie?" he suggested, hoping to extend the magic of the day while battling the turmoil within.

Rachel's face lit up at the idea. "I love that! I could definitely use a good meal after all that hiking," she replied, her enthusiasm infectious.

Polly's eyes sparkled with delight. "Count me in! I don't think I could walk another step right now," she laughed, stretching her arms wide as if to emphasize her point.

Ivan grinned, rubbing his neck. "Yeah, a shower sounds amazing after today's adventure, especially if we're going out again," he added with a chuckle, his playful banter easing the weariness of the hike.

"Very well then," Jacob said, his voice warm yet tinged with the weight of his unspoken feelings. "Let's all head home, get cleaned up, and meet back at the café around six." The thought of spending more time with Rachel filled him with excitement, but the heaviness in his heart lingered, a constant reminder of the truth he hadn't yet shared.

As the group began to disperse toward their cars, Rachel felt an irresistible pull towards Jacob. She reached for his hand, drawing him closer, her heart racing as their eyes locked in a moment charged with unspoken words. Without thinking, she leaned in, their lips meeting in a gentle yet electrifying kiss. The warmth between them radiated, and in that instant, the world around them faded into a soft blur.

"See you later, Jacob," Rachel whispered, pulling away, her cheeks flushed and her heart pounding. She searched his eyes, looking for a reflection of the emotions they had just shared and found warmth and affection mirrored back at her.

Jacob smiled, his heart thudding in his chest, the thrill of their kiss lingering on his lips. Yet, the heaviness of his unspoken secret weighed heavily on him, clouding the joy of the moment. He watched her walk away, feeling the warmth of their connection radiating through him, but also the tight grip of anxiety in his chest. As he turned to his car, the beauty of the day and the promise of the night made him feel alive, yet the fear of what lay ahead lingered ominously in the background, a shadow he couldn't shake.

As Jacob and Ivan settled into their seats in the car, Jacob took a deep breath, attempting to calm his racing heart. The lingering warmth of Rachel's kiss danced on his lips, yet it was overshadowed by the weight of the secret he had yet to divulge. He glanced through the windshield, watching Rachel share laughter with Polly, their joy infectious, but a growing tension tightened in his chest.

What if she didn't feel the same way? What if revealing

his true feelings jeopardized their friendship? Jacob's mind spiraled through daunting scenarios, each one more unsettling than the last. He had known Rachel for years, their bond blossoming from friendship into something deeper, but the fear of losing her held him back from taking the leap. He often found himself daydreaming about moments like the one they had just shared, each glance and touch electric with potential, but the uncertainty gnawed at him relentlessly.

He closed his eyes for a moment, trying to summon the courage he knew he needed. Rachel deserved to know how he truly felt. She deserved to understand the depth of his emotions, the way his heart raced when she smiled, how each shared moment felt like a step toward something beautiful. Yet, the fear of vulnerability gripped him, an unbreakable chain.

With a sigh, he started the car, the engine rumbling to life as he pulled out of the parking lot, his thoughts still swirling. The drive home blurred past him, the scenery a haze as he replayed the day's events—the laughter, the breathtaking views, the effortless camaraderie. Each memory was tinged with the bittersweet awareness that something profound was blossoming between him and Rachel, but he remained tethered by his fears.

As they drove, Ivan glanced over at Jacob, a teasing grin spreading across his face. "So, did you tell her yet that you're the crown prince of Slovitia?" he asked, his tone playful.

"No, it's just that I can't find the right time," Jacob replied, his voice tinged with frustration.

Ivan raised an eyebrow, clearly unconvinced. "Come on, Jacob. You're going to have to tell her sooner or later. It's a pretty big deal."

"I know," Jacob sighed, gripping the steering wheel tightly. "But you know my mother will do everything she can to stop me from pursuing her if she finds out."

"I get that, but isn't that all the more reason to tell Rachel?" Ivan pressed, his tone serious now. "She deserves to know the truth about who you are, especially if this thing between you is real."

Jacob's heart raced at the thought. "I want to tell her, I really do. But what if she doesn't want that kind of life? What if she decides it's too much to handle?"

"Then at least you'll know, and you won't have to keep living this lie," Ivan replied, his voice firm. "You can't keep hiding from who you are. It'll only get harder the longer you wait."

Jacob took a deep breath, the weight of Ivan's words sinking in. He knew his friend was right; the longer he kept this secret, the more complicated things would become. But the fear of losing Rachel, of having her pull away because of his royal obligations, was paralyzing.

"I just wish it were easier," Jacob admitted, glancing out the window as they drove down the interstate. "I don't want to scare her away."

"Trust me, Jacob. If she truly cares about you, she'll understand. But she can't do that if you don't give her the chance," Ivan urged, his voice supportive yet firm.

"Okay," Jacob said, his voice firm. "I'll tell her tonight. No more waiting."

Arriving home, Jacob paused to gather his thoughts. Stepping into his townhouse, the familiar surroundings offered comfort but felt stifling. He paced the living room, running a hand through his hair, trying to quell the storm of emotions within. The echoes of his friends' laughter lingered in his mind, reminding him of the happiness they shared and the closeness they had built.

He knew he needed to talk to Rachel, to share his heart with her, but how could he find the right words to express the whirlwind of feelings that had taken root within him? He thought of the way she looked at him, the softness in her eyes, and how her laughter lit up the world around them. It was a connection he cherished, yet it now felt like a fragile thread, one he feared might snap if he pulled too hard.

As the clock ticked closer to six, Jacob made the decision to take a shower, hoping the warm water would wash away his anxieties. He stepped under the cascading spray, letting the steam envelop him, a soothing balm against the whirlwind of emotions swirling inside him. Closing his eyes, he envisioned the evening ahead: the café, the food, the movie—but most importantly, Rachel.

In his mind, he pictured her smile, radiant and genuine, lighting up the room like the sun breaking through the clouds. He could hear her laughter, a sound that danced in the air, wrapping around him like a comforting embrace. He imagined the way her eyes sparkled with excitement when she talked about her passions, each glimmer drawing him in deeper, igniting a warmth in his chest.

As the water flowed over him, Jacob allowed himself to dream about what could be moments spent together, shared glances that lingered a little too long, and the possibility of a future where he could be open about his feelings. But along with those dreams came the gnawing fear of the truth he had yet to reveal. Would Rachel feel the same? Would she accept him for who he truly was, crown prince and all?

With a deep breath, he let the steam clear his mind, focusing on the present moment. Tonight was important, and he needed to be ready. He envisioned walking into the café, seeking Rachel's gaze, the connection between them palpable. He wanted to feel the courage to express everything that had been weighing on his heart.

Emerging from the shower, Jacob dressed with care, opting for a simple yet sharp outfit, wanting to look his best for Rachel. He glanced in the mirror, searching for the confidence he needed to confront his feelings. "You can do this," he murmured to himself, his reflection showing a mix of hope and trepidation.

As Jacob stood in front of the mirror, searching for the courage to tell Rachel the truth, Ivan exited the bathroom, a towel wrapped around his waist, his hair still damp from the shower.

"Are you still trying to find the perfect words?" Ivan asked, a teasing lilt in his voice.

"Yes, it's the hardest thing I've ever had to do," Jacob admitted, his gaze fixed on his reflection, feeling the weight of the moment pressing down on him.

Ivan leaned against the doorframe, arms crossed, his expression shifting to one of earnest support. "Jacob, you can do this. Just be yourself."

"I know, but it's not that simple," Jacob replied, running a hand through his hair in frustration. "What if I mess it up?"

"Listen," Ivan said, his tone firm yet encouraging. "I've seen the way Rachel looks at you. I know for a fact she's in love with you, Polly has told me several times. You just need to be completely honest with her so she can make that decision for herself."

Jacob's heart raced at Ivan's words, a flicker of hope igniting within him. "You really think so?"

"Absolutely," Ivan affirmed, pushing off the door and stepping closer. "The only thing standing between you two is this secret. Once you tell her, everything else will fall into place. But you have to take that first step."

Taking a deep breath, Jacob nodded slowly. "You're right. I can't keep hiding who I am. Rachel deserves to know the truth."

"Exactly," Ivan said, a proud smile spreading across his face. "Now go out there and be honest. You've got this."

With renewed determination, Jacob straightened his posture, feeling a rush of resolve. "Thanks, Ivan. I really needed that."

"Anytime, man. That's what friends are for." Ivan replied, giving Jacob a supportive pat on the back as he headed out the door.

As Jacob took a final look in the mirror, he reminded himself of the warmth of Rachel's smile and the laughter they shared.

Meanwhile, Rachel and Polly were getting ready for the evening, the air filled with excitement.

"Can you help me with my makeup?" Rachel asked, a hint of nervousness in her voice.

"Heavens, yes! Let me have at it!" Polly replied enthusiastically, grabbing the makeup bag and settling into a comfortable rhythm as she worked on Rachel's look.

As Polly applied a light shimmer to Rachel's eyelids, she couldn't help but giggle. "You and Jacob make such a cute couple," she said, her eyes sparkling with mischief.

Rachel smiled, her cheeks flushing slightly. "When I kissed him today, it just felt so right, like we were always meant to be together."

Polly paused, her eyes wide with excitement. "Have you told him how much you love him?" she asked, a teasing smile on her lips.

"Well, I don't want to be too forward," Rachel said, her blush deepening as she looked down, fiddling with her hair.

"Oh girl, you have to tell him! You two keep dancing this crazy dance around each other," Polly insisted, applying a touch of blush to Rachel's cheeks. "It's time to stop tiptoeing."

Rachel bit her lip, contemplating Polly's words. "Well, he did tell me today that he loved me."

"What? You didn't say anything? That is huge! You need to let him know that you love him too!" Polly exclaimed, her excitement contagious.

"I know, but what if he doesn't feel the same way?" Rachel replied, her heart racing at the thought.

"Trust me, Rachel. If he told you he loved you, then he's just as invested as you are. Don't hold back; take that leap!" Polly encouraged, finishing up Rachel's makeup with a flourish.

Rachel looked in the mirror, taking a deep breath as she absorbed Polly's words. The thought of being open with Jacob filled her with both excitement and fear. "You're right. I can't keep dancing around my feelings. I just need to be brave."

"Exactly! Now, let's get you ready for your big night," Polly said, a conspiratorial grin on her face. "You're going to knock his socks off!"

Chapter 27

When Secrets Collide

As Jacob and Ivan drove to the café, the evening air filled with a mix of anticipation and nervous energy. The car was quiet for a moment, the hum of the engine punctuating the silence as they navigated the streets. Jacob's mind was racing, each thought swirling with excitement and anxiety about what lay ahead.

"Are you ready for this?" Ivan finally broke the silence, glancing over at Jacob, who was gripping the steering wheel tightly.

Jacob nodded, though uncertainty flickered in his eyes. "I think so. It's just… I've never had to share something like this before."

Ivan leaned back in his seat, his expression earnest. "You're not just sharing a secret; you're sharing a part of yourself. That's what makes it so significant. But you've got to trust that Rachel will understand."

"I know," Jacob replied, the weight of Ivan's support providing a small comfort. "It's just scary. What if she doesn't react the way I hope?"

"Then you'll deal with it, just like you've dealt with everything else," Ivan said, his tone encouraging. "You can't let fear hold you back from being happy. You owe it to yourself and to Rachel to be honest."

As they approached the café, the warm glow of the lights welcomed them, illuminating the sidewalk filled with people enjoying their evening. Jacob felt his heart quicken at the sight, a mix of excitement and nervousness bubbling within him.

"Remember, just be yourself," Ivan reminded him as they parked the car. "You're a great guy, and Rachel's lucky to have you."

"Thanks, Ivan. I really appreciate your support," Jacob said, feeling a renewed sense of determination.

They stepped out of the car and made their way to the entrance of the café. Jacob took a deep breath, the aroma of coffee and pastries filling the air as he pushed open the door. The familiar sounds of laughter and chatter enveloped him, and he immediately scanned the room for Rachel.

There she was, seated at a table with Polly, her laughter brightening the atmosphere around them. In that moment, Jacob felt a surge of hope.

As Jacob stepped into the café, the lively atmosphere wrapped around him like a warm blanket. The soft chatter of friends catching up, the clinking of cups, and the rich aroma of freshly brewed coffee filled the air, creating a perfect backdrop for what he hoped would be a pivotal evening.

His gaze landed on Rachel, and his heart swelled at the sight of her. She sat comfortably at a small table, her hair cascading over her shoulders, laughter dancing in her eyes as she spoke with Polly. There was an effortless beauty about her, and in that moment, Jacob felt a rush of gratitude for having someone like her in his life.

"Let's go," Ivan said, nudging Jacob gently, bringing him back to the present. With a determined breath, Jacob walked toward the table, each step feeling heavier yet more purposeful than the last.

"Hey, you made it!" Rachel exclaimed, her face lighting up as she spotted him. The warmth of her smile sent a rush of confidence coursing through him.

"Of course! Wouldn't miss it for the world," Jacob replied, taking a seat across from her. As he settled in, he tried to focus on the conversation, but his mind kept drifting back to the secret he carried.

"You look great," he added, genuinely admiring her. "What are you two up to?"

"Just catching up and planning our evening. Polly's been helping me with my makeup," Rachel said, glancing at Polly, who grinned with pride.

"It's true! She's going to steal the show tonight," Polly said playfully, giving Rachel a thumbs-up.

Jacob chuckled, grateful for the lightheartedness. But as the conversation flowed, he felt the familiar weight of his secret pressing down on him. He knew he couldn't put it off any longer.

"Rachel, there's something I need to talk to you about,"

he said, his tone shifting as he leaned forward slightly, trying to gauge her reaction.

Rachel's expression softened, and she nodded encouragingly. "What's on your mind?"

Just then, Ivan interjected, sensing the intensity of the moment. "Why don't we order first? I'll grab us some drinks," he said, standing up. "You two can have a little chat."

"Good idea," Jacob replied, grateful for the distraction but also feeling a mix of relief and anxiety. As Ivan walked away, he turned his full attention to Rachel.

"Jacob?" Rachel's voice was gentle, her eyes searching his. "You seem serious. Is everything okay?"

He took a deep breath, the moment feeling both exhilarating and terrifying. "I've been meaning to tell you something important. Something about who I am."

Rachel's eyes widened slightly, curiosity mixed with concern. "What is it?"

Jacob hesitated for a heartbeat, weighing his words carefully. "I haven't been completely honest with you. There's more to my life than you know."

Her brow furrowed slightly, but she remained patient. "Okay… I'm listening."

Just then, Ivan returned to the table, balancing four steaming mugs of hot chocolate and a selection of pastries. "Have I missed anything?" he asked, a playful grin on his face as he set the treats down.

"No, Jacob was just about to tell Rachel something big," Polly chimed in, her eyes sparkling with mischief.

Jacob felt a mix of anticipation and nerves at the mention of his earlier confession, but before he could continue, the café door swung open, and in walked Patricia, accompanied by Princess Penelope.

Chapter 28

A Royal Mess

The atmosphere shifted instantly as the two entered, their presence commanding attention. Patricia, dressed in her usual stern suit, scanned the room before her gaze landed on Jacob and his friends. Princess Penelope, youthful and radiant, followed closely behind, her demeanor serious and intent.

"Alexander!" Patricia called out, making her way toward the table. "There you are! I'm glad to see we have finally found you."

Jacob's heart sank as he saw his mother's personal assistant, Patricia, striding toward them, Princess Penelope following closely behind. The moment felt surreal, as if time had slowed down.

"Oh, Prince Alexander! It is so good to see you again," Patricia called out, her voice cheerful yet smug.

Rachel's expression shifted from confusion to shock as she turned to Jacob. "Why is she calling you Alexander?" Her voice was barely above a whisper, but it carried the weight of disbelief.

Jacob's throat tightened, the implications of the moment crashing down on him. He felt exposed, as if the truth he had been steeling himself to share had just been ripped from his grasp.

"Polly looked at Ivan, her eyes wide with shock and bewilderment. "Ivan, what is going on? Who is this?"

Jacob stumbled for words, his mind racing. "Rachel, this is my mother's personal assistant, Patricia Jackson," he said, forcing the words out. "And the lady with her is Princess Penelope, an old friend."

The realization hit Rachel like a wave, and her face transformed, reflecting pure shock and betrayal. "You… you're not just Jacob. You're Alexander? A prince?"

"I—" Jacob began, but the weight of her gaze made it difficult to continue. He could see the hurt in her eyes, and it pierced him deeply. "I didn't want to keep this from you. I thought I could tell you when the time was right."

Rachel's expression hardened, her voice trembling with emotion. "You thought you could hide this from me? All this time, you let me believe you were just… Jacob. Why didn't you tell me the truth?"

The tension in the café escalated, and Jacob felt a burning need to explain. "I was going to! I just didn't know how. I wanted to have a normal connection with you, without the weight of my title looming over us."

"Normal?" Rachel echoed, disbelief etched on her face. "How can anything about this be normal? You're a prince! You didn't trust me to tell me the truth! That changes everything!"

Patricia, sensing the rising tension, stepped forward. "Perhaps this is a good time to clear the air," she suggested, trying to navigate the situation diplomatically. "Alexander has a lot on his shoulders, and it's understandable that he wanted to protect his personal life. After all, women are attracted to his title and wealth."

But Rachel shook her head, her eyes glistening. "Protect? Or deceive? I can't believe you didn't trust me enough to be honest from the beginning."

Jacob's heart ached at her words. He desperately wanted to bridge the gap that had suddenly formed between them. "I never meant to deceive you, Rachel. I was afraid of losing you if you knew. I thought you might see me differently. "

Princess Penelope, who had been quietly observing the exchange, finally spoke up, her tone shifting to one of condescension. "His mother, Queen Isabella, thought it would be best if Alexander was reminded what a real lady looked like," she said, her eyes flicking dismissively toward Rachel.

Jacob felt a rush of anger and embarrassment on Rachel's behalf. "Penelope, that's not fair!" he interjected, trying to defuse the tension. "Rachel is amazing, and you know nothing about her."

"Is she, though?" Penelope shot back, her tone dripping with sarcasm. "She seems quite shocked to discover that her boyfriend is a prince. Perhaps she can't handle the pressure of the royal life."

Rachel turned slowly, her expression a mixture of hurt and indignation. "I can handle plenty, thank you very much. My worth isn't defined by royal expectations or appearances."

"Then why did you look so betrayed?" Penelope asked, crossing her arms defiantly.

"Because he deceived me!" Rachel replied, her voice rising slightly. "He didn't trust me enough to be honest about who he is. That's not something you can gloss over!"

Jacob felt caught in the crossfire, the weight of the situation pulling him in multiple directions. "This isn't about you, Penelope," he said, frustration creeping into his voice. "This is about Rachel and me, and what we were building together until this moment."

Patricia, sensing the escalating conflict, stepped in to mediate. "Let's all take a breath. This is a complicated situation for everyone involved. Alexander, perhaps you could take this opportunity to apologize for the misunderstanding."

Jacob nodded, turning to Rachel with sincerity. "I'm really sorry for how I've handled everything. I should have been open with you from the start. I never wanted to hurt you."

Rachel's eyes softened slightly, but the hurt was still evident. "It's not just about the secret, Jacob. It's about trust. I thought we had something real, and now I feel like you've been hiding an entire part of yourself from me."

"I do care, more than anything," Jacob said, desperation creeping into his voice. "I just didn't know how to navigate this world while also being with someone I genuinely like. I thought I could protect you from the complications of my life."

"Or maybe you just wanted to protect yourself," Penelope interjected, her tone still sharp. "You thought you could have a normal relationship without considering the reality of your responsibilities."

Jacob turned to Penelope, frustration boiling over. "And what do you know about normal? You've been raised in a palace your entire life! You don't get to judge what I experience outside of that."

Rachel watched the exchange, her expression thoughtful. "I just need space to think," she said finally, her voice steady but tinged with sadness.

Jacob's heart shattered as he watched Rachel walk away, each step echoing the weight of his regrets. The air felt heavy around him, filled with unspoken words and lost chances. "I should go," Polly said, her voice barely above a whisper as she glanced at Ivan, uncertainty etched on her face. The tension in the air was palpable, a storm brewing on the horizon. "I'll call you later," Ivan replied, his gaze now locked on Patricia, a mix of anger and concern swirling in his eyes.

"Let them go," Princess Penelope said, her tone dripping with disdain. "They're just common Americans."

Jacob felt a surge of anger rise within him, heat flooding his cheeks. "There's nothing common about her!" he retorted, his voice laced with defiance as he glared at Penelope, the fire in his eyes reflecting the depth of his feelings for Rachel.

"Now, now," Patricia interjected, her tone attempting to soothe the brewing tension. "This is for the best. She was going to find out eventually, and you know you must marry someone of royal lineage as our laws dictate." The cold practicality of her words felt like a dagger, twisting deeper with each syllable.

Jacob's fury grew more intense, a tempest of emotion swirling inside him. "This was mother's idea, wasn't it?" he said, his voice rising, the accusation hanging in the air like a thunderclap.

"Don't blame your mother," Princess Penelope said, inching closer to Jacob, her voice smooth yet insistent. "She only wants what's best for you, and that's me. You must have known we were always meant to be together." Her words felt like a chain tightening around him, suffocating the very essence of what he wanted.

"Leave me alone!" he shouted, the raw pain in his voice betraying the turmoil within. "I want no part of this madness. Come on, Ivan, we're leaving!"

"Alexander, stop being so stubborn!" Patricia yelled, frustration lacing her voice as they turned away.

Jacob stormed out, his heart racing and fists clenched,

with Ivan trailing closely behind. Each step felt like a battle against the chains of obligation pulling him back, and as they hurried to the car, the weight of his decisions loomed heavily over him, mingling with the lingering image of Rachel's hurt expression. He knew deep down that the choice ahead was more than just about duty; it was about choosing the life and love he truly wanted.

"I need to go find Rachel," Jacob said with urgency, his voice thick with emotion as he and Ivan fastened their seatbelts. The weight of his decision settled heavily on his shoulders, every second that ticked by feeling like an eternity.

"Jacob, I really think you should give Rachel some space for now," Ivan replied, concern clouding his features. "She's just been through so much. Let me call Polly and see if Rachel has cooled off and had a moment to herself."

Jacob pressed his forehead against the steering wheel, the cool leather a stark contrast to the turmoil inside him. "I love Rachel, Ivan. I can't lose her," he confessed, his voice cracking, revealing the vulnerability hidden beneath his bravado. The thought of her hurt and disappointment twisted in his stomach like a knot.

"I know, my friend," Ivan said gently, placing a reassuring hand on Jacob's shoulder, grounding him momentarily in the whirlpool of his emotions. "But rushing in right now might push her further away."

Just then, out of the corner of his eye, Jacob spotted Princess Penelope and Patricia emerging from the café, their demeanor radiating an air of superiority. The sight of them ignited a fresh wave of anger within him. "Prince Alexander, stop!" Penelope called out, her voice dripping with condescension.

In a surge of adrenaline, Jacob slammed the car into reverse, tires screeching against the pavement as he pulled out of the parking spot with reckless speed. The engine roared to life, filling the air with a deafening sound that matched the pounding of his heart. He felt a mix of fear and exhilaration, but the thought of Rachel's face, the hurt, the disbelief spurred him on.

"Jacob, be careful!" Ivan shouted, gripping the dashboard as they jolted back onto the road. "You can't let your emotions drive you to reckless decisions!"

"I know!" Jacob replied, his voice taut with determination. "But I can't let her slip away. Not like this." His hands tightened around the steering wheel, knuckles white as he navigated through the streets, weaving through traffic with a singular focus.

With each turn, memories flooded his mind—Rachel's laughter, the warmth of her smile, the way her eyes sparkled with life. He could still feel the connection they shared, a bond that felt both exhilarating and terrifying. He had to find her. He needed to tell her everything, to show her that his love was worth fighting for.

As they sped through the city, streetlights blurred into streaks of color, mirroring the chaotic emotions swirling inside him.

"Let's go home," Ivan urged, his voice steady but laced with concern as he tried to console Jacob. He could see the turmoil etched on his friend's face, the way his eyes darted with urgency and pain. "Let's just go back home, and I'll call Polly to set something up."

Jacob clenched his jaw, the thought of returning home feeling like a retreat from the battle he was determined to fight. "I can't just sit around and wait, Ivan! What if she's hurting? What if she thinks I don't care?" His frustration bubbled over, the fear of losing Rachel amplifying his anxiety.

"I know you care, Jacob. That's why you need to give her some time," Ivan replied, his tone calm yet firm. "Rushing in without a plan might make things worse. Let's regroup. We can figure this out together."

Jacob took a deep breath, the tension in his shoulders settling slightly as he weighed Ivan's words. Deep down, he understood the need for patience, but the ache in his heart urged him to act now. "But what if she doesn't want to see me anymore?" he murmured, vulnerability creeping into his voice.

"She will. You just need to show her that you're willing to fight for her," Ivan reassured him, his gaze steady. "Trust me, we'll find a way to make this right. But we can't do it while you're in this state. Let's go home and come up with a plan."

After a moment of silence, Jacob nodded reluctantly, the weight of his emotions still heavy but tempered by Ivan's support. The streets whizzed past, but his mind was fixated on one thing: finding a way to reach Rachel and mend the rift that had opened between them.

As they made their way home, the anticipation of what lay ahead mingled with the uncertainty of their next steps. Jacob's heart was still racing, but now there was a flicker of hope, hope that with Ivan's help, he could find a way back to Rachel and show her just how much she meant to him.

Chapter 29

When Everything Changes

Back at Polly's apartment, the atmosphere was thick with tension as Rachel entered, her emotions still raw from the encounter with Patricia and Princess Penelope. "Who do they think they are?" she snapped, frustration bubbling to the surface.

"Come on, girl. Let's get something to drink to calm us down," Polly suggested, her voice soothing as she led Rachel toward the kitchen. She could see the hurt etched on Rachel's face, the way her brows knit together in disbelief. "I can't believe Jacob is a prince and he didn't trust me enough to tell me," Rachel continued, her voice trembling with emotion. "I feel so betrayed."

"I know," Polly replied, pouring steaming mugs of hot chocolate, the rich aroma filling the air and momentarily distracting them from the turmoil. "And if he's a prince, what does that make Ivan? Those boys have a lot of explaining to do." She tried to inject some levity into the situation, hoping to lighten the mood a bit.

As they settled into the cozy living room, mugs in hand, the warmth of the hot chocolate began to seep into their bones, but the emotional chill remained. "I just don't know what to do," Rachel admitted, her voice small as she wrapped her hands around the mug, seeking comfort in its warmth.

Polly sat down beside her, leaning in with genuine concern. "You need to take a step back and breathe, Rachel. You're feeling a lot right now, and it's okay to feel confused. But you need to give yourself some time to process everything."

Rachel sighed, her thoughts a whirlwind of emotions. "I thought we had something real, Polly. I thought we were building a foundation of trust, and now I don't know if I can look at him the same way again."

"Relationships are complicated, especially when secrets are involved," Polly replied, her tone empathetic. "But you know Jacob cares about you. He wouldn't have kept this from you lightly."

Rachel took a sip of her hot chocolate, letting the warmth spread through her, but it did little to quell the storm inside her heart. "It just feels like I was living in a fantasy, and now I'm left with this harsh reality. How can I trust him again after this?"

Polly reached out, placing a comforting hand on Rachel's knee. "Trust takes time to rebuild, but it's not impossible. You need to decide what you want. Do you want to talk to him? Are you willing to hear him out?"

Rachel bit her lip, contemplating Polly's words. "I don't know, Polly. Part of me wants to confront him and demand answers, but another part of me is scared. What if I can't forgive him?"

"Then take your time," Polly encouraged gently. "You don't have to make any decisions right now. Just focus on how you feel and what you want moving forward. You deserve to be happy, and you deserve honesty in your relationships."

As they sat together, the warmth of their friendship enveloped them, and Rachel felt a glimmer of hope amidst the chaos. She knew she had a lot to figure out, but having Polly by her side made the burden a little lighter.

As they continued their conversation, Rachel's phone began to ring, cutting through the heavy atmosphere in the room. "It's probably Jacob calling," Polly said, casting a sympathetic glance at her friend.

"I don't know if I'm ready to talk to him," Rachel replied, her voice shaky as she stared at the screen, torn between her emotions. The phone continued to ring, each chime echoing her uncertainty.

Finally, curiosity overcame her hesitation, and she flipped the phone over to see who was calling. "It's my mom," she said, her heart racing as she dried her tears, trying to compose herself for the conversation.

"Hi, Mom," Rachel answered, forcing a brightness into her voice, though the tremor betrayed her inner turmoil.

"Rachel, I'm so glad I got hold of you," her mother's voice came through, strained and filled with urgency.

"Mom, it's late there. Are you alright?" Concern flooded Rachel's voice, the previous tension momentarily forgotten as her mother's distress became the focal point of her thoughts.

"It's your father," her mom sobbed, and Rachel's heart dropped. "We're in the ER. He's had a heart attack."

Rachel felt the world around her tilt, her breath catching in her throat. "Oh no, Mom! Is he going to be alright? What did the doctors say?" Panic surged through her, drowning out everything else as tears streamed down her cheeks, each drop a mix of fear and helplessness.

"He's in surgery right now, but they haven't told me much," her mother replied, her voice choked with emotion. The uncertainty hung between them like a heavy cloud, thickening the air.

Rachel's heart shattered at her mother's words, the weight of the situation crashing down on her. "I'm on my way, Mom. I'll be there as soon as I can," she said, her voice firm despite the fear swirling inside her.

"No, Rachel, it's late. You don't have to rush," her mother insisted, but Rachel could hear the worry lacing her words.

"I need to be there for you. For Dad," Rachel replied, determination igniting within her. "I'll find a way to get to you. Just keep me updated, okay? I love you."

"I love you too, sweetheart," her mother said, her voice tinged with both gratitude and fear. "Just be safe."

As they hung up, Rachel felt a surge of urgency coursing

through her veins. She looked at Polly, her eyes wide and filled with tears. "I have to go. My dad… he had a heart attack."

Polly's expression shifted from concern to immediate support. "Of course, let's get you packed and figure out how to get you there."

Rachel wiped her tears away, her heart racing not just with fear for her father, but also with the realization that life was too fragile and unpredictable. The weight of her earlier worries about Jacob felt so insignificant in the face of this new crisis.

Rachel's heart raced as she processed her mother's words, the gravity of the situation crashing down on her like a tidal wave. The cozy apartment that had felt like a refuge just moments ago now felt suffocating. "I can't believe this is happening," she whispered, her voice shaking as panic clawed at her insides.

Polly moved quickly, sensing the urgency in Rachel's demeanor. "Okay, let's get you ready. Do you have everything you need? Clothes? Your ID?" She rushed to the bedroom, gathering items as Rachel stood frozen for a moment, grappling with the enormity of the news.

"My dad… he's always been so healthy," Rachel murmured, trying to make sense of the situation. "How could this happen?" The tears continued to flow, a mixture of fear for her father and guilt over her earlier emotional turmoil with Jacob.

"Sometimes these things come out of nowhere," Polly said gently, returning with a small bag in hand. "But right now, you need to focus on getting to him. Everything else can wait." She handed Rachel her phone, ensuring it was charged. "Keep this close. You'll want to be in touch with your mom."

Rachel nodded, taking a deep breath as she wiped her eyes. "You're right. I can't fall apart now." The determination in her voice began to take root as she realized she needed to be strong for her family.

"Do you want me to come with you?" Polly asked, her eyes soft with concern. "I can drive you to the airport or wherever you need to go."

Rachel shook her head, the thought of burdening Polly with her problems weighing on her heart. "No, I don't want to impose. I'll manage. I just need to get there."

"Rachel," Polly said firmly, stepping closer. "You're not imposing. You're my best friend, and I'm here for you. If you need me, I'll drop everything to be by your side. Just say the word."

The sincerity in Polly's voice struck a chord, and Rachel felt a rush of gratitude. "Thank you, Polly. I appreciate it."

Polly nodded, respecting Rachel's decision, though her eyes reflected the worry she felt for her friend. "Just promise you'll keep me updated. I'll be here waiting for your call."

"I promise," Rachel said, her voice steadier now. She quickly gathered some essentials—a couple of outfits, her toiletries, and her father's favorite book, knowing he would want something to read during his recovery.

As she packed, her mind raced with thoughts of her dad. Memories flooded back: family dinners filled with laughter, him teaching her how to ride a bike, the way he would always know how to make her smile even on her worst days. "Please be okay, Dad," she whispered to herself, clutching the book tightly as if it could somehow bridge the distance between them.

With her bag slung over her shoulder and a sense of purpose igniting within her, Rachel took a deep breath. "I'm ready," she said, her voice more resolute than before.

Polly gave her a supportive smile. "Let's get you to the airport. You've got this, Rachel. You're stronger than you think."

As they made their way to the car, Rachel's heart raced with hope and fear intertwined. She knew she had a long journey ahead, both to her father's side and in the emotional turmoil she had been navigating. But one thing was clear: family came first, and she would fight through whatever it took to be there for him in this moment of need.

Polly drove the car with determination, the headlights illuminating the road ahead as they made their way to the airport. The night sky was a deep indigo blanket, punctuated by countless stars twinkling like distant beacons of hope. Rachel leaned back in her seat, her gaze drifting upward, searching for solace in the vastness above.

"Look at how beautiful the stars are tonight," she said softly, her voice barely above a whisper. The beauty of the night seemed to contrast sharply with the turmoil in her heart, yet it offered a moment of peace amidst the chaos.

"They really are," Polly agreed, glancing briefly at Rachel before focusing back on the road. "It's like they're reminding us that even in the darkest times, there's still light."

Rachel nodded, letting the words wash over her. "I've always loved looking at the stars with my dad. He used to tell me stories about constellations and how they connect different cultures and histories. It made me feel like we were part of something bigger, you know?"

"Yeah, I get that," Polly replied, her voice warm. "It's comforting to think about how the same stars have been shining down on people for centuries. No matter where you are, you're never truly alone."

Rachel took a deep breath, trying to harness that sense of connection. "I just hope he's okay. I can't bear the thought of losing him." The knot in her stomach tightened again, but she fought against it, focusing instead on the memories of laughter and love.

"I remember the time we all went camping?" Rachel said, trying to lighten the mood. "My dad made this ridiculous campfire story about the 'Great S'more Monster'?"

Rachel chuckled through her tears, the memory

warming her heart. "He had us all convinced that if we didn't roast our marshmallows properly, the monster would come and take our snacks!"

Polly laughed, the sound brightening the atmosphere in the car. "And then he proceeded to burn his own marshmallow! I thought he was going to cry over it!"

"Classic Dad," Rachel said, smiling as she wiped away a tear. "He always knew how to make the best out of any situation."

As they neared the airport, the bright lights of the terminal came into view, a contrast to the calm of the night sky. Rachel felt a surge of anxiety mixed with determination. "I need to be there for him, Polly. He's always been there for me. I can't let him down now."

"You won't," Polly reassured her, pulling into the airport parking lot. "You're strong, Rachel. You have so much love to give, and he knows that. Just be there for him—sometimes that's all they need."

Rachel nodded, feeling a renewed sense of purpose as she prepared to step into the unknown. "Thank you for being here with me, Polly. I don't know what I'd do without you."

"Always," Polly replied, her expression steadfast. "Now let's get you checked in. We'll make sure you get to your dad, no matter what."

As they parked and Rachel gathered her things, she took one last look at the shimmering stars above, feeling a flicker of hope. No matter what challenges lay ahead, she knew she would face them head on just the way her parents had taught her. Her heart longed to have Jacob by her side, but for now, she knew more important challenges lay ahead.

Chapter 30

Between Love and Duty

Jacob and Ivan pulled into the driveway of their home, the engine's hum fading into an uncomfortable silence. As they stepped out of the car, a storm of emotions brewed within Jacob. "I can't believe Mother sent Patricia here with Princess Penelope," he erupted, his voice sharp with frustration. The walls of the house felt as if they were closing in on him, amplifying his anger and sense of betrayal.

He marched inside, unable to contain his feelings any longer. Jacob slammed the door to his room and flopped down onto his bed, the weight of his thoughts pressing heavily on his chest. He felt like a puppet, tangled in strings he couldn't cut. In a moment of impulse, he grabbed his phone and typed a message to his mother: How could you do this to me? The text felt inadequate, but it was the only way he could express the torment within.

Back in Slovitia, King Frederick walked past the ornate dining table where Queen Isabella had carelessly left her phone. The royal household was typically so orderly; this moment of disarray caught his eye. Curiosity piqued, he glanced at the screen and saw Jacob's message flash before him. "What has my wife been up to?" he murmured, concern knitting his brow. Feeling the urgency of the situation, he retreated to his study, a room filled with leather-bound books and the scent of polished wood. Picking up the phone, he dialed Jacob's number, his heart heavy with worry.

"Hello?" Jacob answered, his voice trembling with a mixture of anger and hurt, betraying the storm inside.

"Jacob, what is going on?" King Frederick's tone was calm but firm, a steady anchor amidst the chaos.

"It's Mother," Jacob replied, his voice barely above a whisper, the pain slicing through him. "She sent Patricia here with Princess Penelope to ruin my life." The words hung in the air, heavy with frustration and helplessness, as if he were pleading for understanding.

"Oh," King Frederick said, realization dawning on him. "Maybe you should come home, Alexander. We can discuss this together, figure it all out."

"I may never come back, Father!" Jacob shot back, defiance flaring in his chest. "I can't live someone else's life. I need to make my own decisions!" His voice cracked, a mix of rebellion and despair spilling out. He felt trapped in a gilded cage, watching others shape his fate while he longed to break free.

"I'm sorry, Alexander," the king replied, his voice softening with regret. "I warned your mother about meddling in your social affairs. I will have a serious talk with her today." He paused, allowing Jacob a moment to absorb his words. "You need to rest, and we will talk again when you've had some time to think things over."

Jacob dropped the phone onto his bed, feeling a wave of

despair wash over him. How could he ever regain Rachel's trust after this? The thought gnawed at him, a relentless ache in his heart. He felt lost, adrift in a sea of expectations and obligations. Just then, Ivan entered the room, his expression a mix of concern and understanding. He sat down beside Jacob, the weight of their friendship grounding him.

"I know how much you care for Rachel," Ivan said softly, placing a hand on Jacob's shoulder. "You'll find a way through this. You just need to breathe and think."

As Jacob stared at the ceiling, he felt a flicker of hope amidst the turmoil. Ivan, feeling a surge of urgency, grabbed his phone and dialed Polly's number. The phone rang several times, each ring echoing his growing anxiety. Finally, her voice came through the line, slightly breathless as if she had just hurried to answer.

"Hello?" Polly said, her tone sharp and inquisitive.

"Ivan," she replied, trying to keep her voice steady despite the fluttering in her stomach. "We need to talk. You have a lot of explaining to do."

"Ivan," she said, her tone shifting to one of concern. "What's going on? Are you a prince as well?" She asked this as she walked back to her apartment building, her mind racing to make sense of the whirlwind of events.

"No, no," Ivan quickly assured her, sensing her disbelief. "I'm Jacob's bodyguard," he explained, trying to ease the tension that hung in the air like a thick fog.

"Why didn't you tell me?" Polly pressed, her voice

rising slightly. The disappointment was palpable, and Ivan could hear the frustration beneath her words.

"It's complicated," he replied, running a hand through his hair. "I had to keep Jacob's identity a secret to protect him. It was the only way to ensure people would leave him alone."

"So is it Jacob or Alexander?" Polly shot back, clearly still trying to piece everything together.

"It's both," Ivan said, his voice firm yet gentle. "His full name is Jacob Alexander Frederick Kingston the Third." He could almost hear her processing the information on the other end of the line.

Polly finally reached her apartment and pushed the door open, stepping inside and closing it behind her. She leaned against the door for a moment, trying to catch her breath, the weight of the night's events crashing down on her as she made her way to the couch. She sank into the cushions, her mind racing with the implications of what Ivan had just revealed.

As she sat there, the reality of Jacob's situation began to settle in. The royal lineage, the expectations, the pressure, it was all so overwhelming. She glanced around her warmly lit apartment, seeking clarity as she tried to absorb the gravity of the situation. "So, what does this mean for him?" she finally asked, her voice softer now, laced with concern.

"I don't know yet," Ivan admitted, his tone serious. "But he needs support now more than ever. There's so much at stake, and he's feeling lost."

Polly nodded, even though Ivan couldn't see her. "I'll help however I can," she promised, her resolve strengthening. "He deserves to have someone in his corner."

"Thank you, Polly," Ivan replied, relief flooding through him. "I think he'll need all the friends he can get."

"Is Rachel with you?" Ivan asked, his voice filled with a hint of urgency.

"Oh no, you don't know, do you?" Polly replied, a tremor of concern threading through her words. Ivan could sense that something was gravely wrong.

"What do you mean?" he pressed, anxiety creeping into his chest.

Polly took a deep breath, steadying herself as she prepared to deliver the news. "We had just been home a short while when Rachel's phone rang. Her father, Max, suffered a heart attack." The weight of her words hung in the air, heavy and suffocating.

Ivan's heart sank. "What? Is he okay?" He felt a rush of panic, his mind racing at the thought of Rachel facing such a crisis alone.

"I just got home from dropping her off at the airport," Polly continued, her voice shaking. "She was so excited to see her dad at graduation, and now…" Her words trailed off, the gravity of the situation settling between them like a thick fog.

"I can't believe this is happening," Ivan murmured, his thoughts racing.

Jacob sat on the edge of his bed, his heart racing as he listened to Ivan speak on the phone with Polly. Each word Ivan exchanged felt like a lifeline, yet the tension in the air was palpable. "Is Rachel alright?" Jacob finally asked, his voice laced with worry, the uncertainty gnawing at him like a persistent ache.

Ivan raised his hand, signaling Jacob to be still as he continued his conversation, his brow furrowed in concentration. Jacob watched him intently, feeling the seconds stretch into what felt like an eternity. Every passing moment heightened his anxiety, and he couldn't shake off the feeling that something was terribly wrong.

After what felt like an eternity, Ivan ended the call and turned to Jacob, his expression somber. "Rachel's father has suffered a heart attack," he said quietly, the gravity of the news weighing heavily in the room. Jacob's heart sank, a cold wave of dread washing over him.

"What? Is he… is he going to be okay?" Jacob asked, his voice trembling, the reality of the situation crashing down on him like a tidal wave.

Ivan took a deep breath, trying to find the right words. Polly just got home from dropping her off at the airport. Rachel is on her way back to Tennessee to be with her father and family." The finality of Ivan's words hung in the air, filling the room with an overwhelming sense of helplessness.

Jacob felt a mix of emotions roiling within him—fear, guilt, and an aching desire to be there for Rachel. "I should be with her," he said, his voice barely above a whisper. The thought of Rachel facing this crisis alone filled him with despair.

Chapter 31

Unseen Consequences

In the grand halls of the Slovitia palace, King Frederick wandered with purpose, his heart eager to find his beloved wife, Queen Isabella. As he entered her drawing room, he found her seated gracefully in a chair by an arched window, her gaze lost in the beauty of the gardens outside.

"I have been looking for you, my love," he said, his voice warm and filled with affection as he stepped into the serene atmosphere of the room.

Isabella turned to him, her face lighting up as she set her delicate tea cup down. "I've just been enjoying a little time to myself," she replied, her smile radiating a sense of comfort that wrapped around him like a warm embrace.

Frederick reached out his hand, revealing her phone, and a playful smile tugged at his lips. "I found this and thought you might want it back."

Her expression brightened with joy as she accepted the phone. "Thank you, my love! I had completely forgotten where I laid it down," she laughed, the sound like music that lifted his spirits.

But as he watched her, a shadow of concern crossed his face, and he took a step closer. "I noticed Alexander had texted you," he said, his tone shifting to one of seriousness.

"I saw the message he sent."

Isabella's smile faltered, and a flicker of worry crossed her features. "Oh, did you? It was just a casual message, nothing to worry about," she replied, though her voice lacked its usual lightness.

Frederick's heart ached at the sight of her concern. "Is that so? But I thought we had talked about giving Alexander some room. He seems very upset with you," he said gently, his eyes searching hers for understanding.

Her brow furrowed, and she looked away, the weight of his words pressing on her. "I didn't mean to upset him," she said softly, her voice tinged with regret. "I just want Alexander to make the right choice."

"Oh my darling, I love you, but you have to let Alexander be his own man," King Frederick said gently, his voice laced with both affection and concern. He stepped closer, the weight of his words hanging in the air between them. "He is upset now and is talking about not returning to Slovitia. I tried to warn you that interfering in his love life will only push him away."

Isabella's heart sank at his words, a mix of worry and guilt swirling within her. "But he has to marry someone of royal lineage," she replied, trying to convince both Frederick and herself. "It's the way things are done. I just want what's best for him."

Frederick nodded, understanding the burden of duty that weighed heavily on her shoulders. "I know you mean well, but love cannot be forced, my dear. It has to come naturally. If you try to dictate who he should be with, you risk losing him altogether," he said softly, his eyes searching her face for understanding.

Isabella felt a swell of emotion, the conflict between her desires for Alexander and her love for Frederick tearing at her heart. "I only want to protect him," she insisted, her voice trembling slightly. "He deserves to find happiness, but he also has a duty to fulfill."

Frederick squeezed her hands, grounding her in the moment. "And so do I, Isabella. But we must allow him the space to make his own choices. He's not a child anymore; he needs the freedom to forge his own path, even if it doesn't align with tradition."

The tension in the room hung thickly as Isabella processed his words. She could feel the truth in them, yet the fear of losing Alexander loomed large in her mind. "What if he chooses someone who isn't suitable?" she murmured, her voice barely above a whisper.

"Then that is a risk we must accept," Frederick replied firmly, yet tenderly. "He has to learn and grow, just as we did. Trust him to make the right decisions for himself."

"So, do you want to tell me what you have done so I know what is going on when I talk to Alexander?" King Frederick asked, a hint of frustration creeping into his voice. He looked at Isabella, seeking clarity amidst the turmoil.

Isabella took a deep breath, her gaze shifting to the

window as she gathered her thoughts. "All I did was send Patricia along with Princess Penelope to America," she confessed, her tone defensive yet tinged with a hint of pride. "I thought it would remind Alexander of how beautiful and sophisticated Princess Penelope is. I mean, how is he to know which one he truly wants if they are oceans apart? I simply wanted him to be able to compare the two choices right before him."

Frederick's expression hardened, the weight of her words settling heavily in the air. "That would explain his anger," he said, shaking his head slowly. "You should not have done that. He needs to make his own decisions without feeling pressured or manipulated."

Isabella felt a pang of regret, her heart sinking as she realized the implications of her actions. "I just wanted what was best for him," she replied, her voice softer now, tinged with guilt. "But I see now that I may have misjudged the situation."

Frederick sighed, running a hand through his hair in frustration. "I have a feeling Patricia may not have done you any favors. It seems that the plan has exploded," he said, his tone serious. "We need to address this before it spirals further out of control."

Isabella nodded, her heart heavy with the weight of her choices. "I never intended to hurt him," she admitted, her voice trembling slightly. "I only wanted to guide him in the right direction."

Frederick stepped closer, placing a reassuring hand on

her shoulder. "I understand your intentions, but we must be careful. Our actions can have consequences we cannot foresee. Let's talk to Alexander together and clear the air. He deserves to know that we support him, no matter what decisions he makes."

Isabella squeezed King Frederick's hand, her eyes reflecting gratitude and admiration. "You are truly a wise king," she said, her voice warm and sincere. "I hope Alexander takes after you."

Frederick smiled softly, the corners of his mouth lifting as he felt the warmth of her affection. "Thank you, my love. It means the world to me to hear you say that," he replied, his heart swelling with pride. "But remember, wisdom comes from experience, and Alexander will find his own way in time."

Chapter 32

Love's Unwritten Story

As the plane landed, Rachel's heart ached with a heavy mix of emotions. The uncertainty of her situation made her stomach twist and knot. She longed for Jacob to be by her side, but doubts crept in. How could she trust him after he had hidden the truth about being a prince all this time? She pushed those feelings back as the plane touched down, telling herself that she had bigger problems to deal with.

Her mind raced with worry about her father. Was he okay? Would he recover from the heart attack? The thought weighed heavily on her, overshadowing everything else. As the plane came to a stop, Rachel took out her phone, her heart pounding in her chest. She needed to reach out; she needed support.

The moment she unlocked her screen, a message from her sister, Sally, flashed before her eyes: "I'm here for you, Sissy." Instantly, tears welled up in Rachel's eyes, a wave of emotion crashing over her. The simple message brought her comfort, a reminder that she wasn't alone in this tumultuous time.

She wiped her eyes, grateful for Sally's unwavering support, and took a deep breath. No matter the uncertainty surrounding Jacob, her father's health, or the secrets that had been revealed, she knew that family would be her anchor. As she prepared to disembark, Rachel made a silent promise to herself: she would face whatever came next with strength and courage, knowing that she had her sister by her side.

Rachel quickly gathered her bag and left the plane, her heart pounding with a whirlwind of emotions. The moment she stepped into the airport, her eyes locked onto Sally's radiant smile, shining like a beacon of hope amidst the chaos. Overcome by relief, Rachel sprinted down the corridor and enveloped her sister in a tight embrace.

"Oh, Sister, I have missed you!" Rachel exclaimed, her voice shaking with emotion as she held Sally close, feeling the warmth and familiarity of her presence.

"I am so happy to see you too," Sally replied, tears streaming down her cheeks, a beautiful mix of joy and worry etched on her face. The sight of her sister's face made Rachel's heart swell, but it also reminded her of the weight they both carried.

After a moment, Rachel pulled back, her eyes searching Sally's face for answers. "How is Father?" she asked, her voice barely above a whisper, the fear tightening in her chest.

"He is stable and in the ICU right now," Sally said, quickly drying her tears, but Rachel could still sense the undercurrent of anxiety in her sister's tone. As those words sank in, Rachel felt a fresh wave of despair wash over her, and tears rushed down her face again, the gravity of their father's situation crashing over her like a tidal wave.

"I just want to be there with him," Rachel murmured,

her heart aching at the thought of their father lying alone in a hospital bed. The helplessness was suffocating.

"Come on, Sis, let's get your bags and get you back home," Sally said softly, wrapping an arm around Rachel's shoulders, grounding her in that moment.

Rachel nodded, grateful for the comfort of Sally's presence. "I feel so lost," she admitted, her voice breaking. "I don't know how to handle all of this."

Sally squeezed her sister's shoulder, her eyes filled with love and determination. "You're not alone in this. We'll face it together like a family. We'll make sure he knows how much we care, and we'll be there for him, just like he's always been there for us."

As they walked through the bustling airport, Rachel found solace in Sally's unwavering support. The bond between them felt unbreakable, and in that moment, she knew that no matter how daunting the challenges ahead seemed, they would navigate through them together, holding onto each other and the love that strengthened them both.

Rachel and Sally made their way through the parking lot, their footsteps echoing in the stillness of the early morning. With each step, Rachel felt a mixture of anxiety and determination swelling inside her. When they reached Sally's pickup, Sally helped Rachel place her bags in the back, the weight of her belongings feeling almost trivial compared to the emotional burden she carried.

As they climbed into the cab, Rachel took a deep breath,

steeling herself for what lay ahead. The engine roared to life, and soon they were barreling down the interstate, the world outside a blur of lights and colors. The rhythmic hum of the tires against the pavement was oddly comforting, a steady heartbeat in the midst of her chaos.

Sally glanced over at Rachel, her expression a blend of concern and strength. "Are you okay?" she asked, her voice gentle and reassuring, cutting through the tension in the air.

Rachel nodded, though her heart felt heavy. "I just can't stop thinking about Dad," she admitted, the words spilling out in a rush. "What if he doesn't recover? What if I never get to tell him how much he means to me?"

Sally reached over, placing a comforting hand on Rachel's knee. "He knows, Rachel, he knows how much you love him. And we're going to be there for him. He's strong, just like you," she said, her voice filled with conviction.

Rachel turned to look out the window, watching the landscape rush by. The trees and buildings blurred into a tapestry of greens and browns, mirroring the swirl of emotions inside her. "I just wish I could take away his pain," she whispered, her voice thick with emotion.

Sally nodded, her grip on the steering wheel tightening a little. "We all do. But being there for him is the best thing we can do right now. We'll show him that he's not alone in this fight."

Rachel felt a flicker of hope ignite within her. Sally's unwavering belief was a balm to her frayed nerves. "You're right. I need to focus on being strong for him, for us," she said, her determination solidifying.

As they continued down the interstate, the weight of the unknown loomed ahead, but the bond between the sisters felt like a shield against the darkness.

As they drove, the rhythmic hum of the engine filled the silence, but Sally's question cut through it. "So, are you still seeing that fella Jacob you've told me so much about?"

Rachel's heart sank at the mention of his name. The thought of discussing Jacob, or Alexander, as he was truly known, felt like a weight pressing down on her chest. She hesitated, the memories of their last fight flooding back, sharp and painful. "It's kinda complicated," she said, her voice catching slightly as she dried her tears. "We had a fight just before I left."

Sally glanced over, concern etched on her face. "It's okay, Rachel. We can talk about it another time," she replied, her tone gentle and understanding. "For now, let's just worry about Dad."

Rachel nodded, grateful for her sister's instinct to steer the conversation away from the turmoil surrounding Jacob. "Thanks, Sally, I just… I don't want to think about anything else right now," she said, her voice trembling.

Sally gave her a reassuring smile, her eyes focused on the road ahead. "I get it. We have enough on our plates without adding more drama. Let's just focus on being there for Dad and supporting each other."

Rachel felt a wave of relief wash over her. Sally's ability to redirect the conversation to their father felt like a lifeline in the turbulent sea of her emotions. They drove on in companionable silence for a while, the weight of unspoken words lingering in the air, but Rachel found comfort in knowing that her sister was by her side.

As they neared the hospital, the glowing lights of the building began to emerge in the distance, casting a soft, reassuring glow against the morning sky. Rachel's heart raced, a mix of anticipation and dread swirling within her. She glanced over at Sally, who was focused on the road, her expression calm yet determined. In that moment, Rachel felt a deep sense of gratitude for her sister's unwavering support.

"Do you remember when we used to sneak into Dad's room to 'borrow' his old books?" Rachel asked, trying to lighten the mood as they pulled into the hospital parking lot. The memories provided a brief distraction from the heaviness in her heart.

Sally chuckled softly, her eyes sparkling with nostalgia. "How could I forget?

Rachel smiled, the warmth of those memories momentarily easing her anxiety. "Yeah, we were so sure we were going to be doctors or lawyers one day. It feels so far away now, doesn't it?" she said, her voice tinged with a hint of sadness.

"Maybe not as far away as you think," Sally replied, her tone encouraging. "You've always had that passion for helping people, just like Dad. You can still follow that dream, Rachel. Dad was so proud of you when he learned that you had passed your finals."

Rachel nodded, appreciating Sally's words, but the reality of their father's condition overshadowed her thoughts. "I just wish he could see how much he means to me right now. I want him to know that he's not alone," she said, her voice breaking slightly.

As they parked the pickup and stepped out, the sounds of the hospital surrounded them, the faint echo of hurried footsteps, the distant beeping of machines, and the low murmur of conversations. It was a world filled with urgency and hope, and it both frightened and comforted Rachel.

Sally took Rachel's hand, giving it a reassuring squeeze. "We'll face this together. Just remember to breathe. He's stable, and that's what matters right now," she said, her voice steady and calming.

Together, they walked toward the entrance, the cool morning air brushing against their skin. Rachel's heart pounded in her chest, each step bringing her closer to the man who had always been their rock. As they entered the hospital, the bright lights and sterile smell enveloped them, a stark reminder of the seriousness of the situation.

They approached the reception desk, and Rachel's nerves began to flutter again. "I hope he's awake," she whispered, her fingers fidgeting with the hem of her shirt.

Sally leaned in closer, her presence a steady anchor. "No matter what, we need to be strong for him. He'll feel our love when he sees us," she said, her eyes full of determination.

After checking in, they were directed to the ICU waiting area. Rachel's heart raced as they made their way down the long corridor. The walls were lined with photographs of families, smiles captured in moments of joy that felt worlds away from their current reality.

When they finally reached the entrance to her father's room, Rachel paused, her hand hovering over the door handle. "What if he's in too much pain? What if he doesn't recognize us?" she asked, the fear creeping back in.

Sally turned to her, eyes softening. "Then we'll be there for him. We'll remind him who he is, who we are, and how much we love him. That's what matters," she said firmly.

Taking a deep breath, Rachel nodded, steeling herself for the moment. She opened the door, and the sight of her father lying in the hospital bed, surrounded by machines, hit her like a wave. But even in his vulnerability, she could see the love and warmth that had always defined him.

"Dad," she whispered, stepping forward with Sally by her side, ready to face whatever came next together.

As Rachel stepped into the room, her eyes locked onto her father, and a rush of emotions flooded her. Max, her father, lay in the hospital bed, his face pale but still radiating warmth. The moment he saw Rachel, a bright smile broke across his face, illuminating the dimness of the room with a beam of joy that cut through the tension.

"Rachel!" he exclaimed, his voice a mixture of surprise

and delight, despite the weakness that lingered in his tone. The sight of his daughter was like a balm to his spirit, and it was clear that seeing her brought him comfort amidst the sterile surroundings.

"Hey, Dad," Rachel replied, her heart swelling at the sight of him. The familiar spark in his eyes made her feel as though she had stepped into a safe haven, even as the reality of the hospital weighed heavily on them all.

Sally moved to Rachel's side, her own expression filled with love and concern as she watched the reunion unfold. "I came as soon as I could," Rachel said softly, stepping closer to her father's bedside.

Max attempted to sit up a little, his smile unwavering. "I'm so glad you're here. I was worried about you," he said, his voice a little hoarse but filled with warmth. The love in his gaze made Rachel's heart ache with both joy and pain.

"Dad, I was so worried about you," Rachel said, her voice thick with emotion. She reached out, taking his hand into hers, feeling the familiar roughness of his skin that had always brought her comfort. "You scared us."

Max chuckled lightly, a sound that seemed to lift the heavy atmosphere in the room. "Just a little hiccup, that's all," he replied, trying to lighten the mood, but Rachel could see the faint shadow of fatigue behind his bravado.

Sally squeezed Rachel's shoulder, offering silent support as they both stood by their father's side. "You're going to be okay, Dad. We're here for you," Sally affirmed, her voice steady as she leaned in for a hug.

Rachel watched as her father embraced Sally, the warmth of the family moment wrapping around them like a comforting blanket. In that instant, the worries and uncertainties seemed to fade away, replaced by the strength of their bond.

As Max released Sally, his gaze shifted back to Rachel, his eyes shining with pride and love. "You two are my greatest treasures. I just need to get better so that I can get back to the farm," he said, a hint of that familiar sparkle returning to his eyes.

Rachel felt tears welling up again, but this time they were tears of hope. "We'll have plenty of time for the farm, Dad. Just focus on getting better. We're right here with you," she promised, squeezing his hand tighter.

Max nodded, the joy of seeing his daughters bringing light to the room. For a moment, the world outside faded away, and in that hospital room, surrounded by love, Rachel felt a flicker of hope ignite within her. They would navigate this challenge together, as a family, and no matter what lay ahead, they would face it hand in hand.

Chapter 33

Between Heartbeats

Meanwhile, back in Utah, the atmosphere in Jacob's home was heavy with unspoken thoughts and simmering emotions. Ivan moved about the kitchen, attempting to keep the air light as he prepared breakfast. The smell of sizzling eggs and freshly brewed coffee filled the space, but the warmth of the moment felt overshadowed by Jacob's lingering sadness.

"I know you miss Rachel, but you have to have faith that if you two are meant to be together, it will happen," Ivan encouraged, glancing over at his friend as he plated the food. He could see the turmoil etched on Jacob's face, the way his brows furrowed in deep thought.

Jacob sighed, running a hand through his hair in frustration. "I just wish I had told her the truth sooner," he confessed, his voice heavy with regret. "Every moment we spent together felt so real, and then I ruined it by hiding who I really am."

Ivan set the plate down in front of Jacob, his expression sympathetic. "You were trying to protect her, Jacob. You thought it was for the best, but now you're both left with this uncertainty. Just remember, it's not too late. You can still make things right," he said, hoping to offer some comfort.

Jacob looked away, his thoughts racing. "I still can't believe Mother sent Patricia and Princess Penelope here. It feels like everything has spiraled out of control," he muttered, frustration coloring his tone. The arrival of his mother's personal representatives had added another layer of complexity to an already complicated situation.

"Maybe it's a sign," Ivan suggested, trying to find a silver lining. "Perhaps it's time to confront your feelings and the reality of who you are. You can't let fear dictate your choices anymore."

Jacob took a moment to absorb Ivan's words, the weight of his friend's wisdom resonating with him. "You're right. I can't keep running from this. I need to talk to Rachel, to explain everything to her," he said, determination flickering in his eyes.

"Exactly," Ivan replied, a small smile breaking through the tension. "And when you do, just be honest. She cares about you, Jacob. She deserves to know the truth."

As they sat together, the breakfast forgotten for a moment, Jacob felt a renewed sense of purpose. He knew the path ahead wouldn't be easy, but the thought of Rachel and the love they shared ignited a fire within him. He needed to fight for that connection, to bridge the gap that had formed between them.

"Thanks, Ivan. I appreciate you being here for me," Jacob said, gratitude lacing his voice.

"Always, my friend. Now, eat up. You'll need your

strength for what's to come," Ivan replied, nudging the plate closer to Jacob with a grin.

"I am going to see Polly today to make things right with her," Ivan announced, determination clear in his voice. He looked at Jacob, gauging his friend's reaction. "Will you be alright here by yourself?"

Jacob nodded, a sense of resolve beginning to settle within him. "Yes, yes, I need to work on my speech for graduation anyway," he replied, forcing a smile to reassure Ivan. "You go and see if you can work things out with Polly."

Ivan studied Jacob for a moment, sensing the weight of everything that had been happening. "You know, if you need anything at all, if you want to talk or if you need help with your speech, just let me know."

Jacob leaned back in his chair, a hint of guilt creeping in. "I'm sorry my situation has caused you so many problems," he said, his tone sincere. He felt the burden of his own turmoil and how it had affected everyone around him, especially his friend.

Ivan waved a hand dismissively, brushing off the apology. "It's not your fault, Jacob. Life gets complicated, and we all have our messes to deal with. What matters is that we're here for each other," he replied, a reassuring smile breaking through his concern.

"Thanks, man," Jacob said, feeling a swell of appreciation for Ivan's unwavering support. "I'll be okay. I just need to focus on what I want to say to Rachel and how to explain everything."

"Exactly. Just speak from your heart," Ivan encouraged, placing a hand on Jacob's shoulder before standing up. "I'll check in later, and I hope everything goes well with Polly. You deserve to find happiness, too."

As Ivan gathered his things and headed for the door, Jacob felt a mix of emotions swirling inside him. He was grateful for Ivan's friendship, but he also felt the weight of his own decisions pressing down on him.

"Good luck, Ivan. I hope you two can work things out," Jacob called out as Ivan stepped outside, the door closing softly behind him.

Alone in the quiet of the house, Jacob took a deep breath, trying to muster the courage he would need for the conversations ahead. He glanced around the room, his eyes landing on his graduation cap and gown hanging on the wall, symbols of both achievement and the uncertainty he now faced.

With renewed determination, he pulled out his notebook and pen, ready to begin working on his speech. He knew he had to confront his feelings, not only for Rachel but also for himself.

As Ivan approached Polly's apartment, he felt a knot tightening in his stomach, each step growing heavier with anticipation. The weight of their unresolved issues hung in the air, and he knew that today was crucial for both of them.

Taking a deep breath, he knocked twice on her door, the sound echoing in the silence of the hallway.

"Coming!" a voice called out from inside, and Ivan's heart raced as he waited. A few moments later, the door swung open, revealing Polly standing there, her expression a mix of surprise and apprehension.

"Hello, Polly," Ivan said, trying to keep his voice steady. "Can I come in?"

"Yes," she replied, her tone cautious but inviting. "You have a lot to answer for," she said with a hint of determination as she motioned for him to step inside.

Ivan stepped into the apartment, the familiar scent of her favorite candles wafting through the air. The space felt both welcoming and charged with tension. He could sense the weight of the conversation that lay ahead.

Polly closed the door behind him and turned to face him, her arms crossed defensively. "I didn't expect to see you today," she said, a mix of emotions flickering across her face. "After everything that happened, I figured you'd want to avoid this."

"I know I haven't been the best at communicating," Ivan admitted, his voice earnest. "But I came here to talk—to explain and hopefully make things right between us."

Polly raised an eyebrow, the skepticism evident in her expression. "You think just talking will fix everything? You left me hanging, Ivan. I felt completely blindsided," she said, her voice rising slightly with frustration.

"I understand that, and I'm really sorry," he replied, his heart racing as he searched for the right words. "I didn't handle things well. I was overwhelmed with everything going on, and I should have been more honest with you about what I was feeling."

Polly's gaze softened slightly, but the hurt was still present. "You could have at least tried to reach out. I felt like I was the only one invested in our relationship."

"I know, and that's my fault," Ivan said, stepping closer, trying to bridge the gap between them. "I realize now how important you are to me, and I want to show you that I'm committed to making this work. I want to be there for you, to support you, and to communicate better."

She studied him for a moment, and Ivan could see the conflict in her eyes. "It's not that easy, Ivan. Trust takes time to rebuild," she said, her voice softening but still guarded.

"I'm willing to put in that time," he replied earnestly. "I care about you, Polly. I don't want to lose what we have because of my mistakes. I want to learn from this and grow together."

Polly sighed, the tension in her shoulders beginning to ease ever so slightly. "I appreciate your honesty, but it's going to take more than just words," she said, her voice firm yet compassionate. "If we're going to move forward, I need to see that you're serious about making changes."

"I promise you, I am," Ivan said, his heart pounding with sincerity. "I'll do whatever it takes to show you that I can be better. I want to understand your needs and be the partner you deserve."

Polly considered his words, her expression shifting as she processed what he was saying. "Okay," she finally said, her voice tentative. "Let's take it one step at a time. But I need you to be all in, Ivan. No more half-measures."

"I'm all in," he affirmed, a sense of relief washing over him. "I won't let you down again."

Polly looked at Ivan, curiosity flickering in her eyes. "So, is your real name Ivan, or do you have another name back where you come from?"

"No, no, my name is Ivan," he replied, shaking his head slightly. "I had to keep Jacob's secret. You see, a lot of women chase after princes like Jacob, not for love but for the privileges of the crown. It's a complicated world."

Polly listened intently, her arms uncrossing as she leaned against the kitchen counter, intrigued by the depth of the situation. "What do you mean?" she asked, wanting to understand more about Jacob's life.

"Jacob and Princess Penelope have known each other since almost birth, but Jacob doesn't love her," Ivan explained, his tone serious. "Rachel has Jacob's heart. Unfortunately, he's required to marry into a proper royal lineage, and that puts him in a difficult position."

"That sounds so unfair," Polly said, her expression softening with sympathy. "So, he's stuck in a situation where he has to choose duty over love?"

Ivan nodded, feeling the weight of the truth in his words. "Exactly. And that's why I suspect Queen Isabella decided to interfere and sent Princess Penelope here. She wants to ensure that Jacob fulfills his royal obligations, regardless of his feelings for Rachel."

Polly frowned, her mind racing with the implications. "That sounds like a lot of pressure for him. No wonder he's been struggling."

"Yes," Ivan agreed, his voice filled with concern. "It's a lot for anyone to bear, especially when love is involved. Jacob is torn between what is expected of him and what he truly wants."

Polly sighed, understanding the complexity of Jacob's predicament more clearly now. "So, what do you think he should do? Just accept what's being thrust upon him?"

Ivan pondered her question for a moment. "It's not that simple. Jacob needs to figure out what he values most. If he truly loves Rachel, he has to find the courage to fight for her, even if it means going against tradition. But that's a huge risk."

Polly nodded, feeling the weight of the situation. "And what about you? You're caught in the middle of this too, helping him keep secrets while trying to navigate your own relationships."

"I've realized that I need to be supportive of Jacob, but I also need to be honest with myself and with you," Ivan said, his voice steady. "I'm here because I care about you, and I don't want my friendship with Jacob to complicate what we have."

Polly looked at him thoughtfully. "I appreciate your honesty, Ivan. It's refreshing to hear you speak so openly about everything. I can see how much you care for Jacob, but I need to know that you're committed to us, too."

"I am," Ivan assured her, sincerity in his eyes. "I want to make this work, and I'll do everything I can to show you that I'm serious about us."

Polly smiled softly, the tension easing further between them. "Okay. Let's take this one step at a time, just like we talked about. I want to be here for you, but I need to see that you're with me too."

"I promise, I'll be here," Ivan said, feeling a sense of hopefulness return. "We'll figure this out together, no matter how complicated things get."

As they stood in the kitchen, the air between them felt lighter, and for the first time in a while, both Ivan and Polly felt a renewed sense of connection.

Ivan leaned on the counter, letting out a light laugh. "You know, things would be easier if Rachel came from a royal family instead of being a farmer's daughter."

"I know," Polly replied, sipping her coffee, a smile tugging at her lips. The thought was amusing, and the warmth of their conversation made the weight of their earlier discussions feel lighter.

"Hey, wait a minute," Polly said, her eyes brightening with sudden inspiration. "What if there's some distant relative who was royalty in her past?"

"I don't know, I guess it depends on how distant the past is," Ivan chuckled, enjoying the playful banter. "But it's an interesting idea."

"Do you know much about Rachel's deceased parents?" Ivan asked, his curiosity piqued.

"Not really," Polly admitted, shaking her head. "But I know that Rachel and I were planning to go downtown and do some research about her family history. Maybe we could dig up something interesting."

Polly's face lit up with enthusiasm. "We could do it together! It would be fun to see what we can uncover about her heritage," she said, a smile spreading across her face.

"Absolutely," Ivan replied, grinning back at her. "Count me in!"

"Well, grab your coat and let's go!" Polly exclaimed, her excitement infectious. She moved to the hallway, quickly retrieving her jacket while Ivan followed suit, his heart racing with anticipation for the adventure ahead.

As they stepped outside, the crisp air greeted them, invigorating and fresh. Polly glanced at Ivan, her eyes sparkling with enthusiasm. "I really think we might find something interesting. You never know what hidden stories are out there."

"Exactly," Ivan replied, feeling a sense of hopefulness. "And who knows? Maybe Rachel's family history could bring her closer to Jacob in a way we never expected."

Chapter 34

The Strength to Choose

As Jacob sat at his cluttered desk, surrounded by scattered papers and half-finished thoughts, he felt the weight of the world pressing down on him. Graduation should have been a time of excitement and hope, yet his heart was heavy with sorrow and regret. His mind was consumed by thoughts of Rachel, her laughter echoing in his ears like a haunting melody. He longed to turn back time, to find the courage to reveal his true self to her. How different things might have been if he had just spoken the truth! The image of her face when she had seen Patricia and Princess Penelope flashed in his mind, the hurt and confusion in her eyes cutting deeper than any royal duty ever could.

The burden of being the crown prince of Slovitia felt like a relentless storm raging inside him, each thunderclap a reminder of the expectations he could never escape. His mother's persistent insistence on a royal union loomed over him like a dark shadow, suffocating his spirit and turning what should have been a celebratory moment into a suffocating burden.

Suddenly, the doorbell rang, a sharp sound that pierced through the silence and shattered his thoughts. Jacob took a deep, shaky breath, trying to steady the whirlwind of emotions swirling within him. As he approached the door, anxiety gripped him, each step heavier than the last. When he finally opened it, he was met with the sight of Patricia, her expression a mix of annoyance and superiority, standing alongside the innocent Princess Penelope, whose wide eyes sparkled with unearned curiosity.

"Jacob Alexander," Patricia scolded, her voice slicing through the air like a blade, filled with a sharpness that sent a chill down his spine. "Are you going to invite us in, or just stand there like a statue?"

"What do you want, Patricia? Haven't you done enough to ruin my life today?" Jacob snapped, his voice cracking as frustration and pain bubbled to the surface. The heat of anger flushed his cheeks, but beneath it lay a deep vulnerability, a fear of losing everything he held dear.

Patricia brushed past him with a dismissive wave, her presence filling the room with an oppressive air of authority that made him feel small and powerless. "This is no way for a royal prince to behave, especially not the crown prince," she declared, her tone dripping with condescension, as if she reveled in his discomfort.

She took Princess Penelope by the hand, leading her further into his home as if it were her domain, leaving Jacob standing at the threshold, frozen in a whirlwind of emotions.

He felt his heart racing, the walls of his sanctuary closing in around him, each breath becoming harder to take. The chaos that was unfolding felt like an impending storm, and he grappled with a desperate need to break free from the shackles of his royal identity, even if just for a fleeting moment. How could he make them understand the turmoil within him? How could he escape the suffocating expectations that threatened to drown him? In that moment, all he wanted was to be seen for who he truly was, just Jacob, not the crown prince of Slovitia.

As Jacob stood at the threshold, watching Patricia and Princess Penelope invade his space, a mix of emotions churned within him like a tempest. The air felt thick, heavy with unvoiced words and unfulfilled dreams. He fought the urge to slam the door and retreat to the safety of his room, where he could drown his sorrows in solitude. But he knew that wouldn't solve anything; the reality of his life, the expectations that chained him to a destiny he hadn't chosen, wouldn't just disappear.

Patricia turned, a triumphant smirk on her face as she surveyed his modest town home, a stark contrast to the opulence of royal life. "You really should take better care of your surroundings, Jacob. A crown prince's quarters should reflect his status," she said, her voice dripping with disdain. Each word felt like a dagger, twisting in his chest. It reminded him of how trapped he was, how every facet of his life was scrutinized under the unforgiving gaze of tradition and expectation.

Princess Penelope, blissfully unaware of the tension, began to explore the living room, her small fingers tracing the outline of a family photo on the mantel. Jacob's heart ached at the sight; there was a time when he felt free, before the responsibilities of royalty weighed him down. He remembered sitting and studying in the library with Rachel, laughter spilling from his lips as he studied with Rachel, their bond untainted by the constraints of his title. Those memories felt like a distant dream now, overshadowed by the looming pressures of royal duty.

"Honestly, Alexander," Patricia continued, her voice snapping him back to the present, "you need to start acting like the prince you are. Your indecision is embarrassing, and it's time you embraced your role. The kingdom deserves a strong leader, not a brooding boy lost in his thoughts."

Her words ignited a fire within him, a mix of anger and despair. "You don't understand," he replied, his voice rising. "You don't know what it's like to be trapped in a life that isn't yours. Every choice I make feels like it's already been decided for me."

Patricia's eyes narrowed, the smirk growing as she relished the gravity of his turmoil. "What do you mean?"

"I mean," Jacob said, his voice trembling with emotion, "that I want to live my life on my own terms. I want to love who I choose, to be more than just a title. I want to be Jacob, not just the crown prince."

For a moment, silence hung in the air, thick and palpable. Jacob's heart raced as he laid bare his feelings, exposing the vulnerability he had kept hidden for so long. He watched as Patricia's expression shifted from annoyance to something more contemplative, perhaps even sympathetic.

Princess Penelope, sensing the tension, turned to Jacob,

her innocent gaze piercing through the heaviness. "But you're the prince, Alexander! You're supposed to protect the kingdom, and that is a life of duty," she said, her voice filled with a childlike sincerity that made his heart ache even more.

He knelt down to her level, searching for the right words. "I want to make everyone happy, Princess. But I also have to be true to myself. If I can't do that, then how can I be a good king?"

Patricia crossed her arms, considering his words. "You're young, Alexander. You'll learn that sometimes duty comes first."

Patricia glared at Alexander, her eyes narrowing with a mix of frustration and determination. "You've had your adventure here in America," she said, her voice steady but laced with urgency. "Now it's time to set aside these foolish and childish feelings and accept the responsibility of the crown. You must marry for advantage, that is what royals do."

Jacob felt a stab of indignation rise within him. "You think I want to be a pawn in some political game?" he retorted, his voice rising slightly. "What about love? What about happiness?"

Patricia waved her hand dismissively, her expression hardening. "You and Princess Penelope were born to be together for the sake of both your kingdoms. This isn't just about you, Alexander. It's about the future of Slovitia and the alliances we must forge. A royal life has its sacrifices, and you must learn to embrace that."

"Sacrifices?" Jacob echoed, incredulity flooding his voice. "You mean sacrificing my chance at real happiness? My chance to choose who I love?" He took a step closer, his heart pounding with emotion. "You don't understand what it's like to feel so trapped. All I see is a life dictated by duty, with no room for personal desire."

Patricia's gaze hardened further, her resolve unwavering. "And what about this mere commoner? What stability or benefits does she offer the kingdom? None, I tell you!" Her voice rose, edged with the fervor of her convictions. "She's not of our world, Alexander. She can't bring the alliances, the power, or the respect that we need. You must think beyond your heart and consider the greater good."

His heart sank at her words, a mixture of anger and sorrow swirling within him. "You're reducing everything to politics and power, Patricia. What about the people? What about the love they deserve to see in their future king?"

Patricia crossed her arms, her expression unyielding. "Love doesn't save kingdoms. Duty does. You need to rise above your emotions and see the bigger picture. You were raised for this, Alexander, you know what's at stake."

Jacob's fists clenched at his sides as he battled with his thoughts. The weight of her words felt suffocating, but he couldn't shake the feeling that there had to be a way to honor both his heart and his duty. "You act as if I'm not capable of being a good king while still being true to myself. But what kind of king would I be if I couldn't be honest about who I am?"

"An ineffective one," Patricia shot back, her tone sharp as a whip. "You need to show strength, not weakness. You need to be decisive, not lost in this fantasy of romance. The crown is not just a title; it's a responsibility that requires sacrifice."

Jacob took a deep breath, trying to rein in his emotions. "And what if my sacrifice means living a life devoid of love? What if I can't be the king my people need without being true to myself?"

A silence fell between them, thick with tension. Jacob could see the flicker of uncertainty in Patricia's gaze, a crack in her armor. She was unwavering in her beliefs, but perhaps, just perhaps, there was room for compromise in her rigid worldview.

"Look," he said, softening his tone, "I understand the importance of duty. But I believe that a ruler can find strength in love, not just in obligation. Can't we find a way to honor both?"

Patricia opened her mouth, then hesitated, her fierce expression faltering as she considered his words. "You're asking for a lot, Alexander. The world doesn't work that way."

"Maybe it should," he replied, his voice steady. "Perhaps if we lead with our hearts, we can inspire our people in ways we never imagined."

Princess Penelope approached Jacob, her eyes sparkling

with nostalgia. "Don't you remember the fun times we had at the palace?" she asked, her voice bright with the innocence of their childhood. "Running around the garden while our parents attended to their royal duties? Those were the best days!"

Jacob took her hand gently, a wave of warmth flooding through him as memories of their laughter and carefree days washed over him. "We were eight, Princess," he said, his gaze locking onto hers with a seriousness that belied their lighthearted past. "But let me ask you something, would you still want me if I were not a prince?"

Her brow furrowed in confusion as she searched his eyes for meaning. "What do you mean?"

"If I were to forsake being a prince, to leave behind the life of the royal court, would you come to live with me here in America?" he asked, his voice steady yet filled with an underlying vulnerability.

Princess Penelope looked at him, her expression shifting from curiosity to disbelief. "That is ridiculous!" she laughed, shaking her head. "You are the crown prince of Slovitia! Why would you not want to enjoy a royal life?"

Jacob squeezed her hand tighter, a surge of emotion coursing through him. "Answer me, Penelope. If I were to give up my royal life and choose to live here, would you come with me?"

She chuckled, her laughter light but tinged with an edge of concern. "No, no, you're acting silly! Of course not! You need to stop this foolishness and come back to accept your role as the crown prince of Slovitia."

As her words sank in, Jacob felt a sharp pang of disappointment. He released her hand, the warmth of their connection fading into the air between them. "That's why I can't be with you," he said quietly, his heart heavy. "My title means more to you than I do."

He turned away, walking back toward the door, the weight of her laughter ringing in his ears like a painful reminder of the divide between them. He felt the sting of tears threatening to surface, but he fought them back, unwilling to show the vulnerability that came with his heartache.

"Alexander, wait!" Princess Penelope called out, her voice laced with urgency. He paused, but didn't turn around. "I didn't mean it like that. I just… I don't understand why you would want to give up everything."

"Everything?" he echoed, his back still turned to her. "You see it as everything, but to me, it feels like a cage. A life dictated by duty, where my heart has no say. I want more than just a title and a throne. I want to live, Penelope, truly live."

Silence fell between them, and Jacob could feel her presence behind him, a mixture of confusion and concern. He knew she cared for him, but he also knew that her upbringing had shaped her views on duty and loyalty in ways he couldn't fully accept.

"Alexander," she said softly, "I don't want to lose you. But you have to understand the importance of your role. You're meant to lead."

"And I can't lead if I'm not being true to myself," he replied, finally turning to face her. "If I'm just fulfilling a role, then I'm not the leader my people deserve. I need to find my own path, even if it means stepping away from the crown."

Her eyes shimmered with unshed tears, and for a moment, they stood in silence, each lost in their own thoughts. Jacob felt his heart ache for the bond they once shared, but he also knew that it was time to make a choice, one that aligned with his true self, even if it meant walking away from the life he had always known.

As Jacob stood at the door, the weight of his decision pressing down on him, Princess Penelope took a step closer, her voice trembling slightly. "Alexander, please don't do this. You can't just walk away from your responsibilities. You're meant to lead Slovitia!"

He turned to face her, his heart racing. "And what kind of leader would I be if I'm not true to myself? I can't wear a crown that doesn't fit, Penelope. You know that."

"But you are the crown prince! You have a duty to your people!" she insisted, her frustration bubbling to the surface. "They're counting on you to be strong, to make the right choices. You can't just abandon them for… for what? A fantasy?"

"It's not a fantasy!" Jacob exclaimed, his voice rising. "It's my life! I want to live it, not as a puppet on strings. I want to find love, real love, not one arranged for political gain."

Princess Penelope crossed her arms, her expression a mix of anger and hurt. "So you think Rachel is some kind of fairy tale? You think she can give you the stability and respect you need as a king?"

Jacob's chest tightened at her words. "It's not just about that. It's about having someone who sees me for who I am, not just my title. Someone who loves me, not what I represent."

"Alexander, think about your legacy!" she pleaded, her voice softening. "What will you leave behind if you turn your back on your royal duties? A king must think of the future. You have the chance to unite our kingdoms, to bring peace and prosperity."

"And what if I'm miserable while doing it?" he shot back, exasperated. "What if I end up resenting everything, even you? I can't lead with a heart full of regret!"

Penelope stepped forward, her eyes searching his. "But you don't have to do this alone. You can have both! You can be with me and still fulfill your duties. You just have to find a way to balance it. We can learn to love each other, even as our parents. "

Jacob shook his head, frustration boiling over. "You don't get it! This isn't just about finding a balance; it's about being true to who I am. I can't pretend to be someone I'm not. If I marry for political gain, I'll always wonder what could have been."

"Isn't that selfish?" she asked, her voice breaking. "What about the people who look up to you? What about the sacrifices that come with being royal? You were raised for this!"

"And I've had enough of being raised for it!" Jacob shot back, his voice thick with emotion. "I've spent my whole life being groomed for a role that doesn't reflect who I truly am. I'm tired of living for everyone else's expectations."

Princess Penelope's expression softened, her eyes glistening with unshed tears. "I don't want to lose you, Alexander. I've always admired you, not just as a prince but as my friend. I thought we would face this together."

Jacob's heart ached at her words, the bond they once shared hanging by a thread. "I care about you, too, Penelope. But I can't be the person you want me to be. I need to find my own path. If that means stepping away from the crown, then so be it."

"Can't you at least give it a chance?" she implored, her voice wavering. "Come back, try to embrace your role. You might find that you can be happy in it, or at least find a way to make it work."

He sighed, the weight of her words pressing down on him. "Maybe I need to find out who I am outside of that life first. I can't make decisions based on what everyone else wants anymore."

"Alexander …" she began, but he could see the struggle in her eyes.

"Please, Penelope," he said gently, "understand that this is not just about me. It's about my future, my happiness. I hope one day you can see that."

With a heavy heart, Jacob opened the door wider, motioning for Patricia and Princess Penelope to leave. "I think it's best if you both go," he said, his voice steady despite the turmoil inside him. "I need time to think without the weight of your expectations hanging over me."

Patricia bristled, her expression a mix of disbelief and irritation. "You can't be serious, Alexander! You're throwing away everything for a whim. This is not how a prince behaves!"

"I'm not throwing anything away," Jacob countered, his voice firm. "I'm trying to find myself, to figure out what I truly want. And right now, that doesn't include the crown or the royal court."

Princess Penelope shifted uncomfortably, glancing between Alexander and Patricia. "Alexander, please don't do this," she pleaded, her eyes filled with a mix of concern and sadness. "We're only trying to help you see the bigger picture."

"The bigger picture?" Jacob echoed, a hint of bitterness creeping into his tone. "The bigger picture is that I'm suffocating under the weight of expectations that don't reflect who I am. I can't be your prince if I'm not being true to myself."

Patricia stepped forward, her voice lowering to a more serious tone. "You need to understand the consequences of your actions, Alexander. Walking away from your responsibilities could have repercussions not just for you, but for your entire kingdom."

Jacob met her gaze, his resolve unwavering. "I understand the stakes, Patricia. But I refuse to live a life dictated by fear and obligation. I have to make my own choices, even if they're difficult."

"Fine," Patricia said, her frustration palpable as she crossed her arms. "But don't say I didn't warn you when things go awry. The crown is not just a title; it's a commitment to your people."

"I know that," Jacob replied, a hint of sadness in his voice. "But right now, I need to be committed to myself. Please, just go."

Penelope stepped closer to him, her voice trembling. "Jacob, I don't want to lose you. You mean so much to me, and I don't want to see you throw everything away."

Jacob's heart ached at her words, but he knew he had to stay firm. "I'm not throwing it away, Princess. I'm trying to find a way to build a life that I can be proud of. If that means stepping away from the crown, then so be it."

She looked down, her shoulders slumping as the reality of his words settled in. "I just... I wish things were different," she whispered, her voice barely above a breath.

"I do too," Jacob said softly, his heart breaking for the friendship they once shared. "But I need to do this for me. I hope you can understand that one day."

With a heavy silence hanging in the air, Patricia finally turned toward the door, her expression a mixture of annoyance and resignation. "Come along, Princess Penelope," she said, her tone clipped. "We're leaving."

As they stepped outside, Jacob felt a mix of relief and sorrow wash over him. He watched as they walked away, their figures growing smaller against the backdrop of his home. He knew he was making a difficult choice, but deep down, he felt a spark of hope igniting within him, a hope for a future where he could be true to himself.

As the door closed behind them, Jacob leaned against it, taking a deep breath. The weight of their departure settled heavily on his shoulders, but he also felt a flicker of freedom.

Chapter 35

Unveiling the Past

Meanwhile, in the bustling heart of downtown, Ivan and Polly stepped into the genealogy research center, both feeling a thrill of anticipation coursing through them. The air was thick with the sounds of enthusiastic conversations, as fellow visitors shared their hopes of uncovering their family histories. Each story resonated with the desire for connection, filling Polly with an exhilarating sense of possibility.

Amidst the crowd, an older woman named Sophia approached them, her kind eyes sparkling with understanding. "Hello there! How may I assist you today?" she asked, her voice a soothing melody in the lively atmosphere.

Polly's heart raced as she responded, "We were hoping you could help us discover more about our family heritage." Her voice trembled slightly with excitement. "I've always wanted to know where I come from."

Sophia smiled warmly. "Of course! I love helping people connect with their roots. What do you already know about your family history?"

Ivan, feeling a mix of excitement and nervousness, chimed in, "Not much, really. Just a few names passed down through my family." He glanced at Polly, who was practically vibrating with enthusiasm. "But Polly's really keen to find out more."

Polly nodded eagerly. "I've heard stories from my grandmother about our ancestors, but I want to dig deeper and see if I can find any records."

Sophia nodded knowingly. "It's a wonderful journey. Let me show you how to navigate our database. It's filled with stories waiting to be uncovered." She led them to a computer station, and Polly leaned in closer, her eyes wide with anticipation.

As Sophia began explaining the system, Polly interrupted, "What if we find someone famous in our family? I mean, that would be amazing, right?"

Ivan chuckled, "Or maybe we'll find out we're descended from royalty! Wouldn't that be something?"

Sophia smiled, "You never know! Let's start with what you do have. Do you know your grandparents' names?"

Polly quickly replied, "Yes! My grandmother's name was Margaret, and my grandfather was Henry Harris."

"Great! Let's start there," Sophia said, her fingers deftly typing into the computer. "Now, let's see what we can find about them."

After several minutes of instruction, Polly and Ivan exchanged glances filled with excitement. "Okay, I'm ready," Polly said, her voice barely containing her eagerness.

"Let's see what's out there!"

Ivan nodded, "Yeah, let's do this!" He took a deep breath, feeling the weight of history pressing down around them. As they began typing, Polly leaned closer to the screen, her heart pounding with anticipation.

"Look!" Polly exclaimed, pointing at the screen. "I think I found a record of my grandmother's birth!"

Ivan leaned in, his excitement palpable. "That's incredible! What does it say?"

Polly read aloud, her voice trembling with emotion. "It says she was born in 1920, in a small town in Ohio. Oh, I can't believe this!" Her eyes sparkled with joy. "I'm really discovering my family!"

Sophia watched them with a smile, sensing the bond growing between the two as they navigated this journey together. "Keep exploring, and remember, every name you find is a story waiting to be told."

As they continued their search, Polly felt a rush of connection to her ancestors, while Ivan marveled at the unfolding tapestry of history that was now coming to life before them. "This is amazing," he said, his voice filled with awe.

As they experimented with the database, Polly and Ivan decided to search for Rachel's lineage. "What was Rachel's mother's name?" Ivan asked, curiosity sparking in his eyes.

Polly furrowed her brow in thought. "I think it was

Elizabeth," she replied, her fingers flying over the keyboard as she typed it in. "Let's see what we can find."

Ivan leaned closer, his voice filled with hope. "Do you know when she was born?"

Polly shook her head, her expression turning somber. "No, I never bothered to ask. All I know is that they were killed in a car accident in New York City." As the weight of her words settled in, both their faces fell, disappointment washing over them.

Ivan sighed, feeling a twinge of sadness. "That's really tough. I wish we could have found something happier."

Polly nodded, her heart heavy. "Yeah, it was a good idea," she said, her voice tinged with disappointment. "I guess we will have to dig a little deeper ourselves if we are to help our friends."

"Don't give up, Polly," Ivan encouraged, trying to lift her spirits. "I'll play detective and find out more. We can dig deeper into Elizabeth's life and see if we can uncover anything about her past."

Then, as they continued their search, an idea sparked in Ivan's mind. "Wait a minute," he said, a glimmer of excitement in his eyes. "The court has royal historians who specialize in this kind of research. They do this all the time! Maybe I can enlist their help."

Polly's eyebrows shot up, intrigued. "Really? Do you think they would be willing to assist us?"

"Why not?" Ivan replied, his confidence growing. "If we can present our case clearly, they might find it interesting. After all, uncovering family histories is what they do best!"

Polly's face lit up with renewed hope. "That sounds like a fantastic idea! If anyone could help us trace Rachel's lineage, it would be them."

Ivan nodded, already formulating a plan. "I'll reach out to them and see what resources they have. They might have access to records we wouldn't be able to find on our own."

Polly leaned closer, her eyes sparkling with excitement. "This could really work! Imagine if we could get in touch with someone who knows how to dig deep into the archives. It might lead us to something incredible about Elizabeth."

"Exactly!" Ivan said, his enthusiasm contagious. "I'll draft an email as soon as I get back home, outlining what we're looking for. We just need to be clear about Rachel's family and the tragedy that struck."

Polly nodded vigorously. "And we can include everything we've found so far! That way, they have context. I can help with the details and make sure we don't miss anything important."

As they worked together to outline their approach, the atmosphere shifted from disappointment to determination. They felt invigorated by the prospect of enlisting the help of experts who could shed light on a story that had long remained shrouded in darkness.

"Let's do this," Ivan said, a fire of resolve in his voice. "We're going to uncover the truth, no matter what it takes."

Polly smiled, her confidence renewed. "Together, we can make it happen! I can't wait to see what we find."

Chapter 36

Facing the Storm

In Tennessee, the sun shone brightly as Max finally made his way home, having been released from the hospital after his recovery. Sally and Polly were practically bubbling with excitement, their hearts light at the thought of having their dad back where he belonged. Meanwhile, Max's wife, Kathy, had been busy preparing the house, ensuring everything was perfect for his return.

As Polly and Rachel drove Max home, the familiar roads flashed by, and Max gazed out the window, taking in the scenery. "Wow, everything looks so different from the back seat," he chuckled, a hint of nostalgia in his voice.

"I'm glad to see you still have your sense of humor," Rachel replied, her laughter mingling with his, lightening the mood.

Max smiled, a genuine warmth radiating from him. "I don't believe I've ever ridden in the back of my own car before," he said, his tone playful, though a glimmer of seriousness lingered beneath.

Rachel glanced at him, feeling a mixture of joy and concern. She knew that the heart attack had changed everything for her dad; life would be different now. "It's just a new chapter, Dad. We're all here for you," she reassured, her voice steady but filled with emotion.

Max turned to face his daughters, his eyes softening. "I know, and I appreciate it more than you can imagine. I wouldn't want to go through this without you two by my side."

Sally, sitting in the front seat, chimed in, "We've got your back, Dad. Together, we'll make sure you take it easy from now on." Her determination echoed the love they all shared. As they continued their drive, the laughter and warmth filled the car, but Rachel couldn't shake the feeling that their lives were now intertwined with new challenges. She glanced at Max, noticing how his demeanor was slightly more reserved, the weight of his experience evident in the lines etched on his face.

"Just remember, we'll take it one day at a time," Rachel added softly, wishing to lift the burden of worry off his shoulders. "You've got a whole team of us to help you adjust."

Max nodded, gratitude shining in his eyes. "Thank you, girls. It means the world to know I'm not in this alone."

As they pulled onto the long dirt road leading to the farm, delicate snowflakes began to fall gently upon the car, creating a serene and picturesque scene. Polly glanced out the window, marveling at the way the white flakes danced in the air, blanketing the landscape in a soft layer of winter beauty. "Looks like we made it back just in time," she remarked, her voice filled with a sense of wonder.

Rachel nodded, her gaze fixed on the familiar surroundings. The vibrant leaves that once adorned the trees had long since fallen, leaving behind bare branches that swayed gently in the crisp breeze, testifying to the impending winter. "It's beautiful in its own way," she said, a hint of nostalgia in her voice. "It feels like it's preparing to be a long, cold winter."

Max smiled, taking in the sight with a mixture of appreciation and reflection. "You know, there's something peaceful about this time of year," he said, his voice steady despite the changes he faced. "The quiet of the snow can be comforting."

Sally, feeling a sense of warmth and unity, added, "It's like nature's way of telling us to slow down and appreciate what we have. We're all together again, and that's what matters most."

As they drove further down the road, the familiar sights of the farm came into view, each landmark sparking memories of laughter, hard work, and love. The barn stood proudly against the winter sky, its red paint a vibrant contrast to the white landscape. Max felt a wave of gratitude wash over him, reminding him of the strength of family and the support that surrounded him.

Rachel turned to her father, her heart swelling with affection. "We made it home, Dad."

Max nodded, feeling the warmth of his daughters' words wrap around him like a comforting blanket. "I couldn't ask for anything more," he replied, his voice filled with sincerity. "Being back here with you all is the best gift I could have ever hoped for."

As they parked the car and stepped out into the crisp winter air, the crunch of snow beneath their boots echoed around them.

As the car doors opened, Kathy burst out of the house, her face lighting up with joy at the sight of Max. "Oh, how I have missed you, my love!" she exclaimed, rushing toward him with open arms. She enveloped him in a tight hug, her heart swelling with relief and happiness.

Max wrapped his arms around her, feeling the warmth of her embrace chase away the lingering chill from the winter air. "I missed you too, Dear," he said, his voice thick with emotion. The comfort of her presence reminded him of the love that had always been a cornerstone of his life.

With a gentle smile, Kathy took Max by the arm, guiding him carefully toward the house. "Let's get you settled in," she said, her voice tender as she led him inside. The familiar scents of home enveloped them, and Max felt a wave of familiarity wash over him.

Once inside, Kathy helped Max to his recliner, a cozy spot that had always been his favorite. "Here you go, right where you belong," she said, adjusting the blanket over his lap with a soft touch. She looked into his eyes, concern mingling with love. "You take it easy now. I'll get you something warm to drink."

Max settled into the recliner, sinking into the comfort of the chair that had cradled him through many seasons. "Thank you, my love. It feels so good to be home," he replied, his voice steady but filled with emotion.

As she moved to the kitchen, Polly and Rachel exchanged a glance, both feeling the palpable bond between their parents. "They're so happy to have each other back," Rachel whispered, her heart swelling with warmth.

Polly nodded, her smile reflecting the joy in the room. "It's beautiful to see, especially after everything that's happened. They deserve this moment."

Kathy returned with a steaming cup of coffee, carefully handing it to Max. "Here you go, just how you like it," she said, her eyes sparkling with affection. As he took a sip, the warmth spread through him, bringing a sense of comfort that only home could provide.

Max looked up at Kathy, his gratitude evident. "You always know how to take care of me," he said softly, his heart full.

Kathy smiled, brushing a strand of hair behind her ear. "It's what we do for each other, right? We're a team."

As Rachel stood watching her parents, Max comfortably tucked into his recliner with Kathy beside him, a wave of warmth washed over her. The sight brought a smile to her face, filled with love and nostalgia for the moments they had shared. "I think I will walk down to the mailbox and get the mail," she announced, pulling on her coat.

Sally looked up from the kitchen, a smile spreading across her face. "Okay, how about I fix us some hot chocolate to sip on when you get back?"

"Oh, that would just make my day," Rachel replied, her

smile brightening even more as she stepped outside into the crisp winter air.

As she walked down the long dirt driveway toward the mailbox beside the main road, the gentle snowflakes continued to fall, creating a serene blanket over the landscape. The quiet of the moment wrapped around her, but as she reached the mailbox and pulled it open, her heart began to race.

Inside, she found a handful of bills, and as she flipped through them, her stomach dropped. Stamped on several of the envelopes were the ominous words "past due" and "final notice." Each one felt like a weight pressing down on her chest.

"Why didn't they tell me they were struggling?" Rachel whispered to herself, her voice barely audible over the soft sound of snow settling around her. The realization hit her like a cold wave, and she felt a mix of concern and frustration.

She stood there for a moment, the world around her fading away as she processed the news. How could they be facing such challenges without confiding in her? A sense of urgency began to build within her. She wanted to protect her family, to offer help and support, but how could she do that if they kept this burden to themselves?

With a deep breath, Rachel turned back toward the house, the bills clutched tightly in her hand. As she walked, her mind raced with thoughts of how she could approach Max and Kathy. She wanted to be there for them, to reassure them that they didn't have to face this alone.

When she finally stepped back inside, the warmth of the house enveloped her, but the weight of the mail lingered heavily in her heart. "Sally, can you help me with something?" Rachel called out, her voice steady despite the turmoil she felt inside.

Sally looked up from the kitchen, concern etching her features. "Of course! What's wrong?" Rachel handed the stack of overdue bills to Sally, her hands trembling slightly.

"Did you know that Mom and Dad were in financial trouble?" she asked, her voice barely above a whisper.

Sally took the bills, her expression shifting to one of concern. "I knew things were a little tight," she admitted, glancing down at the ominous stamps. "It hasn't been the best year for the farm."

Rachel felt a sinking feeling in her stomach. "But why didn't they tell me? I had no idea," she said, struggling to hold back her tears. The weight of the situation pressed heavily on her chest, making it hard to breathe.

Sally sighed, a hint of sadness in her eyes. "You know, Dad. He always wanted to do what was right. He wanted someone in the family to get a college education. He thought if he could help, it would make a difference."

Rachel's heart ached as she processed this new information. "I had no idea he took out a loan on the farm to help pay for my college," she said, her voice trembling. "He shouldn't have had to do that for me."

Sally put a reassuring hand on Rachel's shoulder. "You were always the smart one, and Dad knew it. He believed in you and wanted you to have opportunities he didn't. But now… what will they do?"

The weight of uncertainty pressed down on Rachel like an anchor. "I don't know," she replied, her voice filled with worry. "What if they lose the farm? This is everything to them."

Sally nodded, her brow furrowed with concern. "We need to talk to them. Maybe we can figure something out together. They don't have to face this alone."

Rachel wiped away a tear that had escaped, her resolve settling in. "You're right. We have to support them, no matter what. We're a family, and we'll find a way through this together."

"I guess it's time to put this college education to work," Rachel said, a determined smile forming on her lips despite the heavy weight of the situation. "I'll go down to the bank tomorrow and see if I can't get an extension. After all, Christmas is just a few weeks away. They wouldn't foreclose on the farm right before Christmas, would they?"

Sally looked down at the foreclosure letter in her hands, her heart racing with anxiety. "I hope not," she replied, her voice trembling as she tried to restrain her tears. "That would be so cruel. But… what if they do? What if we can't stop it?"

Rachel placed a comforting hand on her sister's shoulder, attempting to instill a sense of hope. "We won't let that happen. I'll talk to the bank manager and explain everything. There must be some way to buy us some time. We just have to be honest with them about our situation."

Sally nodded, though her eyes glistened with worry. "I just hate that Mom and Dad are already dealing with so much, and now this. They deserve to enjoy Christmas without this hanging over their heads."

"Exactly," Rachel said, her voice firm with resolve. "We can't let this ruin their holiday. We'll find a way to help them. We're stronger together, and we can figure this out."

Taking a deep breath, Rachel felt a surge of determination. She knew this was a critical moment, and she was ready to step up for her family. "Let's come up with a plan tonight. We can brainstorm ideas on how to support them, and I'll start with the bank tomorrow."

Sally wiped away a stray tear and managed a small smile. "Okay. Let's do it together. We'll make sure they know they're not alone in this."

Chapter 37

Shattered Dreams

As the days slipped by following graduation, Jacob found himself ensnared by memories of Rachel, each thought a bittersweet reminder of what once was. King Frederick and Queen Isabella, deeply concerned for their son, made every effort to divert his attention from the heartache that seemed to envelop him.

"I believe it's time for you to come home now, Alexander," Queen Isabella urged, her voice soft yet firm. "It's essential to set this chapter behind you and embrace the future."

"Mother, I'm not sure I ever want to return," he snapped back, frustration and sorrow intertwining in his tone.

King Frederick felt an overwhelming sense of empathy for Alexander, his heart aching at the sight of his son's grief. He could perceive the depth of love Alexander held for Rachel, a love that now felt like a heavy weight upon his shoulders. "Isabella, let him come home when he's ready," he said, his tone imbued with compassion. "We will be here for you, Alexander, whenever you choose to return."

"I feel like I can't win with you two," Queen Isabella interjected, a mix of exasperation and love evident in her words.

"Thank you, Father," Alexander replied, gratitude mingling with sorrow in his voice. "Your understanding means a lot to me."

"I was a young man once, too, facing my own trials," the king said, his voice a soothing balm to Alexander's fractured heart, offering a glimmer of hope amidst the shadows of despair.

After ending the call with his parents, Alexander sat in solitude, his gaze fixed on the soft, swirling snowflakes that drifted down outside the window. The world beyond was transformed into a serene white canvas, yet inside, he felt a heavy storm brewing in his heart. The silence enveloped him, amplifying the ache of longing for Rachel, whose absence felt like a gaping void in his life.

A few minutes later, Ivan bounded down the stairs with an infectious energy that momentarily broke the spell of melancholy. "You're up early again this morning, Jacob," he exclaimed, his voice bright and buoyant as he entered the kitchen. "Have you heard from Rachel?"

"Nothing today," Jacob replied, his voice tinged with sorrow, each word laced with the weight of his concern. "I know she's going through so much right now, and it makes me feel so useless and powerless to help her." The helplessness gnawed at him, a relentless reminder of his desire to support her in her struggles.

Polly had been their lifeline, providing updates about Rachel's family issues, but the information felt inadequate in alleviating their worries. Ivan leaned against the counter, his brow furrowed with empathy. "It will be alright, Jacob. You just have to be patient and give Rachel some space to figure this out on her own," he reassured, rummaging through the fridge in search of ingredients.

In an effort to uplift the atmosphere, Ivan added, "How about I make us some omelets?" His enthusiasm was palpable, a welcome distraction from the heavy air that lingered.

Jacob couldn't help but smile at his friend's initiative, grateful for his unwavering support. "Thanks, Ivan, that sounds great," he replied, feeling a flicker of warmth in the midst of his worries. "Maybe after that, we can swing by Polly's and see if she has any news about Rachel."

"I think that's a fantastic idea," Ivan agreed, his voice brightening as he grabbed eggs and vegetables from the fridge. As he began to cook, the sunlight streamed through the kitchen window, casting a warm glow and gentle shadows across Ivan's smooth, chiseled chest. The scene was almost cinematic, a stark contrast to the heaviness in Jacob's heart.

The sizzling sound of eggs in the pan filled the room, mingling with the aroma of fresh herbs, creating a comforting ambiance that slowly began to ease Jacob's anxiety. In that moment, surrounded by the warmth of friendship and the simple joy of cooking, he felt a sense of connection that reminded him he was not alone in his struggles.

Rachel threw herself into a whirlwind of activity,

hoping to silence the turmoil that roiled within her. Each morning, as the sun peeked through her window, she awoke feeling as if her heart were shattering into a thousand pieces, memories of Jacob crashing into her like waves against a rocky shore.

His laughter echoed in her ears, his smile burned in her mind, and she ached for the warmth of his presence. Yet a bitter sting of betrayal lingered in the air between them. How could she trust him when his faith in her felt so tenuous, so easily shaken?

In the quiet hours of the night, when the world outside faded into silence, she wrestled with the tangled swirling inside her. She began to understand the weight he carried, the burden of his hidden royal identity that had compelled him to retreat into shadows. But every time she thought of it, a sharp pain pierced her heart, making her wonder if she had somehow pushed him away, if her own insecurities had driven him to conceal the truth.

As December settled over the landscape, the once-vibrant fields now lay barren and bleak, mirroring the emptiness that enveloped her soul. The frostbitten earth, stripped of its life, seemed to echo her despair as the holidays approached. The festive lights in town served as a stark reminder of the warmth and joy she so desperately craved but felt slipping further from her grasp with each passing day. Amidst this emotional turmoil, the urgent reality of her responsibilities loomed large. The farm her sanctuary was in jeopardy, and with it, the very essence of her childhood.

Each corner of the land held a memory: her father teaching her to plant seeds, her mother baking bread in the kitchen while the scent of wildflowers drifted through the open windows. The thought of losing it all felt like a cruel twist of fate, as if the universe conspired against her. With every passing moment, the weight of her parents' health and the looming threat of the bank tightened around her chest like a vise. They had nurtured this land together, pouring their hearts into every inch of soil, and she couldn't bear the thought of it slipping away.

As Christmas approached, Rachel found herself longing for a miracle—something to breathe life back into the barren fields and restore hope to her heart. The idea of life without the farm was a bleak abyss, a future devoid of the warmth and familiarity that had cradled her for so long. The mere thought sent shivers down her spine, igniting a fierce determination within her. She would not let go without a fight; she would dig her heels in and protect her home, clinging to the memories that defined her. With every ounce of strength, she vowed to save the land that had shaped her, refusing to allow it to slip away into the shadows of her past.

As Rachel sat at the breakfast table with Max and Kathy, a heavy silence settled over them, thick with unspoken worries and fears. The clinking of cutlery seemed to echo in the quiet, amplifying the tension that hung in the air. "I'm going back in to see John Johnson at the bank," Rachel finally said, her voice filled with a mix of resolve and trepidation. "I need to find out if he's made any progress on getting us an extension."

Max's gaze dropped to his plate, a shadow of guilt washing over his features. "I'm so sorry that you're having to carry this weight," he murmured, his voice heavy with regret.

"Father, please don't blame yourself. If anyone is to blame, it's me," Rachel replied, her throat tightening as emotions threatened to spill over. "I thought I could manage everything, but now… it feels like it's all slipping away, and I'm terrified."

Max sighed deeply, his eyes reflecting a mixture of pride and sorrow. "I just… I was so proud of you when you got accepted into that fine college. I vowed I would do whatever it took to make sure you had a shot at your dreams." His words hung in the air, a bittersweet reminder of the hopes they had built together.

Rachel reached across the table, her hand finding his.

"And you did, Dad. I appreciate everything you've sacrificed for me. But this is my fight now; I have to do this for us. I can't let you down."

Kathy leaned in, her voice gentle yet firm. "You're stronger than you realize, Rachel. I've seen you rise to challenges before. Your parents would be so proud of the woman you've become." Her smile was warm, but Rachel could see the concern in her eyes, the unspoken fear of what losing the farm would mean for their family.

Rachel struggled to hold back the tears threatening to spill. "I just wish they were here to help guide me. I feel so lost sometimes, like I'm carrying the weight of the world on my shoulders."

Max looked up, his eyes brimming with love. "You're never alone, Rachel. We're all in this together. You have their strength inside you, and you've got our support. You're a part of this family, and we'll face whatever comes our way."

"I know," she whispered, the ache in her heart softening slightly at his words. "But what if Mr. Johnson doesn't give us the extension? What if I fail?"

"Then we'll figure it out together," Kathy reassured her, leaning forward with a fierce determination. "You've faced challenges before, and you've always come out stronger. Just take it one step at a time, and don't lose sight of who you are."

With a deep breath, Rachel glanced at the clock, her heart racing like a drum in her chest. "Well, I'd better get into town before Mr. Johnson goes on lunch," she said, trying to push away the knot of anxiety tightening in her stomach.

Max stood up, his chair scraping against the floor. "Wait, let me walk you to the door." Kathy smiled warmly, her eyes glistening with unshed tears.

As they walked to the door, Max placed a hand on her shoulder, his grip firm and reassuring. "You've got this, Rachel. Just be honest with him. It's all you can do. And remember, no matter what happens today, we love you."

"I will," she promised, her heart swelling with emotion as she felt the warmth of their support envelop her like a comforting embrace. "I won't let you down." With that, she took a deep breath, steeling herself for the daunting task ahead, ready to face whatever challenges awaited her.

As Rachel drove down the snow-kissed dirt driveway, she stole a glance back in the rearview mirror, where the warm glow of her home faded into the distance. "You got this, girl," she whispered to herself, the words a gentle mantra meant to bolster her courage. The chill of the air seeped through her car, but a fire ignited within her, fueled by the determination to fight for her family and their farm.

After about thirty minutes, she pulled into town. The scene that unfolded before her was a picturesque winter wonderland, with festive wreaths adorning every shop front and twinkling lights draping the trees along Main Street. Snowflakes danced in the air, swirling gently around her car, as if nature itself was adding a touch of magic to the moment. It was beautiful, yet it felt bittersweet, a stark contrast to the turmoil in her heart.

As she drove further down the street, the bank loomed on the horizon, its imposing structure a reminder of the weight she carried. The building felt both familiar and intimidating, a place where futures were shaped and dreams could be crushed in an instant. Rachel could feel her pulse quickening as she approached, each beat echoing the mix of hope and anxiety bubbling inside her.

Rachel stilled herself as she stepped out of the car, the

chill of the air wrapping around her like a tight embrace. With determined strides, she walked toward the bank, her heart pounding in her chest. As she pushed through the glass doors, the warm air inside contrasted sharply with the cold outside, but the bustling scene was enough to make her feel a little more at ease.

The bank was alive with the holiday spirit; tellers were bustling about, helping customers with their transactions, laughter and chatter filling the space with a sense of community. Yet, the festive atmosphere felt distant to Rachel, her stomach tightening with each step she took toward the counter. She approached one of the tellers, who recognized her instantly. "Is Mr. Johnson in today?" Rachel asked, trying to keep her voice steady.

"Let me check for you, Rachel," the teller replied, her smile warm but tinged with sympathy. After a moment, she returned with a nod. "He's actually in his office and asked for you to just go on in."

"Thank you," Rachel said, her heart racing as she steeled herself for the conversation ahead. With a deep breath, she made her way to Mr. Johnson's office, her footsteps echoing softly in the hallway.

As she entered, Mr. Johnson looked up from his desk, his expression shifting from concentration to a welcoming smile. "Hello, Rachel," he said, rising to greet her. "Please, have a seat."

"Thank you, Mr. Johnson," Rachel replied, her voice betraying a hint of the underlying fear that churned within her. She settled into the chair across from him, her palms clammy against her jeans. The walls of the office felt like they were closing in, amplifying her anxiety as she prepared to plead her case.

Mr. Johnson's demeanor was kind but professional, and he gestured toward the stack of papers on his desk. "I understand you're here to discuss your situation with the farm. I want you to know that I'm here to listen."

Rachel took a deep breath, her heart racing as she gathered her thoughts. "Yes, I am. I know things have been tough, and I'm really worried about the upcoming deadline. I'm hoping we can find a way to secure an extension. I don't want to lose everything my family has worked for." The words spilled out, raw and honest, revealing the depth of her fear and determination.

Mr. Johnson studied her, his expression thoughtful. "I

appreciate your honesty, Rachel. It's clear how much this means to you and your family."

As he spoke, Rachel felt a flicker of hope igniting within her, battling against the anxiety that had gripped her since she arrived. She knew this conversation could change everything.

"I really hope you have some good news for me," Rachel said, her voice trembling slightly as she sat down in the chair across from Mr. Johnson. She tried to mask her anxiety with a hopeful expression, but the weight of her situation bore down on her.

"Please, sit," Mr. Johnson said, motioning for her to take a seat. Rachel complied, her stomach churning with anticipation. "I'm sure if we can get an extension by summer, I can get the farm back in shape," she added, her optimism shining through the cracks of her worry.

However, as Mr. Johnson's expression grew grim, her heart sank. He leaned forward, his tone serious. "Rachel, I know you are a smart girl, and you love your aunt and uncle, but the bank has been very generous with your uncle over the past few years. I don't think you understand the true situation that the farm is in."

The words hung heavy in the air, each syllable striking like a hammer against her hope. "The bank just doesn't feel that an extension is appropriate any longer," he continued, his voice steady but firm. "It will take more than one good season to turn things around."

Rachel's heart felt as though it had just been ripped from her chest, the pain sharp and immediate. The world around her began to blur, the festive decorations outside the bank window turning into a distant memory. Everything she loved, the farm, her family's legacy, her childhood dreams, now seemed to be slipping away like sand through her fingers.

"Mr. Johnson, please," she said, her voice breaking slightly. "I know the farm has struggled, but I'm willing to work harder than ever. I can find ways to bring in new resources, to make it thrive again. I just need a chance."

She could feel tears pricking at the corners of her eyes, but she fought to hold them back. "I can't let my family's legacy end like this. It means everything to me."

Mr. Johnson's expression softened for a brief moment, but he quickly masked it with professionalism. "Rachel, I admire your determination, but the bank has to consider the financial realities. This isn't just about you; it's about the risk involved."

The reality of his words crashed down on her like a wave, and for a moment, she felt utterly lost. "But what can I do?" she asked, desperation creeping into her voice. "Isn't there any way to reconsider? Any options I haven't explored?"

Mr. Johnson looked at her with a mix of sympathy and regret. "I wish I had better news for you. It's a difficult situation, and there are many factors at play. I want to help, but there is nothing more I can do."

Mr. Johnson leaned back in his chair, his expression grim yet professional. "I'm sorry, Rachel. The farm will have to go on the auction block," he said, his voice heavy with the weight of the news.

Rachel felt as though the ground had shifted beneath her feet. "I really am sorry, Rachel, but the bank has done all it can." His words echoed in her mind, each syllable cutting deeper than the last.

Tears streamed down her cheeks, the reality of the situation crashing over her like a tidal wave. "When will it happen?" she asked, her voice quivering with a mix of fear and disbelief.

"I'm sorry, I really am," he replied, his voice tinged with genuine regret. "But it goes to auction on December 24."

Rachel's eyes widened, a mixture of sadness and despair flooding her expression. "That's next week! That's Christmas Eve!" she exclaimed, her voice rising in pitch, the panic evident in her tone. The weight of the holiday felt like an additional burden, emphasizing the loss that loomed just around the corner.

Mr. Johnson nodded, his gaze sympathetic but resolute. "I know this is devastating. It's a tough time of year, and I wish there were another way. But the bank has made its decision."

Rachel felt her heart shatter, each piece cutting into her. Christmas had always been a time of joy and togetherness, filled with laughter and warmth. Now, it threatened to become a day marked by loss and despair, the day she would lose everything her family had worked for.

"Please, is there really nothing more that can be done?" she pleaded, desperation clawing at her throat. "I can find ways to turn things around, I just need more time."

Mr. Johnson's expression softened, but he shook his head. "Rachel, I wish I could give you more time, but the bank has strict policies. The decision is final."

With every word, Rachel felt the walls close in around her. She had fought so hard to hold onto the farm, to keep her family's dreams alive, and now it all felt like it was slipping through her fingers. "I can't let this happen," she whispered, the weight of her emotions crashing down on her.

Then Mr. Johnson leaned in closer, his voice lowering in a sincere tone. "I will work with whoever buys the farm to give you as much time as I can to get you and your family resettled. I'm truly sorry; that is all I can do."

Rachel felt a flicker of gratitude amidst her heartbreak. She wiped her tears, trying to mask her true emotions with a brave face. "Thank you, Mr. Johnson. I'm sure you have done everything you can, and I do appreciate your support," she replied, her voice steadying as she fought to keep her composure.

Mr. Johnson stood up, his expression filled with genuine regret. "I really am sorry that there is nothing more I can do," he said, extending his hand toward Rachel.

With a heavy heart, Rachel shook his hand, feeling the warmth and sincerity in his grip. "Thank you," she whispered again, the words barely escaping her as she turned to leave the office.

As she walked through the bustling bank, she struggled to maintain her composure, each step feeling like a monumental effort. The customers around her were engaged in their holiday transactions, laughter and chatter floating through the air, blissfully unaware of the storm swirling inside her.

Rachel felt like a ghost among them, invisible and detached from the joy that surrounded her. With each step toward the exit, the weight of her loss pressed down harder, her heart aching with the thought of the farm slipping away forever.

Outside, the cold air hit her like a splash of reality, and she paused for a moment, taking a deep breath to steady herself. The festive decorations that had once filled her with joy now seemed like cruel reminders of what she was about to lose.

As Rachel drove home, her heart ached with every mile. The weight of the devastating news pressed heavily on her chest, making it difficult to breathe. How could she tell her parents about the farm going to auction? The thought of shattering their hopes filled her with dread.

She longed for Jacob to be by her side, to share the burden of her pain. Memories of their time together flooded her mind. Quiet afternoons spent in the library, laughter echoing during their hikes, and that blissful day on the lake when everything felt perfect. She could still feel the warmth of his embrace, the way he made her feel safe and cherished. Now, sitting alone in the car, the loneliness enveloped her like a thick fog.

Rachel's thoughts spiraled as guilt gnawed at her insides. She felt responsible for her parents' sacrifices, their dreams tied to her future. They had worked so hard to give her a chance to go to college, to chase her ambitions, and now it felt like she was letting them down. She couldn't shake the feeling that this was all her doing, a betrayal to their love and support.

With each passing moment, the nightmare of her reality deepened. It was as if she were trapped in a dark tunnel, with no light at the end to guide her. The joy of the holidays felt like a distant memory, overshadowed by the impending loss of everything she held dear.

Tears stung her eyes as she navigated the familiar roads leading home. The landscape that had once brought her comfort now felt foreign and cruel. She missed the laughter of her family, the warmth of their support, and the unwavering belief they had in her.

As she pulled into the driveway, the sight of her home made her heart ache even more. The house stood silent, adorned with few festive decorations that seemed to mock her despair. Taking a deep breath, she steeled herself. She knew she had to face her parents, to share the truth, no matter how painful it would be.

With a heavy heart, Rachel stepped out of the car, the cold air biting at her skin. She walked toward the front door, each step feeling like a monumental task, and prepared to share the news that would change everything. She hoped that, somehow, together as a family, they could find a way through the darkness that threatened to consume them.

As Rachel stood at the front door, she hesitated for a moment, her hand poised above the doorknob. The warmth of the house beckoned her inside, but the weight of the news she carried felt like a leaden anchor. She could hear the faint sounds of her parents moving about inside, her mother humming softly as she prepared dinner, her father's deep voice carrying from the living room, where he was likely watching the evening news.

Taking a deep breath to steady her racing heart, Rachel finally turned the knob and stepped inside. The familiar scents of home enveloped her, cinnamon, pine, and the comforting aroma of her mother's cooking, but they only served to intensify the ache in her heart. She forced a smile as she entered the living room, where her parents were settling in for the evening.

"Hey, sweetheart!" her mother exclaimed, her face lighting up with joy at Rachel's arrival. "How was your day in town?"

"Hi, Mom. Dad," Rachel replied, her voice wavering slightly. She could feel the tension building within her as she tried to muster the courage to share her news.

Her father looked up from the television, his expression shifting to concern as he noticed the somber look on Rachel's face. "Is everything okay, Rachel? You seem a bit off."

Rachel swallowed hard, feeling the lump in her throat swell with her emotions. "Um, can we talk for a minute?" she asked, her voice barely rising above a whisper, trembling with the gravity of what she was about to reveal.

Her parents exchanged glances, their expressions shifting from curiosity to concern, and Rachel felt her heart race as she prepared to share the news that would change everything for their family. This was the moment she had dreaded, yet she knew she had to confront the reality of the situation head-on.

As Rachel spoke, she noticed her mother's eyes widen with concern, and her father's face shifted to an expression of dread. They both sensed the weight behind her words, the gravity of the moment thickening the air around them. Rachel felt her heart pounding painfully in her chest, each beat echoing the urgency of what she was about to say.

"Of course, dear," her mother replied, her voice trembling slightly. "Is something wrong? You can tell us anything."

Rachel took a deep breath, her mind racing as she tried to assemble her thoughts into something coherent. She felt as if she were standing on the edge of a precipice, about to plunge into an abyss of despair. "It's about the farm," she began, her voice quaking. "I went to the bank today to talk to Mr. Johnson about getting an extension on the loan. I thought there might be a chance to save it."

Her father leaned forward, his eyes narrowing with concern. "And… what did he say?" he prompted, a sense of foreboding creeping into his voice.

Tears brimmed in Rachel's eyes as she continued, "He told me that the bank has decided to put the farm up for auction. They believe there's no option left to extend the loan any longer." The words fell from her lips like stones, each one a painful reminder of the reality crashing down around them.

Her mother gasped, her hand flying to her mouth in shock, disbelief etched across her features. "Oh, Rachel…" she whispered, the weight of the news settling heavily over them.

"I'm so sorry," Rachel choked out, feeling the burden of her parents' sacrifices pressing down on her. "I know you've both worked so hard for this, just to give me a chance at college. I never wanted to let you down."

"Sweetheart, this isn't your fault," her father said firmly, reaching out to take her trembling hand. "You've done everything you could. We always knew that keeping the farm afloat would be a struggle, especially with everything we've faced."

"But the auction is Christmas Eve," Rachel replied, her voice rising in desperation. "It feels like everything is falling apart when we're supposed to be celebrating together, as a family."

Her mother moved closer, pulling Rachel into a tight embrace. "We'll figure this out, honey," she said, her voice quivering with emotion. "We're a family, and families face tough times together. This isn't the end; it's just another obstacle we have to confront."

Rachel clung to her mother, feeling the warmth of her embrace but unable to shake the chill of despair creeping in. "I just feel so powerless," she admitted, her voice muffled against her mother's shoulder. "I thought I could make things better, but now it feels like I'm losing everything."

Just then, the sound of gravel crunching under tires echoed from outside, signaling the approach of Sally's truck. Rachel felt a mixture of relief and dread wash over her. "Well, I guess it's better to let everyone know what's going on," Kathy said quietly, wiping away the remnants of her tears with a shaky hand. The decision to share the news felt monumental, but it was necessary.

As Sally stepped through the front door, the warmth of the house seemed to shift, and she immediately sensed the tension in the air. The atmosphere felt heavy, laden with unspoken fears and heartache. Rachel could see it in Sally's eyes; the moment she walked in, she knew something was amiss.

"Hey, everyone. What's going on?" Sally asked, her cheerful demeanor faltering as she took in the somber expressions surrounding her. The jovial spirit that usually accompanied her visits was nowhere to be found, replaced instead by an unsettling sense of desperation.

Rachel's heart raced as she exchanged glances with her parents, silently communicating the weight of what they were about to share. This was a moment none of them had been prepared for, and the fear of breaking the news to Sally loomed over them like a dark cloud.

Kathy took a deep breath, steeling herself for the task ahead. "Sally, we need to talk," she began, her voice trembling slightly. "It's about the farm."

Sally's brow furrowed with concern, her body instinctively tensing as she stepped further into the room. "What about the farm?" she asked, her tone shifting from curiosity to apprehension.

Rachel felt the lump in her throat grow as Kathy continued, "The bank has decided to put the farm up for auction… next week, on Christmas Eve."

The words hung in the air, heavy and foreboding.

Sally's face paled, and for a moment, it seemed as if time had stopped. The gravity of the news settled over them, suffocating and raw.

"No… no, that can't be right," Sally stammered, shaking her head in disbelief. "What do you mean? The farm has been in your family for generations! We can't just let that happen!"

"I wish there was something more we could do," Rachel said, tears streaming down her face as she felt the weight of despair pressing down on her. Her voice trembled, breaking under the strain of her emotions. "Maybe if we had more time… maybe we could find a way to save it," she added, her heart aching with the thought of losing everything she had ever known.

Sally, sensing the depth of Rachel's anguish, moved closer and hugged her tightly. "We will get through this," she said, her voice firm yet soothing as she tried to console everyone in the room. The warmth of her embrace offered a small measure of comfort amidst the chaos of their emotions.

Then, Max, gathering all his strength, took a deep breath and stilled himself, commanding the attention of those around him. "Now, everyone listen," he said, his tone steady and resolute. "Yes, this place has been our home for generations, and it holds countless memories. But times and circumstances change. We have to accept that."

Rachel looked at her father, sensing the depth of his conviction. "Wherever we are as a family, that will be home," he continued, his voice gaining strength. "A home is more than just a house; it's more than wood and shingles. A home is wherever family is, and as long as we have each other, we will survive this."

His words hung in the air, resonating with a profound truth. Rachel felt a flicker of hope igniting within her, bolstered by her father's unwavering belief. The tears still flowed, but they were now mingled with a sense of determination.

"We'll find a way to make this work," Rachel said, her voice steadier now, infused with the strength of her family's spirit. "We'll stand together, no matter what happens.

We'll create a new home, wherever that may take us."

Max smiled, pride swelling in his chest at the resilience of his family. "That's the spirit. We're not alone in this. Together, we can face whatever comes our way."

As they stood united in their shared resolve, Rachel felt a renewed sense of purpose. The road ahead would be difficult, but they were not just fighting for a piece of land; they were fighting for their family, their memories, and their future. And together, they would rise to meet the challenges ahead, no matter how daunting they seemed.

As night fell over the farm, a blanket of darkness enveloped the landscape, and Rachel found herself sitting alone on the porch swing, the cold air biting at her skin. She wrapped her hands around a steaming cup of hot tea, trying to find solace in its warmth, but her thoughts raced uncontrollably. Memories of her family flooded her mind, intertwining with thoughts of Jacob and the moments they had shared. The guilt gnawed at her, and she scolded herself harshly. *How can you even think about anything other than your family?* she chastised internally, feeling a wave of self-reproach wash over her.

Just then, the screen door creaked open, and Kathy stepped outside, wrapping her shawl tighter around her shoulders as she joined Rachel on the swing. "A penny for your thoughts," she said gently, noticing the worry etched across Rachel's face.

Rachel sighed deeply, her chest tightening with emotion. "I just feel so powerless," she admitted, her voice cracking. "This is all my fault." Tears streamed down her cheeks, each drop a testament to her anguish.

Kathy immediately moved closer, placing her hand gently on Rachel's leg in a comforting gesture. "Rachel Rodgers, listen to me," she said firmly yet softly. "We are going to be alright. Miracles happen to everyday people all the time. Somewhere out there, our miracle is just waiting to happen."

The warmth of her mother's touch and the strength in her words began to penetrate Rachel's despair. "Don't lose faith," Kathy continued, her tone imbued with hope. "There is still time for God to send us our miracle, and Christmas miracles are said to be the best."

Rachel wiped the tears from her eyes, her heart swelling with gratitude for her mother's unwavering support. "I love you, Mom," she said, her voice barely above a whisper, but filled with sincerity.

"I love you too, sweetheart," Kathy replied, her eyes shimmering with emotion. "And no matter what happens, we'll face it together. Remember, we're a family, and that means we're stronger than any challenge that comes our way."

In that moment, as they sat together on the porch swing, Rachel felt a flicker of hope igniting within her. The night may have been dark and cold, but the warmth of their bond served as a beacon of light.

"I guess I'm going to head upstairs and turn in for the night," Rachel said softly, wrapping her arms around her mother in a warm embrace. The comfort of her mother's presence was a balm for her troubled heart.

"I think I'll go watch some television with your father," Kathy replied, hugging Rachel back tightly. As they made their way inside, Kathy turned and locked the door behind them, a protective gesture that added to the sense of safety within their home.

"Goodnight, Rachel," she called out as Rachel began her ascent up the staircase.

"I love you, Mom," Rachel replied, her voice echoing softly down the hall.

As she climbed the stairs, Rachel took a moment to absorb her surroundings, each familiar sight feeling more poignant than ever. The family photos lining the walls, the worn wooden banister, and the faint scent of lavender from her mother's air freshener all wrapped around her like a comforting embrace. It was as if she were saying goodbye, even though she desperately hoped she wouldn't have to.

Once she reached her room, Rachel changed into her pajamas and crawled into bed, the sheets cool against her skin. Feeling restless, she reached for her phone and dialed Polly's number, her heart racing slightly as she waited for her friend to pick up.

"Hello?" Polly answered, her voice bright and eager. "How are things going on the farm?"

Rachel took a deep breath, thankful for the chance to share what was weighing on her mind. "Hey, Polly. It's… It's been a rough day," she admitted, the emotions she had been holding back threatening to spill over once more. "I just found out that the bank is putting the farm up for auction next week. It feels like everything is falling apart."

"Oh no, Rachel! I'm so sorry to hear that," Polly responded, her voice filled with concern. "What are you going to do?"

Rachel felt a wave of vulnerability wash over her as she continued. "I don't know yet. We're trying to figure out a plan, but everything feels so overwhelming. I just wish there was something more I could do."

"Listen, I'm here for you, okay? We'll figure this out together," Polly reassured her. "You're not alone in this. Do you want to talk about it more?"

Rachel smiled faintly, grateful for her friend's

unwavering support. "I'd really appreciate that, Polly. Just talking helps. I feel like I'm drowning in all this uncertainty."

"Not to bring up another sore subject, but have you spoken with Jacob? Does he know what's going on?" Polly asked gently, her voice laced with concern.

Rachel felt a pang of guilt as she replied, "No, no, I haven't. I texted him yesterday, but I'm just so confused right now. With everything going on, I feel so helpless, and I don't want Jacob to see me that way."

"You need to talk to Jacob, Rachel," Polly insisted. "You two are meant to be together. He deserves to know what's happening."

Rachel chuckled lightly, though it was tinged with sadness. "You are just the best, Polly, but you know I'm no princess. He has to marry royalty," she said, her voice breaking slightly. "I can't be the one who keeps him from growing into the king he's destined to be. I can't be that person."

Tears streamed down her face as the weight of her emotions crashed over her. "What if I'm the reason he struggles? What if he feels like he has to choose between me and his future? I don't want to hold him back."

Polly's heart ached for her friend. "Rachel, you're not holding him back. Love doesn't work that way. If he truly cares for you, he'll want to support you, just as you would for him. You're both still figuring things out, but that doesn't mean you shouldn't talk."

"I just don't know how to face him," Rachel confessed, her voice trembling. "What if he sees how overwhelmed I am? I don't want him to feel burdened by my problems."

"Rachel, you're stronger than you realize," Polly reassured her. "Being vulnerable is a part of love. It's okay to show him your struggles. It'll bring you closer, not push you apart. You have to give him the chance to be there for you."

Rachel took a shaky breath, grappling with her feelings. "I wish I could believe that. I just don't want to drag him into this chaos. He deserves better."

"Better doesn't mean perfect," Polly replied gently. "It means being real with each other. You both need to support one another, especially now. Don't shut him out. You'll regret it if you do."

Rachel wiped her tears, considering Polly's words. Deep down, she knew her friend was right, but the fear of vulnerability loomed large. "I'll think about it," she finally said, her voice softening. "I just need to figure out how to say everything."

"Take your time, but don't wait too long. You owe it to him to share this with him," Polly urged. "And remember, you're not alone. I'm here for you every step of the way."

"Thank you, Polly," Rachel said, her heart swelling with gratitude. "I really appreciate you being here for me." Jacob lay in bed, staring at the ceiling, unable to shake his restless thoughts. His mind was consumed with memories of Rachel—the laughter they shared, the way her eyes sparkled with genuine joy, and how she had always seen him for who he truly was, not just as a prince. She didn't care about royal titles or the expectations placed upon him. In her eyes, he felt free to be himself.

But now, a heavy weight of regret pressed down on him. He had been wrong not to tell her the truth about his impending responsibilities—the pressure to return to Slovitia and fulfill his family's expectations by marrying someone of noble birth. Patricia had cast a long shadow over his heart, ruining everything he had hoped for with Rachel.

Just as he was lost in thought, his phone buzzed on the nightstand, pulling him from his reverie. Glancing at the screen, he saw Polly's name flashing. Why would she be calling so late at night? His heart raced with anticipation and anxiety. What news could this bring?

He answered the call, his voice a mix of curiosity and concern. "Polly? Is everything okay?"

"Jacob! I'm so glad I reached you," Polly said, her voice slightly breathless with urgency. "I just got off the phone with Rachel, and she's really struggling right now. I think you need to talk to her."

His heart sank at the thought of Rachel in distress. "What's wrong? Is she alright?"

"She's overwhelmed with everything happening at the farm," Polly explained quickly. "But it's more than that.

She's feeling helpless and scared. I think she needs you now more than ever. You two need to be honest with each other."

Jacob felt a swell of emotions, fear, worry, and a deep yearning to be there for Rachel. "I want to help her, but I don't know what to say. I've made a mess of things."

"You need to be open, Jacob. Don't let your fears hold you back. She needs to know she's not alone and that you care about her. You both deserve the chance to share your truths," Polly urged.

He took a deep breath, weighing Polly's words in his mind. "You're right. I've been avoiding the conversation, but I can't do that anymore. I care about her too much."

"Thank you, Polly. I appreciate you looking out for her," Jacob replied, feeling a renewed sense of purpose.

Chapter 38

The Lost Duke

The thought of returning to Slovitia without having fought for her was unbearable. He couldn't let fear dictate his future, not when it came to the woman who had captured his heart.

Jacob laid his phone on his bare chest, the warmth of the device a comforting reminder of his connection to Rachel. "Tomorrow, I'm going to find a way to fix this mess I've made," he murmured to himself, feeling a spark of determination ignite within him.

With a deep breath, he placed his phone back on the nightstand and settled into his pillow, allowing his mind to drift. As he closed his eyes, memories of Rachel flooded his thoughts, the way her laughter could light up a room, the warmth of her smile, and the moments they had shared that felt so genuine and real.

In the quiet of the night, the shadows of uncertainty began to fade, replaced by the soft glow of hope. He envisioned her standing in the sunlight, her hair cascading around her shoulders, and the way her eyes sparkled with mischief and joy. Those memories wrapped around him like a warm blanket, soothing his worries as he surrendered to sleep.

As he drifted off, Jacob felt a sense of clarity washing over him. No matter the challenges ahead, he was resolved to fight for Rachel, to show her that their love was worth pursuing, despite the obstacles. With her laughter echoing in his mind, he slipped into a peaceful sleep, ready to face the new day and the promise it held for them both. As the first light of dawn crept over the horizon, the winter day felt particularly bleak, with the heavy gray clouds casting a somber shadow over everything.

Ivan lay in bed, cocooned in warmth, stretching his arms wide as a yawn escaped his lips, a reluctant signal that it was time to wake. He blinked against the dull light filtering through the curtains, still tethered to the remnants of sleep.

Suddenly, his phone on the nightstand began to buzz energetically, the vibrations rattling against the wood. Startled, Ivan fumbled for it, feeling the cool surface beneath his fingers. "Hello," he croaked, his voice thick with sleep as he propped himself up against the headboard.

"Hello, Ivan! It's Eurick," came a familiar voice, bright and full of energy, cutting through the morning haze. "I wanted to give you some updates on the project we discussed."

Ivan's pulse quickened at the mention of the project. "Oh! Hi, Eurick! Did you uncover anything useful?"

"Yes, my friend! We managed to dig up a wealth of information about the two individuals we were investigating," Eurick replied, his tone laced with enthusiasm.

A spark of excitement ignited within Ivan, chasing away the last remnants of grogginess. "That's fantastic! I can't wait to hear all about it."

Eurick's voice took on a teasing note, hinting at something thrilling yet to be revealed. "I think you're going to be very intrigued by what we found out. Trust me, it's worth your attention."

As Eurick began to unfold his story, Ivan's eyes sparkled with excitement. "Are you suggesting this is somehow connected to the tale of the Lost Duke of Antirok?" he asked, his voice tinged with disbelief and eagerness.

"That's exactly what I'm suggesting!" Eurick replied, his enthusiasm infectious.

Ivan leaned forward, his heart racing. "This is incredible! I need you to email me everything you have. I have to let Prince Alexander know about this at once!" His voice rang with urgency, the thrill of the discovery igniting a fire within him.

"Absolutely, I'll send over all the documents and details right now," Eurick assured him. "This could change everything for the prince, and for the kingdom."

"I can't believe it," Ivan exclaimed, his mind racing with the implications of their findings. "If there's a connection to the Lost Duke, it could shed light on so many mysteries!"

"Yes, and we must move swiftly," Eurick insisted, his

voice taking on a more urgent tone. "This information is crucial, and we need to act quickly before it's too late, given what you've shared with me."

"Agreed! Send me everything you have," Ivan replied, feeling a surge of responsibility. "I'll make sure Prince Alexander gets this as soon as possible."

"Right. I'll be in touch," Eurick said, his voice resolute.

With that, Ivan hung up, a sense of purpose enveloping him as he raced to gather his thoughts and prepare for the monumental task ahead.

Soon, Ivan's phone began to buzz again as the documents started coming through.

Ivan eagerly sifted through the various documents Eurick had sent, his heart racing as each page revealed tantalizing details. The thrill of discovery coursed through him, and he could hardly contain his excitement. Without a moment's hesitation, he dashed into Jacob's bedroom, practically bursting with energy.

The early morning light filtered through the curtains, casting a warm glow in the room. Jacob lay sound asleep, his peaceful expression a stark contrast to Ivan's fervor. "Jacob! Jacob, wake up!" Ivan called out, his voice ringing with urgency and excitement.

He leaned over Jacob's bed, shaking his shoulder gently at first, then more insistently as he felt the weight of the moment pressing down on him. "You won't believe what I just found! You have to see this!" Ivan's words tumbled out in a rush, filled with the promise of adventure and revelation.

"What has gotten into you?" Jacob groaned, rubbing the sleep from his eyes as he tried to make sense of Ivan's frantic energy.

"I have some really important news that you need to know about!" Ivan exclaimed, his excitement bubbling over. He could hardly contain himself, the words spilling out as he paced the small room. "It's about the Lost Duke of Antirok! You won't believe what I just discovered!"

Jacob's curiosity piqued, he sat up, now fully alert. "The Lost Duke? What are you talking about?"

Ivan leaned closer, his eyes shining with enthusiasm. "Eurick sent me documents that connect everything! This could change everything for you and Rachel!"

Jacob's eyes widened with excitement as he sat up in bed, the remnants of sleep fading away. Ivan quickly handed him his phone, and Jacob began scrolling through the documents, his curiosity igniting further.

"Where did you get all this?" he asked, astonished by the wealth of information before him.

"I had Eurick at the Royal Historians Institute help me track down information about Rachel's parents," Ivan explained, his voice steady with conviction. "And I think they hit the jackpot. The connections in these documents could lead us to the truth we've been searching for all along!"

Jacob's expression shifted from surprise to determination as he absorbed the details, a spark of hope igniting within him. "This is incredible! I need to call my father and share this with him!"

Jacob reached eagerly for his phone, his heart pounding with a mix of excitement and anxiety as he dialed King Frederick's number. He could feel the weight of the moment pressing down on him, knowing that what he was about to share could alter the course of their lives forever.

"Hello, Alexander, " the king's voice came through, rich and authoritative, yet laced with curiosity.

"Father, it's Alexander," he said, trying to steady his voice despite the whirlwind of emotions inside him. "I have news that you really need to hear!"

"Alexander, what is it?" King Frederick replied, his tone shifting to one of genuine interest and concern.

"It's about Rachel," Alexander continued, urgency flooding his words. "I've been working with Ivan and the royal historians, and they've uncovered something truly significant. But we're running out of time—Rachel's home is set to be auctioned off on Christmas Eve!"

A heavy silence enveloped the line, and Jacob could almost hear the king processing the gravity of the situation. The anticipation was thick, each second stretching into what felt like an eternity. "What did you find?" King Frederick finally asked, his voice steady but tinged with curiosity.

Taking a deep breath, Jacob poured out everything Ivan

had disclosed, each detail flowing from him like an unrelenting tide. He could feel the king's interest piquing, and when King Frederick let out a surprised chuckle, it felt like a ray of hope breaking through the storm. "Well, this will certainly shock your mother!" the king laughed, a mixture of disbelief and amusement filling his voice. "I will contact the royal historians and review everything. If what you say is true, I'll handle it."

"Thank you, Father," Alexander replied, his voice trembling with relief and gratitude. "This could change everything for Rachel. She deserves a chance at happiness, and we can't let this slip away."

As he hung up, a surge of determination coursed through him, igniting a fire in his belly. This was more than just a mission; it was a fight for love, for a future that felt both fragile and exhilarating. He turned to Ivan, his eyes filled with resolve. "We need to get ready. I'm heading to Tennessee as soon as I can!"

"There's no way you're going alone," Ivan said, his face lighting up with a determined grin. "I need to call Polly and arrange for us to get three tickets to Tennessee!"

Jacob felt a rush of relief wash over him. The thought of tackling this mission without Ivan by his side had been daunting, but together they could face anything. "You really think she'll help us?" Jacob asked, a hint of uncertainty in his voice.

"Absolutely! Polly loves a good adventure, and this one is right up her alley," Ivan replied, already pulling out his phone. He dialed Polly's number, his excitement palpable. Jacob watched as Ivan's expression shifted from anticipation to joy when Polly answered, her voice crackling through the speaker.

"Polly! You won't believe what we've discovered. " Ivan exclaimed, his enthusiasm infectious. Jacob couldn't help but smile as he watched his friend animate the conversation, describing their plan to save Rachel's home.

"Great! Just let me know when you can be ready to leave," Ivan said, wrapping up the call. He turned to Jacob, his grin wider than ever. "Polly's on board! She's already looking for the best flights."

"Fantastic!" Jacob replied, his excitement bubbling over. " With Ivan's energy and Polly's enthusiasm, they were ready to take on the challenge. Jacob felt a renewed sense of purpose as they began to plan their trip, each detail bringing them one step closer to helping Rachel and changing their lives forever.

"I will start looking for the next flights we can get to Tennessee," Ivan said enthusiastically as he left Jacob's room, the energy in his voice propelling Jacob forward.

With a sense of urgency, Jacob quickly hopped into the shower, letting the warm water wash over him, clearing his mind of any lingering doubts. He emerged feeling refreshed and invigorated, ready to tackle the challenges ahead.

He grabbed a leather duffel bag, its sturdy exterior a reminder of countless adventures past. As he packed, he carefully selected each item: a few comfortable shirts, a warm jacket for the crisp Tennessee air, and his favorite pair of jeans. With every piece of clothing he added, his excitement grew, along with the hope of reuniting with Rachel.

Jacob's mind raced with thoughts of her, the way her eyes sparkled when she laughed, the warmth of her smile, and the connection they shared that felt so rare and precious. He wanted to be there for her, to help her through this uncertain time, and to show her that they could face the world together.

After packing, he took a moment to glance at himself in the mirror, brushing his hair back with a mix of determination and anticipation. As he zipped up his duffel bag, a sense of clarity washed over him. He was ready for this adventure, ready to stand by Rachel's side, and ready to face whatever came their way. With Ivan already working on the logistics, Jacob felt a surge of excitement coursing through him as he prepared to embark on this journey.

"I have the plane tickets ordered, and Polly is packing as we speak!" Ivan called out as he hurried past Jacob's room, his excitement palpable even in his rush to get ready.

Jacob's heart raced at the news. "That's amazing!" he shouted back, a grin spreading across his face. The reality of their impending journey to Tennessee was sinking in, and it ignited a fire of anticipation within him.

He quickly made some final adjustments to his packing, ensuring he had everything he might need for the adventure ahead. The thought of being reunited with Rachel filled his mind, pushing him to move faster. Knowing that Polly was on board and already preparing for the trip made it feel even more real and exhilarating.

As he finished up, Jacob could hear Ivan's footsteps echoing in the hallway. "We should probably meet up in a bit to go over our plan," Ivan suggested, his voice filled with eagerness. "I want to make sure we're all on the same page before we head out."

"Absolutely! I'll be ready in just a few minutes," Jacob replied, feeling a wave of determination wash over him. He wanted to make sure they had everything planned out, not just for the flight but for what awaited them in Tennessee.

With his duffel bag in hand, Jacob took a deep breath, reminding himself of the purpose behind this journey.

As they rushed out of the house, Ivan turned to Jacob, a reassuring smile on his face. "It's going to be alright, Jacob. Just take a breath," he said, his tone lightening the tension in the air. "Maybe you should let me drive us to pick up Polly," he joked, a playful glimmer in his eyes.

Jacob chuckled, nodding in agreement. "You may have a point! I'm a little too excited to be behind the wheel," he replied, excitement beaming from his face. The energy between them was palpable, a shared anticipation of the journey ahead.

As they climbed into the car, Jacob could hardly contain his enthusiasm. The world outside felt vibrant and alive, mirroring the thrill building within him. With Ivan at the wheel, they set off, the rhythm of the road echoing the pulse of his racing heart.

"You know," Ivan said, glancing over at Jacob, "this is going to be a trip we won't forget. This is the most exciting trip we may ever set out on."

"Absolutely," Jacob agreed, his voice filled with conviction. "I wouldn't want to do this with anyone else. You really are the best friend a guy could ask for."

As they drove, laughter and banter filled the car, the excitement of what lay ahead swirling in the air. Jacob felt grateful for Ivan's support and the bond they shared.

As Ivan navigated through the bustling streets, the anticipation in the car grew. Before long, Polly's apartment building came into view, a familiar sight that sparked a wave of excitement in both Jacob and Ivan.

"Look, there she is!" Ivan exclaimed, pointing ahead as they pulled into the parking lot. Polly was standing outside, her vibrant energy radiating as she waved her arms enthusiastically, a big smile plastered across her face.

Ivan couldn't help but smile at the sight of her. "She looks ready for an adventure!" he said, laughter bubbling up in his voice. Jacob felt a surge of happiness at the sight of his friends coming together, each of them contributing to the spirit of the journey they were about to embark on.

As they parked the car, Jacob quickly jumped out, eager to greet Polly. "Polly!" he called, waving back at her. She rushed over, her excitement infectious.

"Hey, you two! I can't believe we're finally doing this!" Polly exclaimed, her eyes sparkling with enthusiasm. She tossed her bag into the back seat and then turned to Jacob, her expression turning serious for a moment. "Are you ready for this?"

"More than ever," Jacob replied, feeling a rush of determination. As they settled into the car and prepared to head out, the atmosphere was charged with anticipation.

"I still can't believe the news about Rachel," Polly said, her eyes wide with excitement. "She is going to be so thrilled to hear what you found out! I can't believe all this is real!"

"I know," Ivan replied, his tone filled with enthusiasm. "This adventure just keeps getting better. It feels like we're on the brink of something incredible."

Jacob nodded, feeling the weight of Polly's words. "This really will change Rachel's life," he added, his voice steady with conviction. The thought of him and Rachel finally getting the opportunity they deserved filled him with joy and excitement.

The car filled with a sense of camaraderie and determination as they drove towards their destination. Jacob could feel the excitement building, and with each passing moment, he knew they were one step closer to making a real difference in Rachel's life. Together, they were ready to embark on this journey filled with hope, friendship, and the promise of a brighter future.

Chapter 39

The Auctioneer's Hammer

As Christmas Eve morning unfolded, the atmosphere in the house was thick with unspoken fears and quiet determination. Rachel stood at the doorway, her heart heavy as she watched her mother, Kathy, working tirelessly in the kitchen. The smell of breakfast, bacon sizzling, eggs cooking, was both comforting and bittersweet, a reminder of the countless family meals filled with laughter and shared stories.

Kathy tried her best to keep her composure, but Rachel could see the strain in her mother's eyes. Tears silently slipped down her cheeks as she stirred the ingredients, each movement tinged with the weight of impending loss. Rachel felt a pang in her chest, knowing this might be the last time her mother cooked in their beloved home, a place built upon so many cherished memories.

Max, ever the steady anchor, stepped in and wrapped his arms around Kathy, pulling her close. "It's going to be alright," he murmured, his voice laced with warmth and reassurance as he gently squeezed her hand. "We've made it through tough times before." His words were a balm, but the anxiety in the air was palpable, a reminder of the uncertainty that lay ahead.

Rachel watched as her parents leaned into each other, love radiating from their embrace despite the storm brewing around them. This is all my fault, she thought, guilt gnawing at her insides. She had never fully grasped the financial strain her education placed on them, nor had she realized the sacrifices they had made to give her that opportunity. The weight of her unasked questions pressed heavily on her heart.

She felt like a spectator in her own life, longing to reach out but feeling frozen in place. As she stood there, tears threatened to spill from her own eyes. The sight of her parents, vulnerable yet strong, stirred something deep within her, a fierce desire to protect them, to lighten their burden.

Taking a deep breath, Rachel stepped into the kitchen, determination coursing through her veins. "Mom, Dad," she said softly, her voice trembling with emotion, "I'm here for you both. We can get through this together."

As Rachel settled into the kitchen, the familiar surroundings began to resonate with a sense of purpose. The walls, adorned with photographs of family gatherings and milestones, whispered stories of laughter and love. Each snapshot captured moments that felt distant yet ever-present, fueling her resolve to cherish what remained and fight for her family's future.

Kathy wiped her tears with the back of her hand, her focus shifting back to the task at hand. The rhythmic sounds of chopping vegetables and clinking utensils were soothing, but Rachel could sense the undercurrent of anxiety still simmering beneath the surface. She moved closer, offering to help with the breakfast preparations, hoping to lighten her mother's load, even if just a little.

"Let me handle the pancakes," Rachel said, stepping in front of the griddle. Kathy hesitated for a moment, then nodded, a flicker of gratitude crossing her face. The simple act of cooking together felt like a balm, a way to connect amidst the turmoil swirling outside their kitchen walls.

As they worked side by side, Max kept the atmosphere light with jokes and stories from past holidays, reminiscing about the chaos of family gatherings, his infamous attempts at making the perfect turkey, the time the dog stole the Christmas ham, and the laughter that followed. The sound of his voice, rich with warmth and humor, began to weave a comforting blanket around them, easing some of the tension in the air.

Rachel realized that these moments, however fleeting, were precious. They were a reminder of the foundation her family had built together, one rooted in love, resilience, and the ability to face adversity with grace. She felt a surge of determination, vowing to do everything in her power to keep that foundation strong.

As breakfast neared completion, the aroma filled the air, pulling them together like a magnet. The table was set with care, each plate adorned with carefully arranged food that sparkled with color and warmth. Rachel took a moment to appreciate the sight, her heart swelling with gratitude for these shared rituals.

When they finally sat down to eat, there was a palpable shift in the atmosphere. The tension that had once hung heavily over them began to dissipate, replaced by the comforting rhythm of clinking forks and shared smiles. They exchanged stories, laughter bubbling up as they recounted cherished memories and dreams for the future.

Rachel felt a renewed sense of hope as she watched her parents find solace in each other's company. The love that enveloped them was a powerful force, one that could withstand any storm. In that moment, she made a silent promise to herself: she would do everything she could to support them, to honor the sacrifices they had made, and to keep their family intact.

"Is Sally coming today?" Rachel asked, her voice tinged with hope.

"Oh yes, she is. Should be here any minute now," her mother replied, offering a reassuring smile.

Just then, a car followed by a van made its way up the long driveway. As it came to a stop in front of the house, Rachel's heart sank as she recognized Mr. Johnson from the bank, accompanied by another gentleman. Her gaze shifted to the van, where she noticed two men stepping out and walking down the road, erecting auction signs. A wave of despair washed over her; the reality of their situation hit hard.

"Well, I'd better go outside and see to our company," Max said, pushing himself away from the table. Rachel could see the grief and anxiety etched across her father's face, a reflection of the weight they were all carrying.

"Let me come with you," she said, her voice firm despite the turmoil in her heart. She didn't want him to face this moment alone, to confront the reality of their impending loss without her support.

Max paused, looking at her with a mixture of gratitude and concern. "Are you sure, Rachel? It might be tough out there."

"I am sure," she replied, determination shining in her eyes. "We're in this together, Dad."

As they stepped outside, the chill in the air seemed to mirror the heaviness in their hearts. The sight of the auction signs being planted along the road was a stark reminder of what they were facing. Rachel took a deep breath, trying to steady herself as they approached Mr. Johnson and the other man.

"Mr. Johnson," Max greeted, his voice steady but strained. "Good morning, Max," Mr. Johnson replied, his tone professional yet sympathetic. "I wanted to come by personally to discuss the situation. I know it's a difficult time for your family."

Rachel stood close to her father, feeling the tension radiating from him. She could see the weight of the world resting on his shoulders, and it made her heart ache. She wished she could lift that burden, to take away the pain of uncertainty that loomed over them.

"Thank you for coming," Max said, trying to maintain

composure. "I appreciate it."

The other gentleman introduced himself as Mr. Bennett, a representative assisting with the auction process. Rachel felt a pang of anger at the thought of strangers coming into their home, assessing their life and memories, ready to strip away what had been built over the years.

"Is there any way to postpone this?" Rachel found herself asking before she could think twice. "We need more time. We can find a solution."

Mr. Johnson exchanged a glance with Mr. Bennett before responding. "I understand your feelings, Rachel, truly. However, the timeline has been set. The bank has made its decision based on the current circumstances."

Rachel felt a wave of frustration swell within her. "But this is our home! There has to be something we can do." Her voice trembled, caught between desperation and determination.

Max placed a reassuring hand on her shoulder, grounding her. "We're all in this together, Rachel. We will figure it out."

As they continued to speak with Mr. Johnson and Mr. Bennett, Rachel's mind raced with possibilities. She would find a way to fight for her family, to make sure that their story didn't end here. The bond they shared was unbreakable, and together, they would navigate the storm that lay ahead.

"I guess the best place to set up is inside the barn," Max

said, leading Mr. Johnson and Mr. Bennett toward the weathered structure that had stood for generations. The barn, filled with memories of laughter and hard work, seemed to hold a weight of its own, and Rachel felt a knot tighten in her stomach at the thought of it being used for such a purpose.

"Rachel, I think you should go back in and be with your mom," Max suggested, his tone gentle yet firm. He was trying to shield her from the harsh reality of the situation, to protect her from the difficult conversations that would unfold.

"I can't just leave you out here," Rachel protested, unwilling to retreat into the house while her father faced this daunting moment alone. "I want to be here for you."

Max turned to her, concern etched across his face. "I know, but this part is going to be tough. Your mom needs you right now, and I want you to be there for her. We'll handle this together."

Rachel hesitated, torn between her desire to support her father and the instinct to stay close to the family unit. She knew her mother was feeling vulnerable, and the thought of leaving her alone was unsettling. But she also understood the need for Max to focus on the task at hand, to negotiate on their behalf without the added weight of her emotions.

"Okay," she finally relented, her voice softening. "But promise me you'll keep me updated. I want to know what's happening."

"Of course," Max replied, his expression softening at her resolve. "I'll let you know everything. Just go be with your mom, okay?"

With a heavy heart, Rachel turned and made her way back to the house. Each step felt like a tug of war between wanting to be strong and the urge to collapse under the weight of their situation. As she entered the warmth of the kitchen, she found Kathy sitting at the table, her hands clasped tightly together, staring off into space.

"Mom?" Rachel said softly, moving to sit beside her. "How are you holding up?"

Kathy looked up, her eyes glistening with unshed tears. "I'm trying, sweetheart. It's just so hard to face this." Her voice trembled slightly as she spoke, the weight of their reality pressing down on her.

Rachel took her mother's hands in her own, squeezing gently. "We'll get through this together, I promise. Dad is talking to Mr. Johnson and the other man right now. They're working on it."

Kathy nodded, though her expression remained troubled. "I know, but it's just so overwhelming. I keep wondering how it all came to this."

Rachel felt a surge of compassion for her mother. "It's okay to feel that way. We're all scared. But we still have each other, and that means something."

Kathy managed a small smile, the warmth of Rachel's words providing a little comfort. "You're right. We've always been a strong family. We'll find a way."

As they sat together, Rachel felt the bond between them deepen. She wanted to reassure her mother that they would face whatever came next with love and unity. They could weather this storm, just as they had done countless times before.

Meanwhile, outside in the barn, Max was doing his best to navigate the conversation with Mr. Johnson and Mr. Bennett. He was determined to advocate for his family, hoping to find a solution that would allow them to hold on to their home and the life they had built together. The stakes were high, but he was resolute in his commitment to protect his family at all costs.

"Max, I promise I will talk to whomever buys your property to work with you to give you some time to get resettled, but that's the best I can do," Mr. Johnson said, his voice steady yet laced with sympathy.

Max nodded, appreciation mixed with frustration swirling in his heart. He knew that Mr. Johnson was trying to help within the confines of the bank's policies, but the reality of their situation felt insurmountable. As the two men from outside brought in an auctioneer's podium and began to set it up inside the barn, the atmosphere grew heavier with each passing moment.

Rachel stood at the window, watching her father walk back toward the house. His shoulders were slumped, and his eyes were clouded with grief, a stark contrast to the man she had always known, strong, steadfast, and unyielding. In that moment, her heart ached for him. She wished she could take away the burden he carried, to shield him from the pain of losing their home.

As Max reached the house, Rachel hurried to meet him at the door. "Dad," she said softly, stepping outside to meet him. "How did it go?"

He paused, taking a deep breath as he looked into her eyes. "It's not good, Rachel. They're moving forward with the auction, and there's little room for negotiation." His voice cracked slightly, revealing the weight of his emotions. "But Mr. Johnson is going to try to talk to the buyer about giving us some time to get ourselves sorted."

Rachel felt a mix of hope and frustration. "That's something, at least," she replied, trying to muster a sense of optimism. "But it doesn't change what's happening."

"No, it doesn't," Max admitted, running a hand through his hair. "I wish I could do more. I wish we could find a way to keep this place."

Rachel stepped closer, wrapping her arms around her father in a tight embrace. "We'll find a way, Dad. We'll figure it out together. You're not alone in this."

He held her tightly, finding solace in her words. The strength of their bond provided a flicker of hope amidst the darkness that surrounded them. "I just hate feeling so helpless," he murmured, pulling back to look at her. "I always wanted to protect you both from this."

"You have protected us, Dad," Rachel replied earnestly.

"You've given us a beautiful life here. No matter what happens next, we'll always be a family. That's what matters most."

Max nodded, the love in his daughter's eyes reminding him that the fight wasn't over. Together, they would face whatever challenges lay ahead. "You're right. We'll lean on each other." Together, they headed back into the house, ready to confront the uncertainty of their future.

Soon, Sally arrived, and Rachel hurried outside to greet her sister, a wave of relief washing over her. "Oh, Sis, I'm so glad you made it!" she exclaimed, holding back tears that threatened to spill over.

"Oh, Rachel," Sally replied, tears streaming down her face as she enveloped her sister in a tight embrace. "I've been so worried. How are Mom and Dad holding up?"

Rachel pulled back slightly, looking into her sister's eyes, which mirrored her own pain. "They're trying to be brave, but I can see the grief in their eyes," she admitted, her voice trembling. "It's hard to watch them go through this. I feel so helpless."

Sally nodded, her expression somber. "I can only imagine. I wish I could have been here sooner." She glanced toward the barn, where the auction podium stood ominously, a stark reminder of their current reality. "What can I do to help?"

Rachel took a deep breath, trying to steady herself. "I think we need to be there for them, to show them that we're united. We can come up with ideas together, maybe look into resources, or talk to people who can help us."

"Absolutely," Sally agreed, her determination shining through her sadness. "We're stronger together. Let's go inside and talk to them."

As they moved toward the house, Rachel felt a sense of comfort in having her sister by her side. Together, they would face the challenges ahead, drawing strength from one another and their family.

Once inside, they found their parents sitting at the kitchen table, looking weary but grateful to see their daughters. Rachel and Sally exchanged a glance, silently agreeing to keep the atmosphere as positive as they could.

"Hey, Mom, Dad," Sally said gently, her voice filled with warmth. "We're here. We'll get through this together."

Kathy looked up, a flicker of relief in her eyes as she wiped her tears. "Oh, my girls," she said, her voice heavy with emotion. "I'm so glad you're both here."

Max nodded, feeling the weight of their family's shared grief. "We've been talking about how to move forward, and we could use your help. We need to brainstorm some ideas."

Rachel felt a surge of hope as they all gathered around the table, united in their resolve to face the uncertainty together. "We can explore options for support," Rachel suggested, her voice steadying. "There are community resources we can tap into, and maybe we can reach out to local organizations that help families in need."

Sally chimed in, "And we can look into temporary housing options if it comes to that. We won't let this break us. We'll find a way."

Kathy nodded, a look of gratitude washing over her face. "Thank you, both. Your strength means everything to us right now."

Max added, "With all of us working together, we can tackle this challenge head-on. We'll figure it out."

In that moment, surrounded by the people she loved most, Rachel knew they would face whatever came next with courage and determination. No matter how daunting the road ahead, they would walk it together, hand in hand, heart to heart.

As the day wore on, Rachel found herself drawn outside, unable to tear her eyes away from the unfolding events in the barn. The sound of the auctioneer's hammer echoed in her ears like a relentless drumbeat, each strike marking the sale of the only life she had ever known.

She stood at the edge of the barn, feeling an overwhelming sense of loss wash over her as she watched her beloved horse, Zorro, being led away. The sight of him, usually so spirited and full of life, now looked bewildered and anxious as he was sold off to strangers. Her heart ached at the thought of him leaving, a symbol of all the joy and freedom she had experienced growing up in this place.

One by one, the other livestock followed, each sale feeling like another piece of her childhood being stripped away. The men in suits, with their calculated bids and businesslike demeanor, felt like intruders in her world. They were buying more than just animals; they were purchasing cherished memories—family barbecues in the barn, early morning rides through the fields, and lazy afternoons spent playing with her sister in the sunshine.

With each sold item, Rachel felt her heart break a little more, the weight of guilt pressing heavily on her chest. This is all because of me, she thought, the accusation echoing in her mind like a haunting refrain. She recalled the conversations about her education, the sacrifices her parents had made, and how she had been so focused on her future that she hadn't fully grasped the impact it would have on their lives.

Tears streamed down her face as she fought against the overwhelming sense of helplessness. She wanted to scream, to fight against the injustice of it all, but there was nothing she could do to stop it. Each hammer strike felt like a reminder of her inadequacy, a whisper of failure that gnawed at her insides.

Taking a deep breath, Rachel stepped away from the barn, needing to escape the reality that surrounded her. She wandered toward the edge of the property, where the trees stood tall and resolute, offering a brief sanctuary from the chaos. Leaning against one of the sturdy trunks, she closed her eyes and allowed herself to feel the weight of her emotions.

"Why is this happening?" she whispered to the wind,

feeling lost and alone. "I didn't want this for us. I never meant for any of this to happen."

As the breeze rustled the leaves above, she slowly opened her eyes and looked out over the land that had been her home. Despite the pain, she could still see the beauty in it, the sun filtering through the branches, the vastness of the fields that had once been filled with laughter and adventure.

Rachel turned back toward the barn, where her family was gathering, ready to support her parents. With each strike of the gavel, the reality of their situation became more unbearable. She watched as everything that had defined her childhood, her horse, the livestock, and now the family home, went up for sale on the auction block. Each item sold felt like a piece of her heart being ripped away.

When the gavel came down on the sale of the family home, Rachel's composure shattered. She wept openly, her sobs echoing the anguish that filled her heart. It felt as though her very soul was being pulled out, leaving a void that seemed impossible to fill. Memories of laughter, warmth, and love flooded her mind, intertwining with the sorrow of what was being lost.

Max, feeling the weight of the moment, did his best to be strong for his family. He wrapped an arm around Kathy, who was also struggling to hold back her tears. He could see the pain in both of their faces, the heartache that came with watching their life slip away. "We'll get through this," he whispered, trying to project a sense of hope even as his own heart ached.

Sally, standing close to Rachel, gripped her sister's hand firmly. "It's going to be okay," she reassured, her voice steady despite the turmoil surrounding them. She knew they needed to lean on one another now more than ever.

Rachel looked at her sister, tears streaming down her cheeks as she fought to find comfort in Sally's words. "I kept hoping for a Christmas miracle," she confessed, her voice choked with emotion. "But I'm afraid it's over now."

Sally's grip tightened, a gesture of solidarity. "It's not over, Rachel. This isn't the end. It's just a new chapter, even if it doesn't feel that way right now. We're still here, and we still have each other."

Rachel felt a flicker of hope in her sister's words, though it felt fragile amidst the overwhelming grief. "But how can we move on from this?" she asked, her voice barely above a whisper.

Max, overhearing their conversation, stepped closer, his expression softening. "We may not have control over what has happened today, but we do have control over how we respond to it. We need to hold onto each other and find strength in our love. We're still a family, and that means everything."

Kathy nodded, wiping her tears with the back of her hand. "We've faced challenges before, and we can face this one too. It won't be easy, but we will find a way, together."

Rachel took a deep breath, feeling the warmth of her family surrounding her. The pain of their loss was still raw, but the love they shared provided a glimmer of light in the darkness. "You're right," she said, her voice steadier now. "We'll find a way to make it through this."

As the last items were auctioned off and the reality of their situation settled in, Rachel realized that while they were losing their home, they were not losing each other. Their bond was unbreakable, forged through shared experiences and unwavering support. Together, they would navigate this new path, allowing their love to guide them as they faced whatever challenges lay ahead.

Chapter 40

A Prince to the Rescue

As night enveloped the farm, the snow began to fall again, each flake a soft whisper from the heavens, blanketing the farm in a soothing silence. Inside the barn, the air was thick with memories and unspoken sorrow as Rachel and Sally nestled close to their parents. The weight of their loss, a home filled with laughter, warmth, and love, pressed heavily on their hearts, each breath a reminder of what they were leaving behind.

Max, ever the anchor in their turbulent sea of emotions, looked at his daughters with a mixture of love and anguish. "It's going to be alright," he said softly, though his voice trembled slightly, betraying the turmoil within. They began to share stories, fragments of joy that felt both distant and achingly close. Sally's laughter rang out when she recounted her first attempts to ride a bike, the thrill of wobbling down the path, her tiny hands gripping the handlebars tightly while she used the fence as her trusty safety net. Her innocent joy was infectious, lighting up the dim barn with a flicker of warmth.

Rachel, however, felt a pang of bittersweet nostalgia as she remembered her time with Zorro, the spirited horse that had terrified her at first glance. She recalled the way her heart raced as she climbed up, her hands shaking with trepidation, yet somehow, the exhilaration of riding him had transformed her fear into something beautiful, something she longed to hold onto. They laughed together, but the laughter was tinged with a profound sadness, a yearning for the days that seemed so simple and bright.

Then, as if the universe had conspired to shatter their fragile moment, Sally's gaze drifted to the road outside. The headlights of approaching cars cut through the darkness like a harbinger of doom, and a cold shiver ran down Rachel's spine. "Who could be coming at this hour?" Sally asked, her voice quivering with uncertainty. Rachel tried to mask her own rising dread, forcing a casual tone. "Probably someone who forgot when the auction was." But deep down, fear gripped her like a vice. What if it was the new owners, coming to claim their sanctuary, their memories? The thought struck her like a lightning bolt, paralyzing her with the weight of impending loss.

As the first car rolled to a stop, two figures emerged, their outlines stark against the snowy backdrop. "Rachel, are you out there?" a voice called, cutting through the thick silence, echoing with familiarity and warmth. Rachel's heart leaped, her pulse racing as recognition washed over her like a wave of relief. "Polly, is that you?" she shouted back, her voice breaking with a mixture of disbelief and joy, as if the name itself could chase away the shadows of despair that loomed over them.

In that moment, the chill of the night felt less oppressive, replaced by a flicker of hope. The warmth of reunion began to thaw the icy grip of fear, igniting a spark of possibility amidst their heartache. Rachel's heart swelled with emotion, the promise of connection and love piercing through the darkness, reminding her that even in the depths of sorrow, there was still light to be found.

"Yes, we're all out here!" Rachel bellowed, her voice bursting with joy as she felt the weight of her sadness momentarily lift. The sound echoed through the chilly air, wrapping around her like a warm blanket. Without hesitation, Ivan and Polly raced toward the barn, their figures illuminated by the glow of the headlights, bringing a rush of familiarity and comfort.

As Polly entered, Rachel's face lit up with happiness, a radiant smile breaking through the shadows of her grief. "Polly! It's so good to see you!" she exclaimed, her heart swelling at the sight of her dear friend. There was an unspoken understanding between them, a bond that transcended the heartache they all felt.

"How are you?" Polly asked, concern etching her features as she stepped closer, ready to embrace Rachel.

"I've had better," Rachel replied, her voice wavering slightly as she fought to regain her composure. She longed to share her feelings, but the emotions were still too raw, too fresh.

Ivan stepped forward, a gentle smile spreading across his face. "Hello, Rachel," he said warmly, as Rachel and Polly embraced, their laughter mingling with the crisp night air, momentarily washing away their worries.

"It's so good to see you, Ivan," Rachel said, her heart racing as she faced him. Yet, a wave of guilt washed over her, weighing heavily on her heart. "I'm so sorry I acted the way I did at the café. Can you ever forgive me?" The words tumbled out, thick with sincerity, as she stepped forward and wrapped her arms around Ivan.

His embrace was warm and reassuring, a balm for her troubled soul. "Of course, I forgive you," he replied softly, his voice steady and filled with compassion. "We all have our moments."

With a renewed sense of joy pulsing through her, Rachel pulled back from Ivan's embrace, her heart brimming with warmth. "Let me introduce you to my family!" she exclaimed, her eyes sparkling with enthusiasm as she turned to her sister and parents.

"Sally, come here!" Rachel called, motioning for her sister to join them. Sally, her cheeks glowing from the cold, stepped forward, her eyes wide with curiosity. "This is Polly and Ivan, my friends!"

Polly stepped forward, her smile bright and welcoming. "Hi, Sally! It's so nice to finally meet you!" she said, her voice bright with sincerity.

Sally's face broke into a grin, her initial shyness melting away. "Hi! I've heard so much about you both!" she replied, her excitement bubbling over.

Then, Rachel turned to her parents, who had been watching with warm smiles. "Mom, Dad, this is Polly and

Ivan," she said, her voice laced with pride.

Rachel's mother stepped forward, her eyes glistening with gratitude. "It's wonderful to meet you both. Thank you for being here for our Rachel during this difficult time," she said, her voice filled with warmth and sincerity.

Rachel's father nodded, a gentle smile on his face. "You're welcome anytime. Friends are what help us get through tough times," he added, his voice steady and reassuring.

As introductions were made, the atmosphere in the barn shifted, filled with laughter and the warmth of companionship. The weight of the day's sorrow began to lift, replaced by the bonds of friendship and family. As Ivan and Polly exchanged a knowing wink, a spark of excitement danced in the air. "We have someone else who wanted to talk with you," Ivan said, his tone playful but laced with an undercurrent of seriousness.

Rachel's heart raced, her eyes lighting up with a mix of hope and apprehension. "Is it Jacob?" she asked, her voice barely above a whisper. The mention of his name sent a wave of anxiety crashing over her. She felt a familiar grip of fear around her heart, as memories of their last encounter flooded back, the hurtful words exchanged, the way she had reacted to his news. How could she even begin to apologize for her response?

Polly noticed Rachel's change in demeanor and stepped closer, a reassuring hand resting on her shoulder. "He's been worried about you," she said softly. "He really wants to talk."

Rachel took a deep breath, trying to steady the whirlwind of emotions churning inside her. She felt a twinge of guilt mixed with longing, wishing desperately to make things right. The thought of facing Jacob, of seeing the hurt in his eyes, made her stomach twist. But deep down, she knew she had to confront this, she owed it to him and to herself.

"Okay," Rachel finally said, her voice steadier than she felt. "I'm ready." She glanced at her family and friends, seeking their support, and found their encouraging smiles bolstering her courage.

As Ivan and Polly stepped aside, Rachel's heart raced with anticipation and fear. She took another deep breath, feeling the warmth of her loved ones surrounding her, and prepared to face Jacob.

"I give you Prince Alexander!" Ivan announced with a dramatic flair, his voice echoing through the barn, filled with playful reverence.

Rachel's heart skipped a beat as she turned to see Jacob stepping out from the shadows, the soft glow of the barn lights illuminating him like a figure from a storybook. Snowflakes danced around him, dusting his royal uniform in a delicate layer of white. As he walked slowly into the barn, each step seemed deliberate, the air thick with anticipation.

Max and Kathy, sensing the significance of the moment, stood up, their expressions shifting from surprise to respect.

They watched as Jacob approached, his presence commanding yet warm, exuding an aura that drew everyone's attention. There was a quiet strength in him, a nobility that felt both reassuring and friendly, as if he was fully aware of the weight of the moment.

Rachel's breath caught in her throat as she took in the sight of him. Memories flooded back, the laughter they had shared, the trust that felt so solid, and then the painful distance that had formed between them after their last encounter. She felt both excitement and trepidation, knowing that this moment was a chance to bridge the gap that had grown between them.

Jacob's eyes met Rachel's, a mixture of warmth and understanding shining through. As he drew closer, she could see the concern etched on his face, a reflection of his own struggles. The silence in the barn was palpable, filled with unspoken emotions and the weight of shared history.

"Rachel," Jacob began, his voice steady yet gentle, "I've been hoping for the chance to speak with you." Each word felt like a lifeline thrown into the turbulent waters of their relationship, and Rachel could feel her heart beginning to soften despite the fear that still gripped her.

"Jacob," she said softly, her voice barely above a whisper, filled with a mix of vulnerability and hope.

As their eyes locked, Jacob's expression brightened, and his gaze sparkled with warmth. He reached out, taking her hand in his, a gentle gesture that sent a rush of comfort through her. It felt like coming home.

"Do I call you Jacob or Prince Alexander?" she asked, her voice playful yet nervous, a faint smile tugging at her lips.

"I will always be your Jacob," he replied, his gaze unwavering as he looked deeply into her eyes. In that moment, the fear and anxiety that had gripped her heart began to melt away, replaced by a warmth that spread through her, igniting a flicker of joy.

Rachel turned slightly, her heart swelling with pride as she introduced him to her family. "Mom, Dad, this is my friend Jacob. I've told you so much about him."

Max stepped forward, a broad smile on his face as he reached out his hand. "It's a pleasure to meet you, Your Majesty," he said, his voice respectful yet friendly.

Jacob took Max's hand firmly, a genuine smile lighting up his face. "The pleasure is all mine, sir. Thank you for welcoming me into your home," he replied, his tone warm and sincere.

Kathy stepped forward next, her eyes filled with kindness. "It's wonderful to finally meet you, Jacob. Rachel has spoken so highly of you," she added, her voice laced with warmth.

Jacob turned to Rachel, his expression earnest and filled with emotion. "I don't want to lose you, Rachel. You mean everything to me," he said, his voice steady yet soft. He slowly placed his hand on her cheek, his touch gentle and reassuring. "I cannot see my life without you in it."

Rachel felt her heart flutter at his words, a warmth spreading through her. "I love you," he confessed, his eyes searching hers for understanding.

"I love you too," she replied, her voice trembling with sincerity, but a shadow of sadness crossed her face. "But I know that we can never be. You have to marry into a royal line, and I'm just a simple country girl from Tennessee." She lowered her head, the weight of reality pressing down on her.

Jacob chuckled softly, lifting her chin gently with his fingers. "Rachel, you are the most uncommon woman I have ever met. Your heart, your spirit, they are what I cherish most." His smile was warm and affectionate, his gaze unwavering. "I know that you love me not for the crown, but for who I am."

Tears brimmed in Rachel's eyes as she absorbed his words, but the ache in her heart remained. "Your parents would never allow us to marry," she said, a hint of desperation in her voice. "And I won't be the one to hold you back."

Jacob's expression shifted, a mixture of determination and sadness. "I won't let anything come between us, Rachel. We can navigate this together." There was a sincerity in his voice that made her chest tighten and her heart swell with hope.

"But the reality is," she said, her voice barely above a whisper, "the world we live in is complicated. Your duty is to your family and your kingdom."

Jacob chuckled and grinned, the tension in the air shifting slightly. "You have no idea how complicated things really are," he said, his tone lightening just a bit. "But hear me out; there are some things you need to know." He then looked at Ivan and nodded, signaling him to make the next introduction.

"I give you Queen Isabella!" Ivan announced, his voice filled with a mix of excitement and reverence.

As the barn doors creaked open wider, Queen Isabella entered, her presence commanding yet graceful. She moved slowly, her royal attire flowing elegantly around her as she approached Rachel. The atmosphere shifted, and Rachel felt both awe and apprehension at the sight of the queen.

"Your Majesty," Rachel said, her voice barely above a whisper, her heart racing as she met the queen's gaze.

Queen Isabella smiled warmly, yet there was a seriousness in her eyes. "I feel I owe you an apology, my dear," she said, her voice rich and melodic. Rachel was caught off guard by the queen's unexpected remarks.

"I never meant to place you in such an uncomfortable position," the queen continued, her tone sincere. "The weight of my crown can sometimes blind one to the feelings and lives of those not in the royal sphere. I realize now that my actions may have caused you pain, and for that, I am truly sorry."

Rachel blinked, processing the queen's words. She had expected formality, perhaps even judgment, but the queen's vulnerability softened the edges of her apprehension. "Your Majesty, I—" Rachel began, but the queen held up a hand gently, signaling for her to pause.

"Please, let me finish," Queen Isabella said, her expression earnest. "Jacob speaks of you with such admiration and love, and it has opened my eyes to the importance of following one's heart. Love should never be stifled by duty alone."

Jacob watched intently, his heart swelling with pride for the queen's understanding and compassion. Rachel felt a mix of emotions—surprise, gratitude, and a flicker of hope.

"You are a remarkable young woman, Rachel," the queen continued, her voice filled with warmth. "You have the strength to shape your own destiny, and I would never want to come between you and the life you envision for yourself and my son."

"I don't understand," Rachel said, trying to get a grip on the unfolding scene. Her mind raced with questions, and the weight of the moment felt overwhelming.

Jacob squeezed her hand once more, grounding her as he looked deeply into her eyes. "I know this is a lot to take in," he said softly. "But Ivan and Polly got the idea to see if they could learn more about your parents, and well, they found something you need to know."

Rachel's eyes lit up with excitement, a spark of curiosity igniting within her. She was eager to understand what secrets lay hidden in this unexpected turn of events.

Polly was practically bouncing on her toes, her enthusiasm palpable. "We couldn't believe it when we found out!" she exclaimed, her eyes wide with anticipation.

Jacob smiled, sensing her eagerness. "What they discovered might change everything," he said, his voice filled with intrigue. He looked at Ivan, who nodded, ready to share the news.

"Rachel," Ivan began, stepping forward, "we learned that your parents have a history that ties back to royalty, something you might not have known."

Rachel's eyes lit up with a mix of shock and curiosity, but the weight of the revelation made it hard to fully react. She could hardly process the information as Jacob continued, a warm smile on his face.

"Was your mother's name Elizabeth Ann Edwards?" he asked, watching her closely.

Rachel turned to her parents, her heart racing. Max and Kathy exchanged glances, and Kathy wiped away a tear from her cheek. "Yes, that was her maiden name," she confirmed softly.

"She married a man named Thad Lichten?" Jacob prompted, his expression eager.

"Yes, that is correct," Kathy replied, her voice steady yet filled with emotion.

Jacob took a deep breath, preparing to unveil the layers of mystery surrounding Rachel's lineage. "Well, you see,

Thad Lichten was more than he appeared. It turns out that Thad is who we call the Lost Duke of Caledonia."

Rachel's eyes widened, her heart pounding as Jacob began to reveal things she had never known. The words hung in the air, a tapestry of history unfolding before her.

"The legend of the Lost Duke of Caledonia is a love story about a young prince who ran away from the royal court to marry a commoner," Jacob explained, his voice rich with intrigue. "Thad Lichten's real name was Prince Thaddeus Leopold von Lichtenstein, the only son of King Edward Gabriel Leopold of Caledonia."

"Thaddeus met your mother on a trip to America, and they fell madly in love," Jacob continued, his voice filled with a deep sense of reverence. "Their connection was so extraordinary that Thaddeus was willing to flee the royal court, abandoning everything to be with her. He even went as far as to legally change his name to hide from the royal court and to forge a new life with your real mother, Elizabeth."

Rachel felt her heart racing, each word pulling her deeper into a past she had never known. The idea that her mother had fallen in love with a prince, a man who had left everything behind for love, was both thrilling and surreal. But as Jacob's expression shifted, the gravity of his words settled heavily upon her.

"Unfortunately," he continued, his voice thick with emotion, "when you were just an infant, tragedy struck. They were both killed in an automobile accident in New York."

The breath left Rachel's lungs as the weight of his revelation crashed over her. A sharp pain pierced her heart, a deep sorrow for the parents she had never really known, but felt an undeniable bond with. "My parents…" she whispered, the realization washing over her like a tidal wave, leaving her gasping for air.

Jacob stepped closer, his eyes filled with compassion as he watched her struggle with these newfound revelations. "Your aunt and uncle adopted you, as they were your only known relatives," he said gently. "Then your records were sealed, and the royal court has been unable to locate what happened to Thaddeus until they started to track your lineage."

Tears streamed down Rachel's cheeks, each drop a reflection of the heartache that had suddenly engulfed her. The loss of her parents, the secrets of her heritage, it all felt too much to bear.

"Oh, Jacob, I love you," she sobbed, her voice trembling as she leaned into him, seeking comfort in his embrace. The warmth of his body against hers felt like a lifeline, grounding her amidst the chaos of her emotions. She could feel the steady beat of his heart, a reminder that she was not alone in this moment.

"I love you too, Rachel," he replied, his voice a soothing balm to her troubled soul. He wrapped his arms around her, holding her tightly as if to shield her from the pain of the world.

"There is someone else you need to meet," Jacob said,

his voice steady yet filled with a sense of gravity. As Rachel looked up, two figures began walking toward her, their presence commanding and regal.

"This, Rachel, is my father, King Frederick of Slovitia," Jacob introduced, his pride evident. "And this is your grandfather, King Edward of Caledonia."

Rachel's heart raced, a whirlwind of emotions swirling within her as she wiped the tears from her eyes, trying to focus on the approaching figures. King Frederick stood tall beside his son, his demeanor dignified yet warm, while King Edward moved with a grace that spoke of a lifetime spent in royal courts.

As they grew closer, Rachel felt a mixture of awe and trepidation. King Edward reached out for her, his expression softening as he drew near. "You are as beautiful as your mother," he said gently, his voice laced with emotion.

Tears rolled down Rachel's face as she stared into King Edward's eyes, searching for any trace of the father she had lost. His face, though older, radiated kindness and a sense of familiarity that tugged at her heart.

"I'm so sorry for how we treated your mother," King Edward continued, his voice thick with regret. "It was a mistake I thought I would never be able to apologize for." The weight of his words hung in the air, carrying the burden of years lost to misunderstanding and pride.

Rachel's heart ached for the mother and father she never knew, a couple who had loved fiercely and had paid the price for their choices. "Thank you," Rachel managed to say, her voice quivering with emotion. "I've always wanted to know more about them."

As King Edward gazed upon her, his eyes glistened with tears of his own. "You know you have your father's eyes," he said softly, his gaze filled with a mixture of pride and sorrow. "Every time I look at you, I see his spirit living on."

In that moment, Rachel felt a profound connection to her past, as if the pieces of her life were finally coming together. The presence of her grandfather brought a sense of belonging she had longed for, a bridge to a family history that had been shrouded in mystery. Rachel turned to Jacob and enveloped him in a heartfelt embrace, pouring every ounce of love and emotion into that moment.

"I love you, Jacob," she sobbed, her voice trembling with the weight of everything that had transpired. "I just wish you had come sooner; maybe things would have been different." Tears streamed down her cheeks as she felt the ache of all they had lost, the years, the family, the connections that might have been.

Jacob's eyes glistened with unshed tears, and his voice cracked with raw emotion. "I'm here now," he said softly, his sincerity wrapping around her like a warm blanket.

In that moment, King Frederick stepped forward, handing Jacob a small wooden box, its surface polished and engraved with intricate designs. Jacob took a deep breath, steadying himself as he turned back to Rachel, his expression transforming with purpose. He took her hand gently, then knelt down on one knee.

"Rachel Rodgers," he began, his voice steady yet filled with emotion, "will you do me the pleasure and the honor of being my wife?"

A gasp escaped from Polly as tears rolled down her cheeks, her joy palpable. She reached over and grabbed Ivan's hand, their shared excitement electrifying the air around them. Rachel stood there, frozen for a moment, her mind racing with a whirlwind of thoughts and feelings.

She looked at Queen Isabella and King Frederick, seeking their approval. Queen Isabella smiled softly, her eyes filled with warmth and understanding. "You have my blessing, Rachel, if you will still have my son to be your husband."

Rachel's heart soared, yet uncertainty lingered as she looked back at Jacob, who sat motionless, his face glowing with anticipation. The world around her faded into the background, leaving just the two of them, suspended in time.

"Yes! Yes!" she finally exclaimed, tears cascading down her cheeks, a rush of joy and relief flooding her heart.

Jacob's face lit up with a brilliant smile as he carefully took the ring from the small box, sliding it gently onto Rachel's finger. The ring glistened in the soft light of the barn, its beauty breathtaking. Decorated with rows of diamonds, emeralds, and sapphires, it was a masterpiece, and at its center sat a stunning blue stone, proud and striking against the gold setting.

"It's amazing! Truly fit for a queen!" Rachel exclaimed, her heart swelling with happiness. She marveled at the ring, feeling the weight of its significance. "What is the stone in the middle?" she asked, her curiosity piqued as she examined the unusual hue of the gem.

Jacob's smile widened, his eyes sparkling with pride. "It's a blue diamond," he replied, his voice filled with joy. "A rare symbol of love and commitment, just like our bond."

As Rachel looked at the ring, she felt an overwhelming sense of gratitude and love for Jacob, for the journey they had taken together, and for the promise of a future filled with hope. In that moment, surrounded by the warmth of family and the love of her life, she knew she was exactly where she was meant to be.

Then King Frederick stepped up to Rachel, his presence commanding yet warm. "Alexander informed us of the events happening here," he began, his voice steady and reassuring. "Knowing we would not get here in time, I had some business associates come to the auction today. As a wedding gift to my future daughter-in-law and soon-to-be future Princess of Slovitia, I would like to give you your farm back, along with everything that belongs to your family."

Rachel's breath caught in her throat, her heart racing as she struggled for words. The enormity of his gesture washed over her like a tidal wave. She glanced at Max and Kathy, who reached out for each other's hands, their expressions a mixture of disbelief and joy.

"I had my associates buy everything, and as our wedding present, we will give you back everything," King Frederick said, his eyes filled with sincerity and compassion. The weight of his words was profound, and Rachel felt tears welling up as gratitude swelled in her chest.

King Edward stepped forward, his gaze shifting to Max. "I see that you will need help in maintaining such a large farm," he said kindly. "I'm here to let you know you have the backing of the crown to hire helpers to work this farm as my wedding gift to Rachel."

Max and Kathy burst into tears at the offer, their emotions overwhelming them. "Thank you! Thank you!" Max exclaimed, his voice thick with gratitude as he looked at the king, unable to fully express the depth of his appreciation.

King Frederick shook Max's hand firmly, a gesture of respect and camaraderie. "It is the least I can do. You have raised a wonderful lady," he said, his voice filled with admiration.

Rachel felt a rush of warmth and love at her father's words, a sense of belonging that she had longed for. The weight of her burdens began to lift, replaced by the hope of a new beginning. The thought of reclaiming her family's farm, the land that held so many memories and dreams, filled her with an overwhelming sense of gratitude.

"Thank you both," Rachel finally managed to say, her voice quivering with emotion. "This means more to me than I can express. You've given me back not just the farm, but a piece of my family's legacy."

King Frederick smiled, his eyes crinkling with warmth. "You deserve to have your roots restored, Rachel. Your family's legacy is important, and we are here to support you in every way we can."

Tears continued to flow freely down Rachel's cheeks, but now they were tears of joy, of hope, and of a future that felt brighter than ever. Jacob stood beside her, his hand intertwined with hers, and she felt a surge of love for him as well, the love that had brought them to this moment, that had united their families.

When spring arrived the following year, Slovitia held a grand wedding that was said to be the wedding of the century, a magnificent event uniting Slovitia and Caledonia in a celebration of love and alliance. The air buzzed with excitement as townsfolk adorned the streets, their faces beaming with joy and well-wishes for the couple.

Royal carriages glided gracefully down the cobblestone paths, decorated with flowers and ribbons that danced in the gentle spring breeze. The sounds of laughter and music filled the air, creating a festive atmosphere that wrapped around everyone like a warm embrace. Colorful banners fluttered in the wind, heralding the union of two families and two kingdoms.

As the majestic cathedral loomed before her, Rachel felt a wave of emotion wash over her, the delicate fabric of her long white dress flowing around her like a soft cloud. With every step she took, guided by her beloved grandfather, King

Edward, she felt the weight of love and legacy enveloping her. His wise smile and gentle pride made her heart swell as they walked together toward Jacob, who stood at the altar, his face aglow with joy and anticipation.

In that moment, as their eyes met, the world around them faded into a blur. Jacob's heart raced, captivated by the beauty of the woman he adored, her presence illuminating the sacred space. Surrounded by their cherished family and friends, they stood together, their hands intertwined, feeling the warmth of a love that had blossomed through trials and triumphs.

As they exchanged vows, their voices intertwined like a melody, each promise a testament to their unyielding devotion. Rachel's words danced through the air, filled with passion and dreams of a future together, while Jacob's vows resonated with unwavering commitment and adoration. With each shared glance, they ignited a spark of magic that enveloped the cathedral, culminating in a kiss that ignited their souls and sealed their love, echoing through the ages as the beginning of their forever intertwined journey.

When they sealed their vows with a kiss, the crowd erupted into cheers, and Rachel felt a rush of joy as they turned to face their family and friends. It was a day filled with love, laughter, and the promise of new beginnings—a day that would forever be etched in their hearts as a testament to the power of love and unity.

Rachel and Jacob ruled over their country with grace and compassion, embodying the ideals of love and respect towards their subjects. It was said that never had there been two people who loved each other more; they were rarely seen apart, their bond a shining example of devotion to all. They worked tirelessly for the betterment of their people, and their reign was marked by peace and prosperity.

As stories of their love spread throughout the kingdom, the people rejoiced in the happiness of their beloved rulers. Everyone lived happily ever after, united in the joy that Rachel and Jacob brought to their lives, except for Patricia Jackson. As a final gesture of justice and closure, Queen Isabella exiled Patricia, ensuring that the shadows of the past would not tarnish the bright future that lay ahead for Rachel and Jacob.

THE END